Storm Front

Storm Front

Belle Reilly

Renaissance Alliance Publishing, Inc.
Nederland, Texas

ISBN 1-930928-19-X

First Printing 2001

9 8 7 6 5 4 3 2 1

Cover art by Linda A. Callaghan
Cover design by Mary Draganis

Published by:

Renaissance Alliance Publishing, Inc.
PMB 238, 8691 9th Avenue
Port Arthur, Texas 77642-8025

Find us on the World Wide Web at
http://www.rapbooks.com

Printed in the United States of America

For all those who face life's impossible challenges, and dare to make them possible.

Chapter
1

"Okay people, let us through. Clear this area." Pressing his way through a panicked, frightened airport crowd, James 'Mac' MacArthur held his Orbis Airlines Strategic Operations ID high above his head, as though he were flying his colors into battle.

MacArthur was a big man, going at about six foot two and 220 pounds, just ten pounds or so over the "playing" weight he sported when he was attached to the FBI's Washington D.C. office.

"Mommy, is there a bomb?"

Mac hesitated only briefly to watch a harried looking young woman sweep an angelic-faced little girl up into her arms.

"I don't know, honey," she said, glancing furtively over her shoulder. "But we're leaving."

"Mommy, I'm scared," the tot cried, reacting to the confusion and fear in the rush of people around her.

Mac picked up his pace as the wails of the child faded away behind him.

Shit.

After twenty years with the bureau, he'd been just six months into his retirement, sipping Budweiser and catching small-mouth bass on Lake Winnetonka in upstate New York. Then the call came from his old buddy Cyrus Vandegrift. He and

Cyrus had shared casting lures one hot summer's day on a muddy riverbank outside of Twin Forks oh, fifteen years ago now, and they'd been fast friends ever since. They made it a point to rendezvous at least once every summer for a bit of fishing and a bit of bullshit in the Finger Lakes region. Far away from jobs, spouses, and hot showers, they loved every minute of it.

Cyrus had asked Mac if he'd consider talking to this Catherine Phillips. As a favor. Would he simply drive into town and meet with her—just once? That was all. Phillips was putting together some brand new unit at Orbis, dedicated to tracking and preventing terrorist activity.

Hell, MacArthur was retired. Hadn't he earned his pension and gold-plated desk set from the bureau? He was through taking orders from anybody, much less a woman.

But oh, what a woman, MacArthur thought, watching his boss cut her way through the mass of people as though she were the prow of an icebreaker slashing through frozen seas.

Ten minutes.

All it had taken was ten minutes with Phillips, and he knew he wanted to work with her if she'd have him. Her biting, pointed questions. Her studied indifference. Her cold, hard stare reading him. Judging. And he'd asked her a few questions of his own, too. What was her background? What was her stake in this?

She had answered him quickly, concisely, and with a command of clarity and purpose that he'd rarely come across in his days with the Bureau. He was impressed: a United States Air Force Academy grad, a top-notch pilot with Desert Storm experience, plus training in special ops and covert deployment. And, he knew, his buddy Cyrus Vandegrift thought the world of her. Cy did not bestow such status often, if ever.

In the end, they had sat silently for a moment, staring at one another across the great expanse of Phillips' desk, piercing blue eyes locked on hazel. And then the tall woman had stood and thrust out her hand to him, offering him a job.

To his wife's subsequent consternation, Mac had heard the sound of his own voice accepting a position as the unit's chief investigator. That had been three months ago. He'd scarcely had the time since then to figure out just what madness had gotten into him. Damn that Cyrus Vandegrift to all hell.

It had been four months since Flight 2240's hijacking, and since that time tensions had been running high not only at Orbis, but at other air carriers as well. After a solid three months of investigative work, they still were no closer than they had been that first day to determining who was ultimately responsible for funding and supplying the hijackers.

They couldn't have done it alone, the boss lady insisted, and MacArthur had to agree with her. Those Albanian "patriots," with their expensive clothes, impeccable bogus identification, and high-tech weaponry that had managed to escape security detection. The M.O. bothered Mac, a lot, and he could see that Phillips fretted over it as well. Who knew when the terrorists might decide to strike again? And where?

They were almost at the entrance to the terminal now. It had taken them just ten minutes to get there from the nearby low-rise office building where Orbis housed their flight and security operations. The alert had come in loud and clear: "suspicious parcel," as airport security called it. A bomb scare by any other name. The parcel was a black Adidas duffel bag, left sitting unattended near a washroom trash bin. A cleaning attendant had first noticed it about an hour ago. As time passed by and no one claimed it, the attendant had done the right thing—reported it to management.

"Hey, watch it, you jerk."

Mac heard the epithet at the exact moment when his elbow accidentally slammed into the shoulder of a thin, well-dressed businessman. Dressed in charcoal and sage pinstripes and wearing tiny, oval-framed glasses, the man had been more preoccupied with staring towards the drama at the terminal's entrance than with where he was walking. He'd cut directly into MacArthur's path and, with the force of the impact, the computer case he had slung on his arm went careering off onto the ground.

"Sorry," Mac tossed off behind him, but he kept going.

"Asshole."

Any other day, Mac would've stopped dead in his tracks and given that tight-assed little shit what-for. But not today, or Phillips would have his head. And so he kept moving. They had just now reached the top of the concourse, where an NYPD patrolman stood guard.

"I'm sorry, ma'am, but you can't go any further—"

"Save it," Catherine Phillips growled. She flashed her ID without breaking stride.

"Wha—*hey.*" The patrolman lunged after her.

"Easy, buddy." Mac placed a beefy hand on the young man's shoulder. "We're with Orbis Strategic Ops," he said evenly, giving the officer time to read his ID. "Phillips, there," he nodded towards the tall form moving down the concourse, rapidly leaving him behind, "is the director."

"Well, okay then," the cop said, mollified. He turned his eyes to stare reproachfully after Kate. "Lieutenant Rossi radioed you were on your way."

"Thanks." Mac smiled faintly and jogged after his boss. Another rough moment smoothed over.

It was a familiar routine for him now, though at first it had taken some getting used to. Phillips was a hell-raiser, no doubt about it. And he, Special Agent James MacArthur (Ret), was left to sweep away the debris left in the wake of it all. When it came to incident analysis, critical thinking, working leads, and cutting to the chase, there was none better than Phillips. But somewhere along the line, the usual niceties of social behavior eluded her.

He was able to kid her about it from time to time at least, point out her to the way she blew into a room and took no prisoners. She would laugh and flash him a crooked smile, telling him she wasn't in this job to make friends.

Mac inwardly chuckled. *No danger of that.*

"Good thing that kid's orders weren't shoot-to-kill," he gasped, catching up to Kate's side.

"Hrmph" She kept her gaze straight ahead. "He was so wet behind the ears I think there was something growing back there."

"Cauliflower?" Mac suggested his favorite vegetable.

"Nah, he was too green. Broccoli, I think," Kate said, curling up the corner of her mouth in a half grin.

The concourse had been cleared of all civilian traffic; gate after empty gate flashed neon departure and arrival information, all marked "delayed" or "cancelled." A variety of official personnel dotted the walkway: airport security, police officers; Kate noticed the airport manager, Liz Furey, jawing it out with a florid-faced, middle-aged officer.

Whatever the officer was saying to the executive, it was obvious there was a difference of opinion. Her cheeks were reddened, her eyes narrowed, and her mid-length brunette hair looked windblown. "That is a load of crap, and you know it," she shrieked, just as Mac and Kate came upon them.

"Hi, Bill," Mac interrupted. "You know Catherine Phillips here, don't you?" he struck a thumb at the tall woman.

"Sure," the officer boomed, gratefully seizing upon the opportunity of escaping the airport manager.

"Lieutenant Rossi," Kate proffered her hand, "what have we got?"

"What we've *got,*" Furey said, her dark eyes flashing, "is twenty-four gates in this concourse completely shut down, air traffic stacked up from here to Albany, and revenue bleeding away out my ass. Oh, and did I mention the pissed off passengers?"

"No," Kate studied the executive coolly, "but you're pissing *me* off."

"Don't start with me, Catherine. Just because your little Orbis unit hasn't been able to get to the bottom of that hijacking." She put a hand on her hip. "You've got this whole God-damned airport on pins and needles. Disrupting schedules. Upsetting our passengers. Hell, I feel like I can't even take a shit without notifying security."

"Can we discuss your bowel problems at another time, Liz?" Kate asked, "Because the sooner you let me do my job, the sooner all that revenue will stop bleeding out your ass."

The smaller woman's face purpled. "You just wait. Vandegrift will hear about this."

"How embarrassing for you," Kate replied, her voice hard and even. She watched the smaller woman turn on her heel and storm back up the concourse, tucking a sheaf of papers under her arm as she went.

"What a piece of work," Mac muttered, shaking his head after the retreating woman. "You shouldn't let her get to you."

"Oh, she didn't. Not by a long shot," Kate said. "She ain't

seen nothing yet. Now," she turned to Rossi, "how long has it
been since the parcel was first detected?"

"We're not sure, but based on when the attendant believes
they first noticed it," the officer consulted his notepad, "we
think about an hour and fifteen minutes."

"Bomb squad deployed?"

"Yup. And they're ready to go. It's the men's john just past
gate 16."

The officer pointed towards a spot farther down the terminal. The immediate area and a good fifty yards around it was
completely clear, save for a group of men gathered near the open
space in front of the restrooms. They wore the gray, "space suit"
type garb that marked them as members of the bomb disposal
unit.

"Just say the word." He held up a walkie-talkie.

"Not yet," Kate said, taking off towards gate 16. "I want to
be there."

"No." Rossi's Adam's apple bobbed. "You—you can't. Not
without a protective suit."

"Then get me one."

"Oh, Christ." The lieutenant turned to Mac. "Can't you stop
her?"

MacArthur lifted his hands helplessly and grinned. "Nope.
Wouldn't even think of it."

* * * * * * * * * *

"All right, ma'am, now before we go in, there are just a few
things I need to review with you."

"Fine," Kate said, her voice sounding hollow and muffled
inside the helmet of her bomb protective suit. It was a strange
sensation, compounded by the fact that the voice of Officer
Andre Broome of the NYPD Bomb Disposal Unit was sounding
both through the headset she wore, and naturally, through the
insulation of the suit.

Broome was shorter than her by a few inches, wiry and
dark, with a pair of deep-set penetrating eyes. He looked at her
intently as he spoke, his voice flat and without emotion. Whether

he resented her presence or merely tolerated it, she could not tell.

"Our goal here is to utilize a series of low risk options in order to ultimately execute a safe operation, in keeping with our neutralization procedures. The position of the device has eliminated our election of a remote response—"

"Meaning you can't get a robot in there, right?" Kate tugged uncomfortably at the thick gloves she wore.

Correct, ma'am. Therefore, our technical support for this event will include manual intervention and manipulation, screening and possible disruption, with transfer of the device to a total containment vessel."

"So you go in, check it out, and get it the hell to the bomb disposal truck before we're blown to smithereens."

"Yes, ma'am. And I would add that I have not been blown to smithereens, yet." His voice was serious, professional, but through the faceplate of his suit Kate could detect the hint of a twinkle in his dark eyes. "Now, if you'll just stay close behind me and do as I say, we'll get along fine."

"You're the boss." Kate swallowed hard, fighting the butterflies in her stomach.

The remainder of the unit's support team stood in a semicircle on the main concourse, outside the bathroom holding the suspect package. Kate had seen the looks on their faces when she had demanded to be a part of the operation. To them, she was just another "suit," throwing her weight around.

Oh, she knew she could've just sat back and waited for a report on the incident, like a Liz Furey would do. Kate sighed at the thought of the airport manager. They'd butted heads more than once as her investigations had proceeded. And, though the pilot hated to admit it, Furey was right. She *was* angry that her unit had produced zero results so far. Unacceptable, by her standards. They needed a break, and soon.

Now, as she and Officer Broome cautiously entered the restroom, she came clean with herself. The truth was that she hoped by getting close to this device, by seeing it as the perpetrator had left it—the way he or she had configured it—she would get inside their head. See things through their eyes. Find something—*anything*—to go on.

She glanced back over her shoulder one last time. Through the picture glass of gate 16, she could see the reflection of the red flashing lights of emergency vehicles and the bomb disposal truck. Farther away, up the concourse, there was Mac, standing a head above Lieutenant Rossi. He saw her look his way, and gave her a thumbs up.

She lifted her thick-gloved hand in response. James Mac-Arthur was a good guy. She was glad he was on her team. Cyrus had not steered her wrong.

"All right, ma'am," Broome's voice crackled in her ear, "please stay low and close behind me, and keep your sound and movement to a minimum."

"You've got it," Kate said breathlessly, and she watched Broome set to work.

Urinals lined one wall, a series of stalls stood opposite, and at the end of the room was a row of sinks beneath a narrow mirror. A trash can, wedged in a corner between the urinals and sinks, was filled to overflowing.

They inched their way along the sticky linoleum floor, and there it was. Just to the right of the waste bin, beneath a sink, was a black Adidas gym bag, trimmed in purple.

"I have the package on visual," Broome notified his colleagues.

"10-4 unit 2. Keep us informed."

Broome squatted down about five yards from the bag and motioned Kate down as well. She drew up behind him and watched him silently open his kit and run his hands over the equipment it contained. He paused and gazed around the men's room, squinting up at the artificial lighting as though he were a sea captain testing the wind. "Not enough room in here to take a picture," he said, referring to the portable x-ray machine he carried. "I'm going in for a listen."

"10-4."

Broome was a young man, barely thirty Kate estimated, yet he moved with a deliberate steadiness and maturity more common to one far beyond his years. The pilot idly wondered just what it would take to get the man excited, and she wasn't sure she wanted to find out at the moment.

Kate noticed the shape of Broome's hands as he reached into his kit and withdrew an electron stethoscope; they were thin, delicate, almost womanly. The hands of an artist. He lifted the front flap of his helmet and slid on the single ear piece.

Slowly, with a barely perceptible motion, he placed the stethoscope's chrome bell against the side of the bag.

Kate held her breath, waiting. She felt the perspiration trickling down the side of her face, inching down the middle of her back, but there was no way to easily get at it, not in these suits. They were ventilated, but a fat lot of good that did, she considered, here on her haunches in an airport men's room. She could smell it now, the stink of too much piss and sweat, and not enough cleanser. *God, the life of a cleaning attendant. No wonder they weren't sure how long the package had been there. Judging by the overflowing trash can, it could've been hours.*

"I'm picking up a low-frequency emission," Broome said softly, quietly.

Oh, shit. "What now?" Kate dared not raise her voice to more than a hoarse whisper.

"I'm going to see if I can't take a look inside."

"Steady, unit 2. Be safe."

"Roger that, command 1," Broom replied, withdrawing the stethoscope and replacing it in his kit. Next, he produced a flat-screen display, a small control board, and a narrow cord of tubing.

"What's that?" Kate wanted to know.

"A fiber optic inspection kit," Broome explained, in a voice as kind and patient as though he were speaking to a small child. "See how the zipper is open there?" He pointed to the edge of the bag where, indeed, there was a narrow opening. "I'm going to slip the video end of this tubing through that hole, and I'll be able to receive an image of the contents of the package here on this display."

"Reminds me of when they're checking for ulcers," Kate joked, trying to calm her own frayed nerves. "But I guess I don't have to tell you about that in this job, right? All this stress."

"The technology is the same," Broome said, calmly flipping

on the equipment, "but I'm afraid I don't know what you mean about stress."

"Never mind." Kate shook her head. "Never mind." Damn it. Broome was showing her up. She needed to calm her ass down. It was the damn suit. So restrictive, so confining. She'd never thought herself prone to claustrophobia, but now...Aw, hell. After all, it *was* just a gym bag. Probably had nothing more in it than a pair of dirty sneakers and a wet towel. Oh, and a device emitting a low frequency sound, ready to blast them all to kingdom come. Nothing to worry about. On the other hand, some small part of her hoped that the package *was* related to the terrorist activity, if it would bring them that one step closer to their trail.

Broome expertly guided the tubing into the bag, and on the monitor Kate was able to see the rough, textured edges of the inside of the duffel.

"We've got your picture out here, unit 2," the command post squawked. *"Proceed with caution. Bomb basket on standby."*

"10-4, command 1. Will keep you advised."

Wow, Kate thought, *this is one cool customer. He sounds as though he's reporting on the weather.* She scooted a little closer behind him, feeling awkward in the bulky suit.

"Getting close to the source of the frequency," the officer said, and Kate wondered now whether the young bomb disposal expert could pick up on the wild pounding in her chest.

At that inopportune moment, the air conditioning in the bathroom decided to kick on. A great gust of air rushed in from a vent directly above them. Kate's mouth fell open in a silent scream as the current blew a crunched film box onto the bag. The image on the screen wavered at the soft *thunk* of the impact.

Oh, Fuck. Kate's heart stopped.

Andre Broome's hands froze in mid-air. "A foreign object has intruded upon the operation zone," he reported in a smooth, silken voice. From nowhere he produced a small pair of tweezers, and plucked the box away. "The event has been contained."

"Easy for you to say," Kate gasped, barely remembering to breathe.

"You know what the motto of my unit is, don't you?" Broome calmly continued his fiber-optic exploration.

"No," Kate shakily replied, finally giving in and pushing up under the front flap of her helmet piece in an attempt to brush the stinging sweat out of her eyes. Thank God at least she'd braided her hair back this morning, anticipating another stifling New York summer's day.

"Initial success or total failure."

"Nice," the pilot groaned, having succeeded only in poking herself in the right eye with an oversized gloved thumb.

Now visible on the screen was a large field of white, lying just beneath a darker, deeply ridged mass.

"Sneakers"

"Perhaps," Broome said, reluctant to commit.

The angle of the tubing changed, and suddenly, there it was. An oversized numeral 1. Broome pulled back on the zoom, just as a second hand swept into view.

"A wristwatch." Kate's voice was flat, unwilling to believe that they were out of it yet.

"Possibly." Activating the small grippers within the tube, Broome gently clipped on to the watchband and slid it back through the bag. The communication channel was silent, and the only sounds Kate could hear were her own harsh breathing and the hiss of the damnable air conditioning through the vents.

Not a peep from Broome.

After long, painful seconds, the possible watch came into plain view. Broome drew it closer, eyeing it carefully. And then, in a gesture that rocked Kate backwards on her heels, he released the watch with a flip, catching it with a gloved hand in mid-air.

"What the *fuck* are you doing, Broome?" Kate shouted, landing hard on her backside in a urinal.

He turned to her then, his white teeth flashing in a broad grin. "Yep, it's a watch all right. A sports watch." He dangled it out to her, laughing as she shied away. "Can you use one?"

"I don't work out," Kate muttered darkly, scrambling to her feet. Trying desperately to keep her tattered dignity in place, she stalked out of the men's room, the sound of Broome's laughter still buzzing in her ear.

Chapter
2

Catherine Phillips closed her eyes against the bright fluorescent lights of the elevator. Tired to the bone, she sagged against the rear of the car as it lifted her to her destination: the 42nd floor. At this late hour, nearly 2300 hours, she traveled alone, and was grateful for it. She was not in the mood for company, and even less so for conversation. Not after the day she'd had.

She felt the familiar lurch as *42* flashed on the overhead indicator. The heavy doors spilled open, and she gained admittance to the more subdued, discreet lighting of the apartment building's hallway. She walked soundlessly on deep-pile carpet past closed doors—the silent, cold barriers keeping her out, and whatever and whoever lay beyond them, within. And that was fine with Kate. She didn't know her neighbors, didn't care to.

She'd chosen this luxury high-rise on the upper west side not because of the security, the array of personal services available, or the status her address gave her in the eyes of some, but rather as a matter of simple convenience that the location gave her. She had privacy, easy access to transportation, and she was able to live in the city without completely feeling a part of it, being consumed and smothered by it.

Not up on the 42nd floor.

She paid more for it, she knew that, but it was worth it. She had to have it—the view. Not of the stunning panorama of the city below that others might prize. No. For Kate, the vista she valued was of the sky above. The closer she was to it, the more at ease she felt. On some days, when the clouds rolled in heavy and low off the Hudson, she swore she could reach up and touch the fuzzy edges of them with her bare hands. And on some nights since passed, when her soul was tired and her heart weary of the pain, she'd sat alone on her starless balcony and thought she just might try.

But something had held her back during those bleak days, a dogged stubbornness perhaps, and she was glad of it now. Glad that she'd happened to be piloting that Orbis Flight 2240 those four months ago. Not only because the fates had put her in a position to be able to help save the aircraft from those hijackers but also, thanks to a certain young flight attendant crewing that day, her own life had been salvaged as well.

It's been some shitty day, Kate thought, as she fumbled in her shoulder bag for her keys. She looked down at the wrinkles in her beige linen slacks; the matching blazer slung over one arm hadn't fared much better. And she was missing a button off the sleeve of her white blouse—probably lost somewhere inside that damn bomb suit.

It took some doing to find her keys amidst all the paperwork she'd brought home from the office, work that hadn't gotten done during the day. Her unexpected absence during the afternoon's bomb scare had seen to that.

Her fingers seized upon the cold hardness of her keys, and as she turned the proper one in the brass lock, she thought about the appointment she'd blown with Josh Greenfield, from the CIA. Dottie West, her office assistant, had rescheduled the appointment, bless her semi-retired senior citizen's heart. Unfortunately, the well meaning woman had forgotten to remind her of it in the first place. Dottie had been provided to her courtesy of the Orbis administrative pool, and Kate had instantly taken a liking to the big-hearted, motherly secretary.

Dottie had five grown children of her own, and Kate and her colleagues had become immediate additions to that extended family. Dottie was wonderful on the phone, calm and soothing, and even better in person—warm and good-natured. But Kate, Mac, and Rory Calverton, the other investigator on staff, had found out the hard way that the older woman was earnestly forgetful—diligently scatter-brained. Kate didn't have the heart to let her go, not when Dottie seemed so attached to them all. And, truth be known, the pilot and her team felt the same way.

Home at last. *Well, today can't get any worse.* Kate pushed open the door of her darkened apartment and blindly tossed her bag on a small hall table, as she had done countless times in the past.

She blearily reached for a light switch while at the same time she heard a splintering *crrrunch.*

"Damn it," she hissed, as the lights flickered on.

Her shoulder bag lay on the table.

Still.

Guilty.

Kate slowly picked up the bag, knowing what she would find there.

What had been a delicate, small crystal elephant, was now nothing more than a pile of shattered glass. She gazed upon it morosely for a time, resenting the intrusion of this foreign object into her personal space. She was angry with herself at having carelessly broken it, and missing like hell the woman it belonged to.

God, she sighed, *when is Rebecca coming home?* She slowly retrieved a dust pan from the kitchen and cleaned up the debris.

Home. And it was a home, she considered, now that Rebecca Hanson was in it. Just when had the petite blonde flight attendant moved in? They had never talked about it, not really. It just sort of happened. After each of the younger woman's successive shifts, particularly ones that took her to her Los Angeles base where her family was, more and more things would mysteriously appear in Kate's apartment.

The toothbrush, toiletries, and changes of clothes made perfect sense. Nothing wrong with that, of course.

Rebecca loved music, especially when they were together, and so the small stereo system and CD tower were naturally added to Kate's bedroom.

With the start-up of the Strategic Operations unit, the pilot had taken to using her spare bedroom as an office, and Hanson had happily helped her with that, setting up a small but high-powered computer and peripherals, and selecting solid, ergonomically sound office furniture. Nothing alarming about that.

But how to account for the framed museum prints that now dotted her previously barren walls, the potted ficus and dwarf palms that had suddenly sprung up throughout the apartment? And Kate did not even want to think about the controlled chaos that was now her kitchen.

The crystal elephant collection had been the latest tangible evidence that she now had a roommate. *God, how Rebecca loves those elephants,* Kate thought, as she finished sweeping up the deceased animal. The younger woman had been collecting them since she'd been a kid. "Trunks up" was the only way to go, she would say. An elephant with its trunk up, waving in the air, signified happiness and good luck.

Oh well. Kate examined the pieces of crystal in the dust pan as she walked it to the kitchen. It had been one of Rebecca's favorites, an Indian elephant, festooned with a brightly colored *howdah* in a style reminiscent of the days of the Raj.

Even now, the rich colors of broken glass shimmered in the apartment's subdued lighting, and Kate grimaced as she whisked the remains of the poor beast away, into the trash.

Done.

But Rebecca would be devastated.

Too tired to eat, Kate opened the refrigerator and took out a cold bottle of mineral water. Popping the cap, she moved back into the living room and collapsed onto the white leather sofa. She kicked off her shoes and propped her feet up on a chrome and glass coffee table, taking care to move her long legs to one side in order to avoid the small coleus plant thriving in the center of the glass.

The pilot struggled to marshal her energy reserves as she sipped at the water and debated her next move. The paperwork that awaited her? Her mind told her it needed to be done: budgets, scheduling, reports. How she hated the mind-numbing but necessary tasks. Or, should she tank on the work at hand, and pursue the sleep her deeply exhausted body told her she craved?

Funny. Tired as she'd been these past seven days since Rebecca had taken off, she'd found no respite in sleep. She'd tossed and turned, with her eyes snapping open at the break of dawn after the end of each restless night. It was always that way anymore, whenever Rebecca was gone. She felt unsettled...incomplete, without her.

Kate sighed, reached one hand behind her head, and tugged her hair free of the plait that tied it back. Her eyes drifted to the top of a bleached pine bookcase; prior to Rebecca's arrival the shelves had been two-thirds empty, now they were chock full of books on a variety of subjects. Someday, Kate resolved, she'd take a look to see what was in there. But for now, she was captured by the accusing gaze of another crystal elephant perched atop the case, slightly larger than the one lately of the hall.

The elephant was of clear crystal, simple in design, trunk raised. Still, it was as if it somehow knew of the death of one of its brethren. And if given the chance, she suspected it would have designs on rising up as a darkened, avenging shadow in the night, evening the score.

"That's right," Kate's blue eyes glittered as she stared the animal down, "I'm a murderer. Whatcha gonna do about it, big guy?"

You are losing it Phillips. She shook her head, and took another swallow of the cool water, enjoying the feel of it as it slid down her throat. There was utter silence in the apartment, save for the faint hum of the air conditioning. The luxury apartments had been well-built, with high ceilings and thick, soundproof walls that suited Kate just fine. She relished the quiet. Craved it, normally. But now...Christ, when was that little Rebecca Hanson due back? And why hadn't she heard from her in the last two days, three hours and twenty minutes?

The young Californian was quickly weaving herself into the fabric Kate's life, and during these absences when Rebecca was working, the pilot helplessly felt herself become...unraveled. It was something she'd sworn she'd deal with. Work her way through. After all, it had to be hard on Hanson, too. But damn it, this time, it seemed as though she'd been gone forever. And each time she had to say goodbye, it was becoming harder and harder to let her go.

God, how she missed her.

Kate yearned for the sound of her voice, her softness, the gentle, capable way she soothed her rough edges into oblivion. The longer she was gone, the more difficult it was for the pilot to endure—to hang on to that shred of self-worth, of value that the young blonde had reawakened in her.

Perhaps that was why she had pushed it today, gone where she really had no business going, instead of just letting the experts do their jobs. She was feeling the heat, the pressure she'd put on herself, to validate her purpose through results.

"Goose-egg" was a score the pilot had no taste for.

Kate's thoughts continued to whirl from one subject to another, and she was unaware of just when her eyes had decided to close and when her grip on the water bottle had loosened.

The *rrrrrrinnnggg* of her phone roused her from her doze.

She bolted upright like a shot, and the water bottle tipped over in her lap.

"Fuck." She lunged for the phone before her machine could pick up. "Hello."

"Uh...hi," came a familiar voice across the line. "Did I wake you up? I forget, it's still early here."

Kate turned a bloodshot eye to her wristwatch. Nearly 2345 hours. Where had the time gone? "Ah, no," she said, clearing her throat. "So, how are you? *Where* are you?"

"Here in Los Angeles, at my parents' place. I thought I'd stay with them tonight, do some catching up, before I head back tomorrow." Muffled laughter and a bit of static, and then, "Mom and Dad say hi."

"Oh, hi back," Kate said gruffly, feeling a pang of jealousy that Rebecca was having fun, spending time with these important people in her life. People whom she'd never met.

Another thing they hadn't talked about.

"So, you're definitely coming back tomorrow?" Kate pressed, her voice more harsh than she'd intended. "I wasn't sure. I mean, you haven't called since Tuesday."

The dark pilot heard a sigh at the other end of the phone. She could just imagine young Hanson running a hand through her short blonde hair. "I called your office yesterday and left a message with Dottie. Didn't she tell you?"

"Noooo."

"And today, too, Missy. She said you were out on some bomb scare at JFK? What was *that* all about?"

"I didn't get the messages. Sorry," Kate said, her voice low. "And it wasn't a bomb after all. I helped defuse a pair of old Nikes, a dirty tee shirt, and a sports watch. But I'll save that gem of a story for you when you get home."

Silence for a moment, just a distant hum on the line, and then, "I miss you, Kate."

"I miss you too, Rebecca." Kate was scandalized at the sound of a catch in her voice at that.

"Kate," Becky sounded worried, "are you okay?"

"I'm fine. I—it's just hard...without you."

"For me too," Becky said, softly.

Suddenly, Kate couldn't help it. The guilt overwhelmed her. "I broke one of your elephants."

"Oh, no. Who—don't tell me it was King Tusk?"

"No."

"Belle?"

"No."

"C'mon, Kate, spit it out. You're killing me here."

"It was Raj. I'm...I'm sorry, Rebecca. It was an accident." *Damn it,* Kate thought, *what's the matter with me?* There was a tightness in her throat, a heaviness in her chest. She could barely get the words out. All over a stinking glass elephant?

"It's okay," Becky said, sensing her lover's distress. It *was* hard, this being apart.

"If I knew where to get you another one—"

"Don't worry about it, Kate, really. As long as *you're* in one piece, that's all I care about."

There was more muffled conversation at the other end of the line and then, "Look, Kate, I've got to go. We're meeting Johnny and Eileen and the kids for dessert and coffee. "I'm wheels down at three-thirty tomorrow. Can you meet me?"

"Ah...I don't think so," Kate said, half-desperate now. "I've got some damn appointment, I think."

"No problem," Becky said quickly. "I'll swing by the office. Okay?"

"Okay."

A pause, and then, "I love you, Kate."

"Goodnight, Hanson," the pilot replied, her voice strangled, hoarse.

The connection died in her hand, and she briefly held the phone against her forehead before slowly replacing it in the receiver. Kate pushed herself to her feet, ignoring the uncomfortable wetness of the mineral water on her lap, and she walked over to the floor-to-ceiling sliding glass doors that dominated the apartment's living room. She pushed aside the thin gauze curtains that stood closed during the day, shielding the thick beige carpet from direct sunlight. Kate flipped open the lock and eased one door open, stepping out into the muggy night air.

Even at this height, at this hour, the faint breeze provided no relief from the relentless heat that had plagued New York all week. The wind stirred Kate's hair as she lifted her head to the sky, probing. Searching. Not a star in sight. The clouds were rolling in. If she tried, she'd bet she could touch them, even now. She breathed in deeply, and she could smell it, taste it, on her lips, her tongue, the back of her throat. Her senses told her it was coming, long before her mind could even process that singular thought.

A storm front was moving in. And there would be hell to pay.

****

Kate decided to take a cab to the office early the next day, after another long, restless night. The skies had opened in the early morning hours—suddenly, fiercely. The pilot had lain in her bed and watched the lightning cut jagged, scarred streaks against the blackened sky, exposing the heavy, boiling clouds as though they were a nocturnal predator revealed in a camera flash. Now, it merely rained steadily, the thunder and lightning a distant, near-mystical memory.

As Kate stood inside the doorway of her building, waiting for the sleepy doorman to hail her a cab, she debated whether she should retreat back upstairs for a raincoat. This was the worst kind of rain in New York, one that provided no relief from the heat, and instead fell warm and sticky through the polluted air, landing on the dirtied streets and sidewalks, creating a toxic, primordial soup of puddles and streams.

It would be just a short dash from the building to a cab, the pilot reasoned, and another quick leap from the cab to the J.P. Fleet building housing the Orbis offices. Kate decided she'd take a chance, and forego the raincoat. Holding her leather bag over her head, the tall woman jogged to the taxi hailed down for her, getting only moderately wet in the process.

It was barely 0630 hours when they arrived at the Fleet building, just missing the first rush of passengers for the day heading to the nearby Kennedy airport. The Strategic Operations office was on the eighth floor of the ten story building, and Kate quietly let herself in.

She was not surprised to find herself alone; as a rule she was always first in, last out. And that was saying something, considering how competent and dedicated MacArthur, Calverton, and Dottie were. But it was this time of day, in the early-morning quiet, that she did her best thinking.

Fat lot of good it had done her lately, she considered, turning on the coffee maker and winding her way towards her office. She chose to leave the lights off and sat down behind her desk, enjoying the natural light, dim though it was, creeping through the windows.

She could see the planes taking off and landing from her vantage point; activity at the airport was picking up. *Liz Furey will be pleased*, Kate thought archly.

The pilot could not help it; she felt a bit wistful watching the big birds lumber through the sky with a sublime grace. The power of flying, the feel of the stick in her hand, the thrust of the engines at take-off—she missed it. Oh, she'd kept herself sharp in the flight sim, doing her time as per FAA regulations; she could captain a flight today if she wanted to. All she had to do was ask Cyrus. He'd promised her that if she needed that "break," felt the urge to fly, he'd make it happen.

But Captain Catherine Phillips had already made up her mind that she had a job to do. She would never give up. She would complete the mission at hand, as she'd promised Cyrus—and herself—that she would. There was no turning back.

A light rap on her door. "Katie?"

"C'mon in, Cyrus." Kate felt a grin work its way across her face, chasing away some of the shadows. "I should've known you're the only guy who'd get up early enough in the day to still beat me."

"You won today, kiddo," the older man boomed, pushing the door open wide. A smile crinkled at the corners of his blue eyes, and he held two steaming mugs in his hands. "I smelled the coffee when I came in down the hall."

Kate laughed at that. "Still can't make your own, eh?"

"With you around, why should I?" Cyrus Vandegrift, Director of Flight Operations for Orbis Airlines, handed Kate a mug before sitting down with a comfortable familiarity in a leathered chair opposite the pilot's desk. "This weather is gonna be a bitch today if it keeps up."

"I thought the worst of it was over?"

"It is," the former Air Force colonel responded, "here, anyway. Just rain the rest of the day. But another band of rough weather will be moving through the Midwest. There'll be delays up and down the line, from Cleveland to Chicago."

"But that shouldn't affect any trans-con flights, right?" Kate's thoughts skipped to Rebecca out in LA.

"Not unless the equipment they intend to fly out on gets socked in elsewhere, first." Cyrus took a sip of his coffee. "Why? Expecting someone?"

Kate swung her head from the window to gaze squarely at her boss. Pale blue eyes sparkled impishly at her from behind a coffee cup.

"Maybe."

More than a mentor, more than teacher from her fighter pilot training days at Luke AFB, Cyrus Vandegrift was a friend. A confidant. Someone she trusted with her life.

Tall, barrel-chested, and still sporting a military buzz-cut, there was not an ounce of fat on the tanned, silver-haired veteran. A nose he'd broken some years ago left his deeply lined face slightly off-kilter, yet it did nothing to diminish the rakish good looks and confidence that attracted women's admiration and men's respect. He'd never told Kate the story of how his nose had been broken, though he threatened to do so one day if she were able to get him drunk enough.

It had been Cyrus who offered her the job at Orbis when she'd quit the Air Force, after her brother, Lt. Brendan Phillips, had been killed. And Cyrus, too, who had managed to talk her into staying when she'd been ready to bail out on the airline. But this particular job had been the ex-colonel's biggest coup yet—talking the mercurial pilot into forming the new Strategic Operations unit. To track down the source of the terrorist activity, stop them in their tracks, expose their network, bring them to justice. So far, her efforts had been a failure on all fronts.

"Well." He leaned back in his chair, regarding her. "Want to tell me about what happened yesterday, Katie?"

Kate sighed. "It was a fiasco. You know the drill. A 'suspect package.' Only it turned out to be smelly sneakers and somebody's watch in a goddamned men's room. Oh, and I looked like an ass—no—make that *fell* on my ass," she waved her hand in the air with a flourish, "in front of the bomb disposal squad."

"What's going on with you, Katie?" Cyrus leaned forward, his eyes grown dark and serious. "Would you rather it *had* been a bomb?"

The pilot thought about that before answering. "Yes." The rain fell more heavily now, pattering against the window. "At least a part of me does. If we just had something to go on—"

"You're pushing too hard, Katie. It will come."

"God *damn it*," Kate swore, slamming her mug down on her desk. Coffee slopped over the side. "I'm *tired* of waiting. Tired of playing this game on his terms." She shoved herself out of her seat and stalked over to the window, clasping her hands behind her back.

Cyrus kept silent, giving her the time he knew she needed, to work things through. Finally, she turned around to him, a pained expression marring her chiseled face. "I know it's him, Cyrus. I can feel it in my gut." She squeezed a fist in front of her belly. "But he's like a ghost. Never leaving a trace of where he's been, or a shred of a clue as to where he's going. Sometimes, I wonder whether he even exists."

"He does Katie, he does. We know that much." Cyrus moved to the tall woman's side, placing a hand on her shoulder. "What did Greenfield have to say?"

"Ha," Kate barked out a laugh, spinning away from her mentor. "I was so busy playing bomb jockey yesterday, I missed our appointment." The pilot held up a warning hand and returned to her seat. "Don't worry. He's rescheduled for this afternoon. Hopefully, he'll give us something we can use."

"Those spooks always do," Cyrus observed. "You don't know where they get their information. You don't *want* to know," he chuckled.

"Abbado El Yousef," Kate whispered, as if to herself. "It's got to be him. It all makes sense."

Just the name of the international terrorist brought a flutter of excitement to the dark-haired woman's stomach, fired in her the thrill of the hunt that sent her blood racing. El Yousef might not have been the hands-on perpetrator of the recent Orbis hijacking, but he certainly could have been the brains and the bucks behind it.

And he had the motive.

Abbado El Yousef was one of forty-two children born to the various wives of a Saudi Arabian oil magnate. A product of the top schools in Switzerland and England, devout Islamic fundamentalism soon drove him to advance his causes through violence and terrorism, rather than through peaceful, political means.

El Yousef vowed to wage a *jihad* against all Western governments, particularly the Great Satan—the United States—and its hated ally, Israel. The holy war was financed by a fabulous fortune estimated in the hundreds of millions of dollars that El Yousef had inherited from his late father, supplemented by bogus businesses and charities based in Switzerland which served as fronts for his illegal operations.

Embassy bombings, warfare in the Balkans, Afghanistan, Pakistan, even the World Trade Center bombings in the US—all had the mark of El Yousef stamped upon them. But nothing could pin him down; the trail was cold. His followers would support him to the death and beyond. And that was a problem for anyone—Catherine Phillips for instance—trying to bring the elusive and powerful terrorist to justice.

"If it is El Yousef," Cyrus said, his face lost in the shadows of the dim room, "he's covering his tracks well. But what else is new?" He drained his mug and turned to leave. "See what Greenfield has to say, Katie. But be careful. Don't rush into something that's over your head."

"I won't," Kate answered, offering the grizzled Air Force veteran a small smile. "That's why you put me in this job, right?"

"Riiiight," Cyrus replied, nodding his gray head as he considered that fact. "Just keep me in the loop."

"You got it, you old buzzard."

Vandegrift closed the door behind him, and Kate continued to sit, quietly, blue eyes staring out at the gray sky at the planes magically appearing and disappearing in the mists.

It would be some time yet before she would finally relent and turn on her office lights.

Before she would allow the darkness to give way to the light.

* * * * * * * * * *

It was another long, dreary day at the Strategic Operations unit, and the soaking weather outside did nothing to lighten the mood around the office. Kate and her team spent the day in a small conference room, poring over Interpol reports. They reviewed for the thousandth time the details of Flight 2240's hijacking, comparing the specs of that case to other terrorist activity world-wide, searching for commonalties and potential links.

Kate paused at one point and pushed back from the table, rubbing her tired eyes. Guns, explosives, suicide bombers,

diverted weapons shipments, chemical warfare, financial maneu-
verings, intimidation, threats—the pilot was amazed at the
countless ways human beings found to hurt and destroy one
another.

And for what?

A misguided cause or a perceived wrong; greed, hatred, or
just for the hell of it.

Kate gazed across the table at James MacArthur. The big
investigator had his shirtsleeves rolled up, exposing beefy arms,
and he was following along intently as Rory Calverton walked
him through a spreadsheet. Mac, with his formerly jet-black hair
graying at the temples, was easily old enough to be Rory's
father.

Rory Calverton was the youngest member of their team,
fresh out of the Wharton School with a Masters degree in international business and finance. He was also one hell of a whiz at
computers. The thin youth, of medium height and build, could've
had his pick of any job on Wall Street, and perhaps he still would
one day. But for now, he found his thrills responding to the
exciting pull he felt from the underbelly of the business world. A
financial cesspool where bad people hid behind anonymous
account numbers and money managers; where criminals laun-
dered their cash rather than investing it; where corporations fun-
neled revenues towards supporting illegal activities rather than
generating a return on investment to stockholders.

Rory had been recruited by the DEA and was ready to commit to that deal, when a buddy of his from Wharton told him
what Orbis was looking for. Working as a key member of a
smaller unit within a larger organization appealed to Rory; he'd
never liked big crowds. He far preferred to spend time in front of
his computer, tracking precious metals futures and offshore
banking activity.

Catherine Phillips had recognized she didn't know a hell of
a lot about computers and finance, but she figured if her unit was
to have any hope of tracking down an international terrorist in
his lair, they needed someone who did. No, Kate was about contacts and experience. About putting together the big picture
through exhaustive investigation and plain old hard work. And if

there was any *special* operation that needed to happen as a part of that, then she was the woman willing to step up and get it done.

Rory Calverton had arrived for his interview sporting shaggy, shoulder length hair of a most unnatural shade of blonde, oversized jeans, a Penn T-shirt and a pierced nose. A Walkman hung loosely around his neck, silent, for the moment. Kate had been a bit taken aback, to say the least. She carefully read through his impressive credentials, talked to him some, and found herself mightily annoyed at the wad of bubble gum he kept popping in her face.

The pilot had taken him out to a computer and asked him to produce a listing of all the financial transactions initiated by, or on behalf of, Stefan Bukoshi, Mishka Rhu, Alexandra Sadrio, and Roberto Andizzi, within the past twenty-four month period. The four individuals had been the hijackers on Flight 2240.

Kate had left the kid alone to get herself another cup of coffee and do some hated paperwork, thinking that was the last she would see of Rory Calverton. Within thirty-five minutes, the young, brown-eyed Penn grad was tapping lightly on Kate's door, casually showing her a printout of the financial activity for the hijackers *and* their immediate families, over a forty-eight month period.

Right then and there, Kate had told him that if he were willing to lose the gum, he'd have the job. He had told her he'd think about it, his eyes blank, his face expressionless.

A week later, Rory dropped by the office as though he'd just stepped out for a cup of coffee, and accepted the offer. Pierced nose and all, she hadn't regretted it since. Of course Dottie mothered him like nobody's business, and even MacArthur had warmed to the young man once he'd seen what the kid could do. With Mac, actions and results spoke louder than looks and words.

Kate threw up both her arms in a stretch, and was just about to wade back into the stack of printouts, when the intercom buzzed.

"*Catherine, Josh Greenfield is here to see you.*"

"Show him to my office, Dottie, I'll be right there."

"Right away, dear," Dottie signed off, and Kate could not help but cringe at the endearment.

"Well boys, I hate to leave this party but..." Kate grinned.

"Don't worry," Mac looked up over the spectacles he'd taken to wearing whenever going over small print, "it'll still be raging on when you're through."

"No doubt," Kate chuckled, heading for the door.

****

Catherine had met with Josh Greenfield a number of times over the past few months. Cyrus had prevailed upon the connections he still had in DC from his Pentagon days, to have the Orbis Strategic Operations unit receive periodic, classified briefings from the Central Intelligence Agency. Although the Agency was not usually the most accommodating when it came to partnering with outside organizations, they'd been hitting the wall, too, when it came to tracking down the funding source of the recent rash of terrorist activity.

And so The Powers That Be had determined that perhaps two organizational heads were better than one. Additionally, a key requisite of the unlikely partnership was a reciprocal sharing agreement. Meaning that, whatever information Phillips and her team came up with, they'd have to relay to the Agency. And who knew? Maybe they'd get lucky.

"Hi, Josh." Kate came striding into her office, offering the agent her hand. "Uh, sorry about yesterday. Bomb scare and all."

"I heard," Josh said, grinning. He stood to greet her. Agent Greenfield was boilerplate Agency issue: average build, average looks, with an above average intelligence. He wore an uninteresting blue suit, the better to complement his medium complexion and unremarkable brown hair. Greenfield was the type of agent who could fit in anywhere. Or simply disappear into nowhere.

He hadn't expected much from this assignment, at first thinking he'd done something to disenchant his superiors. But he'd soon realized that Catherine Phillips and her team had their shit together, even if they presented quite a preposterous picture when gathered together in their small conference room. They would never have made it at the Agency. Not Phillips, whose tall, stunning good looks would turn every head in any room she walked into. Not MacArthur, who though smart and dedicated, could sometimes be like a bull in a china shop. Calverton...well...he had potential, if only he'd consider a Brooks Brothers makeover. And as for Dottie? She was a sweet woman. She just couldn't seem to be able to find the cream for his coffee whenever he visited.

"Whatcha got for me, Josh?" Kate sat down heavily in her chair.

"This." He threw a file onto her desk. "There's a lot of detail in there that you and your boys will want to review. But the reader's digest version is that Abbado El Yousef could definitely be our guy."

"Really?" the pilot said, taking a sip of her coffee. "Tell me more."

"He's headquartered somewhere in Afghanistan now, since his own people, the Saudis, kicked him out. So he isn't too far from all that messy Balkan stuff. Not that that means anything, he never stays in one place for too long. But wherever he goes, he's protected by an armed security force."

"Great," Kate said, shaking her head. "It makes him that much harder to get to."

"*If* we can link him to these 'events,' then yes, it will be hard to get our hands on him, without local assistance. But I doubt that will happen—the assistance, I mean." Greenfield took a swallow of bitter coffee. Black. "He believes he's the Chosen One, destined to lead the *umma*, the worldwide Muslim community. He's got a strong foundation of support, Catherine. Make no mistake of that."

"We've got to find a way to connect him to these events." The pilot ran a hand through her loose, dark hair. "You've looked at his e-trails? The banking end of it?"

"Endlessly. The problem is in tracing his funds. El Yousef invests in about sixty legitimate companies, from banking to agriculture to construction—any one of which could provide a cover for his terrorist activities."

"If not *all* of them." Kate's voice was hard as she drummed her fingers on her desk. "So, if we've still got nothing to pin directly on him, why are you more convinced now that he's our guy? Not that I'm sorry to have you finally agree with me." She gazed levelly at the agent.

"It's in there." He pointed to the file. "Your Calverton will want to really give it a going over. El Yousef uses a system of laptop computers that transmit encrypted communications to his terrorist cells via satellite."

"What?" Kate's drumming stopped, and she sat straighter in her chair. "Who's keeping an eye on these guys? How can you just...just access a satellite?"

"Welcome to the new millennium. How many cars do you think are driving around out there receiving satellite signals on Global Positioning Systems? Or receiving *and* sending on cellular phones? Look," he explained, "if you've got the money, you can get yourself access. Hell, El Yousef could buy himself one, for that matter."

"The connection, Josh," Kate pressed. "Keep talking."

"Last week, one of our listening posts in Madrid picked up a transmission. We think it came from El Yousef. If it did," the agent grimaced, "he's planning something. Big."

"What? Where? Is there a timetable—"

"Whoa, hold on," Josh held up his hands. "We don't have any more details than that. It was only a partial transmission, and encrypted, remember. Our experts couldn't come up with anything more specific. Believe me," his brown eyes grew sober, "I wish they had."

"So a fanatical international terrorist with unlimited funding and 21st century technology, is—how did you put it—planning something big. That's it."

"That's it. I'm sorry." Josh paused. "How about at your end, Catherine? Anything yet?"

"No," Kate said, letting her gaze wander to the window. "We're still analyzing the Interpol reports."

"Uh-huh. Well," the agent stood, "let's keep in touch. If something breaks, it could happen soon, and we'll need to be ready to move."

"Right," Kate replied, her mind whirling. She barely noticed when Greenfield departed her office.

****

An hour later Kate had finished going through the file the CIA agent had left with her, feeling no closer to finding any answers. She tiredly massaged her temples. Her encoding skills were rudimentary at best; still, she had endlessly studied the encryption grid, hoping that something would jump out at her. But no. Greenfield was right. Perhaps Rory Calverton could make better sense of it.

The intercom on Kate's phone buzzed just as her door burst open.

"Catherine, you have a—"

"Hey there, stranger. Can I come in?" A rain-drenched blonde head poked around the doorjamb.

Wordlessly, Kate stalked out from behind her desk, pulled the visitor into her office, and slammed the door shut. In one swift motion, she swept the newcomer up into her arms, hungrily searching out damp lips with her own.

"Wow," Becky said, pulling away breathlessly at last. "It's good to see you, too."

"I missed you so much." Kate dipped down and leaned her forehead against Rebecca's.

"Me too," Becky sighed, unwilling to break the contact, although she knew she was forming a puddle on the floor. "Look, I'm getting you all wet."

"No kidding," Kate rumbled, finally allowing the smaller woman to wriggle herself free.

Rebecca's face turned scarlet. "Kate." Green eyes flashed as the flight attendant shrugged off her trench coat. "I meant the weather."

"Me too." Kate innocently held up her palms, and then swooped in for another kiss. "Mnnn, you smell nice," she said, pushing a strand of damp hair away from Rebecca's brow.

"I don't know why that is." She wrapped her arms around Kate's waist. "I feel as though I've been in these clothes forever.

And we had problems with the climate controls in the tube on the way in—it wasn't pretty. I think my eighteen hour deodorant surrendered after six."

"Yeow." Kate's voice was sympathetic. "Who was Captain?"

"Roger Sheridan," Becky replied.

"A good guy."

"Yeah, he was good," she lightly kissed the tip of Kate's nose, "but I've known better."

Kate lifted an eyebrow and looked down at her young lover. "Flattery will get you everywhere."

"I'm a-hopin'." Becky grinned. "It's Friday, I've got four days off, and I wanna go *home.*"

"You've got it," Kate decided. She grabbed Greenfield's file from her desk, swung her bag onto her shoulder, and came back around to Rebecca. "I'm ready."

"I don't know how you find anything in this office, Kate. It's a mess. My messages are probably in that swamp somewhere." She took a curious step towards the mounds of paper strewn on the pilot's desk.

"Ooooh, no you don't." Kate playfully grabbed at the white sleeve of her Orbis Airlines blouse. "Let's go."

"You don't have a coat?"

"Nope."

"Are you crazy? Kate, it's pouring out there."

"Geez, Hanson, calm down, will ya? I won't melt."

"You..." Becky clicked' her tongue disapprovingly, and allowed Kate to usher her out into the main office.

"Oh, just a sec." The pilot ducked into the conference room where she'd left Mac and Rory. As promised, the "party" was still going on.

"Hey, guys, I'm outta here."

"Party-pooper." Mac threw a pen down on the table. "You're not missing anything. This gig has been dead for a while."

"Yeah," Rory agreed. "We're like...stuck."

"Go home, guys. We get to do it all over again Monday," she said, knowing that she'd probably see them here in the office at least one time or another over the weekend. "Oh," she handed

Mac the file, "Josh left this. Take a look at it. Rory, there's an encryption grid in there you might like to play around with."

"Really?" he said, his eyes brightening. "Cool."

Kate grinned and shook her head. "G'night, guys."

"Goodnight," they chorused back to her, already delving into the contents of the file.

Back in the main office, Becky was just slipping into her trench coat again. "I think there's an umbrella in my bag," she said, reaching for her pull-case.

"Forget it." Kate cut in front of Becky and grabbed the bag. "Let's go." The pilot lowered her head and buzzed next to the young blonde's ear, "I want to get you home as soon as possible." She turned to the heavy-set, gray haired woman who sat near the front office door. "Have a good weekend, Dottie."

"Oh, goodnight, Catherine. And nice to see you again, Becky dear."

"You too, Dottie," Becky leaned down and gave the secretary a peck on the cheek. "And give Mr. Chips a hug from me, will you?"

"Done." The older woman beamed, adjusting the glasses on her face.

With a wave goodnight, Kate and Becky were gone.

"Okay," the pilot said as they headed towards the elevator. "I know I'm going to regret asking this, but *who* is Mr. Chips?"

Becky stopped short, planted her hands on her hips, and cocked her head at her taller companion. "Why, Mr. Chips is her cat, of course. Shame on you for not knowing."

"Rebecca..." Kate shook her head and chuckled as they resumed their trek towards the elevator. "You amaze me. How do you find these things out?"

"It's easy," Becky pressed the button and the doors immediately opened. "I just ask. It's called 'conversation.'" Her nose crinkled at her companion in a teasing grin. "You should try it, sometime."

* * * * * * * * * *

As a taxi took them back to Manhattan, Catherine gritted

her teeth and did the right thing: knowing Rebecca's boundless appetite for a good meal, she offered to stop at a restaurant or grocer's and pick something up. "You don't want to know what's going on in the refrigerator," she said.

"That's okay," Becky replied matter-of-factly, her face betraying no emotion. "We can go out later or just order up something." She kept her eyes on the rain-soaked cityscape blurring by, but she reached out her hand and laid it on the back of Kate's own as it rested on the seat of the cab.

The elevator ride to the 42nd floor was definitely a local, with Becky pausing to chatter happily with the other tenants as they trudged on and off.

"What's it doing out, Becky?" A young man dubiously cast a sidelong glance at the tall, dark, and water-logged form of the pilot. Unfortunately, a renewed cloudburst had occurred just as the cab pulled up at the corner of their building. Kate's leather bag had offered her little protection, and even now she could feel the warm water droplets trickling down her head, her arms, her back.

"Can't you tell?" Becky pointed a thumb towards her companion. "And this one refuses to wear a raincoat."

"It's just a shower," Kate mumbled through wet lips, vowing to take her revenge on Rebecca Hanson at her earliest possible convenience.

At last, their floor arrived. "Let me get it." Becky used her own key, unlocking the door and stepping inside. "Yeah," she said, reaching for the light switch, "I can see now I never should've put Raj on that table. I don't know what I was thinking—"

A strong hand suddenly grabbed hers, preventing her from reaching the lights.

"Rebecca..." Heated breath on the back of her neck in the dark.

"Hmnn?" A hot bolt of desire surged through the flight attendant at the anticipation of what she knew was to come.

"The fuck with the elephant."

They barely made it from the hall to the living room. A dim, opaque glow filtered through the gauze curtains, giving them just enough light to leave a barely discernible debris trail of bags, shoes, a coat, and keys.

"Kate, I want to get out of these clothes," Rebecca weakly protested.

"Good, because *I* want you out of those clothes," Kate growled. She loosened the young blonde's white blouse and pushed it off her shoulders.

"But I need a shower."

"We both just got one." The pilot assaulted the flight attendant with her kisses, her senses igniting with the salty taste of Rebecca's silken skin, the sweet juices of her mouth. At last she saw the blonde's head roll back, eyes closed in surrender, and the small, lithe body melted into hers. "That's right." Kate's voice was hoarse as she gently lowered Rebecca to the floor.

The younger woman relaxed into the thick pile carpeting as though it were a feather bed, and quickly, Kate discarded her own ruined clothing. The climate controls had done their job throughout the hot, muggy day; the air was cool to the point of a chill inside the apartment—just how Kate liked it. She could feel it now, like ice against the wetness on her skin. It energized her, invigorated her—and it didn't stand a chance against the burning inferno, the desire for Rebecca Hanson, a heat that threatened to consume her from within.

The pilot hovered over Hanson in the gloom, one hand tracing the line of the girl's jaw. "Oh, Rebecca, I missed you so much."

Green eyes blinked open, and Rebecca reached out, running her hands over the smooth, muscled skin of the taller woman's arms and back. "I die a little bit inside when I'm not with you. You know that, don't you, Kate?"

The rain continued to tap against the windows, in a persistent drumbeat that matched the pounding of Kate's heart. And in the gathering darkness, as the day slipped away into night, blue eyes were set aflame. "Then don't go. Don't ever go."

* * * * * * * * * *

Catherine Phillips was in the middle of the most deeply

restful sleep she'd had in days. And her unconscious body was
enjoying every moment of it.

Hanson had finally gotten the shower she wanted, after a
fashion, and the pilot had taken diligent, lengthy care to make
sure not a single spot was missed during the cleaning process. A
product of years of military-style discipline, she was nothing if
not thorough.

Later, Rebecca had thrown on a robe to take delivery of
some Chinese take-out they'd ordered. Egg rolls, rice, lo mein,
Szechuan chicken, spareribs, and something called Four Happiness pork—just because Becky liked the name of the dish.

They had talked for a time, Becky catching Kate up on the
doings with her family, and the pilot filling the younger woman
in on her long, frustrating week.

"Oh Lord," Rebecca had groaned, squeezing her eyes shut,
"I can't believe you were trying to defuse a bomb. I can't leave
you alone for a minute, can I?"

"It wasn't a bomb," Kate had protested, licking a dollop of
spicy sauce from the corner of her lover's mouth.

"Yeah, but you didn't know that at the time. Wait." the
younger woman had halted her tirade. "Why should *any* of this
surprise me? Calm," she breathed in deeply, "I must remain
calm."

"Does this help?" Leaning up on one elbow, the dark-haired
woman had reached a hand over to Rebecca's middle, and begun
a slow, circling massage of her flat belly.

"Well," Becky had carefully considered her body's response
to Kate's intervention, "a little."

"You know what they say about Chinese food," the pilot had
said then, flashing Becky a devilish smile as she shoved the
take-out boxes to one side, "you're hungry an hour later."

They'd finally fallen asleep as the night wore on, tangled in
one another, their hunger at last sated. Catherine luxuriated in
having Rebecca near—in her arms, her bed, her heart. Whether
awake or asleep, it was a presence that soothed her, centered her,
gave her life meaning.

She was reluctant to leave this place of warmth, of bliss, not
when she'd just found it again. But there were demands upon

her, people counting on her, calling her...

"Katie. Katie."

No. She would not respond. She didn't have to now. Rebecca was home. She would take care of everything...

"Katie. If you're there, please, pick up. It's—"

"Cyrus?" Kate's voice was thick with sleep and egg noodles as she pushed herself up on her elbows. Disoriented, she ran a hand through her dark hair. "What the hell—?" She picked up her watch from the bedside stand. Nearly 0300hours. Damn. And she hadn't even heard the phone. This had better be good.

The tall woman reached across Rebecca's soundly slumbering form, and grabbed the receiver.

"Talk," she said hoarsely, trying not to wake her bedmate.

"It's bad, Katie, real bad. I need you in here, now."

"Cyrus, my God, what is it?" Alarm ripped through the pilot's guts with the chill and intensity of an ice pick. Beside her, Rebecca was stirring. Sensing Kate's distress, the girl reached out her hand. Kate eagerly clasped it and held it tight.

"We've lost one, Katie. Fell right the hell off the scope with no goddamned warning at all."

The usually unflappable Vandegrift was shaken; Kate could hear it in his voice. A profound feeling of dread seized her. "No...Cyrus..." she shook her head as if trying to clear it.

It couldn't be. Perhaps she had heard wrong...or was still dreaming. "Are you sure?" she blurted out, instantly recognizing the absurdity of that question.

"Katie..." His voice broke. *"We've got a plane down."*

Chapter
3

"No way. Absolutely not." Catherine Phillips stalked about the bedroom, grabbing her travel bag and carelessly throwing a change of clothes and toiletries into it. Her long dark hair fell loose and was still damp from the shower she'd just taken; her blue oxford shirt hung open, and the button of her jeans gapped open.

"Kate, please. If you'd just—"

"Didn't you hear what I just said?" Icy blue eyes narrowed. "There is no way you are coming with me." Kate's face was set like a stone; her jaw was clamped shut, and her normally tanned skin took on a pale, translucent glow in the white light blazing around her. After Cyrus' call, the pilot had stormed through the bedroom switching on every available light. It was as though she'd tried to chase away the phantoms of the nether world, that dwelled so near in those darkened hours between the midnight and the dawn.

Rebecca Hanson crossed her arms in front of her chest, swallowed hard, and shook her head. "I have the time off, Kate. And I don't think you should be alone—"

"What you *think,*" Kate cut her off, "is not the point. I have a job to do, and it doesn't involve you."

Kate sounded angry, that was obvious, but Becky suspected

it was all bluster. She'd already caught sight of the pain and anguish that flickered just behind the taller woman's blue eyes. How she wanted to make it all disappear. There was only one thing for it. She would not let Kate continue on this way, as the woman was no doubt used to doing in the past, shouldering alone a frustrated rage and helplessness that inevitably bled into a numbing withdrawal. No, she would not let Captain Catherine Phillips get away with it. Not this time.

"Now, did you see where I threw that damned bag with the laptop?" The pilot dragged a hand through her hair. "Cyrus said he'd have Rory e-mail me with a manifest of the flight."

"Kate," Rebecca's voice was tired, patient, "do you know how to operate it? I've never even seen you take it out of the bag."

"It can't be too complicated," the pilot replied, miffed that the younger woman had chosen to point out her technical short-comings. "I mean, I have a desk-top model. And I can fly the most complicated planes Uncle Sam has in his arsenal. I think I can get by."

Kate wrenched the zipper on her travel bag shut, grabbed a second smaller, battered suitcase sitting near her night table, and moved towards the doorway.

A small blonde with blazing green eyes stood in it, blocking her path.

"I'm coming with you."

"Don't argue with me, Rebecca." Kate's voice was hard. "Get out of my way."

"No. Not until you say yes."

"Forget it."

The pilot tried to push past her, but Becky reached out and seized her with both hands.

"Then I'll follow you, Kate, I swear I will. Can't you see what's happening to you?"

Kate pulled an arm free of the smaller woman's grasp and glared at her.

"I can see," Becky continued, "and I know you're hurting. That you feel like you've failed, somehow." She could see Kate stiffen at that. "Well you haven't, Kate, not by a long shot," she

said fiercely. "Not in my book, anyway. But you shouldn't be
alone right now. I...don't want that. For either of us."

Damn. Kate released a heavy, hitching burst of air, and
turned her glistening eyes towards the window. The ceiling.
Anywhere but at Rebecca Hanson. For if she did, she feared
she'd never be able to get the words out. "It's going to be awful,
Hanson," she said weakly, in a voice she barely recognized as
her own. "A fucking nightmare from hell, if you must know."
She paused, collecting herself. "The kind of nightmare that'll
haunt you forever. A shadow walking just behind you when
you're awake. Oozing into your soul while you sleep. Nobody
should have to see...to go through that."

At last, Kate's gaze fell upon Rebecca, and she reached out
and briefly rested the back of her fingers against her cheek.
"Especially you."

The flight attendant sighed, understanding that once more
the pilot was trying to look out for her. To protect her. It was a
trait that, while admirable, could be most annoying at times.
"Kate. Let this be my decision to make. Please, baby? We need
to stick together, you and I. Just look at you." She took a step
back and gestured at the tall, dark woman. "You're walking out
of here half-dressed, half-packed, and carrying your flight kit."

Kate's eyes dropped down, noticing for the first time that,
indeed, she'd grabbed her flight case as she'd done thousands of
times before when rushing out of her apartment to the airport.
But that had been when she was flying. And she wasn't piloting a
plane anywhere this dark early-morning. Cyrus had arranged for
an Orbis charter to take her and the rest of the Orbis team to the
crash site.

Kate shook her head and let some of the tension leave her
body as she considered the wisdom of her friend's words. She
released her flight kit to the floor with a *thunk* and curled the
corner of her mouth up in a small, wan smile. "Kinda half-assed,
huh?" She began to button her shirt one-handed.

"Here, let me." Smaller hands reached out. "I can't take you
anywhere, you know that?"

Kate closed her eyes against the warmness of the gentle
touch against her skin. Rebecca's request...it was wrong...all

wrong, and went against every better instinct she possessed. But if there was one thing she'd learned in these past months with Rebecca Hanson, it was that being wrong was sometimes okay. And that sometimes you just had to step aside, to swallow your pride, and trust in something, or someone, else. It was a new process, and one unfamiliar to her, but she was working on it. By God, she'd get it right yet.

"Aw hell." Kate looked down at Rebecca's earnest, upturned face and threw in the towel. "Can you be ready in ten minutes?"

"I'm a flight attendant," Becky said softly. "Watch me."

****

It was a dreary cab ride to the airport, but the rain had stopped, and Kate was not surprised to see that the traffic, even in the muggy wee hours of a Saturday New York morning, flowed steadily around them. People moving, rushing, wrapped up in their own worlds, unaware and uncaring of the disaster that was unfolding in the red spruce and white pine forests of northeastern Maine.

New York, Kate thought ironically, gazing out a smeared window, *the city that never sleeps.* The streets glistened wet, like black ice, and there was a distinct chill in the cab that matched the one in her gut, despite the relative heat of mid-summer.

Trying to shake off the feeling, she swung her gaze to the young woman by her side. Hanson sat quietly, unmoving, her face pale and still, yet determined.

God, what am I getting her into? Kate wondered, and she reached out and slowly took Rebecca's hand in her own. Cyrus had said that she could name her own staff, but this was certainly the last thing she'd had in mind, even if it was for the short term. What if it were all too much for Rebecca?

"You sure about this?"

"Kate," Becky leveled green eyes at her, "I have no doubt that my place is with you. Deal with it, okay?" She offered the pilot a crooked grin.

Kate gave Becky's hand a squeeze. "I'm workin' on it."

It was 0420 hours by the time they arrived at JFK, and it

would be another half hour before the Dornier 328 Cyrus Vandegrift had commandeered from Orbis Express would take off. The
terminal was nearly empty at the early hour; the retail shops
were closed, their shutters pulled down tight. The artificial lighting gleamed unnaturally white against the faint glow of the airport runways outside the picture windows. The runways
themselves were no more than thin shimmering strips of silent
concrete, nearly swallowed whole by the darkened sky above. In
the distance, an empty baggage cart moved towards the edge of
the terminal, a ghostly rider gliding along the tarmac.

A small cluster of Orbis staff gathered near the gate; their
faces were drawn, and they spoke in hushed tones. Cyrus would
not be making the flight, choosing instead to stay behind and run
damage control with the press in New York. He had faith in Kate
and her team, and there would be more than enough people
crawling around the crash site, screaming for answers, without
adding his own voice to the chorus.

Kate let her eyes travel around the assembled group: people
from Orbis' Risk Management Unit; Bo Sample, Orbis' executive vice president of operations, and several of his staffers—PR
people no doubt. The "suits." Sample was nice enough, Kate
considered, from what little contact she'd had with the fellow
since she'd made the job switch. Young, no more than forty, he
dressed exclusively in dark blue business suits and white shirts
that very nearly matched the Orbis corporate colors. Always
quick with a handshake and a smile, the tall, angular executive
was not smiling now. And gone was his formal attire, replaced
instead by khakis, work boots, and a blue polo shirt that looked a
few sizes too big for him. His shoulders were slumped over, as
though he bore the weight of the world upon them. *Maybe he
does*, Kate considered, *the weight of Orbis, anyway.*

Additional travelers on the Orbis Express flight included
two FBI investigators from the Bureau's Manhattan command
post. They were hitching a ride to the crash site, all in the spirit
of inter-agency cooperation. About fifteen people in all, perhaps
half-filling the Dornier 328.

Introductions were made, hands shaken, business cards
exchanged, and what few crash details were known, reviewed.

The FAA and NTSB would already be rushing teams to the accident scene too, with all parties converging in the old-growth forests just outside of Pohassat, Maine, northeast of Bangor. But it would be the FBI who would be running the show, Kate knew, until such time as the "accident" could be termed exactly that. And the pilot had her doubts about the investigation reaching that prospective conclusion. Planes didn't just fall out of the sky.

Rebecca trailed behind Kate, smiling politely when she was introduced, trying to remember everyone's names. As Bo Sample and Kate discussed the weather conditions over Maine, Becky found herself drifting away from the group, edged out by the executive's hangers-on. The flight attendant didn't mind. So far, no one had questioned her purpose, they'd simply assumed she was a member of Catherine Phillips' team. *Maybe I am,* Becky thought wryly, as she shifted Kate's laptop bag from one shoulder to the other. God knew that Kate could use the organizational help. It was at Becky's own insistence that they had fired up the laptop before leaving the apartment, just to make sure the darn thing was working properly and to download Kate's e-mail. Best to clear that stuff out now before the deluge resulting from the crash hit.

E-mail. And then there was that, Becky sighed, as she pushed a day-old newspaper aside and sat down in a seat near the jet way entrance. "Good God, Kate," she'd said when she'd seen the extensive queue of mail sitting out there, "Look at all this older stuff. How often do you go through it?"

"Every day," Kate had replied, looking over Becky's shoulder at the flickering screen. "I've been meaning to set up some separate save files for some of it, but I just haven't had the time."

"Don't worry about it." Becky had held up a silencing hand. "I'll take care of it."

Becky heard one of the FBI men call out to Kate and motion her over. The tall woman excused herself from Bo Sample and walked slowly towards the agent, putting on her best corporate face. *Better let her do her thing,* Becky thought, *and stay out of the way.*

After a moment's consideration, she opened the laptop bag,

flipped open the unit, and turned it on. *Time to start earning your keep, Becky-girl.*

"So, Catherine, has Orbis received any direct threats of violence or sabotage?" Special Agent Hank Danner felt for a packet of cigarettes in his breast pocket. "You know, terrorist stuff?" Danner was forty-something, with a gut hanging over his belt, a reddened nose that was not from lack of sleep, and deep wrinkles that lined his face. *Too much eating, drinking, and smoking,* Kate surmised. She'd met his type before, both in and out of the military.

"We get it every day, you know that," Kate finally replied. Danner would not be the Agent in Charge of the investigation, and just as well, since she'd taken an instant dislike to him when they'd been introduced. "The programmer out in La Jolla who was pissed off when his Orbis stock took a dive after the hijacking. The banker in London who was bumped from his overseas flight and missed his business meeting in New York. And our special friend in Willacoochee, Georgia, who threatens at least once a month to destroy Orbis unless we turn over control of the airlines to the Callistoans."

"Beg pardon?" Danner leaned forward as he took out a pack of Camels.

"Callisto. It's one of the moons of Jupiter. This guy's from there. Or so he says." She gave the robust agent a dry stare.

"Ah...gotcha." Danner shook his head. "You're right. There's always that lot of powder kegs and nut cases. Not to mention," he eyed her carefully, "the 'Abbado El Yousef's' of the world." He waited for a response. "Right?"

"El Yousef doesn't make threats, *Hank,*" Kate said, quickly tiring of the conversation, "he takes action. That's what makes him dangerous." A pause. "And deadly."

"Ah hell," the agent brought a cigarette to his lips, "it's just too damn early to tell 'til we hit the ground up there. Shit, for all we know, they could have run into a flock of Canadian geese or something."

"Not at 30,000 feet. According to Bangor Control, that was when they received the last transmission from Flight 180." Kate checked her watch, wishing it were time to leave. Another ten minutes to go. *Damn.* Under the best of circumstances the pilot hated talking shop, preferring to let her actions do the talking for her. And now, as conversations all around her shifted to speculation and conjecture, she felt her patience waning. Worse, this guy was a talker, too. He didn't know when to stop running his mouth.

Special Agent Hank Danner took out a Zippo lighter.

"It's 'no smoking' in here, you know," Kate said, casting a glance towards where Rebecca was curled up in a seat, playing with the laptop. Kate knew how sensitive her young friend was to second-hand smoke. Her eyes would tear up, and she would immediately become congested. Hell, the first time she'd seen the phenomenon, she'd thought Hanson was coming down with the flu.

"There's nobody around." Danner opened his arms towards the deserted terminal, the unlit cigarette dangling from his lips.

"I'm around."

The agent took a long, hard look at the tall, imposing woman in front of him. They'd be working together over the next few days, weeks even, and given the frosty gaze capturing him now, he decided he'd do well to choose his battles carefully. *Great. Just what I need. Some bitch with attitude getting in my way.*

"Hey, no problem," he said, shrugging his shoulders and tapping the cigarette back into his pack. "Wife says I gotta quit, anyway."

"You should listen to her." Kate turned at the sound of heavy footsteps pounding down the concourse towards the group.

"Hiya, boss."

"Mac." Kate felt some of her irritation flee as her eyes took in the familiar sight of her husky chief investigator. He had a garment bag folded over one arm and carried a light jacket with the other. The wrinkled tail of his sports shirt was working its way out of his putty-colored slacks.

"What's the word on this again?" The big man drew up to her side and ran a hand through his rumpled graying hair. "I was so bushed when you called, all I heard was 'crash, Maine,' and 'airport—*now*.'"

"I know what you mean," Kate replied, gazing fondly at her chief investigator. "I couldn't believe it when Cyrus called me. Didn't *want* to believe it." She paused, glancing out the window into the darkness beyond, before she continued. "The flight originated in Lisbon, stopped in Paris, and was delayed getting out of Charles deGaulle. Three and a half hours late, it finally took off for Montreal." She hesitated. "It never made it."

"Maine, eh?" Mac rubbed the stubble on his chin. "We're lucky it didn't hit in the goddamned ocean."

"No kidding," Kate agreed. "Emergency teams are on site already. Agency types: NTSB, FBI, FAA—us—are on the way. We've even got a couple of your former Bureau colleagues hitching a ride on this flight." Kate nodded towards Hank Danner. "And Rebecca's helping us out too, just with some of the organization and information coordination stuff."

Mac followed Kate's eyes towards where the young blonde sat diligently working on a computer. The big man had certainly become aware over the past few months of how close Becky and his boss were, and it never escaped his notice how the mood of the mercurial Catherine Phillips instantly changed for the better whenever the flight attendant was around. Of course, he'd heard of the smaller woman's bravery during the hijacking of Orbis Flight 2240, and of the ultimate price she'd nearly paid then for her actions.

This would be a rough trip, on all of them. And for Catherine's sake, he was glad Becky would be coming along.

MacArthur turned back towards Kate. "In other words, all that detail shit you hate."

Kate smiled. "You noticed, huh?"

"Hey, I'm an investigator," Mac said. "I'm paid to detect these things." He paused before continuing, his voice more somber now. "Casualties?"

"It doesn't look good Mac," Kate said, noticing for the first time how tired Mac looked—as though he'd just rolled out of bed. Hell, they all had, for that matter. "It's..." She fought to control the emotion in her voice. "There's nothing. No word, so far. Last communication at 0229 hours, 30,000 feet, en route to

Montreal—everything was normal."

"What about the weather?" Mac stifled a yawn. "It's been pretty crappy around here, after all."

"Low rain clouds, but they should've been flying in smooth air at that altitude. No reports of turbulence in the area. Rory's following up on it; he'll keep us posted."

"What a kid." Mac shook his head in wonder. "I left him at the office tonight—last night, I mean—at eight o'clock. Still trying to crack that code."

"I'm worried he might not have to, now," Kate said, stuffing her hands into the pocket of the blue wind-breaker Rebecca had made her wear.

"El Yousef?" MacArthur's eyes glittered in thinly veiled disgust.

"Maybe. It's our job to find out."

They stood together silently for a moment, each considering the implications of the mandate the Strategic Operations unit had been charged with. To protect. To prevent. To save. Had they failed in that duty tonight? Had the 210 souls on board the Boeing 747 paid the price for that possible failure? Or not? Kate struggled with the emotions battling inside of her, pressing upon her with all the force of pulling an 8-G loop. She didn't know which answer she dreaded more.

Chapter
4

The rushing waters of the mountain stream exploded with a churning, primal force, battering solid rock, sweeping away any object living or dead unfortunate enough to be caught in its path. Waters that despite the high summer afternoon, were bone-chilling, mind-numbingly cold, fed as they were by the Hindu Kush to the north and the mighty Himalaya Range to the east. Foaming, twisting, smashing its way along a course that was constantly changing, eroding, as it pursued its timeless assault upon the land; impatiently driven to carve out its own path of least resistance against the battlements of nature.

Down, down the water flowed, through a rugged, hardscrabble landscape whose rocky outcroppings rendered it wholly non-arable. No man watched its passing, nor beast, either. For where once a shepherd might have herded his sheep among the meadow steppes, there were only the occasional small piles of stones marking the locations of unexploded land mines. Where once the wild mountain goat might have ranged free, a gnawing hunger in the valleys below had caused it to be hunted into near-oblivion.

The ancient, glacial waters were no stranger to such human struggles. For the land once known as Bactria had been the target of migrating civilizations and cultures since the dawn of time; from the legions of Alexander the Great, to the armies of Buddhists and Muslims, all left their mark of influence upon the people. In modern times, it was a British King and a Communist Russia's turn to fail against the fiercely independent people of Bactria—Afghanistan.

Relentlessly, tirelessly, the water journeyed past bombed-out villages and burned-out tanks, through a man made badlands pock-marked with craters and graves. But it was no threat from a strange land this time which caused the water to roar and to cry out to its mother earth. To sigh and groan in abject grief at the scars it witnessed upon the land. No, it was a turmoil of the worst sort—one whose seeds were sown from within.

For when the aged Russian bear had at last expended itself and retreated to its lair to the north, licking its wounds, the many factions of the Afghan *mujahideen* turned on one another in a struggle for supreme ruling power. The civil war raged on, bloody and costly, with the former holy warriors all tacitly agreeing to follow the *Shari'a*.

The one point of order they could all agree upon.

And so Islamic Law became the only law enforced in a country that could not decide what country to be; a nation played out of resources, of peace, and of hope.

On and on the water raged, weeping over smoothed rocks, sobbing under broken-down bridges, until at last it tumbled out exhausted and spent in the central highlands northeast of Kabul, near the village of Birat. It was here that the water's progress was thwarted at last, and it pooled into a mountain lake forged millennia ago. The Khyber Pass was still to the south, and there was nothing save more desolation and barren landscape to the west, but here, amidst the dusty hillsides and uneven ground on which the little village perched, there was life, at least.

Low cement-block huts, an occasional concrete block dwelling, a few shops, a small mosque, and the mullah's house constituted the whole of Birat. Small children and their dogs played inside mud-walled courtyards, while women clothed head to foot in traditional Afghan dress tended to the outdoor cook-fires and wash basins found in the rear of each little home. The mid-day meal had just been consumed, and the spicy scent of it still lingered in the hot summer air.

With no running water, no electricity, no phone, and no governmental infrastructure to speak of, Birat was just like a thousand other villages in Afganistan that had been decimated during wars past.

But no longer.

It would be time soon, to turn once again towards Mecca and give glory and praise to Allah, to thank him for his blessings. For Allah had brought hope to Birat, had he not?

He had brought Abbado El Yousef.

The children of the village had full bellies now, for the first time in many seasons. There was firewood—real firewood—to provide fuel for heating and cooking. Not the wormy, dried out scrub brush that was all that remained of the bristle-cone pines which had once flourished in the valley. The last of the stately trees had been harvested by desperate, freezing hands some winters back.

The men of Birat had work of another sort now, keeping strangers away from the encampment that had sprung up at the eastern edge of the village, facing the hills. Feeling proud and powerful with their Kalashnikov rifles slung over their shoulders, they smiled as they walked the dusty streets, chain smoking and talking in their native *Dari.* In spite of the heat, they wore their turbans and *chapans,* long-sleeved cloth coats tied at the neck.

Flighty chickens and balky goats now shared the road with boxy Russian army trucks—Urals—co-opted from the recent invaders. But the armored personnel carriers were new, as were the trailers carrying AT-2 Snapper tank-piercing mortars and Iranian-made surface-to-air missiles.

Drawing closer to the encampment, comprised of two-score or more variously sized tents and hastily constructed outbuildings, one could hear the hum of generators, the rapid-fire *pop-pop-pop* of target practice in an adjacent field, and animated conversations in a variety of languages, including Arabic. More men, armed with AK47s, swaggered through the camp. They wore a hodgepodge of colors, some featuring green or dusky brown fatigues, while others wore more traditional, neutral clothing. They bustled in and out of tents, talking, laughing. Life

here was good, or as good as it could get in this godforsaken corner of Afghanistan—in an alpine valley tucked away in a corner
of the world forgotten by most.

In a massive tent in the center of the compound, the front
flaps were tied open and a large slab of plywood rested atop four
poles driven into the ground at the entrance. It provided a hap-
hazard bit of shade for the small field table and chairs which
rested there, obviously battered, scavenged pieces.

Inside the tent, it was another story. The canvas had been
assembled atop a wooden platform, a rare concession to luxury
in these parts, the better to keep the sudden rain washes which
erupted down the hillsides from streaming in and muddying the
tent floor. Atop the platform, rich Persian carpets had been laid,
ablaze with a rainbow of colors and flaming red medallions. The
furnishings spoke of extravagant comfort as well, with two plush
settees strewn with silken pillows, and a low-footed dining table
arranged in the front of the interior. Towards the rear, there was
a separate work area featuring chairs and a polished table worthy
of a Fortune 500 executive. And nearby, a canopied field bed fit
more for a five-star hotel than for the rugged central highlands.

The hum of a generator just outside the rear of the tent powered lights, a desk-top computer, an air conditioning unit—silent
for the moment—and a satellite-based communications system.

A solitary man sat at the dining table. He was of middle age
and middle height, neither fat nor thin. He wore the flowing
clothes and turban of a traditional Arab man. With long, manicured fingers, he thoughtfully stroked a black beard that traveled
down to the middle of his chest in length. The other hand rested
across his stomach, and he watched silently as two women
quickly cleared away the remnants of his midday repast—a delicious *chalow* of lamb, eggplant, bell peppers, and tomatoes.
Heavy on the garlic and onion, just how he liked it. Together
with *nan,* a coarse bread topped with sesame seeds, it was a local
meal he'd acquired quite the taste for since arriving in the valley
in early spring.

He noted appreciatively how the serving women avoided his
gaze, how they wore the *burqa* shielding their faces, and how
they kept a quiet, respectful distance in his presence.

As it should be.

He pushed back from the table, stretching, and moved to a settee. Dark eyes, bright with intelligence, scanned the tent's interior from a face deeply lined by the sun. Impressive toys, he thought, for a temporary shelter in the middle of the badlands. But the equipment here was nothing compared to the hardware positioned in the caves above Birat. More computers and generators, full climate control, a satellite dish, a communications center, and enough firepower, courtesy of international arms merchants, to take Kabul for himself, if he was of a mind to.

He was not.

No, here in this scarred valley where he'd cultivated the fierce loyalty of the locals, thanks to his *zakat* or "charity," his personal security force, nearly three hundred in number, was nicely supplemented. Exiled by his native Saudis, expelled from the Sudan, Abbado El Yousef had come to a staggering Birat, propped it up, and taken it for his own. All as part of his larger plan to drive the infidels from lands belonging to the people of Allah. He was the Chosen One. Destined to lead the *umma*, the worldwide Muslim community. With enough money to buy and sell Afghanistan a thousand times over, he was committed to his life's work. His obsession. His purpose. And he would not rest, until his work was done.

A rustle at the entrance to the tent.

It was Rashid, his right-hand man. A fellow Saudi, he'd first made his acquaintance at school in Switzerland. It was there they found that their politics and beliefs were nearly identical. And when El Yousef had decided to undertake his own personal *jihad*, Rashid was right there by his side, vowing his undying loyalty. It was common among his followers, that. Death was welcomed, if it was in the service of the Chosen One.

"Come." El Yousef waved an arm.

Rashid's boots were dirty and a trail of dust snaked out behind him. His turban was slightly askew, and he leaned against a post in the tent, struggling to catch his breath. El Yousef smiled. His lieutenant had chosen to hike down the hillside from the communications post, rather than make a call on the 2-way radio system they used to stay in touch within the camp. Good. It could only be positive news, then, for Rashid always liked to deliver that in person. When things were not so good...well, Rashid wisely understood it was best to keep his distance from the Chosen One.

"What news have you, my friend?" El Yousef's dark eyes narrowed, and though he smiled, his jaw was tightly clenched, his face held no mirth.

Waiting.

Above the sound of Rashid's heaving gulps, El Yousef could tell that the target practice had ceased. Now he could hear the tinkling of the bells on the goats as they were ushered in from the meadow, the yelps of a dog barking, the squall of a baby crying.

"We are picking up the first transmissions, Chosen One," Rashid gasped, producing a black and white checkered kerchief to wipe the streaks of perspiration from his face. With his free hand, he formed a fist. "Success."

"Ah." El Yousef's face broke open in a wide grin, revealing perfect white teeth, and the darkness left his eyes. "Thank you. Thank you for that bit of news, my friend."

Rashid, happy to be the bearer of it, bowed slightly and returned the smile.

Abbado El Yousef, leader of the *umma,* steepled his fingers and squeezed his eyes shut. *"Allahu Akbar."*

Indeed, God was great. And this was only the beginning.

****

The Dornier 328 got them to Bangor just as the faint first rays of the rising sun peeked above the horizon. It had been a quiet flight with very little talking; most of the passengers chose to make use of the air time to doze. There would be precious little time for rest soon enough. Gazing across the narrow aisle, Kate noticed that Becky's head was tipped against the window; the girl was fast asleep, and her hands still cradled Kate's laptop. Just in front of the flight attendant, Jim MacArthur's head was flung back, eyes closed and jaw hanging open, lightly snoring.

Kate could feel the slight *thunk* as the Dornier's pilot lowered the landing gear. The plane's air speed dropped off, flaps were lowered; final approach into Bangor. A last sweeping turn, and suddenly the warm, burnished glow of dawn flooded the cabin, bathing the passengers in rich tones of copper and gold. In the stillness, in the calm, in the peace of the moment, all seemed well with the world.

How deceptive it was. Kate shifted uncomfortably in the small seat. She'd stayed awake the entire trip, the true purpose of the flight never slipping from the fore of her consciousness for even a moment.

Illogically, Kate had found herself dreading her arrival at their destination. The clamminess of her palms, the churning in her gut, hell, she hadn't felt this way since she was a kid. Then, there had been times--whether going to the doctor's, or to school on a test day, or to her father's funeral—when she'd squeezed her eyes shut and prayed to God that she'd never arrive. That she might just keep going and going, never stopping. Never having to think. To hurt. To feel.

Childish thoughts.

Childish nightmares.

Sighing, Kate turned to look out her window. This nightmare was all too real, that was the problem. Swaths of green, the open fields surrounding the airport rushed up from below, still shrouded in the wispy remnants of a pre-dawn mist. Cool air blasted her from the vent above her head, chilling her, but she welcomed the sensation of it. It helped to keep her alert. On her guard.

The plane dipped lower, and there was the concrete runway of Bangor, just beneath them now.

Nice...even...steady, the pilot was taking them in, and doing a good job of it. In just a few seconds, they would be on the ground. Kate glanced back across the narrow aisle; Rebecca was stirring. Mac was too, yawning and awkwardly stretching out his long legs under the seat in front of him.

The plane glided over the runway, lower and lower; a light touch of the wheels, then another—harder this time—and they were down. The Dornier shuddered as the pilot immediately applied his brakes, pitching them all slightly forward in their seats. Quickly, the aircraft slowed and taxied towards the terminal.

Becky grabbed the handle of the laptop. "Mnnn...we're here."

"Yeah," Kate said, feeling the tension in her face. She breathed in deeply. Damn it, she had to find a way to get her emotions under control, or she risked burnout. Something she simply could not afford. She had a job to do.

"Hey, are you okay?" Fingertips rested lightly on the sleeve of her windbreaker. "You look a little pale."

"Fine. I...I just don't like being cooped up on these smaller planes," Kate lied. "I'll be okay as soon as we get off."

"I know you. You're a bad passenger. You'd rather be flying this thing."

Kate flicked a hand towards the cockpit. "Ah...he did okay."

"Good morning, folks." As if on cue, the intercom crackled to life. *"Welcome to Bangor, Maine. Sorry it has to be under such tragic circumstances."* A brief pause. *"The local time is 6:15 a.m., and the temperature is 59 degrees. But it'll be another warm one later today, we're expecting a high of 82 degrees. We'll be at the terminal shortly, where I understand there is transportation waiting to ferry you directly to Pohassat. There will be personnel at the gate to guide you."* Another longer pause. *"Ah...our prayers will be with you."*

The pilot turned to Rebecca. Green eyes looked at her, blinking, searching for some sort of reassurance. Kate turned away and stared straight ahead. She had none to give.

****

As promised, a small fleet of 4-wheel drive vehicles, plus a Bangor Emergency Response van, stood ready to transport the aircraft's occupants to the crash site outside Pohassat, an approximate forty-five minute ride away. The SUVs, featuring blue emergency lights on the dashes, were obviously personal vehicles belonging to the region's predominantly volunteer fire and rescue squads.

Kate quickly claimed an older Chevy Blazer for herself,

Becky, and Mac. The vehicle had seen more than a few New England winters, judging by the rusted look of it, although the driver himself seemed barely old enough to have a license. Just a few stray wisps of hair above his lip passing for a mustache, and a worn Pawtucket Red Sox cap jammed on his head. But the gangly, thin-faced youngster wore the orange blaze vest of an emergency worker, and that was good enough for Kate.

"Hello, ma'am." He held out a grimy hand to the tall pilot. "Freddy Comstock, at your service."

"Hi, Fred." Kate shook his hand, and let the youth grab her bag.

"If you give me your gear, folks, we'll get it stowed away and get you up to Pohassat shortly."

Kate climbed into the right front seat of the Blazer, and watched her fellow passengers clamber into the other vehicles. Bo Sample and his staff, plus most of the Orbis Risk Management people, took the van. The pilot was not unhappy to separate herself from that crew. Bo and his people seemed nice enough, but they were "suits," paper-pushers, just the same. She didn't really know them and didn't need to in order to do her job. Corporate politics be damned.

Hank Danner and his younger colleague, Rick Falzone, plus the rest of the passengers on the flight, divided themselves up among the remaining sport utility vehicles. Kate spied Agent Danner awkwardly hefting himself up into the front of a brand new Ford Expedition.

Figures. Kate shook her head. She unconsciously leaned forward in her seat, anxious to get going now. Her dark fears had faded away with the light of the rising sun, and her adrenaline was kicking in. She could feel the tingle of excitement in her blood now; a mission was at hand. The anticipation, the apprehension, the thrill—it was all there for her now, just as it had always been. The energy, the power those feelings summoned, were at her disposal.

Time to get moving. The sun was creeping higher in the sky; it was damn near 0700 hours. Valuable time was wasting away.

Kate swiveled around in her seat. "You people ready back there?"

"Yeah." Breathlessly, Becky hopped into the blazer.

Jim MacArthur ducked his head as he gracefully maneuvered his bulk into the truck. "Ready."

"Why don't we move out, Fred?" Kate said impatiently. "These people don't need to follow us, right?"

"Well...ayuh..." Freddy Comstock gulped hard, and turned rounded eyes to one of the most imposing, intimidating women he had ever seen. "Nobody said in particulah—"

"Good." Kate settled back in her seat, facing straight ahead. "Let's go."

After a moment's hesitation, the young man put the truck in gear and peeled out of the airport lot, following signs towards interstate 95. "We'll only be on the highway for a bit," he apologized, "then we'll have to head east into Hancock County. Some of it's off-road. Pohassat will be that-a-way." He pointed a knobby finger towards the northeast.

"God's country, eh?" Mac grunted from the back seat. He was tired, his leg had a cramp, and he was half-considering using the time on the ride to grab a few extra z's.

"God's country," Freddy repeated, and he wagged his head. "It is that, sir, normally. And a fine country, it is," he paused, "but not today."

A silence wound its way through the Blazer, heavy, cloying, and neither the hum of the wheels grabbing the road beneath them nor the occasional whoosh of highway traffic opposite, heading south, filled the gaping, cold void.

Finally, a warm voice lifted up from the rear. "Thanks for the lift, Freddy. We really appreciate it."

The driver's eyes flickered to the rear-view mirror, and his tired, dirtied face split into a faint smile. "My pleasure, ma'am."

Becky had taken note of the stiffened way the young man carried himself, of the dark splotches under his eyes. It couldn't have been an easy time of it for these local people, she reasoned. To have to deal with a tragedy of such magnitude—how could anyone train...prepare for something like that? In that respect, she didn't feel at any more of a disadvantage than anyone else here, save for the technical experts.

As a flight attendant, much of her training had been focused on lifesaving and crash survival. On a cognitive level, she knew that the worst could—and sometimes did—occur, and one had to be prepared for that. But that was not her role here, she knew. It was to keep Kate organized, to keep the information flowing between Orbis and the crash site as quickly and as smoothly as possible, and...just to *be* there, for the woman who'd grown so important to her over these past few months. At what had to be one of the toughest times in the older woman's life.

Becky knew how seriously the pilot took her new role at Orbis, how she felt responsible, on a personal, visceral level, for bringing the guilty to justice. To prevent incidents like the Flight 2240 hijacking from ever occurring again. At times, Becky worried that Kate had bitten off more than she could chew. There was evil out there in the world, that was for certain. And as long as there was, how could one person, one woman, ever hope to put a stop to it all? Taking on a mission that, realistically, was impossible to fully execute?

In spite of that overwhelmingly negative prospect, Captain Catherine Phillips fully intended to try.

Becky let her eyes rest on the back of Kate's head, admiring how the early-morning sunshine threw flecks of onyx highlights into her hair. Ah, well. Kate had never let superior odds stop her.

Ever.

Becky sighed. She supposed that was one of the reasons why she loved her so.

"Any word on survivors yet, Freddy?" Mac posed the question through a yawn.

"The hospitals are on standby, ready to receive any injured. That's all I know, sir."

"And have any injured been transported yet?" Blue laser beams bored into Freddy Comstock.

"Uh..." another hard gulp, "not that I know of."

More silence, as the Blazer turned off the interstate and picked up Rural Route 2. The trees thickened and draped the land, and a hint of damp moisture hung in the air, the remnants of yesterday's rainfall.

Becky shifted in her seat, determined to keep the young man talking. Anything was better than the quiet, the emptiness. Now was not the time to let her imagination run away with itself, with troubled thoughts of what might lay ahead for all of them. She cleared her throat. "Are you from this area originally?"

"Lived here all my life, ma'am, but I ain't seen nothin' like this." Freddy caught her gaze in his rear-view mirror, and Becky's heart ached at the sight of his bloodshot, moist eyes. "Nevah...anything like this."

* * * * * * * * * *

Freddy Comstock was making good on his promise to get them quickly to the crash site. From interstate to winding country lanes to nothing more than a barely paved cow-path, over roads he'd known since boyhood. They passed through the old mill town of Pohassat, just coming to life on what should have been a lazy summer Saturday morning. But it was not meant to be, as the streets were already clogged with emergency vehicles and the odd news van. Freddy waved to a few pedestrians he knew; they returned the greeting, gazing curiously at his vehicle and the strangers he carried.

"Folks 'round these parts might just be a-figurin' out what all the excitement is about," he observed, turning the Blazer out of town and directing it along a narrow logging road, lined with pines and spruce. Quickly, they were enveloped by the blanket of trees, so thick they nearly blotted out the sun, and the rich, earthy scent of the forest filled the air. The truck bounced its way along the road for another ten minutes, maintaining a decent speed, before the squat body and whirring lights of an ambulance came into view. The Blazer slowed.

"He's from Binghamton," Freddy said softly. "He's come a-ways."

A few more minutes, and they were part of a little caravan of vehicles winding their way towards the site. No one was leaving, not yet anyway, and it was a good thing, Kate thought, based on the narrowness of the road.

"Folks have set up a staging area at the old Sheetz & Campbell logging camp, but ain't nobody worked it for ye-ahs, not since the mill closed down." Freddy clucked his tongue. "My fatha worked there as a young man. The stories he told us..."

The logging road suddenly widened, flaring open towards a
muddied compound clogged with police cars, fire equipment,
and emergency vehicles of every shape and size. A few broken-
down buildings and barracks, tin roofs sagging under the weight
of the elements and the years, were scattered throughout an open
space cleared long ago of its virgin-growth forest. "The
plane...or what's left of it, is about a five minute walk due east
of he-ah."

Freddy cautiously maneuvered his way through the haphaz-
ardly parked vehicles and rushing rescue personnel, and worked
towards a large trailer adjacent to the old barracks. As they drew
close, Kate could see "Bangor City Emergency Response Mobile
Command Unit" emblazoned in a shock of red lettering along its
side. A small satellite dish sat on its roof. The door of the trailer
was open wide, and a constant stream of people flowed in and
out.

"This is where I'm supposed to leave you good people,"
Freddy said, gesturing towards the trailer. "The FBI fella kinda
kicked Sheriff Longworth out of the-ah once he showed up."

"FBI guy?" Freddy suddenly had Mac's attention.

"Big-shot from the city, I suppose," Freddy said, pushing
his cap back on his head. "He's the one in charge now, they say.
Don't sit too well with the Sheriff, I'll warrant, givin' up his
trailer. The 'law' does love his toys."

With a grinding of wheels against gravel, the Blazer pulled
to a stop. "He-ah you ah," Freddy jumped out of the Chevy and
moved around to the back, pulling out their bags as Kate, Becky,
and Mac got out and stretched. From the dead of a New York
night to the rosy glow of a New England dawn, it had been some
journey to get themselves to this point. And the day was far from
over.

"Thanks, Freddy." Becky smiled at him, taking her bag and
the laptop. "You've been great."

"Yeah, thanks," Kate said, echoing her smaller companion's
sentiments. It was an effort for her sometimes, dealing with the
common courtesies. They had always seemed so...trivial to her.
But she'd sworn to herself that she would show Rebecca she was

capable of it.

Mac had drifted off towards the door of the trailer, interested in the loud shouting coming from within.

"I'll leave you folks to it, then." Freddy tipped his hat and blushed, looking every inch the boy he was. "You need anything...a ride, whatevuh, you just ask for Freddy Comstock, you he-ah?"

"You bet," Becky said, giving the young man's hand a squeeze.

With a quick nod, Freddy melted off into the crowd.

Becky sidled closer to Kate. "Wow," she said, looking over the compound, "looks like a war zone."

"Yeah," the pilot replied, letting her eyes take in the scene. "I'll bet every emergency vehicle in the entire state is here."

"And more coming," Becky said, watching a lumbering red fire truck emerge from the forest, followed closely by the van and SUVs from Bangor airport.

Their traveling companions had arrived.

Kate pointed to a break in the trees behind the barracks. "The aircraft has got to be through there." Emergency workers slogged back and forth on the path, sweat-streaked even at this mid-morning hour, caked in mud and soot, bearing ominously bundled burdens on stretchers. Their faces were etched with the horror of what they had seen, or perhaps of what they had not seen; Kate saw nothing which indicated that a survivor might be anywhere in the compound. No ambulances rushing off, sirens screaming, loaded down with patients, and no on-site first aid being rendered, other than to a fireman having a bloodied hand bandaged.

The burly, rugged looking man sat on the back bumper of a rescue wagon. His protective coat hung open, his hair was plastered to his head, and his helmet sat by his side. Like a little child, the big man held his hand out to the EMT for examination and repair.

Make it go away.

Tears ran down his face, and not from the pain. No, there would be no fixing this.

"I'm telling you, this is an FBI-run operation, not the

NTSB's."

The angry words came from within the trailer.

"It's our goddamned jurisdiction." The pounding of heavy footsteps fairly shook the command center.

Kate spun around at the commotion, just in time to see a large, hulking form filling the doorway, holding a cell-phone. His hair was firecracker red, his eyes a pale blue, and his skin a healthy burnished tan, belying his apparently Northern European heritage. The pilot guessed him to be at least several inches above Mac's height, though younger, with shoulders impossibly wide. She wondered whether straight-on, he'd be able to fit himself through the opening. He wore what appeared to be the uniform of the day: jeans, work boots, and polo shirt. A blue windbreaker, with the block letters "FBI" on the back, hung from his hand.

Shaking his great head in pained disgust, the giant caught sight of the three Orbis employees standing outside his door. He motioned to them, waving them into the trailer.

"I don't care if the goddamned president himself shows up, as the ranking Assistant Director in Charge, I say that this is an FBI investigation until such time as the evidence demonstrates to my complete satisfaction that we're not looking at a crime scene." He paused in his tirade to allow the party on the other end of the line to get a few words in edgewise. The man's face was flushed over his summer coloring; his eyes were narrow slits of vitriol.

Kate regarded him intently. FBI "fella" in charge, eh?

"That's bullshit, Mike."

She liked him immediately.

The large man resumed his argument, turning towards a bank of blinking communications equipment lining the far wall of the trailer. A table and bench chairs were built in to the center of the space, and more communications, video, and surveillance hardware filled pre-fabricated work-stations which lined the sides.

Rebecca edged closer to Kate. "Maybe we should come back later," she said in a hoarse whisper.

"Don't mind this guy," Mac volunteered before Kate had a

chance to respond. "For him, there *is* no good time."

Kate lifted an eyebrow. "You know him?"

"Know him, hell. That's Gordy Ballard. He used to work for me in DC on the Bureau's counter-terrorism unit. *Until* he kissed enough ass to get himself promoted out from under me...HEY." Mac smoothly dodged a balled-up windbreaker thrown at his head.

"We don't know yet..." Ballard shouted, raking a hand through his red buzz-cut. "I'll have to let you know..." More pacing. "FINE," he barked, violently cutting the connection. "Damn Feds. I hate 'em."

"You *are* a Fed," Mac said dryly, stepping forward and offering his hand.

"Yeah, not like some retired old bastard I know." Ballard grinned and gave Mac's hand a vigorous shake. "I heard you'd gone private sector and hooked up with Orbis. What—some cushy deal, right? Stock options? Bonuses? "

"I don't know," Mac chuckled, "You'll have to talk to my boss about that." The investigator nodded at Kate. "Gordon Ballard, meet Catherine Phillips, Director of Strategic Operations at Orbis."

"Miss Phillips." Ballard eyed Kate evenly and liked what he saw. "How-do."

"Call me Catherine." Sparkling blue eyes returned the gaze. "And Mac has one *hell* of a deal."

"I'll keep that in mind," Ballard said, smirking.

Mac cleared his throat. "And this is our..." He looked to Kate for help.

"Associate—"

"Associate this trip, Rebecca Hanson."

"Becky, please," the flight attendant blushed, unaccustomed to her new role. *God,* she thought, *what have I gotten myself into, here? Steady, girl.* She swallowed hard. *Just try and look like you know what the hell you're doing.*

"Bo Sample, our EVP of Ops is right behind us," Kate continued, "with something of an entourage."

Ballard raised thick, bushy eyebrows that ran like slashes of rust across his forehead.

"PR. Risk Management types," the pilot explained.

"Great," Ballard said in a hard voice. "As long as they stay the hell out of my way."

"And a couple of your guys hitched a ride with us too, Gordy," Mac said. "Hank Danner and—"

"Good," Ballard interrupted, holding up his hand. He was clearly relieved. "The more people I can put out in the field, gathering data, conducting interviews, the better. Getting a hold of some of these guys, on a weekend, you'd think they were in the witness protection program or something." He shook his head and grabbed a half-cold cup of coffee from the table. "Can't reach 'em."

"You certainly got here pretty quickly," Kate observed, "and a good thing for it."

"Yeah well, I hate to diminish your fine impression of me so soon, Catherine," he said, flashing a white-toothed grin, "but I was already vacationing down in Northeast Harbor. It's only about an hour's drive from here. The wife's family is from Philly and they've got quite a place, right on the water. Boat dock, clam bakes, a hammock—"

"And the kids like it too, right?" Mac chuckled, dropping his garment bag to the floor of the trailer.

"Yeah," Ballard said. "I hated to break up their vacation like that but...what the hell."

"You'll make it up to them, once this is all over," Becky said earnestly.

"That's what I keep tellin' myself, little lady." Ballard shook his head wistfully, and finished his coffee in one swallow. "I hope you're right." He paused, rubbing the palm of his hand over his face, as if trying to erase the horrific images that burned his mind's eye. "You know...there were no survivors." The sorrow, the grief, the loss, wound its way like a snake through his gut, twisting, turning. The pain rolled off him in waves, Kate could feel it. Smell it. Was accustomed to it herself.

"None?" Next to her, Rebecca's voice was a faint wisp of a prayer, and she could see a tremor skip through the smaller woman's body.

Ballard turned to look sadly out the door of the trailer onto the barely controlled chaos that until a few short hours ago was an abandoned, sleepy logging camp. He crunched the styrofoam cup in his paw of a hand. "They're gone. Every goddamned last one of them."

Chapter
5

Assistant Director Gordon Ballard quickly demonstrated to Kate and her companions the skills which had gotten him promoted so quickly through the ranks of the Bureau's best and brightest, finally landing him in charge of the Orbis Flight 180 investigation. Agent Hank Danner and Rick Falzone, his partner, were instantly shunted off to Pohassat to locate witnesses to the crash.

"Fer chrissakes, somebody had to have seen *something.*" Ballard fumed. "*Find* 'em."

"Yes, *sir*," Danner replied, standing as straight and tall as his heaving belly would allow. The man looked as though he might actually salute, before he remembered himself and thought the better of it. He turned on his heel and left, with the younger Falzone trailing closely behind.

And no sooner had the shadows of Bo Sample and the rest of the Orbis group crossed the trailer door, than Ballard had handed them off for a briefing to his deputy or "SAC," Marissa Bello, Special Agent in Charge.

The agent betrayed no emotion at the prospect of baby-sitting the airline staffers; with the features and demeanor of a prim and proper schoolteacher, she took to her assignment with a cool, patient ease, shepherding them out of the trailer towards the barracks next door. Bo Sample remained, though, insistent on touring the crash site with Ballard.

"It's gonna be rough, Mr. Sample," the assistant director warned.

"I know. But for the families, for those people out there, I have to." Sample's narrow, angular face was pallid, but his voice was firm, and Kate found herself respecting the executive for his conviction—and for his intestinal fortitude. "Rough" didn't even come close to describing what desolation awaited them. She knew that much.

Ballard thought about Sample's words for a moment. "Okay," he said at last. "Let's go." He turned towards the door. "You all can leave your bags here for now. I'll just take you along the perimeter of what we believe is the primary debris field. The site's not secure yet, so I can't have you disturbing any evidence," the big man cautioned.

"We understand," Sample said, tugging nervously at the sleeve of his windbreaker. "Lead on."

Kate moved to follow them, when she heard the small clearing of a throat behind her. *Rebecca. Damn.* What had she been thinking? Kate turned to see the young flight attendant standing stock still near the wall of the trailer. Her green eyes were wide as saucers, her face blanched, the line of her mouth drawn tight and thin. The pilot recognized that look of her partner's. The girl was scared stiff, and as bound and determined as ever.

"Rebecca..."

"I'll be fine, Kate," the small blonde said, drawing herself up to her full height and breathing deeply. "Really."

Kate thought fast. "How are you making out on that manifest?"

"Yeah." Ballard paused in the doorway, blocking the sunlight. He looked back to Kate and Rebecca, his blue eyes alert. "Passenger list, crew, cargo, we need to get crackin' on that."

"It should be coming in shortly." Becky shifted her gaze to the laptop she'd set on the table.

"Plenty of dataports in here. Feel free to use 'em, courtesy of Bangor city." Ballard tramped down the steps and out into the compound, followed by Bo Sample and Jim MacArthur.

Kate stepped close to Rebecca and laid a hand on her arm. The young girl was trembling, in spite of the warm, still air inside the trailer. "Why don't you get working on that?" Kate softly suggested.

"But I—"

"Please." Kate bored her eyes into Rebecca's. "It's important. I need your help."

"Well," Kate could see some of the tension leave the smaller woman's body, "if you're sure."

"I'm sure," Kate said firmly, hating herself for having brought her into this horror. "We'll see you in a while, okay?" She brushed the tip of her finger under Rebecca's chin.

"'Kay." The flight attendant smiled faintly, and moved to open the laptop bag. "Be careful."

"I will, I promise," Kate said, watching Becky for a moment as she worked, before turning and pushing out into the bright sunlight where Mac and the others were waiting.

"She's gonna get working on that manifest," Kate said, eyeing them carefully.

"Okay." Ballard pointed towards the break in the trees that led to the crash site. "Let's get going."

"Good thinking, about that manifest," Mac muttered, falling into step next to Kate. The pilot merely looked at him and nodded. She knew what he meant.

Ballard led them at a fast clip along a narrow trail winding through the woods; tire tracks cut into the soft ground that had been protected from the brunt of the last evening's rainfall by the softly swaying canopy of trees overhead. Workers with gravel-filled wheelbarrows and chain-saws were already working on widening the path and stabilizing the surface for the small army of emergency personnel ferrying back and forth.

"Let me walk you through what we've got so far," Ballard said, slowing down a bit. "We know that while there was a misty rain in the area last night, weather conditions shouldn't have been a factor at the altitude where the incident initiated."

"At 30,000 feet, right?"

"That's when the last reported contact occurred, yes."

"Then you're right," Kate said, thinking, her boots crunching along the gravel. "But you can't rule out clear air turbulence."

"No," Ballard replied, "although if that were the case, one would think the captain or copilot would've had a chance to get off an emergency call. And there were no 'maydays' received from Flight 180. Whatever happened was sudden, and catastrophic. We know that much. Of course, once we have a chance to analyze the CVR and FDR, we'll know more."

"The cockpit voice recorder and flight data recorder, you've found them already?" Bo Sample was impressed.

"Yeah." Ballard pushed a low-hanging pine bough out of his way. "We got lucky. A piece of the tail section was recognizable in the debris field, and of course that's where they're located."

"Since the tail is most likely to survive a crash intact," Sample added.

Ballard cast a fish-eye at the executive. "If you say so. But they're in rough shape. We're waiting for them to cool down naturally before we let our people have a look at them. We don't want to rush the process and risk damaging the tapes and telemetry further. Our top priority at the moment," the group stopped to let two EMTs pass by bearing a stretcher loaded with a body bag, "is to recover the victims in a swift, dignified manner."

"Of course," Sample said, chastened. Kate could not help feeling sorry for the man at that moment. He was clearly in over his head. Hell, they all were, for that matter.

"Second," Ballard continued, "is to collect all available evidence from the scene. And it's a helluva scene. The nose cone and a portion of the flight deck were ripped off from the rest of the fuselage by the force of...whatever happened, and the tail section, too. But everything else," Ballard shook his head, "is all over the place. And virtually unrecognizable."

"Have you turned up anything evidence-wise, that could point to what happened?" Kate wanted to know.

"Nothing yet," Ballard said, "but my guys are good. They know what to look for, even in this mess. TWA 800, ValuJet, the Pittsburgh USAir crash—they've been around the block a time or two. If there's something out there that's not 'right,' they'll find it."

"And you'll be working closely with the NTSB, right?" Mac could barely contain a smirk at what he knew had to be a sore point with his friend.

"Yeah, and the FAA too," Ballard replied, his large form moving gracefully through the forest with an athletic ease. "Those NTSB guys aren't too bad, not really," he allowed. "Bob Joseph, the agency's vice-chairman, should be here by noon."

"Ready to take charge," Mac said, winking at Kate.

"Not if I can help it." Ballard's voice was sharp. "I've been to enough crime scenes in my day to know 'em when I see 'em. And by God, Mac," the big man sighed, "this sure as hell looks like one to me. I can feel it in my gut. That's where your data comes in so important, Catherine."

"And you'll have it," the pilot stated. "We'll get you the specs on everyone who had their hands on that 747. Not just the passengers and crew, but the cleaners, fuelers, caterers, baggage handlers, inspectors—everybody—from Lisbon to Paris."

Kate tilted her head into the air, her senses on full alert. They were getting close now, she could tell. On the light breeze there was a thickening scent of wood-smoke, and another, more offensive odor. Burned insulation, rubber, and worse. It stuck in the back of her throat and her eyes watered, but there was no escaping it.

"Once the NTSB types get here," Ballard was saying, "we'll have to have some sort of press conference. "I'm thinking about 3 or 4 o'clock. By then we should at least have something to give 'em."

"I—I'd like to be there."

Ballard stole a quick glance at a pale Bo Sample.

"Fine, although you could take some flak. Frankly, until we *do* determine what went wrong here, you've got one hell of a potential liability. You, Boeing, if there was a structural failure, Pratt & Whitney if the engines malfunctioned—"

"I know," Sample gulped. "But...I--I feel I should be there."

"Be my guest," Ballard said, picking up his pace once more. There was silence for a moment, nothing, save for the crunching passing of emergency workers and the occasional shout through the trees up ahead. "Aw hell, who knows," the assistant director continued, "by that time maybe we'll have somebody taking responsibility for this, eh? And then you guys will be off the hook."

"Not likely," Kate said, in a deep, throaty voice that rumbled out into the damp forest. "Not by a long shot."

With little warning, the trail fell away into a jagged-edged open space within the forest, littered with charred, twisted pieces of aircraft. The shock, the sudden "there" of it, stole the breath from Kate's body. Emergency workers, some already wearing white bio-hazard protective suits, poured over the wreckage, while firemen still hosed down smoldering hot spots. The plane had burned upon impact—that was eminently apparent, taking along with it the surrounding woods. The occasional blackened tree limb jutted out from random chunks of debris, looking for all the world like ghostly, darkened appendages waving for help.

Lining the perimeter of the clearing were trees that had survived the initial impact and fire. Standing as silent witnesses to the horror of those first early-morning hours when Flight 180 fell from the sky, they clearly had had the life seared from them. Their scorched trunks still valiantly stood straight and tall, but their boughs sagged and wept in shades of charcoal and gray, their living, vibrant greens of life, but a memory now. Unlike the sudden death of their fellows, the end for these trees would be agonizingly slow. With limbs unable to take up the nourishment they so desperately needed, they would starve, after a fashion, until finally with a dry, crackling last gasp, they would tumble over dead to the forest floor, perhaps at the hand of a strong wind or winter's storm.

Several smaller emergency trucks were parked at the side of the clearing where the newly forged path flared open to meet it. Ballard led the way towards one, motioning to the EMT standing at the rear of the open vehicle. "How about getting us fixed up with a few masks?"

Immediately, Kate knew what Ballard was doing. The pilot normally had a stomach of iron and a will to match, but already she felt her gut twisting and churning under the assault of the indescribably putrid air she was forced to breathe in. It was almost a solid thing, the force of it, and she could feel it seeping into the strands of her hair, the essence of her memory, the marrow of her bones, and she doubted whether she'd ever be truly free of it. All she could do was be grateful that Rebecca was not here to be marred by it. Kate was content to bear the burden of this scene for the both of them.

"Here you go." Ballard handed each of them surgical-type masks featuring a dab of menthol Vapo-rub on the insides. "There's more if you need it. Sorry we don't have gloves or anything more than this—we've run out at the moment. You really shouldn't be back here without 'em. But since we're just going to skirt the perimeter—"

"What is this?" Bo Sample held the mask out distastefully from his body.

"It's for the smell, Mr. Sample," the big man replied tiredly, patiently. "It'll get to you without it, believe me."

"Is this really necessary? I think I'll be fine—"

"Best put it on, Mr. Sample," Mac said. "Take a clue from the rest of these fine people here." And indeed, throughout the debris field, everyone was similarly protected.

Sample spared a quick look out at the crash site, and then silently did as he was told, his thin bony fingers tying off the mask behind his head.

"Okay then," Ballard said once they were outfitted, "all I ask is that you watch your step and stay out of my people's way."

The assistant director gingerly picked a line that ran along the edge of the debris field and set off, followed closely by Kate, Mac, and Bo Sample.

"You can see that we had a bad burn here," Ballard huffed, "but whether it was a result of the impact or if the aircraft hit the ground already in flames, we don't know. We need to find some *witnesses* to this damn thing," he said quietly, as if to himself. "We *do* believe that the plane was not in one piece when it hit."

"Why do you say that?" Kate asked, as they passed by what her trained eye knew to be a warped fragment of the tail section and rear stabilizers.

"Primarily due to the scatter of the wreckage," Ballard replied, wiping the perspiration from his brow. He stopped. The heat radiating from the still-smoking wreckage was like a burning hot pavement on a blistering summer's day. "You can see where we found the tail. The section of front nose cone we've located is way the hell over there." He gestured towards the far end of the clearing. "I've got a report of an engine in some guy's pasture about five miles from here. Plus a cabin door eight miles away, and reports are still coming in."

"Something happened up there," Kate said, knowing what sort of explosive picture Ballard was painting and not liking it at all. "Something big."

Ballard stepped carefully off again into the sodden soup of the forest floor. "That's the premise we're going on."

Silently, the little group followed in single file, working their way along the edges of the hellish scene. There were flashes of color amidst the barrenness of the destruction, small red spotter flags blowing gently in the breeze, indicating the location of human remains. Scores of them dotted the debris field. Workers moved quietly among the flags, bearing olive green and navy blue body bags, speaking periodically into shoulder mics and walkie-talkies.

After a time, Kate's eyes became accustomed to the blackened, misshapen landscape, and she forced herself to look closely. To take it all in. To remember. For the victims' sakes.

The pilot had seen crashes before of course—back at Luke Air Force Base and during Desert Storm—but nothing like this. Charred seat cushions. An Orbis Airline napkin, untouched by the flames, its soggy blue and white globe logo gazing sightlessly at the sky. Fragments of luggage. A man's shoe, separated from its mate forever. And Kate had to fight down the bile in her throat when she caught sight of what she knew had once been the framework of a child's stroller.

Even through the menthol-daubed protection of her surgical mask, Kate could still detect the foul odor of burned insulation, of oil, of death. It was Abbado El Yousef who was the architect of this killing field; she knew it. And as her clouded eyes rested upon the carnage that he had wrought, she vowed silently to herself and to whatever god was listening, that she would make him pay. *These people never had a chance*, she thought angrily, feeling the blood boil in her veins. They were helpless inside the tube when the moment of disaster hit, lined up agreeably like eggs sitting in a carton, and just as fragile. She could only hope that their final awareness of what was happening was fleetingly, blessedly swift. The alternative was too horrible to contemplate.

As they pressed farther into the debris field, Kate found herself conscious of the unnatural silence that permeated it all. Maybe it was because of a reverence for the impromptu graveyard which spilled out over the landscape, but the emergency workers all moved quietly through it, speaking in low tones to one another:

"Here, now." One would hold up a hand to another who would approach with a red flag.

"I've got one." Another hand raised.

The bodies. Too damn many.

Ballard stopped walking on the far side of the unnatural clearing. "At the same time we recover the victims," his voice was hushed, respectful, "we're trying to put together a schematic of what is being found where. The aircraft's skin, interior, hydraulics, and so on. It'll help us to assemble a complete picture of how this event unfolded."

"Nggggh."

A strangled cry came from behind them.

There was Bo Sample, pointing a shaky arm towards something in the scorched brush just outside the perimeter.

"What the—?" Ballard pushed past Kate and Mac. "Oh God," he said, blanching. He raised his hand for an emergency worker. "Can I have a marker flag over here, please?"

Kate felt herself unwillingly propelled towards the spot; she was powerless to stop her feet from moving, a part of her had to see. There it was, half-hidden in a burned-out bush. She had to look closely at it for a moment, clinically, before her mind was able to fully process the sight before her.

It was a portion of a human leg, the skin of it charred and flaking. Its owner had lost it from just below the knee down to the ankle and heel, but the front part of the foot and toes were missing.

Behind her, she heard Bo Sample retching.

Kate felt her mouth run, could sense her mind reeling

unsteadily. She closed her eyes briefly and swallowed hard, knowing that breathing deeply would do little to help her now. *God*, she thought, thinking of the hapless victim, *no one deserves this.*

Willing herself to regain her balance, the pilot recovered herself just as Gordy Ballard turned back towards them. Above the white line of his surgical mask, his gray-blue eyes were misty wet. The mask moved as he spoke. "This is some god-damned vacation, isn't it?"

"Let's get out of here, Gordy," Mac's voice was hoarse, "we've seen enough." He took a few steps towards where Bo Sample leaned with one hand against a tree, bracing himself. His face was a sickly green, and his soiled mask now hung below his chin. "You okay, buddy?" He laid a hand on Sample's back.

The executive nodded an uncertain affirmative.

"Let's go," he said, helping Sample move out behind Ballard.

Kate was the last to leave, pausing for one last look at the scorched debris field, burning it into her mind's eye, searing her soul. She would never forget it, this steaming, stinking bit of hell on earth.

She would be sure to remember it to Abbado El Yousef.

Personally.

* * * * * * * * *

The group quickly, quietly, made its way back to the logging camp. Each individual alone with their thoughts, digesting what they had seen. As they approached the head of the trail at the main compound, Kate could see Rebecca standing next to the old barracks, her arms folded across her chest, staring. The pilot followed her gaze, and saw that the young flight attendant was focused on a row of body bags that were being loaded into waiting ambulances.

There would be no rush to get them to town, Kate thought sadly. Her heart went out to her friend, knowing how the scene had to be chewing her up inside, she of the gentle, sensitive soul that did not deserve to know of such horror in the world.

As they drew closer, Becky heard their footsteps on the gravel and lifted her head.

Kate could see the protective façade slip into place.

"I've got those files we were waiting for," she said, moving to meet them. "I've printed them out and given them to Agent Bello."

"Good," Ballard said, flicking his eyes towards the sun. "We can get going on that. A complete passenger list?"

"Yes, including flight crew and what background information was available on all of them." Becky briefly lowered her head before continuing. "Plus, the service history of the aircraft, flight log, and a detail of how it spent its last 72 hours."

"Thank you, Rory," Kate said gratefully, thinking of Rory Calverton, their computer wizard back in New York.

A grinding whir of wheels and the sound of a straining engine turned their attention to the logging road leading into the compound. A three-fourth ton pickup truck was hauling a large Winnebago trailer into the clearing.

"That'd be for the NTSB and FAA folks," Ballard observed. "Look," he checked his watch, "it's nearly nine o'clock now. Why don't we get together at noon, all right? We'll go over what we've got so far." Ballard looked doubtfully at Bo Sample. "Mr. Sample, I know the EMTs have set up a rest and recovery area in the barracks. You may want to go in there and check it out."

"Don't mind if I do," the young executive quickly replied, and he wobbled off.

"Catch you later, Mac, Catherine," Ballard said, shaking their hands. "And thanks for your help." He nodded at Becky. "Now," he sighed heavily, "let me go track down Agent Bello."

"She may be back in your trailer by now," Becky called after his broad, retreating back. The assistant director acknowledged her words with a wave.

"Seems like a good guy," Kate commented, turning towards Mac. "Do you miss working with him?"

"Nah," Mac replied, and the big man blushed. "I'm happy where I am. Besides which, I don't envy him this job. Not by a long shot." He paused, and Kate saw him look towards the body bags. "Listen boss, how about I go talk to the recovery people, see what I can find out about the condition of the...remains. Might give us our first indication of what kind of trauma: fire, or—whatever—may have hit them."

"Sounds good," Kate agreed. "Poke around some. See what you can find out. You know," she smiled faintly, "do your 'investigator' thing."

"You've got it." Macnodded, and headed off.

"Phew." Kate took a deep breath of air, trying to shake off her dark mood. Barely 0900 hours, and yet she felt so drained, exhausted beyond measure. "I need something to drink," she said tiredly, swallowing through her parched throat.

"There's a canteen truck set up over here." Becky directed the pilot to a busy area next to the barracks and they walked towards it. "So," she said, looking up into the slightly sooty, sweat-streaked face above her, "how are you?"

"Fine," Kate answered, too quickly. A hand on her shoulder stopped her, and resignedly she turned, gazing down into Rebecca's knowing, probing look. "What?" she exclaimed, averting her eyes.

"How *are* you?"

"I...it...it was bad, Rebecca," Kate sighed, relenting. "I'm glad you didn't have to see it. The sooner we can pin this on that bastard—"

"You will, Kate, you will." Becky could see the anger, the frustration building in the tall pilot. And that was okay, she figured. At least Kate was letting it out, talking about it. That, she could work with. "And there're plenty of people around here able to help you. Who feel the same way."

"Yeah. I know." Kate lowered her head. "You're right."

They started off again towards the canteen, dodging scurrying emergency workers.

"That was good work you and Rory did."

"He's still working on that code thing, too. He wanted you to know."

"We're a little late for that now but...whatever," Kate said, reaching a long arm towards the back of the busy truck and grabbing two bottles of cold water. She handed one to Rebecca.

The blonde twisted open the cap and took a long swallow,

eyeing her tall companion carefully. "Well, I've organized your file system on the laptop."

"Did you?" Kate looked curiously at Becky. "Does this mean I'll never be able to find anything again?"

"You rat." Becky gave her a playful swat on the arm. "Like you ever could before."

"Gimme a break." Kate grinned. "I managed."

"Barely. Anyway, do you want to hear about it, or not?"

"By all means." Kate waved her bottle of water in the sunshine.

"Well, I've organized your file system into new, pending, and closed, and sorted them in date order by author, along the lines of project, operations, technical, personal, staff, and miscellaneous."

"Really," Kate breathed, impressed. "When did you do that?"

"This morning," Becky said shyly, "on the way here."

"Christ, in three months I couldn't get around to doing that. Thanks," she said, noting the blush creep up the cheeks of the smaller woman. Kate knew how important it was for Rebecca to feel useful, needed. Her performance this morning, under the most trying of circumstances, had more than filled the bill.

"Listen," Kate said, swallowing the last of her water, "I'm going to trail after Mac. Why don't you go check on Bo. He had a rough time of it out there, and I'm sure he could use a friendly face right about now."

"Gosh, I noticed he didn't look too well," Becky said, a brow creasing her forehead. "The poor man. With all that responsibility on his shoulders, he's got to feel terrible about all this." She put the cap back on her water bottle. "Let me go find him." And the young woman was off, her caring, supportive nature kicking into high gear.

Kate watched her go, so proud of the woman she cherished more than life itself. "Rebecca," she called after her.

"Mnn?" Becky spun around in the dirt, eyebrows raised.

Kate felt her throat constrict with emotion as she struggled to get the words out. Words she needed to say, and Rebecca needed to hear. "I—I'm glad you're here."

****

"All right, let's review the purpose of this meeting, people."
Gordy Ballard stood at the head of the small table inside the
command trailer, perspiring heavily at high noon, despite the
groaning air conditioning unit behind him. Special Agent-in-
Charge Marissa Bello sat next to him, still and unsmiling, with
not a strand of her limp brown hair out of place. Bob Joseph,
vice-chairman of the NTSB had arrived, as had a team from the
FAA. Bo Sample, apparently recovered from his earlier bout of
stomach distress, had also taken a seat. He nervously played with
a pen, constantly clicking the ball point in and out.

Kate slumped against a wall near the rear of the trailer, as
far away from the table as she could get. Mac and Becky stood
next to her, following her lead. *Best to stay out of that hornet's
nest of "suits,"* Kate thought, eyeing Gordon Ballard sympathet-
ically. The big man dwarfed those around him, and she could see
the jaws of the FAA people slacken and their eyes grow round as
they took him in, wondering what to make of him.

There were entirely too many people in the cramped trailer
for her tastes, but Kate resolved to plant her feet and stay put.
Much had happened over the long morning, and the pilot was
determined to stay up to speed on those events.

Whatever it took to move her closer to her mission objective.

Ballard leaned forward, resting his meaty hands upon the
table. Kate smirked to herself as she noticed Agent Bello
inwardly cringe at the close contact. Big men had never intimi-
dated Kate. She rather enjoyed their company, as a matter of
fact, seeing them as kindred to her own spirit. Dating back to her
father, she supposed with a longing sigh.

"We will have these periodic status updates as needed,
going forward," Ballard stated. "At each meeting we will review
the data collected thus far, and endeavor to ensure that the spirit
of inter-agency cooperation is upheld to the highest degree. The
American people, our employers," he let his eyes roam over the
faces of those seated at the table, "would demand nothing less of
us. There will be a coordinated, cooperative exchange of ideas,

and respect for one another's interests will be paramount," he continued, "and we will focus a critical eye towards maximizing the assets available to help us accomplish our goals. And I believe we are all agreed on just what they are, are we not?" Ballard's face was flushed down to the red-tipped roots of his brush-cut hair.

"We all want to find out what happened, Gordy," Bob Joseph spoke up, looking to his table-mates for confirmation.

"And why." Bo Sample finally laid his pen down on the table.

Ballard nodded. "Let's not forget the most important item of all—"

"Who did it." Kate's voice carried up from the rear of the trailer, and heads swiveled her way.

"*If* there is an individual responsible," the NTSB vice-chairman said, holding up a warning hand. "We're not sure a crime has been committed here."

"I am," Ballard said firmly. "Here's what we've got." The assistant director started talking, in his element now. "The FAA is looking into whether there were other planes in the vicinity of where Flight 180 went down, but the one thing we do know is that all voice and radar contact with the aircraft was lost this morning at 0229 hours when it was at 30,000 feet. No 'mayday' signal was ever received. Wreckage is scattered over a wide-ranging area, and the plane burned upon impact. The CVR and FDR have been recovered, and soon we'll be able to get our first look at what was going on in the cockpit. The FDR will help us determine the plane's altitude throughout the sequence of events, as well as airspeed, heading, and attitude."

"Is that all?" Bo Sample began his nervous pen-clicking again. "I thought that—"

"The FDR on the Boeing 747 records the status of more than 300 other in-flight characteristics that can aid us in this investigation," declared the FAA's Eric Brown. He ticked off a list with his fingers. "Everything from flap positions and smoke alarms, to microphone keying, so we can coordinate and time data from the FDR with the cockpit transmissions."

"Right," Ballard concurred. "Once we've analyzed that

data, Bob's people here from the NTSB can generate a computer animated video reconstruction of the flight, visualizing the airplane's altitude, instrument readings, power settings—the whole nine yards."

"But you think this is a crime scene," Joseph persisted.

"Yes, I do. The scatter of the debris, the sudden and catastrophic loss of contact and power, all point to some sort of on-board explosion."

"Agreed," the NTSB vice-chairman said, removing his owl-framed glasses and rubbing his eyes. "But whether due to mechanical failure, structural failure or a well-placed bomb—"

"We just don't know," Ballard finished for him. "I realize that, Bob. But we'll find out, I assure you. And soon." He paused for a moment, clearing his throat. "A temporary morgue has been set up at a school in Pohassat, and we've got a hangar on stand-by at Bangor International where we'll begin reconstructing the remains of the aircraft as soon as this evening."

"And we've got our people working with the victims' families in Lisbon, Paris, and Montreal," Bo Sample added. "From Flight 180's point of origin through to its final destination."

"We'll want to follow up on that with interviews of our own," Ballard said, his eyes falling on Agent Bello. The woman quickly jotted down a note on her memo pad. "We can't overlook the possibility, however incredible as it may seem, that one of the passengers was involved in the destruction of the flight."

"Whether knowingly or not." Kate stirred. "Terrorists aren't above using unsuspecting 'mules' to get their deadly cargo on board."

"Good point, Catherine." Ballard nodded at her, while the NTSB vice-chairman gave her a sour look.

"That remains to be seen," he said primly, placing his glasses back on his face.

"In the meantime, people," Ballard held up a hand, "I recognize that we are all under a lot of stress and pressure here. The public—and the victims' families—will be looking to us for answers. I appreciate your ongoing professionalism, and I firmly believe that the FBI, working in concert with the National Transportation Safety Board, the Federal Aviation Administration and

Orbis Airlines, can come up with them."

"What's happening the rest of today?" Bo Sample asked, still fidgeting.

"We continue focusing on victim recovery, which is nearly complete," Ballard said. "And looking for witnesses locally, who might have seen something. Concurrent with those efforts are scene reconstruction and pre-event and post-event investigation, with assistance as needed from Orbis and Boeing."

"But you'd said something about a press conference?"

"Oh yeah," Ballard ran a hand through his close-cropped hair. "The press." Clearly, it was not one of his favorite subjects. "We've organized a pool of reporters to be here on location, the better to keep our work-site clear and any potential evidence undisturbed. We'll be having the press conference off-site, for that reason, in the Pohassat town hall. You all are welcome to join us there at three p.m. today."

"No way," Kate muttered under her breath. She turned to Rebecca. "Unless you want to go."

"I'm with you," Becky shivered. "I don't want to hear this stuff all over again."

"I second that," Mac said. "We've got more than enough to keep us busy here. Leave that to the pretty PR types. It's what they get paid the big bucks for."

The meeting broke up, with people filtering out the door into the uncomfortable mid-day heat. Kate could feel the warm air rush into the small space of the trailer, sucking out the last bit of coolness that remained.

"Director Ballard. Sir."

A young federal agent, woefully mis-dressed in a suit and muddied dress shoes, shoved his way into the command post.

"What is it?" Ballard swung around to him, annoyed.

"Turn on CNN, sir," he gasped.

"What the—where's the goddamned TV?"

"Got it," Becky said, calmly stepping forward and flipping the appropriate switches on a video unit.

Kate raised an inquisitive eyebrow to her.

"One of the guys showed me around here when you were out this morning," Becky explained, moving away from the console.

An image quickly flickered into view: a "young turk" male reporter looking solemnly into the camera, the CNN logo discreetly visible in the lower-right corner of the picture.

"*...and our sources tell us that a cabin door belonging to the Boeing 747 was found ten miles east of the primary crash site, an indication that there was an explosion of some sort on board the plane.*"

"It's eight miles, you asshole," Ballard swore. "Where's the volume on this thing?"

Becky fiddled with the controls. "There," she said, as the reporter's voice came through loud and clear.

"*At least one witness says that the plane may have been on fire before it hit the ground.*"

"Fuck." Ballard pounded his fist into the wall, rattling the trailer.

On-screen, the camera pulled back to reveal a balding, paunchy middle-aged man, wearing a tee shirt and jeans.

"*I am standing here with Herbert Ames, a delivery man for a local bakery. Tell us what you saw in the sky early this morning, Mr. Ames, at approximately two-thirty a.m.*" The reporter stuck the microphone in the face of one obviously camera shy delivery man.

"Weeeell," he drawled, "I was on Beverly Road—"

"*And where is that?*"

"Oh," he scratched his head, "*about three miles east of Pohassat.*"

"*What did you see there, Mr. Ames. Can you tell us?*" The reporter's voice oozed with impatient sensitivity.

"*I was on my way to my next delivery at the* Stop 'n Shop, *when I heard this rumble in the sky. Sounded like thunda or somethin'. It was raining on and off a bit, so I didn't think much of it.*"

"*Then what happened?*"

"*I slowed down some, it was so dark, you see, and then came a white flash, then a bright orange flash. Right there, up in the sky. I knew then it weren't no thunda.*"

"*And what did you do next?*"

"*Stopped my truck I did, and got out. Up there in the sky,*" he said, his voice wavering a bit, *"there were all these hot orange fragments you see, falling, dropping like that stuff from a volcano. I didn't know what to think."* The truck driver paused, daubing at his face with a handkerchief.

"And how did you feel, seeing that?" The reporter was nothing if not persistent.

"It was awful. Really, really devastating, I've nevah seen anything like it," Ames choked out, and he was unable to continue. The camera zoomed in on his face as he lifted a shaking hand to cover his eyes.

"And there you have it," came the reporter's sonorous voice, *"an eyewitness account, live from Pohassat..."*

Ballard was ready to blow, Kate could see that. And she didn't blame him. Special Agent Hank Danner and his team were in charge of rounding up witnesses, and here they'd been "scooped" by a network reporter.

Ballard's jaw worked furiously, and the corded veins in his neck stood at attention. "Where the *fuck* is Hank Danner?" Ballard roared, furiously punching in a number on his cell-phone. "Gone fishin'?"

Chapter 6

The afternoon was a nightmarish blur of activity, only briefly interrupted by a breath of a pause at three p.m., when many of the workers gathered around portable radios to listen to the press conference. Kate, Becky, and Mac had chosen to remain in the command center, scrutinizing the data sent to them by Rory Calverton, paying particular attention to the passenger lists and who boarded where.

At 1500 hours, Becky flipped on the television.

The press conference itself was a heated, ugly affair, and Kate was glad she'd chosen to stay away. The worst of it came when that same damned reported from CNN posed a question to Gordy Ballard.

"Mr. Ballard, is it true that this crash is the latest evidence of a consistent, ongoing terrorist war being mounted against the United States of America in general, and Orbis Airlines in particular, by Middle Eastern groups striving for political gain?"

"I don't know where you get your information sir," Ballard said sharply, losing his cool. *"I think it's important that out of sensitivity to the families, we not speculate on what may or may not have happened. Just let us do our job."* And with that, he stormed away from the podium as the cameras clicked and whirred.

Kate did not look up. "Turn it off," she said, her voice hard.

The day wore on and the sun slipped lower in the western sky, shining as a faint glimmer of light now through the thick swath of spruce and pine surrounding the compound.

Kate had given a brief call to Cyrus Vandegrift before she'd stopped to grab a quick bite for dinner from the canteen truck. Cyrus was doing his part, trying to keep a lid on the hysteria and fear brewing in New York.

"Folks here are going to want answers, Katie. And soon."

"I'll get them for you, Cyrus," she'd vowed. "I promise."

She hoped her mentor trusted in the words she did not quite believe in herself.

Later, Bo Sample found Kate propped up against a tree, nibbling at a pasta salad. Her long legs were stretched out in front of her, and the sleeves of her blue oxford cloth shirt were rolled up, revealing tanned, toned arms.

"Look," he said, glancing from her legs to the setting sun, "we're heading back to Bangor tonight. I'll be leaving tomorrow morning. There's not much more I can do here," he said, gazing morosely through the trees to where the downed plane lay.

Kate had to admit it, he was probably right. "Well, see you, then," she replied, unsure of what he expected her to say. She stabbed at a piece of pasta with her fork.

"I've reserved some rooms for you at the Airport Holiday Inn, if you need them."

Kate's fork hovered in mid-air, and she rested her eyes on the young executive, considering how much older his boyish features looked now at the close of day. His designer sportswear was soiled and wrinkled, and his hair stuck out at odd angles from his head.

She doubted she looked much better.

It had been a rough day for all of them, and she appreciated his offer. Frankly, she hadn't given a fig of a thought as to where she'd spend the night. Although she was not ready to leave just yet, and didn't relish a long drive back to Bangor.

"Thanks," she said finally, sensing Rebecca's presence behind her.

"Well," he fumbled, "ah...thanks for all your work here," and he left, trailed to a waiting van by his slightly worse-for-the-wear entourage.

"What was that all about?" Becky sat down beside her with a hamburger and fries.

"He said he has rooms for us in Bangor, if we want 'em," Kate said, chewing on her pasta.

"I—I thought if you wanted to stay closer—"

"Yeah?" Kate glanced sideways at Rebecca.

"I reserved three rooms for us at the Lumberjack Motel in Pohassat."

"Really." Kate grinned broadly. "Rebecca, you *are* good. I figured any local accommodations would've been taken up by all those press yahoos and the like."

"Oh they are," Becky agreed, returning the smile. She bit off the tip of a French fry. "But I made the reservations early this morning, after we drove by the motel in Pohassat. Knowing you, I figured you'd be willing to sleep out here, given half a chance."

"You're right." Kate shook her head, chuckling. " But three rooms?"

"Hey, we have to keep up appearances now, don't we?"

"Yeah, but even with three rooms, I'm not sure we are." Kate's eyes twinkled as Jim MacArthur hauled his tired body next to them. Mac knew of course that she and Rebecca were roommates, and he knew that they were close. How close, he'd never asked, and never would. Although, Kate had toyed with the idea more than once that if he ever did question her, she was not inclined to lie to the man. She'd grown close to him over these past few months, and trusted him. Why not tell him the truth?

No, Mac had never asked. Maybe he didn't need to.

Aaah," he said, collapsing to the ground, cradling his dinner. "I don't know about you ladies, but it feels as though it's *way* past my bedtime."

"Speaking of which, Rebecca was just saying she's made reservations for us at a local motel. So there is that," Kate took a sip of water, "or Sample is holding extra rooms at the Bangor Holiday Inn."

"Do I have a choice?" Mac lifted tired eyes to his boss.

"Of course."

"I can't deal with Bangor again today. Or Bo Sample for that matter, if it's all the same to you, thanks."

It was all Kate could do to withhold the merriment from her eyes. "Don't thank me, thank Rebecca."

"Becky," Mac smiled at the small blonde, "I'd tip my hat to you, if I had one."

"You're welcome," Becky replied. "Glad to be of assistance."

The flight attendant took another bite of French fry and then, sighing, pushed her plate away.

"You okay?" Kate noticed that Rebecca had barely touched her food.

"Fine. I'm just not hungry," the blonde said, leaning back against the tree.

Kate let the subject drop, but she knew that for Rebecca Hanson to walk away from a meal, as uninspiring as it was, after so long a day, something was bothering her.

"We'll go soon," Kate said, noting the exhaustion etched on Rebecca's delicate features. "I promise." She looked past the smaller woman's shoulder to where the last of the victims were being loaded into vans and ambulances.

210 passengers and crew, gone, in a flash of light in a darkened sky. This time last night they were all still in Paris, laughing, talking, perhaps grumbling about the delay in takeoff, but at least they were alive. Now...there was no going back. Not ever.

* * * * * * * * * *

"See you tomorrow morning," Gordy Ballard stood at the bottom of the metal steps to the command trailer. It was the last of twilight, and the light breeze carried on it an evening chill. The sky overhead was a deep, vibrant indigo, and evening stars were twinkling clearly in the crisp Maine air. "You people got a ride?"

"Yeah, thanks," Kate looked to where Mac and Rebecca were loading their bags into the back of a decrepit Chevy Blazer. As promised, Freddy Comstock was once again at their service.

"Well," Ballard shrugged on his FBI windbreaker, "I'm hoping tomorrow will be a better day. The lab boys are taking a look now at a couple pieces of luggage, and a section of a luggage rack."

"Find something?"

"Maybe. The initial field forensic and metallurgical tests look promising."

Kate turned at the sound of the Blazer's engine growling to life, and saw Mac and Becky hop in with a wave "good-bye" to Ballard. "Listen," she began haltingly, "I appreciate all your help today. It means a lot." Until she'd actually met the assistant director, she hadn't expected much. Had planned on fighting for equal time and full disclosure every damn step of the way. But with Gordy Ballard, unexpectedly, she hadn't needed to.

"No problem." The big man smiled faintly.

"Thanks." Kate shook his hand firmly, then struck out for the waiting truck.

"Kate," Ballard called after her, and she stopped, her eyes struggling to penetrate the darkened gloom surrounding the trailer. She could barely make out his hulking form against the side of it, and his voice drifted softly to her from the shadows. "Remember, we're on the same side."

* * * * * * * * * *

It was well after dark by the time they checked in to the Lumberjack Motel, situated on the sleepy outskirts of Pohassat. The old hotel stood along the same road that wound towards the Sheetz & Campbell logging camp. A 1950's style diner sat squat and low in the lot next door, and seemed to be doing a brisk late dinner business. Out-of-state vans and cars filled the parking area, and Kate had no doubt they belonged to the hallowed press corps covering the plane crash.

They said their "goodnights" to Freddy Comstock, after the young man agreed to pick them up the following morning at 0700 hours.

"Oh, God," Mac groaned. "Sorry if I'm not the life of the party here, but I'm hitting the sack."

"Yeah, we all should get some sleep," Kate said, fitting her key into the door of her room. "Long day." The three Orbis employees had adjoining accommodations on the first level of the ancient motel. All the rooms opened out ónto a graveled parking area, and a large, grinning neon Lumberjack stood flashing just outside the motel office, his ax forever frozen in mid-chop over a short-circuited block of wood.

"Not bad," Becky observed, peeking around Kate as the pilot flipped on a light, illuminating a simple, sparsely decorated room.

"It looks clean, that's all I care about," Kate said, smiling tiredly. She reached for the doorknob, and her hand brushed lightly against Rebecca's arm. She held the young blonde's gaze for one brief, longing moment, before her eyes flickered to Mac. "G'night guys," she said, and she disappeared behind the door to her room.

The lights of a pickup truck pulling into the parking lot flashed over Becky as she walked the three steps up to her own door. "See ya in the morning, Mac," Becky said, and the investigator gave her a yawn and a wave in return, retiring into the next room down.

The flight attendant clicked open her door and turned on the light switch. Her room mirrored Kate's: bed up against one wall, a small window looking out onto the rear of the building, and a low table and two overstuffed chairs adjacent to a wood-veneer bureau.

Becky put the laptop on the table, dropped her travel bag to the floor, and flung herself down lengthwise across the bed.

Some day, she thought. Every bone in her body ached, and there was a light buzzing in her head that would not go away. *Probably because I didn't eat much today,* she reasoned, although food was the last thing on her mind right now.

Regardless of whether her eyes were open or closed, she could not blot out the images of the day that flashed across her consciousness. The body bags, the shattered faces of the rescuers who had found no lives to save, the muddied, trampled down wood of what had once been a peaceful, quiet forest.

And the smell in the compound—the foul fumes from the

idling engines of the emergency vehicles, mingling with the choking smoke of the nearby crash site. How were Mac and Kate able to bear it all? Becky marveled at their resolve.

She wasn't sure she could have done what they did today. Just one look at Bo Sample's face when they returned from the debris field was proof enough to her of that.

With a heavy sigh, she pushed herself up to a sitting position, and looked at the wall she shared with Kate's room. The tall, dark pilot was just that far away, yet to Becky, it might as well have been a gaping, yawning chasm with no bridge capable of spanning it.

They had a job to do this trip; they were working, and she had to be a professional. She'd done her part today, hadn't she? Kate and Mac had told her so. Even Gordy Ballard, who didn't know her from Eve, had thanked her. And she'd been there for Kate when the older woman had needed her.

Sure, the pilot was tired now, they all were.

So Kate had spoken few words during the course of the day, so what? That wasn't unusual for her, and besides, when she had spoken, she'd made it count.

The important thing was, that her partner hadn't withdrawn into that cold, darkened part of herself that was frightening to behold.

A place that changed her.

That turned her into a sullen, dangerous being, one who'd been hurt deeply and was uncaring about passing that hurt on to others. No, the woman she'd said "goodnight" to a short while ago was still her Kate. And she was grateful for that.

So then, why the tears? Becky could feel them coming now, pushing up from her chest, into her throat, spilling from her eyes. She should be feeling pretty good about things, right? Her mind skipped back to the manifest. She had it memorized by now. All those passengers' names. Ages. Where they were from.

And the crew.

She'd known two of the flight attendants from one of her recent New York to London assignments. Two women, older than her, but they'd seemed nice enough. Now, she wished she'd been able to get to know them better.

Damn, what's the matter with you, girl? Becky shoved herself to her feet and stripped out of her filthy clothes, feeling dirtier than she had in ages. A thorough shower in the dimly lit bathroom washed away her tears; she paid no heed to the lukewarm water, she was thankful just to be clean again. Quickly toweling off, she threw on an oversized tee shirt and tumbled into bed.

But sleep would not come to the young woman. Tired beyond words, her mind numb, Becky simply lay there, staring at the popcorn paint ceiling of the darkened hotel room. She could hear the hum of the air conditioning units in the other rooms, but she'd been unable to get warm since her shower, and had no desire to make a chilly situation worse. Doors slammed, and cars came and went in the parking lot. Hushed voices and footsteps passed outside her door, but eventually they too, fell silent.

Great. All of Maine is asleep but me. Again, Becky felt a tightening in her throat, the moist drop of a tear forming at the corner of her eye. *Great. Just great.*

The young blonde snuffled at her nose and rolled over on her side, cursing her rotten luck.

Tap-tap.

No. It couldn't be.

Becky bolted upright in bed, listening.

Tap-tap.

There it was again, a light knocking on her door.

Throwing off her bedcovers, Becky flew to the peephole. A bright blue eye, attached to tanned, smooth skin, stared back at her.

Becky threw a hand over her mouth to stifle a cry. Of relief? Of Joy? She could not put a name to it. She only knew that she needed Kate. Badly.

She fumbled with the lock on her door and threw it open. In one swift movement, the pilot slipped inside and took Rebecca up in her arms, holding her, kissing her with a desperate, heated passion that dried the smaller woman's tears, and set her ardor aflame.

Wordlessly, Kate moved her to the bed, pushing her down upon it, and Becky welcomed the invasion; embraced the forceful, knowing caresses of a woman she had no desire to be separated from, not ever, and not on this night, most of all.

Their joining was quick, frantic; each of them driving the other onward, needful of the life-affirming, explosive energy of it all. They pushed closer and closer to their limits, electrified by the touch of skin on skin, of tongues meeting flesh—teasing, biting, dominating, and then withdrawing. When Becky thought she could stand it no more, when she feared that she might be driven insane for want of her release, she heard a distant cry that she recognized as her own. It was the only sound in that darkened room, followed immediately by the feel of Kate joining her in that sweet deliverance. The pilot's body shuddered silently, and then went still; and then there was nothing save for the wild beating of two hearts, and the heaving, gulping breaths of two souls that would not be divided.

Rebecca fell asleep soon after, her consciousness at last willing to discard its grasp on the horrors of the day, content in the knowledge she was held fast and safe by the warm, protective arms that encircled her.

As the flight attendant's eyes slipped shut, as her breathing became deep and even, two blue eyes continued to stare into the night.

Watchful.

Alert.

Later, when the first rays of dawn tickled the dusty window blinds of Becky's room, when the songbirds of the northern woods chirruped to greet the new day, a persistent, lingering chill once again crept into the young blonde's tired bones, fingering the base of her skull.

And she awoke.

Alone.

Chapter 7

I have got to be absolutely insane. Rebecca Hanson's sneakered feet pounded along the soft, springy floor of the forest trail in the woods outside Pohassat. It had been an exhausting day yesterday with very little sleep last night, and here she was, attempting to get in a bit of a workout before the start of what promised to be another brutally taxing day.

All the more reason why you needed to get your rear-end in gear, girl. With her oftentimes-chaotic schedule as a flight attendant, Becky had found that taking the time for a quick workout would always give her an extra boost of energy, helping to get her through those longer hauls. That, and because of the way she loved to eat, was more than enough motivation to keep her committed to a fairly regular exercise schedule. Without it, Becky was sure it would only be a matter of time before she failed to make Orbis' weight regs. *Workout so I can pork out,* she chuckled to herself, enjoying the feel of the cool morning air wicking the perspiration off her skin.

Unlike a certain Catherine Phillips.

There was not an ounce of excess fat on the pilot. She was energy and motion personified, and yet the woman never exercised. A genetic gift from her Irish and Greek forebears, Becky supposed a bit enviously, checking her watch. Fifteen minutes out. Time to turn around. She'd allowed herself a half-hour for the run, then just a few quick minutes to shower and dress before Freddy Comstock would be at their doorstep. *Somewhere in that timetable, there had better be room for breakfast*, she thought, ignoring the impatient grumbling of her empty stomach.

Rebecca dug in and quickened her pace.

She wasn't really an early-morning riser unless she had to be, such as on days like these. And so when she'd found herself awakened as dawn peeked in through her window, she'd decided to make use of the time. Weaving through the parking lot of the *Lumberjack*, filled with cars and trucks sitting silently with their fogged-over windows, she'd quickly found the scenic, multi-use trail crossing the highway about 100 yards down the road from the motel.

Becky had been happy to peel off the main thoroughfare and venture into the woods. She relished the peace and serenity she found there, and greedily drank in the quiet hum of the living forest around her.

A far cry from that hellish piece of the piney woods she'd borne witness to yesterday.

Moving at a good clip now, Becky kept up a steady, even tempo on the relatively level path, falling into an easy rhythm, timing her breathing to match her strides. As she took in the rich hues of green growth around her, the young blonde realized that a lack of rainfall in this region was clearly not a problem. An early morning mist swirled and hugged the trees at the base of their trunks, so that the great limbs seemed to rise up towards the sky not from the earth, but from dewy clouds below.

Becky passed by a small picnic area she had not noticed on the way out; a small chipmunk sat on one of the redwood tables, eyeing her carefully. He kept one beady, black eye on her while he twirled an acorn furiously in his front paws. The black and white racing stripe of fur running the length of his body quivered as he chewed at his prize with tiny, razor-sharp teeth. Beneath him, a small pile of shell-shavings littered the picnic table.

"Hi there, little guy." Becky's breathless voice cut through the morning quiet with all the subtlety of cannon fire to the small chipmunk. Choosing survival over a good meal in the face of this superior giant of an intruder, he skittered away with an indignant squeak, leaving the half-eaten nut behind.

The flight attendant smiled broadly, shaking her head at the chipmunk's retreating tan hindquarters. "Have it your way."

A few more strides, and she was closer to the main road now. Becky could see how the narrow trail widened and sloped gently downhill, and the mists had nearly dissipated here. Breathing in and out the crisp, clean air, her legs pumping and arms held lightly at her side, she was surprised to feel as good as she did after so little sleep. Her run was working its energizing magic once again. That, and the fact that a certain airline pilot she knew had spun a special brand of sorcery, too.

Becky felt the heat rise to her face, setting her nerve endings aflame at the memory of it all. Being with Kate...there was simply nothing else she'd ever experienced in her life that compared to it. The way she felt in her arms, so alive, so safe, so loved. She'd been disappointed to wake up alone, but she figured she deserved that after all, having made the separate room arrangements in the first place.

Funny.

When she'd first told Kate she'd reserved the three rooms for appearances' sake, the pilot had smiled and appeared almost indifferent, as though she hadn't given a damn what the others thought. And if she didn't, did that mean that she, Rebecca, did?

No. No way. Rebecca cleared the trail and turned out onto the macadam highway, heading back towards the grinning neon Lumberjack sign. It was just that this was the first time she'd had to deal with the status of their relationship outside of the comfortable aerie of Kate's apartment, or the familiar territory of the Orbis offices.

When they had returned from Rome some months ago, Kate had thrown herself fully into her new position as head of Orbis' Strategic Operations unit. And Becky had been only too willing to resume her flight schedule routine, anxious to have that touchstone of normalcy after the hell she'd been through. Other than the odd meal out, that had been it.

Although Becky had often talked about Kate meeting her family in Los Angeles, that hadn't happened yet. There was always a reason: Kate's busy work schedule, the timing of the flights, Becky's own informal attitude towards it all. *I need to work on that,* Becky resolved, her feet slapping onto the road with driven purpose, *make it happen.* After all, if the tall dark pilot was such an important part of her life, shouldn't she share that with her family? Oh, they knew about Kate, about their friendship, but they didn't *really* know, other than her sister, Eileen.

And what about Kate? Rebecca knew she had a brother and a mother nearby in Queens, but she never spoke of them. There was a lot of hurt and distance there, and Becky still wasn't entirely sure why. And then there was work. One thing she had noticed was that being an "out" flight attendant was no big deal, although she hadn't yet taken that step herself. But for Kate, working now on the executive side of the aisle, what were the professional implications? Becky simply didn't know, and she supposed she'd had that in mind yesterday as well. Something to talk about with Kate, definitely, once all the horror of this crash was behind them.

Becky slowed to a light jog as she pulled into the gravel parking lot of the motel. The faint smell of breakfast cooking wafted over from the diner next door, getting her immediate attention. Groaning, catching her wind, Becky wondered how she'd ever have enough time to shower, change, and grab a bite to eat before Freddy arrived.

Becky steadied herself with one arm against the wall of the hotel, and pulled her leg up behind her in a stretch. *Damn it, I thought exercise was supposed to kill your appetite.*

"Morning."

A deep throaty rumble buzzed in her ear from behind.

Startled, she released her foot and spun awkwardly around. "Wha—oh God, Kate."

"Sorry." Blue eyes crinkled in the soft morning light. "Did I frighten you?"

"Yes, I mean no, I—Where did you come from, anyway?" Becky sagged back against the motel, tugging her sweaty tee shirt away from her body.

"Next door." Kate nodded towards the diner. "I heard you

leave this morning to go for your run, and figured you could use some sustenance once you got back." The pilot lifted a white paper bag and dangled it in front of the smaller woman's nose. "Coffee, yogurt, an orange," she saw Becky's face fall, "and...a powdered donut."

"Gosh, Kate, thanks," Becky said gratefully, moving towards a bench at the end of the walkway. She dug into the bag, taking a long sip of the strong coffee before peeling back the orange's skin. "So, where's Mac?"

The pilot took a seat alongside her, and propped one blue-jeaned leg against the walkway railing. "Still in the diner, talking with a few of the investigators. Always working." Kate sighed, and turned to look out over the parking lot towards the forest beyond, and towards the grim day that awaited them.

Sensing her mood, Becky was quiet as she munched on her breakfast, working her way quickly through the orange and yogurt. She saved the donut for last.

"Want some?" She waved the powdery confection in front of Kate.

"Well," an eyebrow quirked, "maybe just a bite."

"Go for it," Becky replied, as the pilot leaned forward and bit into the soft dough.

"Mnnn, thanks." Kate grinned, chewing. "Mac told me they were good."

Becky could not help herself, she reached out to thumb away a smudge of speckled powder from the corner of Kate's mouth. "I missed you this morning, you know," she said softly, gazing up into eyes whose love and desire mirrored her own.

"Me too." Kate slid her hand next to Rebecca's and gently stroked the back of it with her long fingers. "I hate it when we're apart but..."

"But," Becky said with finality, as if the qualifier answered her own question.

"But," Kate hesitated before agreeing with her, "at least for now."

"I—I don't want it to be this way forever, Kate." Becky inhaled deeply of the brisk morning air, feeling a chill creep over her dampened skin.

"Don't you?" The pilot cocked her head and looked upon her with a fresh eye, as if filing away this piece of new information.

"God, of course not. You don't think—"

"No...no, I don't," Kate said, pushing herself to her feet. "It's just nice to hear you say it." She checked her watch, avoiding Becky's frank, blinking stare. "I'm going to go find Mac. You'd better get showered. We've got to get moving."

"Right," Becky replied, watching Kate's back retreating into the glow of the rising sun, "I'm right behind you." Her appetite gone, she dropped the remainder of her donut into the paper bag and discarded it into a nearby trash can. She took a last sip of her coffee, hoping it would warm her, but it too had grown cold.

* * * * * * * * * *

What a difference a day makes, Catherine Phillips thought, as Freddy Comstock's balky Chevrolet Blazer deposited them in front of the FBI command post. The morning sun had not yet cleared the towering blue spruce and white pine trees, but the shimmering, golden glow that trickled in between the tall sentinels was enough to show that the Sheetz & Campbell logging camp had become a veritable mobile home park overnight. Trailers and RVs were everywhere, supplementing the aged barracks and office. A mammoth motor unit marked "FBI Crime Lab" was parked near the now-silent sawmill; bright fluorescent lights lit the trailer from within, and heads could be seen moving about. Several large cranes and flatbed trucks completed the picture.

Emergency workers were pouring into the site; indeed, it appeared as though many had never left. The atmosphere in the camp was hushed, but people hurried themselves through the compound all the same, the difference being that today they seemed to move with a greater degree of organization, of purpose. Due in no small part to the rather large managerial hand of Gordon Ballard, Kate knew. It was hard enough working one's way through a disaster site. The key was to keep busy, to stay focused, to not dwell on the immutable consequences of what had occurred. A simple, logical philosophy that was, in the heat of the moment, difficult to adhere to.

The pilot turned to Rebecca, noting how already the younger woman's face had changed since they'd left the motel. She looked more pensive, more withdrawn, somehow. As if steeling herself for the day ahead. "Let's really start to break down that manifest today, okay?"

"Right here." Becky smiled faintly, tapping the black laptop bag. "Rory was going to be sending some more detailed background information on the passengers and the origins of the cargo."

Mac blew out a long breath of air and gazed toward the section of trees that screened the logging camp from the crash site. "If I know that kid, he's been up all night working on it."

"Probably hasn't left the office since yesterday, for that matter," Kate said, knowing how her Wharton School computer genius thrived on the juices of excitement and challenge. She'd seen Rory Calverton like that before, a time or three, when they'd felt they'd been close on the trail of a big lead. Cup after cup of strong coffee, candy bars from the vending machine, and *Nine Inch Nails* blaring from his earphones were all the young man had needed to fuel him through successive all-nighters. Nothing Kate had said had been able to dissuade him; he'd sit in front of his computer, its lights reflecting back off the unshowered sheen of his face, as though he were an addict waiting impatiently for his next information fix. During those times, only the stern voice and firm hand of the motherly Dottie West had been enough to propel him out the door towards a bed and a bath.

"Well, at least Dottie's there to keep him in *KitKat* bars and *Baby Ruths*," Mac chuckled.

"Ugh." Becky turned up her nose up distastefully at that.

"Really? I would've thought that was your speed." Kate planted her tongue firmly in her cheek.

"I do have my standards, Kate," the flight attendant primly replied. "Candy bars are *not* a breakfast food."

"Lunch, right?" Mac stepped up the small staircase to the door of the command trailer. He rapped loudly on its battered exterior.

"Oh, definitely." Becky nodded her head vigorously. "Dinner, too. *And* a midnight snack."

Kate cast a sidelong glance at the smaller woman. "Hmnn. I'll have to remember that," she said in a low, mischievous tone, giving Becky a subtle poke in the side.

The door to the mobile unit burst open, revealing the massive form of Assistant Director-in-Charge Gordon Ballard.

He bolted down the steps, past Mac. "Grab some java if you want at the canteen," he said, his dark blue FBI windbreaker flying out behind him, "we're heading to the lab trailer."

Special Agent-in-Charge Marissa Bello carefully picked her way down the wobbly aluminum steps after him, carrying a clipboard. She studiously ignored the new arrivals.

Catherine used her long legs to match stride with Ballard as he moved across the compound. "Find something?"

"I think so," he replied, rubbing at the back of his neck. "Your people may want to hear this, too."

"Mac, Becky." Kate motioned her team to follow her, never leaving Ballard's side. "The luggage pieces from yesterday?"

"Yup. My people have been working on it all night."

And Ballard himself probably had too. Though clean-shaven, he appeared to be wearing the same shirt and jeans as he had the day before, and his pale blue eyes were puffy and blood-shot.

Quickly, they filtered into the mobile crime lab. The trailer was huge, based out of New York, Kate guessed, and from all appearances sported the best equipment that modern forensic science had to offer. Some of the apparatus was easily identifiable: microscopes, centrifuge, heating devices, x-ray, refrigeration, and a bank of test tubes and labeled bottles and jars. Lights blipped and flashed, computers were humming away, and Kate detected a faint metallic scent in the air that vaguely reminded her of those damned required chem and physics labs back at the Academy.

Smaller worktables and stools were placed in front of the hardware, and a large, stainless steel table stood in the center of the trailer. Several blackened segments of aircraft debris rested on the shiny, silvered tabletop, and lab technicians in white FBI smocks busied themselves over the items, conversing softly among themselves. One gentleman was jotting notes down into a tablet, while another appeared to be staining a microscope slide for analysis.

Agent Bello smoothly moved past Kate and Ballard to join the techs' conversation.

"Wow," Mac said, gazing with wonder around the trailer. "Things sure have changed since I left the Bureau."

"You mean your waistline?" Ballard chuckled.

"Hey. I resemble that remark." Mac's face took on a mock hurtful look.

"Actually," Ballard admitted, his thick fingers ruffling his red buzz cut, "I can barely keep up with this crap myself."

Kate folded her arms across her chest as she took in the high-tech gadgetry. "It certainly is impressive. To think that all this...stuff, is mobile."

One of the white-smocked techs broke off from the huddled group and snapped off his rubber gloves. He was a slight man, middle aged, with thinning light blonde hair. His bespeckled brown eyes were bright and his cheeks were flushed a rosy red, as though he'd just returned from a bracing walk through the woods, rather than having just pulled an all-nighter.

"It's the nature of the discipline. The science we're doing here today rivals the best that the central crime lab was able to do just three or four years ago." He smiled brightly and held a hand out to Kate. "Dr. Farley Leber. Welcome to my playground."

The pilot was surprised at the firmness of the scientist's handshake. "Catherine Phillips, Orbis Airlines Strategic Operations. These are my associates, Jim MacArthur and Rebecca Hanson." She could not help but return his smile. "And I promise not to touch any of your toys."

Dr. Leber continued to hold Kate's hand in both of his, grasping it firmly. "Oh, you can," he replied, his dark eyes twinkling, "as long as you ask permission first."

"You've got a deal." Kate's eyes widened as she realized that the little man was flirting with her. She didn't mind, not really. In fact, she admired his chutzpah. Like the old story of the Dachshund ruling the domestic roost over the German Shepherd; the little dog had never looked in a mirror, and so it simply figured that it was a German Shepherd, too.

Obviously, Dr. Farley Leber could not be bothered with mirrors.

"All right, gather 'round, folks," the doctor said, in a warm voice that sounded as though he were gathering friends to a campfire. "This way...you'll want to take a look at this." Leber barely came up to Kate's shoulder, but he took her elbow lightly in his fingertips, guiding her towards the central table.

The door to the trailer suddenly opened and slammed shut, admitting Robert Joseph, vice-chairman of the NTSB. The official cast a peevish look at Ballard through his owl-framed glasses. "You weren't going to get started without me, were you, Gordy?"

"Not at all, Bob." The big man's tone was cordial. "C'mon in."

"And where's Eric?" The older man huffed in irritation as he swung his head about the trailer.

"Dunno," Ballard replied, addressing the whereabouts of the FAA administrator, Eric Brown. "Must be sleeping in. I'll fill him in later. But we've got to get started now."

Kate examined Ballard's face carefully. There was no malice there that she could detect. The man simply could not be bothered with sidebar issues that had nothing to do with his goal: to find out what the hell had happened to Flight 180.

Focus.

Gordon Ballard had it. Kate's respect for the assistant director ratcheted up a notch.

"Farley." Ballard nodded a "let's go" towards the diminutive scientist.

"Well," the doctor adjusted his glasses and smiled a bit self-consciously, "we've been quite busy here over the last sixteen hours, as you might imagine."

"You guys have been working your tails off, Farley, and we slugs out in the field appreciate it."

Dr. Farley Leber beamed at his superior. "Thanks, Gordy." He pulled on a fresh pair of surgical gloves and stepped closer to the cold metal table. "Now, what we have here is...or used to be...a section of a luggage rack or pallet from the ill-fated flight, as well as material—baggage, cargo, what-have-you, that we recovered in the immediate vicinity."

Ballard turned to Kate. "We're fairly certain these items came from the rear baggage hold, but we'll need to wait for more information to come in to confirm that."

"From the flight data recorder."

"Yeah. That, and when we get our arms around the airframe reconstruction."

"What kinds of...tests have you done on this material so far?" Bob Joseph was barely able to contain his impatience. Kate was nursing a rapidly growing dislike for the man; it was obvious to her that he was all about power and bluster, rather than getting things done. Leave it to the Federal Government to keep promoting arrogant jerks like him up the ladder.

"Oh yes." Leber referred to a nearby tablet. "We've been able to do all sorts of interesting analyses here of the physical evidence. Let's see now..." He scanned the list, refusing to be hurried. "We've been running testing protocols on the pallet and collateral material, including fiber analysis, electronic image scanning, chemical testing, spectroscopy, x-ray powder diffractometry, residual stress and," his eyes peeped over the frame of his glasses, "trace element analysis for accelerants and explosive residues."

"And you've found something." Kate's heart pounded in her chest. Her blood rushed through her ears like a freight train, threatening to drown out the scientist's words. Here was her worst fear in this whole mess, about to be realized.

"As we in the forensic science community like to say," Leber put down the tablet and rubbed his hands together, "yeppers. Big time."

"Talk to me, Farley." Ballard pressed closer to the table, his voice all business. "What have we got?"

"Needless to say," Leber laid a hand on the largest blackened artifact, it looked to be a shorn off rung of a ladder, "these bits of debris will be subjected to additional, lengthy chemical and metallurgical forensic examinations. Scientific method and all that neat stuff."

"But right now?" Ballard's patience with the little doctor was wearing thin.

"Right now, Gordy," Leber gently patted the debris as though he were coddling a newborn puppy, "I'd say your plane was brought down by a high-performance plastic explosive. At least, that's what the residue indicates."

"I knew it," Ballard smacked his fist in the palm of his hand, his blue eyes blazing.

"Sounds a bit far-fetched," Bob Joseph loudly protested. "How can something like that get on board a plane today? With all the security checks we've got?"

"It can happen." Kate was surprised at the deceptive calmness of her voice, in spite of the chill she felt tickling the small of her back. "Remember the hijackers on Flight 2240 used some sort of polymers that got past detection at JFK. God knows what might've happened in Lisbon or Paris." The pilot could see Rebecca paling at her side. "Some plastic explosives can pass undetected through normal airport security checks. The plastique itself can be molded or even flattened into a variety of shapes and sizes...concealed in carryon luggage, for example, and *you* wouldn't even know it."

"You're right, Catherine." Leber spoke as though to a star pupil. "Plastique gives tremendously high destructive power to what otherwise is a relatively compact bomb."

"Ah, can we talk a little about the evidence?" The NTSB executive sported a sour, pinched expression on his face.

"Certainly. Lights?"

As the interior of the trailer grew darker, Dr. Leber flicked on a screen attached to the wall behind him. Immediately, an image popped into view of an object that looked like the surface of some far-away planet: pitted, shadowed, torn apart by some unseen force.

"What the...?" Mac's jaw dropped.

"This," Leber produced a laser pointer, "is a section of luggage pallet framework."

Ballard shifted his weight from one foot to the other. "Looks like it's really been worked over."

"Oh yes," Leber enthused. "We were very excited by this particular item. See," he skipped the pointer along the deep, grooved pits in the image, "here it shows conclusive evidence of a detonating high explosive. Again, our preliminary residue tests confirm it. What you see are pockmarks from flying metal shards, consistent with what a strong bomb blast within the aircraft would inflict."

"And that matches what the EMTs were saying about the victims," Mac said, his voice low.

"Correct," Agent Bello confirmed, her head down, jotting a note on her clipboard. "With the force of such an explosion, the thousands of rivets that held the fuselage together would've shot through the plane like tracer bullets. The trauma, the power of such a blast—"

"Would've torn the plane, and everything in it, apart," Ballard finished.

"Instantly," Leber said, switching off the screen and motioning for the lights. "They didn't feel a thing."

"Maybe." Kate swung her piercing blue eyes from the doctor to Ballard. "When will you be able to listen to the cockpit voice recorder?"

"Not until a member of the pilot's union gets here, right, Bob?"

The NTSB executive nodded. The CVR and flight data recorder were under his auspices. "Right. They have to give approval before we release any kind of transcript."

"Kate's a member." Becky proudly volunteered the information, turning and giving her tall friend a self-satisfied smile.

"Really? How *fascinating.*" Leber suavely edged closer to the pilot.

"Rebecca..."

"Yes," Becky continued, "Kate is also a captain with Orbis airlines."

"Not anymore," the pilot muttered under her breath, taking a step away from Leber's advance.

"Well it has to be an authorized rep," Ballard said. "Sorry, Catherine. I'd use you if I could. Meantime," he captured the room in a blistering glare, "we've got a shitload of investigative work that needs to be done here. More data analysis. Witness interviews. We've got to establish the nature of the explosive device, what it was contained in, its location, and the sequence of events immediately following detonation."

"And all this has to be correlated and independently confirmed," Bob Joseph added firmly, still unwilling to commit to a terrorist event. "It could take a year or more, if ever, before we know for sure."

Ballard bristled at that and had opened his mouth to reply, but a soft, cultured voice beat him to it.

"I'm sorry, you are--?" Farley Leber slowly removed his spectacles.

"Robert Joseph," the older man sputtered, taken aback. "Vice-chairman of the NTSB."

"Well, Bob," Leber offered the executive a benign smile, "with all due respect..."

Uh-oh, Kate chuckled to herself, *here it comes. This doggie has teeth.*

"I don't need a year. A month. Or even a week, for that matter." His words were biting, yet the scientist's tone was something out of *Mr. Rogers' Neighborhood.* "I can tell you within a ninety-eight percent degree of probability that my conclusions will be confirmed. If you care to drag your heels and put your fellow investigators—not to mention the victims' families— through hell for that last two percent, then be my guest."

"Wha—" Joseph recovered quickly. "How dare—"

"Okay, that's it for now, people." Gordon Ballard jumped in to salvage the meeting. After all, these people still had to work together, even if Joseph persisted in bullying his way through the investigation. "Thanks again, Farley. We'll let you get back to your...microscopes." He ushered the visitors towards the door.

"Thank *you,* Gordy." The little man fairly clicked his heels. "It's always nice to have some company once in a while."

Before Catherine knew what was happening, Dr. Farley Leber, he with the heart of a giant, swept up her hand and gallantly brushed it against his lips. "*Enchanté,* Captain Catherine Phillips."

"Ditto," the dark pilot replied, gazing down at the small

man and giving him a playful wink.

The group tramped out the door of the lab trailer and down the steps, with Kate and Rebecca lagging behind.

Casting a quick glance around the compound, Becky grabbed her companion lightly by the arm. "Okay. I am a bit slow on some things, but do you mind telling me what *that* was all about?" Her green eyes flashed with good humor in the morning sunshine.

"Hey." Kate feigned indifference, but her eyes danced merrily at the young flight attendant. "What can I tell you? Good things sometimes come in small packages." A pause. "You ought to know."

"Thanks," Becky shot back. "I think."

"Well, he does good work, anyway," Kate said, sobering.

"Yeah." Becky followed Kate back towards the command trailer. "At least we know what happened. Now all we need to find out is who's responsible."

"I already know," the pilot softly replied, her eyes turning towards the crash site. "What I need is proof."

* * * * * * * * * *

The day wore on with Kate, Mac, and Becky hunched over in the command trailer, studying printouts of the manifest and the supporting reports that Rory Calverton had forwarded. Gordon Ballard popped his head in occasionally, but most of the time the big FBI man worked over at the actual crash site, supervising the removal of the larger pieces of Flight 180's fuselage. A dreary, painstaking process at best. The reconstruction of the downed aircraft in the empty hangar back in Bangor would be critical in the analysis and visualization of just what had happened to the doomed flight. The physical evidence had to be consistent with any theory that Leber, Ballard, or the NTSB, for that matter, developed.

Sometime after one p.m., Becky had stepped out into the fresh air and gone to the canteen truck, retrieving coffee and chicken sandwiches for herself, Mac, and Kate. She and Mac had greedily devoured theirs, but the young flight attendant noted how Kate's sandwich sat virtually untouched amid the snowdrifts of paper. Now, it was past three o'clock.

It would never do, Becky knew, for Kate to deplete her energy resources, not now. She understood how driven her partner was, how her complete focus was centered on pinning the crash on the responsible parties. Still, that could take days, weeks, even longer. *And during that time, even the most superhuman among us need to eat,* she thought.

"Kate, aren't you going to eat that?"

"Why, do you want it?" The pilot never lifted her eyes from the paperwork in front of her as she slid the sandwich in Becky's direction. "Here."

"No," the young blonde sighed, "I mean *you* need to eat it. Now." She pushed the chicken sandwich back.

"Not hungry." Kate took a pencil and scratched little check marks on a list. "Can you believe all the stuff this plane was carrying? Besides all the passengers' luggage, I mean. Cases of wine. International mail. Crates of shoes. Collectible porcelain." Kate wore her hair loose this day, and she absent-mindedly pushed a stray piece of it back behind one ear. Sighing, she eased back in her chair and tossed her pencil down. "We need to look at who had access to the shipments. Who packed them and loaded them—"

"Right," Becky said, "and we will. Meantime," she captured the taller woman in a green-eyed reprimand, "you *will* eat this sandwich. Now. Mac has no intention of lugging your butt around this place if you pass out from lack of food, right Mac?"

"Uh, right," the investigator agreed, enjoying this exchange between the roommates. He never could have gotten away with it himself. Catherine sometimes didn't take care of herself the way she should when they were working, and there was nothing he could really do about it. Becky, however, was another matter. Let her go for it.

"But—"

"Kaaaate." Becky lifted her chin to the pilot, the steadiness of her gaze telling her she would brook no argument.

Kate tried to hold her stare, to challenge her into backing down, but she knew she'd already lost. *Damn.* "Okay, okay,"

Kate grumbled, dropping her eyes and reaching for the wax-paper wrapped sandwich. "She's pushy, isn't she, Mac?"

"Oh yeah," the burly Irishman quickly agreed. "In fact, I'd do whatever she says if I were you."

Becky smiled broadly, basking in the glow of her victory. "Thank you very much, both of you," she said primly, clearing her throat before she returned to her paperwork.

Mac yawned and reached his arms up towards the ceiling, stretching to the sound of several audible pops and cracks. "So no one's officially come forward yet, claiming responsibility?"

"If it's El Yousef, and I *know* it is," Kate said in between bites, "then he won't. For him, it's not about getting the attention, the international spotlight for committing a terrorist act. The act is his end in itself. His satisfaction. This guy is a filthy cockroach." Her voice was hard. "He likes to do his business in the shadows. And that's where we'll find him." Kate paused, surprised at the unexpected fierceness of her last statement. She self-consciously dropped her gaze to the sandwich she was eating, eyeing it cautiously.

"Nice visual." Mac grinned, reaching for his coffee cup. "Glad I'm not the one eating."

"So? What's your point?" Kate smirked and lifted an eyebrow at her older colleague, resuming her attack on the sandwich with a gulping chomp.

"Not a thing, not a thing," Mac chuckled, raising his hands in surrender. He knew when to leave well enough alone.

"Where are we on the passenger list?" The playfulness left Catherine's voice as she swung her eyes from Mac to Rebecca. Back to business.

"Well, Becky and I have split it up and broken it down."

"Yes." Becky reached for a sheaf of papers. "Of the 210 people on the plane when it crashed, 200 were passengers. We know of course that the aircraft originated in Lisbon. There were 147 people on that flight: 7 crew and 140 passengers."

"Hmn, nowhere near a full boat," the pilot said thoughtfully.

"Typical for that run, from what I understand," Becky replied. "Anyway, the plane landed in Paris, refueled, and reserviced."

"Three crew were added at that point." Mac took up the story. "A jumpseat captain for the overseas leg, and two flight attendants."

"The ones who originated in Lisbon stayed with the flight?"

"Yeah." Mac's eyes skipped down a list in front of him. "18 passengers remained on the plane, connecting through from Paris to Montreal. Plus 182 new passengers boarding in Paris. That brings us to our 210 total when the plane went down."

"Have you got those reports on the security in Lisbon?" Kate made room as Mac handed her several sheets of paper clipped together. "Thanks," she added as an afterthought, flipping through the paperwork. "I know the security at Charles de Gaulle is very tough. They've had their share of terrorist problems in the past. But Lisbon...I just don't know. All it takes is one small breakdown—a lapse along the way."

"What about the three and a half hour delay in Paris?" Mac massaged the back of his neck. "What was that all about? Could something have happened then?"

"Possibly," Kate allowed. "I don't want to rule it out. But the delay was due to problems with another carrier—Air Marianne—with whom Orbis shares gates. Took a while to get that straightened out."

"So it was nothing mechanical?" Becky wanted to know.

"No. Not the delay, at least," Kate answered. "Now tell me about those passengers who boarded in Lisbon and stayed on through Paris. Theoretically," the pilot stared at the ceiling, "the 122 passengers who deplaned in Paris would've had all their luggage removed with them."

"Yes, unless it was a carryon piece," Becky reminded her. "They're easy enough to leave behind, and the flight attendants might assume it belonged to one of the passengers traveling on."

"Right. But for the sake of argument, and based on Dr. Leber's initial findings, let's suppose that the device was definitely in the cargo hold. Passengers flying on to Montreal might have gotten off the plane in Charles de Gaulle to stretch their legs, but their actual luggage would've remained on board. Correct?"

"Yes," Becky said, casting a sideways glance at Mac. She

could tell where Kate was going with this.

"So, for those pieces that remained in the hold, what kind of security check did they undergo prior to departure—in Paris, I mean. Was there any additional baggage scanning for fly-throughs?"

Mac consulted his paperwork silently for a time before raising his eyes to his boss. "No. Not that I can see here."

"Okay then." Kate's eyes flashed. She leaned forward into the table. "I want us to concentrate on the passenger profiles, with a particular focus on those who checked in at the Lisbon airport. Let's look for individuals who were traveling alone, or who paid for their ticket in cash. Cross-reference them with Interpol. And let's check the passports of these people. Remember, we're looking for links to El Yousef and his associates. That could mean Saudi, Sudanese, Afghan, hell, even European, if you consider the network of legitimate businesses that help finance his terrorist activities.

"There's a Saudi Arabian man who boarded in Lisbon, Kate." Rebecca circled a name on her list. "Khaled Sadek. He worked for an import/export company. Plus several others...two more Saudis and a Sudanese, who checked in for the Paris-Montreal leg."

"Okay." Kate's voice was grim. "Then this is where we get started. Intensive background checks. Financials. Interviews. The whole nine yards."

"We?" Mac proceeded cautiously, not wishing to spark the dark pilot's infamous temper. Still, it needed to be said. "Listen Catherine, we have to watch our step here, and let the FBI do their job."

Blue eyes flamed to deadly life and burned a hole through Jim MacArthur. The former FBI agent shifted uncomfortably in his chair. "What I mean is—"

"The FBI can do their job," Kate said, sounding like the threatening rumble before a thunderstorm, "and I'll do mine. Understood?"

Mac swallowed hard and nodded. "Got it." *Uh-oh.* There was trouble in store ahead, he just knew it. Lead, follow, or get out of the way, his father had always taught him. And to his great misfortune, Mac knew in his heart of hearts that he'd follow Catherine Phillips wherever she might lead. Goddamn it all.

"Okay," Kate said, the anger still apparent in her voice. She returned her attention to the printouts, shuffling papers without really looking at them.

The awkward silence in the trailer was broken when the hulking, breathless form of Gordon Ballard burst through the door. "Shake a leg," he cried, ducking his head so that the tips of his red buzz cut just missed clipping the top of the doorjamb. "The cockpit voice recorder...we're ready to go."

Chapter
8

"Aaah. How are we looking?"

"That's Dick Resnick, the captain," Kate said softly. The faint sound of a cockpit door closing could be heard in the background. Listening intently, huddled around the recorder in the NTSB's trailer, were Gordy Ballard, Bob Joseph and Eric Brown, as well as Kate and her team. A tall, thin-nosed gentleman was from the Orbis pilot's union; Kate had recalled seeing his name on various correspondences she'd received in the past

"Same-o, same-o. Maintaining flight level three zero zero."

"And Tommy Hall, the co-pilot," she added. "They're at 30,000 feet."

"Roger, good sir. Suzie's got some of the hot stuff brewing back there if you want some."

"Resnick again," Kate said.

"I want some, all right, and it's got nothing to do with coffee."

Kate noticed Rebecca blush at lewd laughter sounding from the tape. And it didn't help matters any that they all knew from the crew profiles that Hall was married.

A tired sigh from Resnick, and then, *"They're all sleeping like babies."*

"Can ya blame 'em?" Hall paused. *"When are you out of*

Montreal?"

"Tomorrow night. Not cutting me too much of a break on the legal rest period. Anyway, I'm on to Vancouver. You?"

"Not 'til Sunday."

"You lucky bastard."

"Yep. Heading down to DC. Fits in perfectly with Suzie's schedule."

The sound of more laughter filled the cabin, and by now all those gathered around the recorder were shifting uncomfortably.

Flight 180 had been an older 747, and so the CVR was running on just a thirty minute magnetic tape loop. It was self-erasing, so that only the most recent thirty minutes could be heard at any one time. The problem was, that it would pick up *any* conversation, personal and otherwise, occurring in the cockpit or over the intercom. The people who flew planes were only human. Other cockpit voice recordings Kate had listened to and read transcripts of in her career had proved that often enough.

"Contact Montreal Approach yet?"

"Still about five or ten minutes away, I'd guess. Ooooh...I can feel that featherbed now."

"Yeah. Long day." Resnick again.

"Shit—long night too, with that goddamned delay."

"Yeah. That gate-sharing crap. Why don't they just lease out what they need and be done with it?"

"Dollars and francs my friend," Hall laughed aloud, *"it's what it always comes down to."*

"No kidding."

An extended period of silence followed, there was nothing save for the hum of the 747's big engines. It went on for at least three or four minutes, Kate estimated. Not unusual in long overseas flights, she knew, when the big birds very nearly flew themselves.

"Raining down below." Co-pilot Hall's voice sounded faintly.

"A bit. But it sure is pretty up here with that moon."

If Captain Resnick had anything more to say, or if Hall ever answered him, they would never know. A sharp crack...a clicking noise, sounded on the tape.

Then...nothing.

"That's it," Bob Joseph said to a solemn gathering. "After that split-second sound, the recording ends." When it came to cockpit voice recorder analysis, this was the NTSB's specialty, and Joseph was clearly in his element. "It's nearly identical to the sound picked up in the cockpit at the conclusion of Pan Am 103's CVR."

"An explosion," Kate said, eyeing the vice-chairman carefully.

"Sadly, yes."

"So there was no indication from the crew prior to the end of the tape that there was a problem." Gordy Ballard stood nearly at attention, his great size dwarfing the others around him. "No sign of engine or mechanical failure, or an aborted mayday."

"You're right, Gordy," the older man agreed.

Now it was Ballard's turn to play devil's advocate. "But the sound burst itself, *could* it have come from a mechanical or structural cause?"

"To the human ear, yes," Joseph said, moving to a large computer screen. "We can't distinguish between the sounds of an explosion: whether it's from a bomb, mechanical failure, or even a fuel problem like TWA 800 had. But this computerized oscilloscope can." He nodded to the lab tech who then typed several commands into the computer. "Show them, Jimmy."

The young tech looked over his shoulder at the group. "Well, as Bob has stated, our ears can't distinguish between high frequency sounds. But here," he tapped the keyboard a few more times and seemed satisfied with the results, "we can see the difference plotted."

Jimmy stepped aside so that the group could have a good view of the screen. "The digitized sound of a bomb produces a sharp spike, at a very high frequency. Other explosive sources—mechanical, fuel, for example—occur more slowly. They plot along a sloping line. Here's a digitized fuel explosion." He pressed a key and, sure enough, a gentle, sloping curve appeared on a graph on the screen.

"And here's what we got when we fed in the sound from

Flight 180's CVR." Another touch of the keyboard, and there was a sharp spike of a line, exploding upwards, nearly off the graph.

"Wow." Kate could hear Mac's low whistle behind her.

The NTSB vice-chairman stepped back to the computer and flicked off the screen. He turned to Ballard, his face drawn and tired behind his owlish glasses. "I guess I owe you...and Farley Leber, an apology."

"Don't worry about it, Bob," the big FBI man said graciously. "You were just trying to do your job. We all are."

"Well," Joseph cleared his throat before he continued, "we're still looking at the flight data recorder information. But it, too, shows no instrument malfunction before the tape went dead. *And* it indicates that many electrically powered devices on the aircraft cut out at nearly the same instant."

"Consistent with a catastrophic explosion," Kate said in a flat, emotionless tone.

"Exactly." The vice-chairman fussed with some papers on a nearby table. "Of course, we'll be releasing this transcript shortly, so you'll want to be prepared for the public's reaction."

"It's gonna get ugly," Ballard said, running a hand over his face. Just the thought of the backlash made his head spin.

Kate turned to Rebecca. The young blonde's mouth was open, a stunned look on her face. The pilot realized this was probably the first time she'd ever heard—in person—a cockpit voice recording. At least one that ended with such dire consequences. It had been a rough weekend for the smaller woman, she could tell, and yet she'd performed admirably, without complaint.

Kate dipped her head next to Rebecca's ear. "I've heard enough," she said quietly, surrendering to her frustration. "I want us out of Bangor tonight."

* * * * * * * * * *

Once Catherine Phillips had made up her mind to leave the crash scene, she couldn't get away quickly enough. As though the devil himself were on her heels, she offered a quick goodbye and thank you to Gordon Ballard, assuring him that the Orbis team would stay in close contact with the ongoing investigation. They both agreed to share information as it was developed, but for Catherine, she had all the facts she needed from the site. Dr. Farley Leber would forward to Rory Calverton the final results of the chemical residue and metallurgical testing, as well as any additional details on the origin of the bomb. But piecing together the trail of it would be a bit more difficult, and Ballard was not optimistic in terms of how long that might take.

"Could be months, Catherine," he'd said before they parted, but the pilot had her own ideas about that. She was anxious to start using the...alternative resources she had at her disposal to move the investigation along. Skills and contacts she'd developed in her past with the military, an expertise she thought she'd never have any use for again.

She'd been wrong.

When they were ready, Freddy Comstock took them back to the Lumberjack Motel so they could check themselves out. As the sun slipped behind the gently sloping western mountains, the Chevy Blazer wound its away along the country roads from Pohassat to Bangor, the highway stretching out before them like a faded ribbon in the dying sunlight. Rebecca had phoned ahead and found that there was an Orbis Express flight departing at 2030 hours, and Kate was determined that she and her team would be on it.

The truck rattled up to Orbis' departures drop-off at 2010 hours, plenty of time to spare.

"Thanks, Fred." Kate took the young man's hand firmly in her own. "You've been a great help."

"Yeah," Mac grunted from the back of the Blazer where he was gathering their bags. "Thanks, buddy. Go 'Sox."

"Ayuh," Freddy agreed, pushing the bill of his Pohassat Red Sox cap back off his forehead. "Havin' a respectable year so fa."

Rebecca stepped up to the tall, thin volunteer fireman and smiled. "I know it's been kind of...crazy for you these last few days. Thanks for lending us a hand."

"Not at all, Miss Hanson," the youth replied, his face flushing. "Glad to be of service."

"Once we're gone," Becky continued, "I'm sure things will get back to normal eventually."

"Oh, I'm sure they will." Freddy lowered his eyes to the pavement. "But things 'round here will nevah be the same."

Becky swallowed, her mouth suddenly gone dry. There was nothing she could say. Freddy Comstock had spoken the truth for them all.

****

It was a quiet ride back to JFK; there were only a handful of travelers on the small jet in addition to the Orbis group. Kate had wanted to detour by the office before heading home, but Rebecca was able to dissuade her. A rumpled Mac tiredly agreed with the flight attendant.

"It's after nine-thirty on a Sunday night, Kate," he said. "It'll all be there in the morning."

"All right," the tall pilot finally agreed. "See you tomorrow, then." She offered Mac a crooked smile. "I'll make the coffee."

Outside the airport, Kate and Rebecca flagged down a taxi whose shock absorbers, as it turned out, had evidently been left behind somewhere on the Queensboro Bridge, by the feel of it. The two women rattled and jounced their way back to Manhattan and Kate's high-rise, while the indifferent driver studiously ignored them. The pilot angrily slammed the door to the cab shut when she departed, throwing a few crinkled bills into the driver's lap. She had half a mind to report the cabby to the department of inspection. Good God, she felt as though a kidney was lodged somewhere near her ear.

"Ohhh."

"What's the matter?" Kate punched the elevator button for the 42nd floor.

"My stomach hurts after that cab ride," the young blonde groaned, clutching at her middle.

"No kidding," the pilot muttered. "I think I lost a filling."

"I'm sure if I get something to eat, I'll be okay." Rebecca cast a hopeful look up towards her companion. "How's that sound?"

Kate sighed and leaned back against the wall of the elevator car. "I'm sorry, Rebecca," she said, shaking her head. "We should have stopped somewhere. Or we could call for takeout. Or—"

"Or don't worry about it," Becky said, reaching out and brushing the back of her hand against Kate's cheek. "I'll fix us something from what we've got."

Kate laughed tiredly. "Good luck." The doors whisked open and the two women padded down the carpeted hallway to Kate's apartment.

"Wow." Becky led the way in and flicked on the lights. "It seems as though it's been ages since we've been home."

"I know," Kate agreed, secretly delighting in the fact that the young flight attendant considered the high-rise apartment her home. Now that Rebecca was in it, it was a home to Kate, too.

They cast their bags aside and Kate quickly moved past Becky and into the living room, where she immediately tapped the blinking red light on her answering machine. There were only a couple of messages, including a final one from Cyrus. He'd heard she was coming back tonight, and wanted her to call him. She reached for the phone.

"Oh no you don't." Becky came up behind her and took the phone from her hand. "It's late, Kate. Tomorrow."

"But—"

"Please." Green eyes gazed into blue. "Let's just have tonight...what's left of it, for us."

Kate thought about that for a moment. "Okay," she said at last, watching Rebecca place the handset back into the cradle. "Unpacking and Cyrus can wait."

"Thanks." Becky placed a light kiss on Kate's cheek. "Now. About dinner."

Rebecca whirled around and fairly skipped towards the kitchen, with Kate trailing after her like a puppy dog.

"Okay, let's see..." Becky ran a hand through her short blonde hair and searched the darkened interior of a cabinet. "A-ha." Out came a box of pasta and a jar of tomato sauce. "Not home-made, but it'll do."

Kate crossed her arms and leaned against the stainless steel double sink, smiling, watching her roommate go to work.

Rebecca put a pot of water on to boil, then headed for the refrigerator.

"Be afraid. Be very afraid," Kate warned. "Remember, you haven't been home for nearly ten days."

"Well, this has got to go," Becky scrunched up her nose and pulled out a carton of Chinese food. Leftovers from their dinner of several days past.

"Whaddya mean?" Kate took the carton from her and sniffed at it. "I was counting on that for breakfast tomorrow."

"Omigod, Kate. No way. You wouldn't—" Becky's scandalized rant sputtered and died into laughter when she caught sight of the wicked gleam in her partner's eyes. "Why you..." She gave Kate a playful poke in the ribs. "Garbage disposal. *Now.*"

"Yes, ma'am," Kate meekly complied, grinning.

Behind her, Becky salvaged several fairly crisp leaves of Romaine lettuce from an otherwise wilted head. From the rear of the produce drawer she produced a tomato and a green pepper that were within hours of reaching the limit of their shelf life. Still, they would do.

"Hey. Where did they come from?" Kate moved behind the smaller woman and dropped her chin on her shoulder, circling her waist with her arms.

"An accident, I'm sure," Becky replied, closing the refrigerator door with a nudge of her knee.

"Mnnn. You smell nice." Kate nuzzled a soft bit of neck, feeling the tension leak away from her body, enjoying the contact.

"It's the olive oil," Becky sighed, closing her eyes for an instant and feeling a shiver of desire race down her spine. "And if you don't stop doing that, there will be no supper."

"I'm willing to pass if you are." Kate planted a light kiss on Rebecca's temple.

"Kaaaate, you *know* how cranky I get when I don't eat." Becky pulled a cutting knife from its butcher-block holder and waved it threateningly in the air.

The tall woman instantly released the object of her assault, her arms raised in the skyward. "You got me. What can I do to help?"

"Stand back." Becky pointed knife at Kate, barely containing her laughter. "And watch a professional at work."

Kate obediently did as she was told, taking up a seat on a stool next to the island. In a few short minutes, a delicious aroma of garlic and tomato filled the air. One drained pot and some chopped vegetables later, Rebecca expertly produced two steaming plates of pasta, together with a light salad. As a final touch, she grabbed a bottle of Chianti from the wine rack.

"Are you sure wine is a good idea?" Kate looked doubtfully at the bottle Becky had handed her to open. "This is gonna make me sleepy."

"That's the point," Becky said, her hands on her hips. "You've barely slept at all this past week, Kate—no don't argue with me, I can tell." She cut off the pilot's protest before she could get a word in. "It's late. You've got to work tomorrow. And it looks like I've got some serious food shopping to do," she said, swinging her eyes around the rather barren kitchen. "Sleep. It's an okay thing. You should try it once in a while."

"You just want to get me tipsy so you can have your way with me," Kate challenged her, pouring the light burgundy-colored vintage into a pair of glasses.

"Well, that's another reason, hot stuff."

They sat side-by-side at a small table tucked in the corner of the kitchen, eating and talking. Words flowed easily from Kate, and it wasn't simply because of the wine. She didn't normally consider herself a talker, far from it. But in spending time with Rebecca Hanson, she'd gotten used to sharing her thoughts, her feelings, her dreams. It was an easy intimacy that in the past she never would have imagined for herself; even now she would never have known its joy were it not for this slip of a girl who had wormed her way into her heart.

"So I'll have to get with Liz Furey sometime this week," Kate said, turning the conversation to business. "Based on what we found out in Maine, I think there are some new security measures we need to put into play at JFK."

"Good luck." Becky took a stab at her salad, remembering the times she herself had been witness to the airport manager's hair-trigger temper. "And remember, be nice."

"Always." The pilot grinned in spite of herself. "Then, I want you to start working with Rory in building a database of the passenger manifest, cross-referencing level-of-risk factors and such. And we'll need to start putting together an interview timetable. Mac can help with that. The Saudi prospect you mentioned who boarded in Lisbon—what was his name?"

"Sadek." Becky slowly lowered her knife and fork. "Khaled Sadek."

"Sadek. Right. We'll definitely want to get in touch with his family and contacts, do some investigation there."

"Kate."

"And then there's the cargo point-of-origins. We can't overlook that either. Let's put together a parallel database for—"

"Kate."

The pilot finally stopped talking, and noticed for the first time the quiet, somber tone of her partner.

"Rebecca?" A knot of fear welled up in Kate's gut, and she let her cutlery clatter to her plate. "What is it?"

"I...I want to fly again. I *need* to fly again. I'm calling in tomorrow to get a new schedule of flight assignments."

"Why?" Kate fought to keep the confusion within her from turning into anger. "You did great this weekend. We work well together. I just thought—"

"But you never *asked* me," Becky replied, her eyes gone dark and still. She reached out across the table and grasped the dark-haired woman's hand. "I have to do this. For myself."

"Rebecca," Kate turned her head away, feeling the despair, the hurt creeping into her voice, and hating herself for it, "I *need* you with me."

Becky lifted her hand to Kate's cheek and forced the pilot to face her. "I love you. I need you, too. And I want you to support me in this, okay?"

No. No. No. Her mind was screaming. "Okay," she replied, her voice a hoarse whisper.

Not knowing what else to say, Becky stood up and loaded the pots and plates into the dishwasher. By the time she turned around, Kate was gone.

****

Kate lay huddled far over on her own side of the king-sized bed, utterly miserable. She knew she'd been unfair in the way she'd treated Rebecca. After all, the girl had a career of her own. Who was she to assume that after only one weekend of working together, she would want to make a more permanent change? *Hell, in the beginning, I didn't even want her along in the first place.*

She owed her partner an apology, she knew that. It was just that after such a pressure-filled weekend, placing so many demands upon herself, she'd gotten used to the idea of relying on the younger woman's assistance. It didn't come easily to her, that willingness to trust, to delegate with confidence, but Rebecca, in her simple, guileless way, had made it easy for her to do so.

And now you've gone and fucked it all up, Phillips, haven't you?

Kate heard Rebecca patter into the darkened bedroom. She blinked open one eye, and watched as the young woman walked over to the blinds and opened them a bit, allowing luminescent streaks of moonlight to paint the room's interior. Quickly, she shrugged out of her clothes, donned a long tank tee shirt, and slipped under the cool, crisp sheets next to Kate.

"Kate—"

"Rebecca—"

"Sssh. Me first." Kate rolled over and threw an arm across Rebecca's middle. "I'm sorry. I acted like a presumptuous, possessive ass. What makes you happy makes me happy. Do what you need to do. Whatever that is, I support you."

"Really?"

Kate could see the moistness of Rebecca's eyes in the moonlight. "Really." She sealed her promise with a kiss. "Now you, Champ."

"Okay," Becky sighed, blowing wisps of hair out of her eyes and facing the ceiling. She seemed to need to gather herself before she continued. "I...I guess what I've been thinking about is that those people on that plane...the passengers, the crew...they could have been us, Kate." She turned towards her partner. "We...could have been them."

"I know." Kate's voice was soft, reassuring. She lifted her hand higher, to Rebecca's shoulder. And there she let her fingers trace around the still-rough edges of the scar that marred the skin. A stark, vivid reminder of what could have been—and very nearly was. "But we're here. We're alive. And we have each other now, don't we?"

"Yeah." Becky released a shaky laugh and scooted closer to the pilot's warm body. "I just need to be up there in the air again. Prove to myself that I can do it."

"I know you can," Kate assured her. "Piece of cake."

"And while I'm away—"

"Yeessss?" Kate tried to control the breath of hope that blew into her soul.

"I'll think about it. And *you* think about it too, okay? How embarrassing if you had to fire me after...like a week, because I re-organized your office and you couldn't find anything."

"Not a chance," Kate vowed, a smile creasing her face in the darkness.

"Oh, that reminds me," Becky's lips were mere inches from Kate's, "did you get that second quarter budget pro-forma done?"

"Hmnn?" Kate's eyes were drooping closed, the combined result of her exhaustion, the wine, and the soothing presence of the woman nestled by her side.

Becky jabbed Kate in the tummy. "Don't you ever read your e-mail?"

"That's what I want to hire you for," Kate protested into her pillow, "Miss UCLA business major. My offer is on the table."

"My people will talk to your people," Becky yawned, letting her hand rest lightly on Kate's hip.

"They'd better," Kate growled, tightening her hold on Rebecca as the two of them drifted off to sleep.

Silence, for a time, and then, "Thanks for understanding." Becky's voice sounded low and muzzy in the dark. "It means a lot."

"You're doing the right thing." Kate kissed the top of her

head. "There's nothing to fear, you'll see. You're one of the bravest people I know."

A soft, satisfied sigh from Rebecca, and then deep, even breathing.

Damn El Yousef and the seeds of fear he sows, Kate thought. *I owe it to those poor people to make it right. Some way, somewhere along the line, He'll make a mistake. And I'll be there, waiting. "*

Chapter
9

"I don't care what the fuck you say, Catherine. I think this is a stinking, steaming load of horse shit, and you know it."

Liz Furey jabbed a threatening finger across the conference table towards her perceived enemy, one patently unruffled Catherine Phillips.

"Fortunately," Kate replied, choosing that moment to closely examine the tips of her own fingernails, "what *you* think doesn't matter." She paused, and then lifted a biting, blue-eyed glare to the flushed airport manager. "Get it?"

"The hell it *doesn't,*" the administrator screeched, throwing her pen down violently onto the cherry wood tabletop. She shoved herself to her feet, her mid-length brunette hair swinging wildly, and stomped over to the large picture window that lined the far wall of the Orbis executive meeting room.

"Wha...ah, Christ."

Kate did her best to withhold a smirk when she saw Furey's young, sallow-faced assistant, Michael Edwards, fail to dodge the spilled, half-consumed cup of coffee that the airport manager's sudden move had set in motion.

"Here you go, son." Cyrus Vandegrift slid a paper napkin his way, and the hapless fellow dabbed frantically at his sodden lap.

Furey was oblivious to it all. She stood with her hands on

her hips, staring out over the JFK tarmac without really seeing, her anger blinding her.

Jim MacArthur swung a sideways, questioning look towards Kate. He had worked with the pilot long enough now to pick up on her moods, most of them, anyway, and had a fairly good sense of how the tall woman liked to operate. And so he caught the barely perceptible nod of a dark head, meant for him alone.

Mac shuffled his papers and cleared his throat. "Liz, what Catherine meant to say, was that while we know that making all passengers de-plane between flights to re-identify and re-scan all carryon and checked baggage does pose somewhat of a hardship—"

"Damn straight." Furey's back was still to the room.

"It provides us with the best possible alternative at this time to better manage our security exposure. Particularly in light of what we now know happened to Flight 180."

The airport manager shot her fingers through her hair before whirling around. "How can any of us forget?" she cried. "It's still in the papers every goddamned day. A bomb in the luggage compartment. With people like *you* still trying to figure out how the hell that happened."

Kate remained silent, but Mac could detect the stiffening of her posture with that last comment. *Uh-oh.*

"Meantime," Furey continued, "I'm still waiting for somebody to tell me how x-raying and physically examining all checked and carryon baggage, with increased screening of passengers, after *every* touch-down—which *far* exceeds existing international standards, I might add—is gonna help me keep our flight schedule intact." She waved her hand back towards the window. "Have you people even seen the chaos you've thrown this airport into? Missed connections. Massive delays. Your partner airlines are up in arms."

"We recognize that these measures may delay some flights up to an hour," Mac said, bravely plunging forward, "but we think the public will, in the long term, accept the inconvenience. We'll simply have to allow for it when planning flight timetables."

"*Nobody* else is doing this," Liz growled, letting her dark eyes roam over the room.

"Nobody else has been targeted by terrorists in the way that Orbis Airlines seems to have been," Kate replied, struggling to keep her temper in check. To lose it now would be to let Furey win, she knew. And damned if she would let that happen.

"Well," the airport manager lifted her chin triumphantly, "that's *your* little problem, isn't it?"

For a brief moment, before Catherine fully regained control of her careening emotions, a vision of herself tossing a still-babbling Liz Furey into the path of an onrushing locomotive flitted before her eyes.

The executive had struck a raw nerve.

It had been weeks since the crash of Flight 180; weeks of tracking down what amounted to a series of frustrating dead-ends that left them no closer to Abbado El Yousef than they were that first terrible, gut-wrenching dawn outside of Pohassat. Hell, even Kate herself had realized that the new security measures might not have detected the plastique explosive that Gordon Ballard and his FBI technicians determined had brought down the doomed flight. After all, no security system was one hundred percent effective, particularly with El Yousef on the loose. But it was better than nothing.

*A bomb in the luggage compartment...*the M.O. was the same as what had happened to Kate's own plane, Flight 2240, when Stefan Bukoshi and his terrorist band had attempted to commandeer the aircraft. The bad guys hadn't won, not that time. But the similarities, including the critical point that both explosive devices used had evaded detection, were too blatant to ignore.

And just why was Orbis being targeted? The pilot had no firm evidence or answer. However, she suspected it was possibly due to the fact that Orbis was the only major airline left flying direct Mideastern flights to nations that El Yousef had labeled as being "imprisoned" by the "infidels." Starve out the commerce, and the invaders would leave, or so the logic went.

"We're keeping the new security protocols in place, Liz. For the good of our passengers," Kate said at last, feeling the first throbs of a pulsing sensation in the center of her forehead. *Damn it. Not another headache.* "We'd like to work with you on this." She folded her papers back into her black leather portfolio, signifying an end to the meeting. "It's your call."

Furey's dark eyes widened at first, and then narrowed. "You bet it is." She reached for the phone. "I'm calling the FAA."

"They already know about it, Liz." Cyrus placed a tanned, weathered hand on top of hers, stilling the phone in its cradle. "We ran it by them prior to implementation. In fact, they're reviewing our recommendations right now. Why, they're even considering making them mandatory for all carriers."

"Jesus Christ, Cy." Furey turned with a vengeance upon Orbis' director of flight operations. "You're just going to sit back and let this...this woman *do* this thing?"

"It's already done." Cyrus crossed his arms in front of his barrel of a chest. "That 'woman,'" he spared a quick glance at Kate, "is who I put in charge. What she says, goes. Sure, it'll create some hassles for us all in the short term. But I think it's a pretty nifty idea, myself." The retired Air Force colonel leaned back in his chair, smiling brightly, feeling quite satisfied.

"Oh yeah? Well, fuck you, Cyrus." Furey's face turned blood red. "Fuck the lot of you." And she stormed towards the door. "Michael!" The thunder of her voice spurred her frozen assistant into action. He leapt to his feet, Adam's apple bobbing, and gathered a pile of coffee-stained papers up into his arms. With a brusque nod to the Orbis people, he trailed after her, trying and failing to conceal the unfortunately located blotch on his trousers.

The door slammed shut behind them, reverberating through the conference room, rattling the expensive landscape prints on the walls. Seconds ticked by and the sound faded away, replaced by the window-glass muted engines of an Orbis jet, gunning for takeoff.

"Well, Katie," Cyrus turned twinkling blue eyes towards his one-time protégé, "I think that went fairly well, don't you?"

****

New York City was in the last dying throes of a hot, humid

summer, and the air conditioning in the J.P. Fleet building, which housed the Orbis offices, labored strenuously to keep the temperature cooled to a tolerable level. But, as Mac and Kate took the elevator the two floors down to the strategic operations offices, the chief investigator could tell his boss was steaming in a way that had little to do with the weather.

"I don't think I've ever seen Furey so 'furi-ous,'" Mac chuckled, trying to lighten the mood. A pissed off Catherine Phillips could make for a long, trying afternoon in the strategic ops unit.

Kate shot a blistering glare towards the big Irishman. An instinctive, immediate response that she quickly sought to rein in, and not without some effort. Mac was not the enemy here. "Yeah," she agreed, relaxing her features into a wry smile. "But on the up side, this means she'll probably stay the hell out of our way for the next few days, at least."

"God knows what her problem is," Mac ruffled his graying hair as the elevator doors slid open. "But I'd like to think her heart's in the right place."

The pilot led the way down the hall to the ops offices. "I have yet to see evidence of that," she said dryly.

"What—that it's in the right place?"

"No." Kate paused outside the Orbis entrance. "That she has one."

"Ouch." Mac shook his head, knowing that his boss had been more than a bit ticked off at the carnivorous Furey. "After you," he bowed, pulling open the door and shaking his head.

"Oh, Catherine, there you are."

Kate lifted a hand to her temple as the sharp, piercing sound of Dottie West's voice stabbed at her ears.

"That nice Mr. Greenfield just arrived. No one was here, and I didn't know what to do. He said he didn't mind waiting in your office, so I showed him in. But I simply could *not* convince him to have a cup of coffee this time. And I just brewed a new pot, too. Anyway, I told him there were cookies in—"

"Dottie." Kate fought to keep the sharpness out of her voice, even as she struggled to keep the pounding drumbeat in her head from escalating its tempo. "It's...it's okay," she said, watching the tentative, harried expression on the secretary's face bloom into a smile. Kate would have preferred that the CIA liaison agent not be in her office, alone, but it was too late for that now. The tiny, gray-haired woman in front of her had done her best, according to her well-intentioned, if somewhat short-sighted, business code.

The pilot took a deep breath, fighting back a lurch of nausea as the scent of Dottie's lethally strong brew wafted into her nostrils. "Just..." Kate squeezed her eyes shut for a moment, as Mac slipped by her. It was obvious that the former FBI man wanted no part of this discussion. They all loved the motherly Dottie, despite her secretarial shortcomings. "...in the future, if guests arrive and we're not available, have them wait out here, will ya?" She dug into her energy reserves and produced a thin-lipped smile for the older woman, trying to put her at ease.

Funny. Back in the Air Force, she'd had no trouble at all busting down any errant airman who happened to get caught in her disciplinary sights. But with Dottie...God, she'd rather stick a steel spike in her eye than hurt the kindly old woman's feelings. Something told Kate that the woman had been on the receiving end of enough of that, from other employers in the past.

"Oh, of course, Catherine. I'll be sure to make a note of it."

True to her word, Dottie plucked a yellow legal pad off her desk, and made an entry towards the bottom of an already long list. Kate was certain she could guess what some of the other items might be: get the phone numbers of all incoming callers, make sure to turn the coffee pot off at the end of the day. And, of course, don't turn off anyone's computers. That one had to be right after the coffee pot notation. Dottie had taken it upon herself to turn off *all* things electrical when she'd been warned about the coffee pot, after having inadvertently scorched the corner of the break room. And so, the next day, she'd turned off not only the offending "Brewmaster," but also all the lights, calculators and computers, including the one Rory had been working on before stepping outside for a smoke.

Data he'd been playing with for the last two hours. Gone.

It was his own fault, Kate had told the howling young man

then, for not backing up his work before walking away from it. If there had been a power surge—a sudden storm—he could just as easily have lost the data that way, as with "hurricane" Dottie. In the end, they all were able to agree that it was simply a lesson hard learned. And, true to her "noting" promise, Dottie had steered clear of their computers ever since.

Kate pushed open her office door in time to see her guest picking his head up from a file he was paging through—one that she knew she'd left closed on her desk. "Hi, Josh," she said evenly. "Sorry I'm running a bit late."

Greenfield did not look surprised to see her; showed no remorse at being caught with his hand in the cookie jar. "Catherine, how are you?" He stood to greet her, smoothly replacing the file on top of the neat stack at the corner of her desk. He let his eyes quickly take in the sight of her. She looked stunning, as always, if a bit flushed. Her attire was simple—just a mid-length black skirt and pumps, together with a black and white patterned short-sleeved blouse—but she brought an elegance to her clothes that spoke of taste and style. Truth be known, he found her damned attractive. Perhaps...another time. Now, he was here on business.

"I'm fine, Josh," Kate briefly shook his hand before stepping behind her desk and sitting down. "What have you got for me?"

"That's a good one, Catherine." Joshua Greenfield, he of the unremarkable looks and remarkable intelligence, turned the corner of his mouth up in a cold smile. "More to the point," he tapped his finger on the file he'd been reading, "what have *you* got for me?"

"Why, whatever do you mean?" Kate steepled her fingers and stared into the deep brown pools of Greenfield's eyes. Two could play at this game.

"Tickets. An itinerary for Saudi Arabia?" He leaned forward in his chair. "What are you up to?"

"Just visiting. You know I was stationed there during Desert Storm. I'm seeing some people I know."

"And some you don't," Greenfield said, his eyes flashing. "Like Khaled Sadek's family and associates—"

"You're jumping to conclusions, Josh." Kate clucked her tongue and swiped the file in question out of the CIA man's reach.

"With you, I can see that it pays to stay a step or two ahead."

Kate released a rumbling laugh at that, and grinned evilly. She did not dislike Greenfield. In fact, she admired his...initiative. "Catch me, if you can."

"Watch yourself, Catherine." Greenfield's face betrayed no emotion. His tone held no promise. No threat. "If you step on some people's toes they might not like it."

Kate held onto his stare. "I know I don't like it when someone steps on mine."

"Oookay." Josh let out a long burst of air, ending the moment. "Now that we've got the 'toe' issue out of the way, I suppose you're up-to-date on how the bomb was transported into the plane, right?"

"Yes." She nodded. "Ballard's been really good about keeping me in the forensic loop. A black, hard-sided Sky King suitcase, right? Clothing packed in the bomb suitcase has been tracked to a Riyadh clothing shop. Men's clothes. A Saudi man bought the items several weeks prior to the bombing. We..." Kate caught herself. "Ballard is still trying to determine which of our passengers—if any—were in the Saudi capitol during that time."

"And was the bag processed out of Lisbon or Paris?"

"Ballard's not sure," Kate sighed, "and he may never know. The force of the explosion just mixed up everything in that hold, like ping-pong balls in a steel cage."

"Well," Greenfield opened his briefcase and produced a thick manila envelope, "this might help."

Kate silently lifted an eyebrow.

"It's a report on the circuit board fragment that was recovered from the wreckage."

"Really?" Kate took the envelope from him, surprised. "I thought Dr. Leber was still working on it."

"Dr. Leber may well still be. But our...independent work is done."

"And?" Now it was Kate's turn to lean closer to her visitor.

"It was part of a sophisticated electronic timer, similar to a type that Italian authorities discovered in the possession of an Albanian political activist last fall." He paused. "Any of this ringing a bell?"

The pilot's pulse quickened, her headache momentarily forgotten. "What else?"

"I'm saving the best for last." Greenfield smiled faintly, adjusting his thin, wire-framed glasses. "The timer was coded to a Swiss electronics firm located in Zurich. Possibly, and I do mean possibly, they could be one of El Yousef's shadow corporations. A front for his bogus business dealings."

"You know the name of the firm?" Kate was already grabbing at the paperwork in the envelope.

"It's all there."

"Good," she said, her mouth forming a tense line. "I want to get Rory working on this."

"Speaking of Rory...and the rest of your team, where's my report?"

"On its way." Kate swept her eyes over her relatively clear desk. "It should be here any minute."

"Thanks," Greenfield said, relaxing back into his seat. He knew he was sharing more information with Catherine Phillips than he had any right to, but if he played his hunch correctly, there was a chance that she just might lead him to El Yousef. Why, that computer whiz kid of hers alone was worth his weight in Intel stock options.

"On our end, we're looking into reasons why Orbis has been targeted," Kate said. "I think we can all agree that it's not just been luck of the draw. We're looking at all the destinations we service in what the State Department considers the 'hot' zones. And," she frowned, "I hate to think that we have a security breach, but that's also a distinct possibility. We've got to consider it. El Yousef may have an inside contact."

Greenfield nodded. "And how is Rory making out with that encryption program?"

"No go, so far. But he hasn't given up on it. If you'd just been able to intercept more of the message...?" She eyed the operative carefully.

"You have all we have," he assured her. "El Yousef's transmitters move so damned fast." Greenfield shook his head. "We've heard some rumors that he's got a new training camp setup in northeastern Afghanistan, but it's just that—a rumor." He fell silent.

They eyed each other closely, well aware that the key to unlocking the damnable mystery of El Yousef might lie within the sensitive information they forced themselves to share with one another.

"Well," Kate said, looking past Greenfield towards the door, "are you sure you don't want any coffee?"

"Uh...."

Kate smiled at the way Greenfield blanched. She knew he'd been subjected to Dottie's super hi-test beverage in the past.

"N—no, thanks." He lifted a hand. "Really."

Kate shrugged her shoulders. "Suit yourself." She turned to watch a JAL 757 steam down the runway, gathering itself, preparing to leap into the air. *Where is that report?* Her fingers itched to press the intercom on her phone. She was through with Greenfield, and wanted him out the door so she could get back to work.

"I must say, Catherine, I had no idea you had such a nice office." The agent was smirking at her. "It looks as though a front-end-loader came through here since the last time I visited. What is it—did you take some seminar on organization and time management or something? Because if I *did* want a cup of coffee," he pointed to her near spotless desk, "at least now there'd be a place to put it down."

"Well, ah...I..." Kate was saved by a knock at the door. "Come in," she called out, relieved.

A blonde head poked through. "Sorry to disturb you, Kate. But I have that report you wanted."

"C'mon in." The pilot motioned to the new arrival. "Rebecca, I'd like you to meet Josh Greenfield, the CIA liaison officer assigned to Orbis. Josh, this is Rebecca Hanson, our Strategic Operations Manager."

"A pleasure." Josh smartly got to his feet and extended a

hand. "Sounds like you've got an important job here." His brown eyes glinted behind his glasses.

"No, not really." Becky dipped her head down a bit, blushing. "It's just a fancy way of saying that I try to keep things pulled together. You know. Take care of stuff."

"I can see that," Josh said, letting his eyes roam around the office one last time. He knew damn right well who Rebecca Hanson was. Knew the backgrounds of *all* the members of the strategic operations unit, in fact. It was his business to know. "Well, thanks for the report, Catherine." He slid the file Rebecca had given him into his briefcase. "I'll be in touch and...remember what I said. Please."

"You too, Josh," Kate replied, lifting her chin slightly as Greenfield turned and left.

Becky watched him leave. "What was that all about?" She turned concerned green eyes towards Kate.

"Ah, nothing," the tall woman said, slipping back down into her chair with a sigh and closing her eyes.

"Don't you 'nothing' me, Catherine Phillips." Becky's voice was firm. "Remember, it's my *business* to know now."

"I'll tell you later," Kate said, rubbing her eyes. Damn, but this had been a lousy day so far. And it was barely half over. She never heard Becky pad out of the office. She only felt the faint displacement of air as the younger woman returned, drawing close to her, placing a cool hand on her brow.

"Here. Take this."

"Hmnn?" Kate blinked open one glazed eye to see a hand before her, holding two white tablets.

"And this." Water. A big glass of it.

"Wha -?"

"You've got a headache, right?"

"Yeah, but...how did you—"

"It's my business to know, remember?" Rebecca's voice was soft. "I take care of you, now."

Kate considered that fact for a moment, before reaching for the pills.

Letting someone take care of her.

It was new.

It was different.

And she was bound and determined to get used to it.

****

"You're sure you don't want Mac to go along with you? Or even me, if you need me." Rebecca Hanson leaned against the bedroom doorjamb, watching Kate pack her bag for Saudi Arabia. Mostly light colored, lightweight clothing, appropriate for the intense, dry desert heat that awaited her. But the flight attendant noticed that Kate took care that her selections were as conservative as possible. Long sleeves, loose fitting, and no shorts.

"Oh, I need you, all right," the tall pilot grinned as she continued to fold her clothes into the bag, "but over the next few days, the office will need you more."

"Kate—"

"I mean it, Rebecca." She paused in her packing to capture the younger woman in a serious, blue-eyed gaze. "You know Rory is up to his ass in alligators, tracking down anyone even remotely affiliated with that Zurich electronics firm. You can help him with that."

"I know, but—"

"And Mac is heading down to Washington to compare Josh's report on the circuit board fragment with what Gordy Ballard and Dr. Leber have been able to come up with."

"You're right." Becky threw her hands into the air and paced. "I know that. It's just...just..." she flounced onto the bed next to the pilot's bag, "I worry about you when you're out of my sight, that's all." Her voice softly trailed off. "I mean, Saudi Arabia..."

"Listen, Champ." Kate quirked the corner of her mouth into a smile, and ruffled the smaller woman's short blonde hair. "The war's over, remember? And I'll only be gone for a few days."

"Oh, all *right*," Becky agreed, sighing. "I'll hold down the fort for you while you're gone, okay? As long as you promise not to...take any chances." She reached out and gave a tanned hand a squeeze.

"Are you kidding?" Sensing the emotions warring within

Rebecca, Kate sat down next to her and put an arm around her shoulder. "Look, the most dangerous thing I'll have to look out for is making sure I can dodge all those Mercedes and Rolls Royces when I'm crossing the street in Riyadh." She hesitated before continuing, but forced herself to ask the question. "Rebecca, you...you're not sorry you took that leave from flight crew to work with me, are you?"

"No, no," the new Strategic Ops Manager responded quickly, firmly. "I wouldn't trade these last few weeks for anything—being able to work with you and Mac and all. And I'll see this 'project' of yours through to the end." Becky's green eyes glistened. "That's the commitment I gave you."

"Okay then. Good," Kate replied, finding herself more relieved to hear it than she had expected.

After they had returned from the nightmare in Pohassat, Rebecca had resumed flying, for a time, just to prove to herself that she could. To exorcise any demons that remained. A couple of weeks later, unannounced, she'd shown up at the strategic operations office with a sheepish grin on her face and an application in her hand.

Catherine had hired her on the spot.

It would be temporary, the young flight attendant had said. But they both knew, and hoped, that it would turn out to be more.

"We'll see," they'd agreed then. And it had been working out spectacularly ever since. Everyone in the office appreciated her organizational and business skills, not to mention her diligent work ethic. And of course, Kate found herself relying on Becky more with each passing day than she would ever admit to.

"Well, I've got to get going here," Kate said, moving to resume her packing.

"Wait—" A small hand on her arm. "Kate, you know...you never talk much about your life when you were in the Air Force. I mean, I know in general what you did, at least I *think* I do," Becky's brow furrowed as she tried to work it all through, "but whenever you talk about it, if you do, it's almost like you're talking about someone else. There's no feeling. No emotion there."

Oh, great. A "feelings" chat. The pilot stiffened. She was definitely not in the mood. "I had a job to do, and I did it." Kate unconsciously pulled her arm away, withdrawing into herself. No. This was a conversation she was not about to have. Not now.

"But you were in Desert Storm right?" Becky continued to probe. "What...what did you *do* there, Kate? What was it like? What kind of people did you—"

"Did I kill? Is that what you're asking?"

The words tumbled out before she could retrieve them. They rode on the crest of a tidal wave of bitter memory that she was forced to expel, lest it choke her. She saw the hurt spring to Rebecca's eyes, felt the flinch of the body next to her as though she'd been struck, and yet she was powerless to stem the tide.

"Oh yeah. The whole goddamned Republican Army. And some innocent women and children, too. Is that what you wanted to hear?" Kate pushed herself up from the bed, away from Rebecca, but she could not elude the past that still nipped at her heels. "And how about our own people? The friendly fire kills? But we did keep them within acceptable limits." She laughed harshly. "Something to be proud of, I guess."

Fuck. The pilot stormed over to the window and pulled up the blinds, blinking sightlessly at the movement of the city so far below. Her breath came in hitching, ragged spurts. She could feel the blood rushing madly through her veins like a runaway freight train, threatening to jump the rails into oblivion.

Damn, she hadn't meant to snap out like that, but the way Hanson kept on pressing, pushing—accusing? Memories that she thought she'd neatly filed away forever had been dredged up in a heartbeat.

"Kate." Warm arms encircled her waist. It was Hanson...Rebecca, slipping behind her. "You're wrong you know, you big idiot." Her voice was low, reassuring. "I was just curious about the kind of people you met while you were there. You know. What were they were like? And if you'll see them again this trip?" The grip around her waist grew more snug. Secure. "That's all."

Double fuck. Kate let her forehead *thunk* into the tinted plate glass of the window, and she kept it there. *What the hell is wrong with me? And what have I ever done in my miserable life to deserve being loved by someone as patient and forgiving as Rebecca Hanson?*

"Ah, Rebecca." Kate deftly spun around in the smaller woman's arms so that she was facing her. "I'm so sorry," she said, finding herself getting lost in the bright green eyes that gazed up at her. "That freaking Persian Gulf War." She took in a deep breath and released it, feeling some of the tension leave her body. "It was called Operation Desert Shield, actually, before it ever became Desert Storm."

Becky silently bade her to continue, knowing that it was important for the pilot to get this out of her system.

Right here.

Right now.

"C'mon," Kate said, wrapping an arm around the young blonde's shoulders and leading her away from the window. "How about I make us a pot of coffee, and I'll tell you about it."

Chapter 10

She was going back. God, she never thought she'd find her way across the seas and sky to the land of shifting sands and blinding sun ever again. Even when she was piloting for Orbis, she'd made it a point never to fly legs that would take her to the Middle East. Too many memories; too few of them good.

New York to London to Riyadh. Over fifteen hours flight time. Plenty of time for the eight years that had gone by to blur away, like footprints in the swirling desert winds.

The people.

The places.

The faces she had tried like hell to forget, knowing deep in her gut she never would, or could.

She had been deployed as a member of Colonel Cyrus Vandegrift's 67th Fighter Squadron, finding herself suddenly grounded in Dhahran Air Base at the outset of Desert Shield. And Captain Catherine Phillips, hotshot pilot, didn't like it one goddamned bit.

It wouldn't be until several years later that the government would officially open combat cockpits to women. And so, during the Persian Gulf initiative, Air Force women were deployed in tanker, transport, and medical evac craft. Where Kate had been an equal to her fellow pilots back in the states, on foreign soil she had to take a step back and watch the F15s and F117 Stealth Fighters scream off the flight line without her.

Fine.

If being a support jockey was what got her into the air, so be it. And Cyrus was happy to let her do it, just to get her off his back. Oh, she'd tried to be more than helpful working as his adjutant: organizing strike packages, scheduling sorties. The mission of the 67th had been clear: kick Saddam Hussein's butt out of Kuwait. And protect the coalition allies in the process.

Targets? Pretty much anything had been fair game in Iraq. Leadership and command facilities. Radar, telecommunications, and air defense systems. The railroads, bridges, and oil production facilities. Hell, even Baghdad itself. And if Saddam happened to get toasted in the bargain, so much the better. Focusing on the mission, on the objective, had helped to ease her pain of getting yanked out of the cockpit.

Until that one afternoon when she'd been standing outside the command post. She'd watched the jet fighters taking off and landing one after the other with dizzying speed, lifting above the shimmering airfield and screeching toward Iraq, or coming home from a sortie. She'd quietly observed it all, trapped on the ground, a falcon with a broken wing, wishing for the thousandth time that she could be up there with them.

And then Cyrus had joined her there, in that oppressive desert heat, where every day was like the hottest she could ever remember back in the states, except that in Dhahran there was the winded effect of a hot hairdryer blowing in your face.

Did she know her way around Scout helicopters and Hueys, her commanding officer had asked?

God, did she ever. In her sleep she could fly those lumbering birds.

And so Cyrus was able to get her out and about occasionally, doing some troop transport and life flights, as well as the odd bit of reconnaissance. It was that last area of operation that she enjoyed the most. And the one that had nearly gotten her killed.

"Can I get you something to drink?"

Kate's eyes snapped open to see the cheerful face of a British Airways flight attendant standing before her. She'd opted to fly on a partner carrier, deciding that this was one trip she didn't necessarily want associated with Orbis Airlines.

"I'm sorry—I didn't mean to wake you."

"I wasn't sleeping," Kate grumbled, sitting up in her first class seat and running a hand through her hair. She swallowed, aware of the dryness of her throat. "I'll take a bottled water, when you get a chance."

"I won't be a moment," the blue and red uniformed woman replied, heading towards the forward galley.

It was all the tall pilot could do to repress a yawn as she gazed out her window into the cold, blackened night outside. The throbbing of the big 747's engines *had* lulled her into...something just short of sleep. That, at least, she would admit to.

Checking her watch, she saw that they were just a couple of hours out of Riyadh. *Good,* she thought, stretching her long legs out before her. This was too damn long a flight to begin with, to not be in the cockpit.

"Here you go."

The flight attendant had returned, and was efficiently placing a bottle of water, glass, and napkin on her armrest drinks tray.

"Thanks." Kate nodded, watching her move to service other passengers in the cabin. First class was only half filled, most likely due to the mid-week timing of the flight, and Kate herself would not have been on it if Cyrus hadn't pulled a few strings to get her visa rapidly approved. To travel to Saudi Arabia, if you were not in the military or directly associated with a business concern, was not an easy thing to do on short notice. And, if you were a woman, so much the worse.

That had been another, solid reason why Kate had not wanted Rebecca accompanying her. She had experienced first-hand the differences in the Saudi attitude towards women, as compared to American culture. The two were dramatically opposed. And the fact that you might be a foreign woman on Saudi soil did not mean you were exempt from criticism.

The wearing of the veil, the not being permitted to drive or ride bicycles in public, the featuring of clothing that would be certain to cover the elbows and the knees—the rule of Islamic law. Although the edicts made perfect sense to the traditional male Saudis, whose women were taught to focus on the value of the family and the nurturing of the home, Kate and her peers found it stifling, to stay the least.

Foreigners were tolerated rather than welcomed in Dhahran and, as a result, very few personnel on the base had ever ended up even seeing any of the locals. By design, they were taught and trained to stay away, the better to maintain the delicate balancing act that was the coalition force's relationship with its host. Only local contractors who supported the military effort—building additional barracks, providing free oil—were allowed on the base at all. That was how she had met Robert.

Robert Ahmad Yamani.

A half-breed, like herself, with two cultures as diverse as her own Irish and Greek heritage. Robert was born to a British mother and Saudi father, raised and schooled in England. Tall and dark, speaking with an impeccable British schoolboy accent, it was hard not to give him a second look. And Kate had.

Along with a third.

Robert had been a mild diversion, something to distract her from the deadly dull routine of her waking hours in-between chopper runs. It could never be anything more than that, never; and so she'd been surprised when Robert confessed to her one night of his hope for a future. She had ended it right then, coldly, without a backwards glance. It was her way. No strings, not her.

But he owed her one, big time, and here she was, flying into Riyadh's King Khaled International Airport years later, hoping to collect. The American air operations had been moved several years ago from Dhahran to Prince Sultan Air Base, about fifty miles southeast of Riyadh. That had been in the aftermath of the terrorist bombing of the Khobar Towers, a residential building housing Americans stationed at the base. Nineteen Air Force personnel had been killed; over 400 wounded. At Prince Sultan, overall security and the facility itself were better suited to the Air Force brass's stepped-up requirements. And so when the U.S. operations had moved, Robert Yamani had moved with them.

And expanded his business into imports and exports, Kate had heard.

Whatever.

So she had treated him like shit back then. Time had passed, and she had changed. She needed him one last time.

She'd already contacted him prior to leaving New York, told him what she wanted and where she would be.

And in the rich, warm, cognac tones of his far-away voice, he'd promised her he would be waiting.

****

Stepping out of the jetway into the King Khaled airport, Kate was struck by how merely that short journey from her comfortable airplane seat, down the ramp and into the terminal, made her feel like Alice in Wonderland tumbling down the rabbit hole. All traces of the prim and proper British flight attendants were left behind. And although a number of the passengers on board were apparently Saudis, during the flight Kate had heard them speaking in soft, accented English, and so the contrast had not been so apparent. But now, passing through the gate after being herded through customs, the pilot found herself being swept along towards the main concourse in a teeming mass of humanity that reminded her of 51st and 7th at rush hour.

The crowds were predominantly men, many wearing traditional light colored Arab dress, but there were quite a few featuring western-style business clothes along with the *gutra*, a head scarf anchored in place with the *aghal*, a circular cord of dark lambs' wool. What few women there were walked in the company of men, and this did not surprise Kate in a land where a female could not stay in hotel or board a plane without written permission from a male relative.

The tall pilot allowed herself to be carried on by the crowd, already feeling their gazes upon her. She stood out among them, that was for certain, with her khaki pants and blouse, work shoes, and long dark hair gathered at the nape of her neck in a copper-colored clasp. A woman alone, not dressed in the required *hijab*. Most unusual.

Although her squadron had been based in Dhahran, Kate had had the opportunity to travel to Riyadh several times with Cyrus, for the occasional briefing or two. But they had never landed at the commercial airport, and even then she'd seen very little of the city itself. She would need someone like Robert to help find her way around, much as she hated to admit it.

Okay. The pilot paused and squinted at the directional signs looming ahead, ignoring the jostling she felt going on around her. The smallish signs featured both English and the distinctive Arabic script that she'd never been able to make head nor tail of. A taxi to her hotel...that's all she needed.

"Catherine. Over here."

A feeling she could not put a name to clutched at her heart. She turned, slowly, and there he was, pushing through the crowds to get to her side. And suddenly, all those years ago were only yesterday.

"How marvelous to see you," he cried, taking her flight bag unbidden and slinging it over his shoulder. He took her hand at first, and then gave her the traditional greeting of a light kiss on each of her cheeks, and she did the same.

"Robert, you shouldn't have come here. I thought we agreed—I'd meet you at the hotel."

"Nonsense." He took her by the elbow and guided her towards the exit. "It's more than 35 kilometers from here to the city, and I don't trust you with those taxi drivers, Catherine." A gleaming white smile emerged from a deeply tanned face. "None of them have standard meters, and I fear by the time you would be through with them, there would be nothing left but skin and bones."

"Ha," Kate barked a laugh. "I've mellowed Robert. That, and I've already heard how...entrepreneurial...the local taxi drivers are."

He waved his hand dismissively. "Still, I would imagine that the citizens of Riyadh are just a bit safer today with me as your escort."

He led the way towards the exit and Kate followed, noting how although he was dressed like so many of his countrymen: black loafers, casual black slacks, open-necked long-sleeved white dress shirt, and white *gutra,* like her, his height set him apart. His "aristocratic advantage," he'd always laughed. Leaving the terminal, the doors whisked open and Kate found herself assaulted by a blast of hot, dry wind. The intensity of it seemed to suck the very air from her lungs, and she nearly staggered in the face of it.

"Christ," she swore. "And I thought we were having one helluva summer in New York."

"Don't tell me, Catherine, you have forgotten our temperate climate?"

"Not bloody likely." Already, she could feel the perspiration breaking out on her forehead, on the small of her back. Her body's natural response. To the weather, of course.

"This way." Over the roar of a Lufthansa jet taking off, the tall Arab directed her towards a gleaming, coffee colored, late-model Mercedes sedan.

"Check it out." Robert quickly tossed her bag in the trunk, and opened the door for her. "Mercedes S-500. Latest model. Designo Espresso Edition. Not yet available."

"Oh God," Kate groaned, sinking back into the buttery soft, light brown leather seat. "How did you get this, then? Or will you have to kill me if you tell me?"

Robert winked a hazel eye at her. "Connections, Lieutenant Catherine, connections."

Kate could not help herself. She smiled that. *Lieutenant Catherine.* How long he'd called her that, in his formal, British way, even after they'd become more than friends. She spared a glance at him as he tooled through the airport traffic and out onto the highway. He hadn't changed much. Just a few flecks of gray were visible in otherwise thick, dark hair, as the wind blew back his *gutra.* A strong face and jaw, with a proud, noble nose sitting just above a nicely trimmed mustache. A pair of designer sunglasses covered the eyes she remembered so well, and there was not an ounce of fat on him yet, that she could tell.

Looking around the luxurious German car, Kate recalled how well Robert had loved his toys, more so than most of the other "big boys" she'd known in her life. Somehow, his desire to play hard and fast had made him all the more appealing to her.

Part of that playfulness had carried over into a desire to work out to keep himself in shape, a departure from many of his peers who were content—as Catherine herself was—to rely on nature taking its course to stay fit.

Or not.

"Portable cellular, GPS navigation—listen to this Bose sound system, will you." Robert was running through the features of his vehicle as though he were some sort of manic car salesman.

Suddenly the unlikely, high-pitched sound of Michael Jackson streamed from the speakers.

Billie Jean is not my lovah...

"Bass...equalizer—" The car swerved slightly as the Arab fiddled with the controls.

"Hey." Kate tiredly lifted a hand to her head. "Keep your eyes on the road, will ya?"

She's just a girl who claims that I am the one...

"Even heated mirrors, Catherine, can you imagine that?"

"Like you need it in this bake-oven."

Catherine reached out a hand to flick off the stereo. She'd had enough. "Please," she protested in the sudden air-conditioned silence that followed, " I'm sold for God's sake. You're giving me a freaking headache, Yamani."

"Aaah." He grinned from ear-to-ear, minding her sharp words not at all. "Just like old times, yes, Lieutenant Catherine?"

****

The Mercedes flew along the highway, wheels humming, stirring up a cloud of dust in its wake. Those damned desert sands. How well Kate remembered them. The winds were always blowing it, driving it into your machinery, your nose, your eyes. It was as relentless as it was inescapable. You breathed it, ate it, slept with it. Combine it with the heat—sometimes it would reach 130 degrees Fahrenheit on the flight line—and the overall effect was maddening. "Sand crazy," they'd called it. It took its toll. But hell, there had been a war going on, and no one had said it would be a cakewalk, escorting Saddam's Republican Guards back across the Iraqi border.

The television broadcasts and letters from home had relieved the stress for some, but not Kate. Television? She'd never had time for it. Letters? Who in God's name would ever write to her?

Her work was her focus. Plain and simple.

The more miserable she felt, the harder she would work. And it was through that work she'd met Robert, one of the local fuel merchants supplying the base. In a goodwill gesture, the Saudi's subsidized the cost of it. But Kate suspected that Robert was careful enough to make sure he got his fair share of the take, and then some.

She'd see him in the command post when his people were making deliveries, and observed him heading in and out of the officers' canteen any number of times with some of the friends he'd made on base. All for the sake of "good business," he'd say. She'd known him generally in passing, that was all. But there had been instances when she'd spied him looking at her across the compound, and times when she'd found herself doing the same.

When he would catch her looking at him, she would busy herself and turn away, content in the knowledge that he meant nothing to her.

Until that night when he made a late delivery, on her shift. He'd driven his tanker in personally, and she'd been the one to sign him in and process his papers. It was chance, she'd told herself then, although there were moments later on, after she'd gotten to know him better, when she wasn't so sure.

In the darkened office, amidst the paperwork and signatures, there were hands touching, stroking; bodies pressing against each other, hard, and lips heatedly seeking out flesh. They met frequently after that, usually in the apartment Robert kept just outside the base, again, for business purposes.

It relieved some of the tension, the frustration she'd felt at being kicked out of her F15. And, though she hated to admit it, there was something to be said for allowing herself to be held, to feel the physical pleasure that accompanied such intimacy. And,

once in a great while, with Robert as she had with others before
him, she would catch a brief, fleeting glimpse of the wonder, the
joy that she'd heard existed in a world where two people claimed
to love each other. A world she hadn't dared to believe was real,
until she met Rebecca Hanson.

She hadn't realized he was falling for her until it was too
late. After all, what was there about her to love? And after he'd
made his heartfelt declaration, when he shared his dream with
her, she had belittled him and turned him away.

Several weeks went by after that night and she hadn't seen
him at all. His trucks rumbled in periodically, as scheduled, and
that was fine with her. She'd nearly forgotten him, or so she told
herself. The Republican Guards were on the move. Surface-to-air
missiles and SCUDs filled the air, in retaliation to the massive
number of sorties being launched from both Dhahran and the
coalition carriers in the Gulf.

She could see what the damned bombs were targeting this
particular night, they all could; the refinery about ten clicks
away.

Yamani's.

She was only supposed to be out on recon that evening,
maybe make a few pickups or transfers, if needed. But then she
heard the report that the perpetrator was a mobile SCUD
launcher, on the move and heading her way. Closer than it ever
should have gotten, unmolested. Hell, with her infrared night
vision, it was nearly close enough to see.

Her chopper wasn't equipped to take out ground targets of
that size. She wasn't authorized to fly into areas where there was
action.

Cyrus would have her head.

But her heart told her there was only one thing for it. She
was the closest asset to a highly dangerous, mobile target. They
could lose the refinery or worse, if the SCUD fired off another
round.

A quick conference with her co-pilot, a young captain from
Texas, "Cowboy," and the decision was made. The Huey had
been modified for the Persian Gulf initiative with two 7.62 mm
mini-guns. She hoped they would be enough.

Drawing closer to the last known coordinates of the SCUD launcher, there was one thing she'd realized quickly: it was easier to move in on a target from 10,000 feet up than from 1,000. The anti-aircraft fire filled the air around them, a deadly barrage of Fourth of July fireworks, pinging against the fuselage, pummeling them with invisible percussion waves that rocked the chopper crazily from side to side.

She kept the bird low, close to the desert floor, so close that she swore she could count the grains of sand. Barren, forbidding, and yet...there was a beauty in it too, that she'd never noticed before. Illuminated by sudden flashes of enemy fire, the ground below was all shadows and light, undulating like silent waves on an ancient ocean.

Bingo.

She'd come upon it so quickly, so unexpectedly, that it took a few seconds for her to regain her breath, to process what it was below her. There was the launcher, being towed along a non-existent desert road, surrounded by its support vehicles. She could see individual motion; at this level there were no invisible victims. But she'd had a job to do, hadn't she?

"Let's make this once and out," she'd told her co-pilot. Pushing forward on the control column she'd swooped in, tracking along a line that brought her down as close as she dared behind the racing SCUD launcher. "Aim for his fuel tanks," she'd cried out, deafened by the sound of the chopper's guns, the scream of the rotating blades, and the pounding of her own heart.

Closer. A transport truck behind the launcher went up in flames. *Closer.* She saw tiny stick figures leaping out of the rear of the truck pulling the SCUD. They scurried away into the night like desert rats, desperate to save their own skins. *Just...a little more.*

Suddenly, the chopper jolted to one side, and she heard an ominous groan emanate from somewhere near the rear rotor compartment. *Fuck. Not yet.*

"Lieutenant. I think we're hit."

"Shut up and keep firing." Kate had sworn, willing the Huey back on course, nearly pushing the rudder pedals through the floor. And what was that acrid stench that had filled her nostrils?

Christ, were they on fire? No...no time for that bullshit. She was right on top of that fucking SCUD now. Could see the darkened, camouflaged faces looking up at her, slack-jawed. And then, in a bright flash as white and hot as the sun, it was gone.

"Fuck," Her co-pilot had shrieked. "Did you fucking see that? Did you fucking see? Adios, motherfucker."

"Good shooting, Cowboy," Kate had said through gritted teeth, even as she desperately yanked on the collective pitch control lever. She needed altitude and speed, in that order. The force of the blast had thrown off her attitude, and by God if there wasn't something wrong with her rear rotor after all.

"We're losing oil, fast, Lieutenant. Ooooh shit."

Somehow, Kate had been able to get the bird to turn around, to nurse it and limp it back to the base.

Well, almost.

Over the whine of her laboring engine, there had been more warning sirens and flashing red lights than she'd ever seen out-side of a training run. Worse, she'd felt the pull of gravity on her aircraft like some invisible force, reaching up out of the dunes and trying to tug her out of the sky.

No. She'd fought it every goddamned step of the way. Curs-ing to the skies. Using every trick she knew, and a few she hadn't known she possessed. She always brought her ride home with her, in one piece. Always. So what if it was shot to hell? No matter.

Cowboy had let the tower know they were coming in hard and low. There. The lights of the base just ahead. Looming out of the darkness.

If she could just...hang...on...

Well.

Having one's aircraft end up in two pieces wasn't so bad, not really. And, okay, so they'd hit just outside the airbase's gates, so what? They were alive, albeit with Cowboy sporting a broken leg he had loved to show off afterwards, and Kate with a bump on her forehead the size of a large Easter egg. But, as Cowboy had proudly proclaimed, there was one dead mother-fuckin' SCUD out there in the desert, thanks to them.

They were lauded as wildcatting heroes for a time, a label

Kate neither sought nor appreciated.

For when she closed her eyes, all she could see were those stark, terrorized faces right before she incinerated them.

Cyrus had pretended to be livid about the whole incident and did his best to keep it quiet. But not before word had gotten back to Robert about what had happened. She may have rejected him, but she'd saved his livelihood and more, and he'd promised her then that he would never forget it.

Now, as Riyadh rose up before them out of the desert like a glittering mirage, Kate knew that the time had come to call in that promise.

Chapter
11

Rebecca Hanson finally gave up the ghost. Cursing the glowing digits of an alarm clock that fuzzily displayed nearly three a.m., she hauled herself out of bed and stumbled down the hall, passing through the living room and into the kitchen, flipping on a trail of lights as she went.

Squinting at the unnatural brightness at this ungodly hour, by sense of touch she found the cupboard where she kept a box of herbal tea bags. Depositing one into a cup of water, she popped the whole works into the microwave and pulled up a stool to wait it out.

Insomnia.

Certainly a pastime she'd never thought belonged on her personal resume, but darn it, here she was, perched alone in Kate's high-rise aerie, with nothing better to do.

Perhaps it was the excitement she still felt at the information she'd gotten today. She had decided to wait until later to call the pilot, figuring she was probably sleeping it off after a tiring overseas flight.

The oven sounded with a piercing *beep,* and Becky removed the cup and pattered into the living room, deciding to let the tea steep a bit as she looked out over the city.

Sinking down into the oversized leather sofa, the flight

attendant released a great sigh and let her head tilt back, thinking of how proud she'd been earlier, when the call had come through. She was surprised that it had all fallen into place so quickly. It had only been a week or so earlier that she'd quietly sent a request for a meeting with Mishka Rhu, through his attorney.

Why not do a little detective work of her own, she'd thought? After all, Kate, Mac, and Rory were working so hard on their own leads—why bother them with a long shot?

She'd read and re-read the reports of the Flight 2240 hijacking countless times, and the one mystery that remained was who had financed the poor rebels from Kosovo to undertake their expensive, hi-tech sabotage mission. Of all the hijackers, Mishka Rhu was the one they owed their lives to. In the end, he hadn't been able to go through with it, and had helped Kate and the others to regain control of the plane.

Unlike Stefan, Roberto, and Alexandra, Mishka had pled guilty from the start, cooperated with the federal prosecutors, and received a reduced sentence for his efforts. Kate and Becky had willingly given testimony on his behalf. But even he had claimed to have no knowledge of where the financing came from. It was all Stefan, he'd said, and Stefan Bukoshi wasn't talking.

Mishka's attorney had been all business on the phone, speaking briskly and cutting to the point. Mishka was being held at a Federal facility in Brooklyn, pending the completion of his accomplices' trial in Federal Court. His testimony was still needed, but once the trials were completed, he'd be shipped off to a maximum security prison out-of-state. If she could get to the facility by two p.m., Mishka would be willing to grant her exactly thirty minutes.

Her heart racing, Becky had flown out the door of the Orbis offices, replaying in her mind the questions about the hijacking she'd already asked herself over and over again that she would pose to Mishka Rhu, if only given the chance. She'd felt a connection with him somehow, back on that plane, felt connected to his heart, his soul, and she knew that Kate had sensed it, too.

Mishka was a good man. He wanted to help them, she was sure of it. Perhaps he just needed to be shown how. Otherwise, why would he have granted her request for an interview?

And when at last she'd sat down in front of him in that cold, bare room, his attorney listening to every syllable, she had known that this was her chance. She'd stared into the sad pools of his eyes, eyes that had witnessed so much suffering in his time, and felt that connection between them thrum to life once more.

They'd begun to talk. Just two people. And oh, what Mishka Rhu had told her. Afterwards, in a cab ride she barely remembered back to the office, she'd wondered if he realized just how much of a help he had been.

Wait 'til Kate hears about this. Becky's heart skipped a beat in anticipation of how pleased her "boss" would be. How she would praise her for her shrewd investigative skills, and thank her for producing results on her own that were bound to help the whole Orbis team.

Now, if she could just get some sleep. Becky inhaled the sweet, comforting scent of her tea and took a sip, blinking her eyes at the twinkling lights of New York.

God, what a view. No wonder Kate had chosen this apartment. So high, so quiet, so...alone.

With a start, Rebecca realized that this was the first time she'd ever spent the night by herself here in the high rise. Without the fiery heat of the tall, dark pilot lying next to her, holding her close, soothing her to sleep.

No.

Could it be...that she missed Kate? Missed her more profoundly than ever before, here, in this place that she'd come to think of as her...their home? Her heart lurched as for the first time she got a taste of what it was that her partner had struggled to tell her so many times before. She would hear it every time she came home from an extended flight schedule.

Kate would fight to get the words out for a bit, and then finally give up with an awkward "I missed you so much," leaving it at that. But Becky had always known that there was something more to it; she could see the storm that raged behind those jewel-like blue eyes of Kate's, but it had simply been more convenient for her—and for Kate, apparently—to let it drop.

God, Becky thought, gasping at the gut-churning ache of it all. *No wonder Kate never pressed the issue. It...it hurts so much.*

One last mouthful of her tea, and then she dimmed the lights in the living room. The cool leather crinkled beneath her as she eased down on the sofa, pulling a throw blanket over her body; it was one she knew Kate had used frequently, when she would sit in this very spot and gaze out at the night. God. She could detect the distinctive scent of her lover on it even now, as she drew it up under her chin, snuggling into its thick weave.

She lay staring out at the skyline, feeling more alone than she had ever thought possible in a city of nearly eight million people.

It would be a long couple of days until Catherine Phillips returned.

****

"Asma Sadek's brother, Ibrahim al-Sayed has agreed to allow us into his sister's home to speak with her." Robert Ahmad Yamani cast a sidelong look towards Kate as he drove through downtown Riyadh. "You realize this took some doing."

"Yes," Kate said, knowing that an Arab woman would never receive strangers in her home without a male present. She kept her eyes on the window, taking in the dizzying kaleidoscope of colors that blurred by: the lush gardens, the sacred mosques, the grand palaces of royalty past and present.

"And there's a business associate of mine in the Qatif *Suq* that I believe may have some useful information for you concerning that Swiss firm you're so interested in—Birktec Electronics, I believe?"

"Yes." A pause. "I appreciate all your help, Robert, really." Kate turned soft eyes to him. "It means a lot."

"You are most welcome, Lieutenant Catherine." He smiled at her. "You are at the Inter-Continental, correct?"

Kate checked her watch. Late morning. "Yes. But if it's all the same to you, I'd like to get started." The sooner she obtained the information she needed, the sooner she'd be out of this land of living memories.

"Are you sure?" Concern skipped across Robert's face, and with one hand he pantomimed the application of face powder. "No...need to freshen up?"

The pilot shot him a murderous glare. "Do I *look* like I need to freshen up?"

"No, darling, no. Not at all." Flustered, the Arab quickly made an adjustment. "First stop, then, that clothing shop you mentioned. It's just ahead."

Uncaring of traffic maneuvering around them on the bustling street, Robert boldly parked the Mercedes directly in front of the store.

"Let me do the talking, please, Catherine."

"Fine," the pilot replied, following her old friend into the establishment. It was a two-story, coral colored building, featuring a selection of men's clothing in both traditional and western styles. The air reeked of fine clothes and new money. Kate was struck by the contrast: Gucci and Armani lining one side of the shop, and *gutras* and *dishdashas* on the other. No intermingling, and yet the shop could cater to the best of both worlds.

She followed Robert across the tiled floor to where a worker stood behind a heavy oaken counter. Immediately, he and Robert began chattering away in Arabic.

"This is the shop owner," Robert finally explained. "He says he's already told the authorities everything he knows."

"Please." Kate ignored the rising volume of the merchant's voice. "If he could just go over a description of the man. How he paid for his purchases..."

Robert tried to get her questions in, speaking loudly himself to be heard over the stream of protest from the obviously agitated shop owner. Other patrons in the store, all male, also gathered together, talking amongst themselves and pointing towards the counter.

"He...he says he was an average looking man. Average height," Robert paused a moment, listening, "mustache, dark hair, wearing the *hijab.* "

"Great," Kate muttered, frustrated. "That describes about ninety-five percent of the local male population."

"And he paid in *Riyal*," Robert added. "No check. No credit."

The rumblings behind them escalated into a bit of shouting and, along with that, the shop owner gestured wildly at Kate, the words flying out of his mouth in a fevered pitch.

"What the hell—" Kate shook her head at the commotion. "What's the problem?"

"He..." Robert's face took on a faintly reddish tint. "He says you shouldn't be in here. Men only."

"What?" The pilot was getting annoyed. She needed information, and the proprietor's attitude wasn't helping things any. "Tell him," she quickly looked at the counter and grabbed a leather wallet, "tell him I'll buy this, and ask him if there was any conversation they had that he can remember. And whether he had any scars or distinctive features?"

Looking as though he were venturing into the lion's den, Robert returned his attention to the now-livid man behind the counter. More arguing, more shouts, and Kate was amused to hear all traces of her companion's upper class British accent melt away.

"No conversation, no scars." he turned to her, shouting above the bedlam. "Catherine, really, I think we'd better leave." The poor man looked desperate now, looking about the shop wildly as the other patrons pressed in close, speaking in clipped, Arabic tones.

If there was one thing Catherine Phillips hated, it was getting shoved around. Cultural differences or not. "I want my wallet." Her voice stubborn, she planted her feet at the counter.

"Please, Catherine." Robert was fairly begging now. "Don't you see? He won't sell it to you. If you'd just—"

Suddenly, Catherine felt a sharp poke in her back. Her eyes widened, and she turned slowly around. Now, all the loud voices in the shop fell silent, save for a new one that had entered the fray. It belonged to a sharp-eyed, beaked-nosed older man, wearing the traditional uniform of the *muttawwiun*. Kate had heard tales of the Saudi "morals police," but she'd never had the occasion to see one from such a close perspective. The *muttawwiun* roamed the streets to ensure that businesses closed at prayer time and that the laws of Allah were honored. Armed with cattle prods, they shamed anyone who offended their sense of propriety.

The morals officer ran his eyes over her from head to toe, disdainfully taking in her western clothing, her defiant posture, her uncovered head and face.

Scandalous.

"Let's leave *now,* Catherine." Robert's low-pitched plea behind her.

The *muttawwiun* took a step closer to the tall pilot, and chastised her in a stream of unintelligible Arabic.

Kate felt Robert's hand tugging on her arm. "Please."

The shifting mob of onlookers pressed in around them, screaming threats in their native tongue. Catherine's eyes narrowed as the wrinkled older officer raised the prod again, ready to give her another poke.

In a motion so swift that, later, the witnesses could not be sure of just how it had happened, the morals officer was relieved of his prod, and there it lay in two broken pieces on the cool, tiled floor of the shop.

"I am not a piece of beef." Kate tensely drawled out the words.

The *muttawwiun* shrank back, nearly falling into the arms of the crowd, his *gutra* tilting askew. Clearly, he had never before been challenged in such a fashion, by so intimidating a female.

Kate swung her eyes around the shop, her cold blue eyes blistering the angry faces, challenging them.

Taking advantage of the momentary lull in the action, Robert moved. Knowing he was taking a risk, he increased the force of his pressure on her arm. "For the love of Allah, Catherine," he spat into her ear. "Do you want to spark an international incident? If we're leaving here in one piece, it must be now."

Fury was bubbling in Kate's veins like a lava flow, firing her senses into overdrive. She sniffed at the air like an animal searching out its prey. She was ready to take the *muttawwiun* on, hell, take them all on for that matter.

Christ—what was it with these people? She'd done nothing wrong. Not really.

Not yet.

"Catherine..."

Through the din of the rage pounding in her ears, deafening her, she heard Robert's voice, imploring her to leave. Struggling to re-route the adrenaline that was pumping through her muscles, she allowed herself to be dragged out of the darkened interior of the shop and into the bright glare of the Saudi sun.

"Step away there, please."

A crowd had gathered around his Mercedes, but Robert quickly shooed them away, pulled open the passenger door, and shoved Kate inside.

"Bloody hell," he swore, slamming his own door shut. He angrily turned over the ignition and stomped on the accelerator, and the vehicle leaped away from the curb and back into traffic.

Horns blared all around them, other drivers angry with his sudden cut in front of them.

Robert paid them no heed. Instead, he turned to Kate, a look of both exasperation and fear on his face. "I haven't heard the last of this, you can be sure of that." His eyes flickered to his rearview mirror. "He's got my tag number. I know it."

"So what?" The pilot grumpily replied, rubbing at the small of her back where the *muttawwiun* had prodded her. "We didn't do anything."

"It was a 'men only' shop, Kate," Robert explained, taking a sharp corner on the fly. The Mercedes' wheels screamed. "I was taking a risk even bringing you in there with me."

"Oh." Kate released a sharp breath of air. "Well. You should have told me."

"Why don't we do this," Robert said, taking out a kerchief and wiping away the sweat that dotted his brow in spite of the cool blast powering from the air conditioning vents. "We're going to the *suq* next. It's men only, however women may enter if accompanied by a male relative."

"That would be you," Kate said flatly.

"Correct." Robert was pleased to see that his one-time lover was finally getting the idea. "For argument's sake, you will be my wife." He smirked. "And just assume, going forward, that *all* public places are restricted, unless I say otherwise."

"Meaning," Kate placed her tongue in the corner of her cheek, "I've got to stick pretty close to you the entire time I'm here."

"Precisely." The Arab stabbed at the air with his index finger. "For safety's sake, of course."

"Of course."

Robert reached over and gave her hand a quick squeeze. "Ah, Lieutenant Catherine," he said, winking. "Such a fiery temper. You haven't changed a bit."

The pilot slapped his hand away. "Neither have you."

****

The Qatif *Suq* was located at the edge of the primary shopping district. It was a riot of brightly colored kiosks, tents, and single story storefronts. There were any number of *suqs* in Riyadh, each one with a unique, specialized identity. Some dealt primarily in foodstuffs, others in furnishings, clothing, or crafts. One had even been designated "women only," where the ladies of the capital city could shop to their heart's content, freed from the watchful stares of their men.

The bazaar in the Qatif section focused on fine leather goods, rich Arabian-weave carpets, and electronics. But all the *suqs* featured tea and coffee houses, as well as food stands, and the rich, delectable scents of roasting coffee beans, steaming stews and baking bread filtered through the air. Catching wind of it, Kate was reminded how long it had been since she'd eaten.

Cautiously, keeping an edgy Catherine Phillips closely tethered to his side, Robert negotiated their way through the *suq*, pushing through beaded gates and past swinging cowbells until he arrived at the electronics emporium of his associate, Samir Khashoggi.

Boom boxes, televisions, radios, Walkmans, VCRs—every available square inch of space in the shop—walls, floor, ceiling, were covered with electronics. A cacophony of sound emitted from the players; songs, music, and videos, in a United Nations' chorus of languages.

The tall pilot groaned and squeezed at the bridge of her

nose. *God. If I get another headache now...*

"Greetings, Samir."

"And greetings to you, Ahmad."

Kate watched the two men embrace one another, and it did not escape her notice how the electronics merchant used Robert's Arabic middle name in salutation.

Wisely, after introductions were made, Robert was able to convince Samir to leave his shop in the hands of his assistant, and accept his invitation to join them for lunch in a nearby café. The rumblings in Kate's own stomach told her not to object to her companion's suggestion.

In no time, Samir, Robert, and his "wife," were seated at an outdoor table, shielded from the sun by a colorful awning. They sipped on rich, strong glasses of dark Arabian coffee, and a side order of pita complemented their main course of marinated lamb and peppers, served on a skewer.

"You just missed the midday *'Salah,'*" Samir said, referring to the prayers all Muslims were required to recite five times per day. "Otherwise," he munched happily on a nugget of lamb, "we would have had to wait to be seated and served."

"Our luck," Kate said dryly, and Samir released a deep, belly laugh. Kate had been pleased to find that, like Robert, Samir Khashoggi was not overly concerned with her western attitude and dress, and spoke to her as an equal.

"Bad for business, to do otherwise" he'd said, his dark, impish features turning out in a smile when she'd questioned him on it.

He too wore black pants, a white shirt, and the *gutra;* a man with one foot in the western world, and one foot firmly planted in the Middle East.

"Now," he said, burping and pushing his plate away. "Ahmad tells me you have some questions about Birktec Electronics, correct?"

"Yes," Kate admitted, getting down to business. "I'm trying to ascertain if Birktec has any local connections, and to a Khaled Sadek, in particular."

"He was killed in that plane crash you are investigating, correct?"

Kate glanced sideways at Robert, wondering just how much he had told the electronics merchant. "Yes. We think he may be involved."

"Birktec is an old company," Samir explained, sitting back in his chair and crossing his legs, clearly prepared to launch into storyteller mode. "I've done business with them a number of times over the years. Good inventory. Prompt delivery. Excellent credit terms."

"Did you know Khaled Sadek?"

"Should I have? Was he an employee of Birktec?"

"No," Kate referred to her portfolio, "not that I'm aware of."

"But you think he might be involved...in what caused your Orbis plane to fall from the sky, yes?" He poured more tea into his glass from the silver pot that rested on the table.

"Yes," Kate said, looking him squarely in his dark, mysterious eyes. "I do."

"Abbado El Yousef." He said the name aloud. "You think he is to blame as well."

The pilot ground her teeth. "It's why I'm here. If he is involved, I've got to find a way to prove it. Find a way to keep him from doing this again."

"I see." Samir took another sip of his tea, nodding his head. "El Yousef is a bastard, I grant you that much," he said, chuckling. "There were not many Saudis who were sorry to see him expelled. Still, there are some who perhaps fell under the spell of his money, his rhetoric. People who are looking for a savior in this life, and are only too happy to accept the nearest excuse for one that they can find."

"Meaning?" Kate was leaning forward now. It was apparent that Samir had something to say, something she could use.

"You do know that in ancient times, Riyadh was no more than an oasis in the desert."

"Yeeess." Kate bit her tongue.

"Once outside of the shade of the palms, away from the sacred wells, one's future amounted to how many days worth of water you could carry on your back, or on your camel. Survival of the fittest. Neighbor fighting against neighbor, if it came down to it. A tribal land, sharply divided. But today..." he waved his arms, "look around you. Beautiful trees, gardens, rising up out of the earth like magic, stopping the march of the desert sands. And great desalination stations draw more water in than we could ever possibly need from the Red Sea and the Gulf. A miracle."

"Yes, it is." Kate looked to Robert for help, but he only smiled in return. He knew that Samir would get to the point eventually and, frankly, he enjoyed watching Catherine having to exercise patience for once. He'd seen it infrequently enough years ago when they'd been together.

"The oceans have brought my country together," Samir continued. "The waters of blue that embrace us on either side, and the black sea of oil that churns beneath us, giving us life. But this unity...this, complacency...comes at a price."

"How so?" Kate's voice was low and hard.

"Today, all around us, the jackals walk with the lambs. Side by side. It is difficult to tell them apart, Miss Phillips. Sometimes, we never know, until it's too late."

Kate's heart was pounding in her chest. Here, even in the shade it was hot, and she could feel the perspiration trickling down the back of her neck. To steady herself, she took another drink of tea, feeling the heat of it slip down her throat, making her that much hotter.

She didn't give a damn.

"Whether Khaled Sadek is the man you're looking for or not, I cannot say. However," Samir tilted his head skyward, reflecting, "I knew a man a few years ago, who worked for Birktec. He doesn't any longer, from what I have heard. He lives primarily in Paris now, and still keeps an apartment here in Riyadh. I understand he was last in town in early March, on business, but I did not see him then."

"His name, can you give me his name?" Kate had her pen in her hand, ready to go.

"Izo Mufti."

"Hmnn." Kate quickly scribbled on her notepad. "It doesn't sound familiar."

"Really?" Samir turned his brown eyes to Kate. "The jackal

and the lamb. They walk together, you know." He paused, and Kate thought that the pounding pulse in her head just might drown out the living, breathing sounds of the bazaar around them: the haggling, the laughter, the bells, the sizzling food.

"Once he had taken a young Frenchwoman as his bride, Izo Mufti found it easier to live in Paris most of the time. She did not convert to Islam, and so Izo and she did not feel welcome here. Whenever he returned to Riyadh, he would come alone."

Kate stared silently at the electronics merchant, her blue eyes begging him to continue.

"Perhaps *her* name will sound familiar: Isabelle Rouen."

A thunderbolt struck Catherine from above, the psychic force of it threatening to cleave her in two. Of course she knew the name. She'd memorized them all.

Isabelle Rouen had died along with 209 other souls when Flight 180 went down.

****

It was a quiet drive from the *suq* to a more residential area of the city where the widow and family of Khaled Sadek lived. For once, Robert took a cue from Kate's mood and remained silent, keeping the finer points of his Mercedes S-500's maneuverability to himself.

Kate simply stared out the tinted windows of the car, watching the scenery change from *suq* to oil commerce to residential. She could see the faint layer of sand that covered the streets, the car windows, the sidewalks. It swirled through the air when the desert winds blew, or when traffic rushed down the narrow streets, and then it gently settled to the earth again, patient.

Waiting.

Timeless dust of the ages, an impartial witness to all that had come before, and of what was yet to be.

But Kate was not so willing to leave herself free of judgment. Damn it, how could she have been so blind? Jumping to the obvious conclusion, holding someone suspect simply because of a name on a passport, the home where he lived? God, thanks to that blunder, the party or parties potentially responsible had been given plenty of time to cover their tracks. Kate felt ashamed, and angry, too. She'd allowed herself to be blinded by the mental baggage she'd been carrying around for so long, since that day years ago when she thought she'd left Saudi Arabia, and Robert, far behind.

How wrong she'd been. Well, she would carry on with her plan to speak to Asma Sadek, simply to bring that chapter to a close—tie up any loose ends. That was it. Then, off to Paris.

If it wasn't already too late.

Robert smoothly directed the Mercedes down a street lined with palm trees and the occasional bristle-cone pine. Children played in spacious front yards, under the watchful eyes of their veiled mothers or minders. The windows of the beige and putty colored stucco buildings were fully latticed, the better to shield the women inside from view. *Modesty in all things*, Kate thought wryly.

"Here we are," Robert said, cutting the ignition and leaping out to jog around and open the car door for her. Very British. "Remember, *please* Catherine," hazel eyes implored her, "follow my lead."

The tall pilot nodded.

A short walk up a cobbled path, a knock on the door, and a dour looking Ibrahim al-Sayed was ushering them past two shy toddlers peaking around a corner, through to an inner room where Asma, the widow of Khaled Sadek, stood ready to greet them. Tall, for an Arab woman, and beautiful, Kate noted, taking in her long, brunette hair, her fine olive complexion, and a pair of dark eyes that told the story of the pain of loss that she bore. Here, in her own home, she kept a *dupatta* or shawl around her head and shoulders, but had removed the veil. She wore a *shalwar-kameez,* a roomy lavender colored pants set with a delicately embroidered black dress.

"May peace be upon you," she spoke in barely accented English. Stepping forward, she greeted Robert and Kate in turn, a light breath of a kiss on each of their cheeks.

"And upon you be peace," Robert replied, keeping a careful eye on the clearly unhappy Ibrahim. In a culture where a man's personal and family honor depended on the conduct of the females under his care, his recently widowed sister was now his responsibility. This meeting was highly irregular, and he never would have agreed to it had not Asma been so insistent. Anything that she could do to advance the cause of finding her husband's killer, she was willing to undertake.

"May we visit you?" Robert's voice was low. Respectful.

"Please, you are welcome in my home," the widow replied, motioning for them to have a seat on the plush blue and white carpet that covered the floor.

"Tea, or perhaps something to eat?" Her grief aside, as a Muslim woman with guests in her home, there were certain responsibilities.

"No, thank you," Robert replied as they settled themselves to the floor. "Another time, *Insha'Allah.*"

After more courtesies and pleasantries were exchanged, Robert at last nodded towards Kate.

The pilot opened her leather portfolio and, with a quick glance towards the taciturn Ibrahim, she began. "Mrs. Sadek, you know why we are here."

"Yes," she replied, her voice barely audible. "You're trying to find out who killed my husband."

"Uh, yes." Kate cleared her throat. "I've...just a few questions here, if you don't mind."

"Please," Asma lifted her eyes to Kate, "I want to help you."

"Well," Kate referred to her list, "your husband worked for a Saudi industrial chemical detergent company, correct?"

"Yes. They manufactured disinfectants, lubricants, detergents, air fresheners and the like. He worked in marketing and distribution. He had business contacts all over the world. On this last trip, I know he had meetings scheduled in Lisbon, and in Canada as well, didn't he, Ibrahim?"

"So his employer has said," her brother replied, his voice a near-growl.

"Have you ever heard him speak of Birktec electronics?"

"No."

"Of Abbado El Yousef?"

"We know he is a criminal," she answered quickly. "My

husband had no tolerance for men of that nature." A pause. "Nor do I."

Kate shifted uncomfortably, but she knew she had to finish this. "Did he ever shop at *Sicco* in Riyahd? A men's clothier?"

"Possibly." She lowered her eyes. "I rarely accompanied my husband shopping."

"Did he own a black, hard-sided suitcase, manufactured by Sky King?"

The question brought a faint smile to the young woman's lips. "No. Khaled was a Samsonite man."

Enough.

The pilot softly closed her portfolio.

"I'm sorry for your loss, Mrs. Sadek."

The widow daubed at her eyes with a handkerchief produced from a pocket in her *shalwar.* "Thank you. It is in submitting to God's will that we gain peace in our lives, both in this world and the hereafter. I will be with Khaled again one day."

Solemnly, she and Robert rose and took their leave of the widow Sadek. Clearly, Kate thought, as the ever-watchful Ibrahim escorted them to the door, although many marriages in Saudi Arabia were still of the "arranged" variety, Asma had truly loved her husband.

"Well?" Robert rested his hands on the Mercedes' coffee-colored leathered wheel. "What next?"

Kate checked her watch. It was late, nearly 1800 hours, and she'd been on the go for nearly a day and a half. She was exhausted, dirty, and hungry. If Rebecca could see her now, she'd have her head. A heavy sigh. "Get me to the hotel."

* * * * * * * * * *

The Riyadh Inter-Continental was located just five minutes from the heart of city. Its coral and rose-colored buildings jutted up from 100 lushly landscaped acres, and the hotel was a favorite among local and foreign travelers alike. Service was personal, top-shelf, and discreet. Its clients would demand no less.

With Robert, her "husband", by her side, Kate had little trouble with the check-in process, and she soon found herself standing inside a plushly appointed luxury hotel suite that she was too bone-tired to appreciate.

"Will you allow me to take you to dinner, at least, Catherine?" Robert carefully placed her travel bag on the king-sized bed that dominated the bedroom. He treated her to a dazzling smile. It had always worked in the past. "For old time's sake?"

The pilot looked distastefully down at her dusty clothes. Moving across the room, she stripped off her shirt, glad to be rid of it, revealing a brief white tank top underneath. She could feel the grit of the day in her eyes and hair, taste it, in her mouth. "Ah..." Kate debated with herself for a second or two. "Yeah, why not. For old times. Just let me take a quick shower."

She turned to unpack her bag, mentally reviewing her fairly productive day, made possible thanks to Robert. No wonder she'd been attracted to the Arab all those years ago. He was a good sort, when it came down to it. And, he'd certainly made a difference in how the day had turned out.

"Thanks for your help today, Robert." She grabbed her toiletries kit. "I really appreciate it."

From behind, warm, callused palms caressed her shoulders. A nuzzling in her neck.

"My pleasure."

Sure hands slowly spun her around, and then lips as hard as granite and as soft as a feather bed were pressed against her own.

Kate found herself whirling down a blinding, spinning tunnel of *déjà vu*.

Saudi Arabia, all over again. She was on her own. With larger powers of government and terror at play.

And here was Robert, working his magic on her body.

She thought about that, for a moment, as the oil broker continued to kiss her. About what it all meant to her then, what he'd offered her, and what that meant to her now, if anything. The answer came to her easily, as the image of an emerald-eyed woman with corn silk hair took root in her mind's eye.

Robert pulled himself away after offering his invitation, knowing that her body had not responded as it once had. Hazel eyes searched blue, hoping to see in them what he most desired: acceptance. Instead, he saw—nothing.

Kate gently removed his hands from her shoulders. "What we had between us has been dead for a long time, Robert. And it's going to stay that way."

"Why?" His eyes clouded over and he moved in again, refusing to accept defeat so easily. "No strings. I promise."

Kate laughed softly, not missing the irony at hearing those words—for a change—from him. "Strings or otherwise," she insisted, "the answer is still no." God he looked so...well. So noble. So damned gorgeous, with those puppy dog eyes, those broad shoulders, the tapered waist. But those attributes would be for some other woman to appreciate, not her.

"Doesn't sound like the Catherine Phillips I remember," he said, chuckling.

She laid a hand upon his cheek. "That woman doesn't exist anymore."

Robert looked at her curiously, and then a flicker of understanding overspread his tanned features. "Bloody hell. There's some other bloke, isn't there? Who would have thought after all this time, you'd let your heart get stolen away?"

"*She* is not a bloke," Kate said, pointedly, throwing discretion to the wind.

Silence, save for the quiet hum whispering from the air vents.

And then, "Really?" Robert gazed upon her anew, folding his arms in front of his chest. "Damn it all." He grinned at the woman he'd loved so many years ago, and knew he'd been beaten fair and square. "So, you've gone for something different, eh?"

"Different? Nah."

Kate playfully shoved her soiled blouse into his middle, before brushing by him and strolling into the bath.

"Better."

* * * * * * * * * *

For the twentieth time that morning, a decidedly tired Rebecca Hanson, sporting dark smudges under her eyes, checked her watch. It was nearly eleven-thirty a.m. That would make it nearly six-thirty p.m. in Riyadh. Plenty of time for Kate to have gotten a good sleep and a bite from room service.

The Orbis office was quiet. Rory had gone out for an early lunch, and Dottie was in the break room, cooking up something in the microwave. Releasing a breath she hadn't been aware she'd been holding, her hand reached for the phone.

Kate would be so pleased. She was sure of it.

Several conversations with foreign operators later, and the Riyadh Inter-Continental rang her through to Kate's room.

"Hello?" It was a good connection after all. Becky was pleased. Only the hotel had obviously put her through to someone else's room, for it was a British man at the other end of the line.

"Sorry," she said. "I must've been connected to the wrong room—"

His clipped, cheerful voice interrupted her. "You were you trying to reach?"

"Uh...Catherine Phillips. If you'd just put me back to the operator—"

"No need. She's here. She's just in the shower at the moment."

"Oh." Rebecca Hanson felt weightless, adrift, and her stomach flip-flopped. The same feeling she'd gotten when, as a young girl, her big brother Johnny had shoved her off the end of the high dive of the pool at the club. He'd thought it would be funny. She'd only just learned how to swim at the time, and was terrified. She'd wondered then if she'd ever hit the surface, and feared what would happen when she did.

Well, she'd survived that, and she would survive this. She was a good swimmer.

"May I take a message, dear?" Across the miles, in the silence he heard on his end of the line, Robert could detect the panic, the uncertainty in the girl's breathing. *She's the one.*

"Ah...no. I mean yes." Becky slammed the heel of her palm against her forehead. "Um...with whom am I speaking?"

"Robert Yamani, an old friend of Catherine's." He smiled, shaking his head as the silence resumed.

He's just an old friend. He's just an old friend, Becky chanted to herself, rocking in her chair.

"And?" The gentrified, British voice again.

"Pardon?"

"The message. Would you like to leave her one? We're just on our way out to dinner."

"I—ah..." *A business dinner, a business dinner. He's just an old friend.* "Tell her," she swallowed hard, "tell her Becky called. And I have some information for her."

"Will do, Miss Becky."

Oh, this was all too much, Robert chuckled silently to himself. He could feel the girl's unmistakable distress on the other end of the line. Hell, he'd once been in her shoes himself, where Catherine Phillips was concerned. "She has your number?"

"Yes," Becky's voice came faintly. "Goodbye." She replaced the phone in its cradle, ending the connection. Her self-inflicted torture, however, continued. She rolled her chair back from her desk and ran her hands through her short blonde hair, wondering what the heck had just happened.

Oh, shit.

****

Catherine Phillips emerged from the bathroom, dripping wet, a thirsty white towel wrapped around her torso. "Did I hear the phone?"

"Yes." Robert leaned back on the bed and grinned.

"Well?" Kate used another towel to dry off her long, dark hair. It shone with flecks of obsidian in the fading sunlight that filtered into the room through the blinds. "Who was it?"

"A young girl named Becky. Says she has got some information for you."

"Who?" Kate froze, staring.

"You heard me." The tall Arab chuckled and fell back onto the comforter. "She sounds quite adorable, if I do say so myself."

"You...you are such an ass, Robert." Kate stormed to the bedside phone, her eyes flashing. "What did you tell her?"

"Not to worry, Lieutenant Catherine." His white teeth sparkled. "I told her you were in the shower."

"Fuck."

"Tsk. Where are the morals police when you need them?"

Kate sat down on the bed and used a straight arm on Robert, shoving him away. "Wait the *fuck* out there, please." She pointed to the sitting room.

"But we'll be late for dinner, darling."

"*Goddamn it,* Robert," she checked her watch and pounded out numbers on the telephone, "will you just do as I ask, for *once?*"

Hands raised in surrender, Robert planted a quick kiss on the top of her damp head and backed out of the room.

Great. Just great, Kate thought, waiting for the connection to go through. She had nothing to feel guilty about, of course, but just the fact that Robert's answering of the phone had put her in this position, made her feel decidedly uncomfortable.

"Hello. Strategic Operations," Dottie West's high-pitched voice yodeled across the miles.

"Dottie, it's Catherine. Give me Rebecca, please."

"Oh, Catherine. How are you? Did you—"

"Now, Dottie, please." Kate tried to keep the impatience she felt from turning into anger.

"Surely, dear. Just a moment."

Click.

"Hello?"

Unexplained relief flooded through Kate, simply upon hearing the sound of her lover's voice. "Rebecca. Ah...it's me. Sorry I missed you earlier. Robert should have gotten me."

"In the shower?" Becky croaked.

"No. Well, I mean, knocked on the door, you know." A pause. "He's an old friend, Rebecca."

"So he said." Becky felt as though she'd hit the water at last and was trying to swim, but darn it, the side of the pool was so very far away. "Anyway, I have some information for you. That's why I called." She plunged forward into her explanation of how she'd contacted Miskha Rhu, and the results of her meeting with him.

Listening to Rebecca describe what she'd been up to, Kate watched passively as droplets of water dribbled from her head onto the mahogany bedside table.

"So Mishka told me that..."

No.

Unacceptable.

The pilot felt an uncontrollable flush rise to her cheeks. She was furious, and she wasn't precisely certain why. Hanson hadn't accused her of anything, but the tone that had been in her voice—God. She could just imagine the reproving look that would've been on her face as she questioned her. And now— what the hell did the kid think she was doing? Going off on her own to some prison, meeting with a convicted criminal, risking...

"Hanson," Kate roared at last, stopping Rebecca in her tracks. "What the hell were you thinking of?" The pilot could hear the anger in her own voice, but she was on a roll now, powerless to stop it. "You could've jeopardized the entire investigation. Tipped our hand."

"*What* hand?" Kate was surprised to hear the flight attendant shout back. "We were stuck. Not getting anywhere, Kate. We had nothing to lose, and everything to gain."

"But going into a prison—do you know how dangerous that sort of thing is?"

"Are you kidding? Where they're holding Mishka?" Becky laughed harshly. "It's a freaking country club, Kate. I think I lowered my handicap two strokes just by walking through the place."

"Still," Kate grumbled, feeling some of the upset leave her system, "if something had happened to you—"

"I'm fine, Kate," Becky snapped. "Now let me tell you what I have, and then you and *Robert* can go have your dinner."

Kate took a deep, steadying breath. God, her head was throbbing again. "Go."

"Okay," Becky said, mollified. "Mishka gave me the name of a friend of his from the University of Pristina. An Ahmed Dushan. He was a fellow technical engineering student, and they collaborated together on the design of those polymers that were able to evade security detection on Flight 2240. They both worked on the design, but Ahmed seemed to be the one with the cash. Mishka wasn't sure where it came from, and they never questioned one another. Those were dangerous times."

"So, why didn't he bring any of this up at the sentencing hearing?" Kate was skeptical.

"Ahmed was a good friend. And Mishka's little sister had taken a shine to him."

"Oh," Kate breathed, remembering. "Natasha. The one who was killed."

"Yes."

Kate could hear Rebecca shuffling papers on her end.

"Anyway," the flight attendant continued, "Mishka was worried that his life would be forfeit if he implicated him in any way, as long as he was still trapped in Pristina."

"But?"

"But he's not there now. After the U.N. peacekeeping forces moved in, Ahmed was able to make a run for it with a group of refugees transported to France. He's there now, working in Paris."

"You're joking." Kate rubbed at her eyes.

Becky ignored her. "Mishka has given me a letter of introduction to Ahmed. He says he would be willing to help us now. He says he's sick over what happened, Kate. He had no idea what the devices would be used for. Mishka never told him. He thought they would be part of the war effort against the Serbs. Not for a hijacking. Mishka himself thought the same thing, until the very end. He feels betrayed."

Silence.

"So?"

Kate still was speechless, a thousand thoughts streaking through her mind. Things were starting to fall in place, at last. Her own blunder had led to a piece of information she never could have counted on in advance—Isabelle Rouen's connection. And here Rebecca, through some independent investigative work that she really shouldn't have undertaken alone, was onto something, too.

"Kate?" Becky was still waiting. "How did you, ah, make out today?" The flight attendant knew she was pressing Kate's buttons, and her own for that matter, but she didn't give a hoot. *Swim, Becky, swim.*

"Isabelle Rouen is our lead suspect now," Kate replied, focusing. "She was married to an Izo Mufti who used to work with Birktec Electronics." She heard a sharp intake of breath at the other end of the line. "Have Rory get working on that right away."

"Will do."

"Where's Mac?"

"He's still in Washington, Kate. Why?"

"I'm going to Paris to interview Mufti, and I want Mac to bring me that letter."

"I can do it, Kate," Becky's voice was firm. "Let me."

"No way," the pilot replied, in equally strong terms.

"Now you listen to me, Catherine Phillips."

Uh-oh, Kate thought. *I think I can hear her stomping her foot.*

"This is *my* lead. *I* gained Mishka's confidence, and he gave *me* this letter for us to present to Ahmed. You're over there, and you shouldn't be alone...*if* you are," Becky muttered. "You didn't even bring your laptop, did you?"

"Damn," Kate snorted. "No wonder it seemed I was traveling light." Leaving without the computer had been no loss to her.

"Kate, you're going to Paris next, right?"

"Yes." the tall pilot lowered her head into her hands. She knew where this was heading. And damn it, the air conditioning in her room was blasting colder than an Arctic wind. She was freezing here, sitting in her damp towel.

"Well." Becky's voice was triumphant. "There you are. I speak French."

"No. I can't allow it."

"Kate." A small voice. A plaintive plea. "Let's see this thing through together. It's only right. You know that it is. Please?"

Kate released a heavy sigh. She hated to see Rebecca put in harm's way. Not again. But hell, this was Paris they were talking about. What could happen?

In the meantime, if Mufti got word they were on to him, he might run. And here she was, in a hotel room in Riyadh, freezing her ass off. On both counts, she had to move fast. A plan formulated in her dark head.

"Okay," her eyes glittered, "meet me in Paris."

Chapter
12

The hot, arid, late summer days of northeastern Afghanistan were quickly growing shorter; already a nightly chill swept down from the mountains, invading Birat like an ancient marauder, determined whether by stealth or by storm to seize hold of the tiny village, and never let it go.

In the military camp hugging the eastern edge of Birat, the constant haze of dust that normally choked the air had settled; the dry blowing winds had ebbed away for the time being, and activity on the makeshift thoroughfares was at a minimum. Bellies were full and eyelids heavy after the main midday meal, and the *dhuhr* had been recited—the required prayers just after noontime.

Abbado El Yousef sat at the battered camp table in front of his tent, choosing this open, public place to confer with his right-hand man and camp commandant, Rashid. It was cooler inside the air-conditioned tent, to be sure, but El Yousef enjoyed putting himself on display in front of his men from time to time. He thrived on seeing the adulation in their eyes, witnessing their unequivocal commitment to his cause.

For he was the Chosen One.

The Taliban might be the tacit rulers of Afghanistan in the capital of Kabul. But here, in the far reaches of the barren northeastern ranges, it was he, Abbado El Yousef, whose rule was absolute. Now, as small groups of his men passed quietly by, he waved to them, nodded, offering encouragement. And why not? He was feeling generous. They had all been successful so far, toiling for the cause, and he saw no reason why they should not continue on that course.

It had been years of hard work, of sacrifice, and of prayer that had brought them to this point. Careful planning and strategizing. Attention to detail. No loose ends. Nothing left to chance.

"Do you see this as a problem, my friend?" El Yousef pushed the papers he'd been studying to one side of the rough-hewn table. Frowning, his long tapered fingers reached for a cup of tea.

Rashid took a checkered kerchief out of his uniform pocket, and he nervously swabbed at the perspiration dotting his forehead. He had known Izo Mufti for years, had considered him a friend. That friendship had been strained when the Saudi had taken an infidel as his bride, but Mufti had sworn that he would remain dedicated to the *jihad,* and he had certainly fulfilled that vow by his subsequent service. His most recent activity against the hated enemy had demonstrated that, most of all.

Still, the reports they had received from their Saudi contacts had been worrisome.

"I cannot say." Rashid shook his head slowly. "We knew there would be questions. A vigorous investigation."

"Yes. But this," he tapped a thin finger on top of the paperwork, "indicates that the inquiries are moving in a rather...uncomfortable direction." El Yousef took a sip of the mahogany-colored tea, swallowed, and pursed his lips. "You know Izo. You trust him."

"Yes. Of course I do. Otherwise I would not have recommended him for the mission." Despite the shade, the sweat was pouring off the commandant in rivulets. Yet El Yousef, clothed in his traditional Arab robes, drinking steaming hot tea, looked as icy cool as a mountain stream.

"He is loyal to us? To our holy cause?"

"I am certain of it."

El Yousef smiled and waved, offering a pleasant greeting to

the pots and pans trader noisily passing by the command tent, leading his overburdened donkey. The old man blushed at the attention and offered a toothless grin in return, bowing so low that he nearly lost his turban. There was no reason for the trader to be this far past the edges of Birat, but it was always this way, among the locals. He was a celebrity, a god in their midst, and any traveling trader or journeyman planning a stop at Birat would make sure it included a pass through the Chosen One's camp.

"Still, regarding Izo," El Yousef continued, not missing a beat, "he took an infidel to his bed, did he not?"

Rashid felt his stomach lurch, sending the goat meat he'd had for lunch into a state of immediate distress. "But she has been eliminated, Chosen One."

"And now, in his mourning for the she-devil, he may be weak. Vulnerable."

"No."

"Leaving *us* weak and vulnerable."

"Please...Abbado, don't." Rashid dared to use El Yousef's given name, as he'd done only infrequently since their school days. He had been content to lose that familiarity, to distance himself from that friendship, for in doing so he'd secured a bird's eye seat to watch what he perceived and hoped to be El Yousef's eventual ascendance to the pinnacle of the worldwide Muslim community.

El Yousef took another swallow of his tea, and turned his dark, dead eyes past Rashid to the hills beyond their camp. Though the landscape looked desolate and empty, he could just see the darkened blotch against the hillside, marking the entrance to the cave housing their communications post and weapons stores.

Things were running smoothly. Results were better than he ever could have imagined, this early in the game. There was too much at risk, too much at stake, to let one man ruin it all.

"I am sorry, my friend." El Yousef made a show of sighing heavily, of coloring his words with sadness and regret. "But if Izo is as loyal as you say, then you know he would willingly give his life to insure our victory in the *jihad,* would he not?"

The muscles in Rashid's jaw flexed as he ground his teeth and lowered his eyes, saying nothing.

"As *you* would, Rashid," El Yousef continued, his voice holding a thinly veiled threat. "As we all would."

"Yes," the commandant at last replied, his voice a hoarse whisper. "You know that to be true."

"I never doubted it." El Yousef showed his teeth in a small, glittering smile. "Then you know what to do. We have another contact in Paris?"

"Several," Rashid said, still examining the wooden table.

"Excellent. Have one of them pay him a visit." El Yousef's voice was calm, cultured, as though he were discussing plans for a social call. "We must...help him to preserve his loyalty. We can afford no doubts at this critical juncture."

Rashid finally lifted pained eyes to his friend—his leader, the Chosen One. He knew his mission. He understood his role. He had accepted that long ago, when he'd decided to follow El Yousef to whatever hell or heaven lay in store. "I will see that it is done. Quickly."

"Excellent." El Yousef's smile broadened. "I knew I could rely on you, my friend. This is Allah's will, after all." He poured more tea into his cup, and motioned to a second one. "Are you sure you won't join me?"

Rashid swallowed hard, feeling the heat of despair coursing though his veins, setting his cheeks aflame, choking off his breath. He was already burned. What did it matter now? Silently, he slid the porcelain cup towards El Yousef, accepting what the Chosen One offered him.

Insha'Allah. He accepted it all.

* * * * * * * * * *

"So, let me be sure I have this straight." Rebecca Hanson closed her eyes, gasping, as teeth lightly nipped at her throat. "Robert is just a friend, right? Nothing more...not now, at least." One hand tightened its grip on the chenille bedspread upon which she lay, while the other wound its way through Catherine Phillip's silken hair.

"Nothing more," came the muffled response from a dark head that dipped lower. "Whatever we had was over long ago."

A pause, and then Becky shivered as a hot, wet tongue slowly circled her navel.

"You believe me, don't you?"

"Hmmn." The flight attendant lifted her gaze to the ceiling, taking in the heavy oak beams that ran from side to side. "I don't know. You've spent the last hour and a half trying to convince me." Becky felt a rumbling vibration begin as the long, lean body lying next to her shook with laughter. "What?"

Kate propped her hands on the young blonde's stomach and rested her chin on top. "Well," she flashed a rakish grin, "how am I doing?"

Rebecca had to admit it; when she'd first arrived at Charles de Gaulle she had been quite peeved at the pilot. Why, the way Kate had lit into her on the phone about her solo investigations, virtually ignoring the useful information she'd uncovered, twisting it all around.

And then there was the matter of a certain British accented fellow who had answered the pilot's hotel room phone in Riyadh. Someone Kate had felt comfortable and familiar enough with to leave him hanging about while she took a shower.

Becky hadn't known which she despised more: being treated like a child or a fool. Either way, that Catherine Phillips had had some explaining to do, and fast. In fact, Becky had been halfway surprised that Kate had met her at the airport, given the shouting match that had been their last phone conversation.

It had been a quiet cab ride, at least at first, from the airport to the hotel. Becky was tired and hadn't had much to say, answering the pilot with little more than grunts and nods. It had been obvious to her that Kate's demeanor had improved somewhat; at least she wasn't angry anymore. Now it was the tall woman's turn to try and use a bit of small talk to lure her companion out of a foul mood, but Rebecca would have none of it.

Good. Let her suffer, she'd thought. *God knows I did, all the way across the Atlantic.*

They had arrived at the hotel Kate had already checked into, the Hôtel de l'Abbaye, on Paris' left bank. Becky had barely noticed the classically arched stone entrance of the hotel, the lush, gardened courtyard, the burbling fountain. She hadn't apologized when her travel case "accidentally" caught Kate in the back of her knees as the pilot led the way from the elevator into a cool hallway. And she'd snorted impatiently when Kate had opened a solid, carved wooden door into a rustic but cozily furnished room that featured a single bed.

"Where are you sleeping?" Becky had asked coldly, throwing her bag onto the mattress and dropping the laptop onto a table.

"All right, that's it, Hanson." The pilot had thudded the door shut behind her. "I—I'm sorry, okay? You did good work tracking down Mishka and getting the name of his contact. And it's not because I don't trust you to do the job, that I didn't want you to come to Paris." She raked a hand through her hair and turned to look out a richly draped window. "It's...it's just that I worry about you, okay? About what I'm getting you into with all this..." she waved her hand uselessly, "...stuff. And as far as Robert goes, yeah, we screwed around."

Rebecca face had fallen, and she'd felt the air rush out of her body like a burst balloon. There it was. The truth she'd been dreading. Kate was owning up to it.

"No...listen to me." The pilot had stepped closer to her, seizing her arms. "That was during the war. Whatever we had," her voice grew ragged, "I killed it long ago. I needed his help this time, Rebecca. And God knows why, but he gave it to me."

Kate had placed her index finger beneath Becky's chin, lifting her head so she could meet her gaze with her own. "There's no one but you, Rebecca," she'd said, her blue eyes wide and moist. "There never *could* be. You've spoiled me for anyone else. You know that, don't you?"

Well.

That had been a record of sorts for Catherine Phillips, Becky thought. More apologies in one long breath than she'd ever gotten out of her over the past six months or so. The pilot had sealed her appeal with a kiss, and Becky had considered it only fair that she accept the overture gracefully, without complaint.

So she'd done so, only to find that Kate seemed quite intent on...demonstrating her apology. With both relief and desire flooding her system, Becky had let her, soon finding her luggage thrown onto the floor and herself flat on her back, experiencing a cure for jet lag that she'd only heard voiced in low chuckles in darkened Orbis galleys during long hauls.

"C'mon, c'mon," Kate persisted, demanding Rebecca's attention, courting her approval like a floppy-eared lapdog.

"Wha—"

The pilot's voice dropped to a low, throaty purr. "I want to know," she lifted a hand to walk long fingers up Becky's middle, taking a finger-step with each word, "have I convinced you yet?" Her finger-walk ended with a slight brush against the younger woman's lips, and she quickly followed the move by pushing herself up and over-top her lover, so that she hovered above her, face-to-face. "Well?"

The flight attendant could see the playfulness in Kate's eyes, but she could see the concern there, too.

The worry.

The uncertainty.

The pilot struggled to hide it, but Becky knew her too well. Understood that no matter how blustery and confident Catherine Phillips seemed, there was also a soft, vulnerable side to her. It was a precious, private thing that Kate gave her glimpses of from time to time. Trusted her with it, in all its naked truth.

God, what the heck had that fight been about, anyway? Of *course* she trusted Kate. No matter what.

"I don't want you to ever *stop* convincing me," she sighed, linking her arms around Kate's neck and pulling her greedily down. "Not ever."

****

"Ooh. Is that the *Jardin du Luxembourg?*"

"Yeah," Kate said, strolling next to Becky along the Rue de Vaugirard. "It's on the way to where I thought we could grab a bite to eat. Wasn't sure if you'd seen it before—"

"No, are you kidding?" Becky tugged lightly on Kate's arm.

"Can we check it out?"

"Sure," the pilot said, allowing the younger woman to lead her into the gardens.

"I never got to see much of the left bank the few times my friends and I got into the city. We stuck with the major tourist sites, you know? Eiffel Tower, the Louvre, that stuff. Rennes was quite a distance away."

"Rennes?"

"West of here. Waaay west," Becky replied. "It's where UCLA had their French seminars. We were there for the whole semester—three months."

"So that's where you learned to speak French so well, eh?" Kate had been very impressed with the few bits she'd heard her companion voice so far, and those natives she'd conversed with seemed to understand her, at least.

"*Oui, mon ami.*" Green eyes sparkled up at Kate in the late afternoon sunlight. "It was sink or swim, baby."

"Keep swimming, Champ," Kate felt a smile nudge its way across her face, "you're doing just fine."

Paris.

The City of Light.

A city like none other that Kate had ever been in. The history, the art and architecture, the cuisine and, of course, the romance. With its intimate cafés, the grand elegance of its boulevards, the timeless beauty of the river that formed its lifeblood, it was the perfect place to fall in love.

Or, to *be* in love.

Funny, Kate thought, how she'd never taken the time to notice that before. Oh, she had appreciated Paris and all it had to offer, making it a point during her past layovers there to strike out on her own and explore the museums, walk the Champs-Élysées, or grab a *café noir* and sit at a street-side table, watching the world bustle around her. Then, she'd toured the city with all the enthusiasm of one taking on a high school science project. It was new. She would study it. Learn from it, and file it away for future use.

In her own clinical way, she and Paris had reached a grudging truce. She knew her way around, could use the metro with

ease, and even picked up a few key phrases of French in the bargain. In return, just for her, the lights at night seemed to twinkle
not so brightly, the soft strains of music filtering from the night-
clubs onto the sidewalk did not beckon her, and the couples passing her by were not impossibly, passionately in love.

But now, she was here with Rebecca. On business.

And Kate was nothing if not entirely focused on the mission
at hand: interview Izo Mufti, and track down Ahmed Dushan; get
him to talk. They would be in Paris for only a couple of days, at
most. Still, when deciding where to stay, Kate had opted for a
smaller, privately run hotel, tucked in a side street in the middle
of the 6th Arrondissement, adjacent to the Latin Quarter. The
Hôtel de l'Abbaye had formerly been a convent, and its soothing
apricot and ochre color scheme and high, vaulted ceilings provided just the sort of old world ambiance that Rebecca Hanson
herself would have selected, given the chance. Even so, the pilot
had told herself that the hotel booking was a matter of convenience, rather than one of making amends to the partner whose
feelings she'd found a way to bruise all the way from Riyadh.

Although the young flight attendant had been quiet, hurt,
during the ride in from the airport, Kate had eventually been able
to get her to snap out of it.

Apologizing. It was new to her, but damn, if it didn't work.

Now, following Rebecca through the sweetly scented formal
gardens, feeling the gravel pathway crunching under her feet,
she grinned at the memory of just how vigorously she had pursued that apology. Of course, she had allowed a few hours in
their schedule for Rebecca to grab a nap after her flight, but she
really hadn't intended for things to work out as they did. Not that
she was complaining. It was all Hanson's fault, really, for being
so damned irresistible.

Ah, well. In spite of that unexpected *divertissement*, they
were on schedule. Maybe another time, when they *had* more
time, she'd bring Rebecca back to Paris, on their own terms. But
for now, they had a lot to do and not much time to do it in.

The local authorities had confirmed for her—in the spirit of
reciprocal information exchange—that an Izo Mufti did in fact
live at the address that Orbis had on file for Isabelle Rouen. Kate

had debated calling him first or just showing up at his apartment, finally opting for the latter. Catching him off guard might work to their advantage.

"Oh, wow. Would my nieces ever love that. C'mon."

Becky fast-walked over to a large pond in the center of the sun-drenched gardens, where a tiny armada of toy boats sailed gently about on a Lilliputian sea. She sat down by the edge of the pond, mesmerized, completely engrossed in the enchanting flotilla. Kate stood behind her, straightening out her shoulders, and breathing in deeply of the clean, fresh air. She enjoyed seeing Rebecca like this: unguarded, happy, with a childlike curiosity that sparked a feeling in Catherine herself that she dared not put a name to.

A stately 17th century palace housing the French Senate overlooked the gardens, ribboned with gravel walkways. The walks were lined with trim hedges, and strolling along them were Parisians and tourists alike, simply enjoying this verdant oasis in the middle of a concrete and stone desert. Jugglers, acrobats, and musicians plied their crafts in return for applause and tips, and the laughter of children tinkled on the air like the delicate chiming of distant church bells.

"We'd better get going," Kate said at last, lightly placing a hand on Rebecca's shoulder.

"It's so beautiful here, Kate," Becky said, sighing. She pushed herself to her feet. "So...peaceful."

"You can rent those boats, you know." Kate guided the smaller woman towards the exit that would take them out onto the boulevard Saint-Michel.

"Really?" A hopeful, upturned face.

"Next time." Kate smiled and gave her arm a squeeze. "Next time."

****

Saint-Michel was a grand boulevard that basically sliced Paris' left bank in half; the fabled Latin Quarter, home of tortured artists and academics for centuries, was on one side, with the haughtier Montparnasse/St-Germain district lying directly opposite. Kate had selected a small brasserie along St-Michel, where she knew the food was good. Hell, in Paris, it was hard to go wrong anywhere. She'd been alone when she dined there before in travels past. But now, with Rebecca, she knew that the younger woman would appreciate the half-timbered walls, the crisp, white tablecloths, and the distinctly "non-tourist" clientele.

They were seated immediately; the brasserie was only one third full. They were quite early for the bulk of the dinner crowd, but Kate had heard the telltale rumbles in her companion's stomach while she dozed, and knew that there would simply be no waiting until 1900 hours or later. In addition, her goal was to catch Mufti at home before he perhaps went out for the evening.

The waiter was prompt and attentive, granting their request for a table on the outside terrace, and Kate let Rebecca have her fun, ordering in French for the both of them.

"Okay, I'm eating what?" Kate quirked an eyebrow.

"Well," the flight attendant began, in her best *haute cuisine* voice, "for the lady, there will be a succulent free-range chicken dish, cooked in wine sauce, accompanied by a delightful array of root vegetables."

"Really." Kate grinned and shook her head. "Sounds...okay."

Becky released a sharp burst of air and slapped her hand down on the table. "Kaaaate," she warned, in a mock-serious tone.

"No, no." The pilot laughed aloud now. "Ya done good. I'm sure it will be delicious."

Becky eased back in her seat, satisfied. "Thank you," she said primly.

"And you're getting...?"

"A mixed green salad garnished with *foie gras.*"

Kate made a face. "Goose liver, right? I thought I caught that. Ugh."

"You're in Paris, Kate." Becky's voice was exaggeratedly patient. "It's about broadening your palate."

The waiter returned with a basket of crusty French bread and a pitcher of the house wine, a rich burgundy. He poured them both a glass before discreetly retreating to a service alcove.

"The only thing I want to broaden," Kate tipped her glass towards her companion, "is my knowledge about what the hell brought down Flight 180."

The instant the words left Kate's mouth and she saw Becky's face fall, she regretted them. But damn it, it was too late to reel them back in. Of course they were here to work. But did that mean she couldn't allow Rebecca to enjoy just one meal without indulging in her own obsession? Wasn't it enough that it haunted her every waking and sleeping moment? Did she need to keep dragging Hanson down into the muck as well?

Becky diffidently shrugged her shoulders, tugging at the pilot's heart. "You're right, Kate," she said, her voice solemn, resigned. "I forced you to let me come; we've got a job to do, and here I am going on like some sort of tourist from hell." Her eyes flickered and she lowered her head.

"No." Kate reached her hand across the table and clasped Becky's. "Listen to me now. I'm glad you're here. I need you with me. I—I never thought I'd be here in Paris, with someone I care about so much."

"Hunting down potential terrorists," Becky laughed tone-lessly.

"You and me...working *together,*" the pilot said gently, "getting to the bottom of this thing. And when it's all over with—"

"If."

"*When,*" Kate insisted. "We'll come back here, okay? I'll show you around. Show you off."

A small smile pushed its way onto the flight attendant's face.

"And I swear," she gave the smaller hand a squeeze, "I'll eat whatever you want me to."

"Anything?" Rebecca's face brightened. "Because—"

"Anything," Kate interrupted, shooting a devilish smirk Becky's way.

"Wha—oh, Kate." The young blonde sharply withdrew her hand, blushing. "You...you." She reached for the bread, roughly pulled off a piece, and chewed on it in earnest.

"Hey," Kate chuckled, enjoying her friend's discomfiture, "you brought it up."

"That's not what I meant, Catherine Phillips and you know it."

"I have no idea what you mean." The pilot opened her palms defensively. "Seems to me that *you're* the one with the naughty thoughts."

"Ooooh." Becky chased back the bread with a mouthful of wine. Finally she laughed, knowing this was a battle she was destined to lose. "Well," she settled her eyes on Kate, "since you're the one who brought up the investigation, let me tell you what Rory found out about Izo Mufti."

Kate sat up straighter in her chair, all business once again. "Like, who he works for?"

"Yeah," Becky replied, opening her purse and removing several folded papers. "Your Saudi contact was right. He doesn't work for Birktec any longer. But, get this: he works *with* them."

"I don't follow you."

"It was just a change in classification, Kate." She pushed her papers towards the pilot. "Officially, he's an independent consultant." She paused. "With only one client."

"Birktec," Kate breathed.

"Uh-huh. It's as if he never left."

"We know the connection between Birktec and the electronic timer on the bomb," Kate said, working it through her mind, "but the fact that Mufti still works exclusively for them, that his wife was on the plane...that's no coincidence. The question is, how can we connect Mufti—"

"Or Isabelle Rouen—"

"To El Yousef," Kate finished, tightly gripping the edge of the table. "We've got no solid proof that Birktec is one of Mufti's operations."

"Well, I'm glad you asked." Becky's voice was proud. "I've been doing a lot of computer work with Rory these past few weeks, you know?"

"I noticed." The pilot smiled faintly. "I think he has a crush on you."

"Well, he *is* kinda of cute."

"What? With that pierced nose?"

"Body art," the young woman blithely corrected her. "Anyway, we know that El Yousef uses a system of laptop computers that transmit encrypted communications to his operatives via satellite, right?"

"Yes. If we could only get our hands on the damn encryption key. It might lead us to his cells, his contacts. Shit, the whole bloody house of cards could come tumbling down." Kate's eyes grew hard and cold as she considered the tantalizing prospect of El Yousef's demise.

"Well, a first step towards that could be a data tap, Kate. Intercept the impulses that travel along Mufti's phone lines."

"A what?"

"We'd need permission from the local authorities, of course, and that could take some time—"

"Slow down, Rebecca." Kate held up a hand. "A data tap. Explain."

Becky cleared her throat. "It's really neat, actually. It does the reverse of what a computer's modem does. A modem takes digital data from the computer and translates it to analog signals that run along phone lines."

"Okay, I'm with you so far." Kate took a sip of wine.

"The data tap intercepts the analog phone line signals, and converts those impulses back to digital."

"Meaning...what?"

"Meaning," Becky continued, "we...er, Rory, can take the digital signals and convert *them*. Kate," she lowered her voice, "we can capture Mufti's individual keystrokes."

The pilot pressed forward. "If Mufti's working for El Yousef, he's got to be using a computer as a means of contact. So we'll know who he's talking to. What he's saying."

"Rory thinks he can bypass the encryption program entirely, Kate." Becky fell silent, locking her eyes on the dark haired woman sitting across from her. The implications were plain. Rory Calverton, computer whiz kid, was proposing an electronic shortcut. One that could possibly short-circuit El Yousef and his entire operation.

Permanently.

"Well," Kate sighed, releasing a breath she hadn't been aware she'd been holding, "sounds like Rory deserves a raise."

"He'll take it in *KitKat* bars, I'm sure." Becky grinned as the waiter arrived with their food. "Speaking of which...God, am I starving."

"Don't forget, there's always dessert." Kate nodded at a passing blueberry tart.

The flight attendant tucked into her *foie gras* with gusto. "*Bien sûr, Madamoiselle. Bien sûr.*"

****

Kate and Becky moved along the boulevard Saint-Germain, studiously avoiding the intriguing bookshops, the chic clothing stores, and the beckoning art galleries. The local police inspector had explained to Kate that Mufti's apartment could be found in an empire-style building just past the point where Saint-Germain intersected with the rue Mazarine.

The pilot had to admit it: the French authorities had been more than helpful, answering her questions, offering to accompany her. She had to wonder if a part of it was that they were anxious to prove the sabotage of Flight 180 had not occurred on their watch. And no wonder, she thought, considering it was looking more and more as though that were precisely the case.

But what if things turned more serious? With a liberal portion of Gallic pride at stake, it would be tough going, to be sure, maneuvering their way along the rocky shores of Paris' infamous bureaucratic machine. The data tap Rebecca had proposed could provide just the break they needed, and yet Kate could envision weeks of petitions and hearings before the authorities might grant such a request—if ever.

Weeks they didn't have.

"Okay, here we are," Kate said, drawing up to an eight story building with an ornately sculpted façade. A deep breath. "Follow my lead, okay?"

"You've got it," Becky allowed, trailing behind Kate as the older woman pushed open an outer wrought-iron gate. They passed through a tiny cobbled courtyard, stopping at a massive oaken door. A buzzer entry system lined the doorway.

The pilot pressed number 7C, noting the listing "Rouen" next to it. "If he's home let him know who we are. Tell him we just want to ask him a few questions."

Trying to control the butterflies rioting in her stomach, Rebecca nodded. *C'mon, get a grip.* She told herself. *This is a piece of cake after your little jaunt to the prison to visit Mishka, right?*

"Oui?" A deep voice crackled through the speaker.

"Bonjour, Monsieur Mufti." Becky shot an anxious look towards Kate. *"Nous sommes des Lignes Aériennes de Orbis. Je suis Rebecca Hanson avec Catherine Phillips. Nous aimerions vous demander quelques-uns questionne."*

"Non. Je dois partir. J'ai un engagement." Mufti sounded agitated. Annoyed.

"S'il vous plaît, le monsieur. Il est important."

"Non."

"He won't do it," Becky said in hushed tones. "Says he's got to go out."

Kate's eyes narrowed. "Tell him we've come a long way to talk to him and we're not leaving. We'll wait." She paused, her mind racing. "Better yet, tell him *we'll* go and come back with some help. Inspector Girard seemed quite willing."

Becky pursed her lips and nodded. *"Monsieur--"*

"All right," an accented English-speaking voice, hissing through the speaker, interrupted her. "You may come up. But be quick about it."

Mufti buzzed them in. As the lock clicked open, a gentleman came up behind the two women and followed them through the heavy wooden door. He was of middle height and of dark complexion, with deep-set brown eyes, and carried a bag of *baguettes.* The scent of a just-smoked cigarette was on his breath and hung on his clothes, and Kate could detect the telltale bulge of a cigarette pack in his breast pocket.

"Bonjour," He greeted them, flashing a white smile. *"Merci."* He dipped his head toward the door while making a show of his full arms.

"De rien." Becky smiled in return, happy to be of assis-

tance.

The man joined them on the elevator, shifting his hold on the bread and fishing into his pocket for a set of keys.

"*Quel étage?*" The flight attendant's hand hovered over the number panel after pressing "7."

"*Sixième, S'il vous plaît,*" he replied, watching carefully as the young blonde touched "6."

The elevator creaked slowly to the sixth floor, finally grinding to a stop. With a nod and another blinding smile, the man exited and moved off down the hall as the doors slipped closed behind him. Even when he heard the elevator continue on its way, he kept walking. Onward, to the stairwell at the opposite end of the corridor. He opened it, and carelessly dropped the bag of *baguettes* to the floor. The steps were dirty with years-old footprints, and the still air was rank and musty; he felt the dust of it clinging to him as he took the stairs to the next level.

He heard a door slam just as he arrived at the seventh floor. Peeking through a yellowed, greasy window, he was pleased to see that the emergency exit was within eye and earshot of Izo Mufti's apartment. Surely it was Allah helping him now, guiding him through on this mission.

He sat down on the landing, reaching into a pocket for his *Gauloises.* So, those American women wanted to see Izo. Worse, they were from that airline. He'd been shocked to hear them buzzing Izo's apartment when he'd stolen up behind them. All he'd wanted was to slip inside the building without warning Mufti of his presence. Now, here were these infidels, wanting to question him. Just what Rashid had told him he'd feared.

Walking down the hall to the elevator, he had half flirted with the idea of taking action right then and there, but no. He had to sort this through. He couldn't afford to make any mistakes now. Rashid would have his head. Plus, that tall dark one had been giving him the fisheye. She was bound to be trouble.

Think, Omar, think. He flamed a cigarette to life and took a deep pull from it, watching the glowing orange tip deepen in its intensity. *First things first.* He released a billowing plume of smoke into the stairwell.

He would deal with Mufti; that was what he came for. He

would find out what the women had wanted, and what Izo might have told them.

And then...well. He had a mission, didn't he? He would do what he must.

For he was the sword arm of the Chosen One.

****

Izo Mufti was a small man. He carried too many pounds on his frame and too few hairs on his head, and had never thought of himself as anything more than an average man. Leave the wealth, the looks, the women to others, not him. If that was the card he'd been dealt in life, then he would play it. Like many of his fellow Saudis, he'd been educated abroad, eventually taking a job with an international electronics company based in Paris. There, he had quietly toiled away, content in his obscurity.

Paris was not the worst place in the world to be, and in fact he secretly preferred it to anything that Saudi Arabia had to offer. He was a foreigner, yes, in an urban melting pot seasoned with a global flavor, and so he felt...comfortable, at least. Particularly when he made a break and decided to part with his traditional Arab garb. There were many times, sitting at a sidewalk café, edging up to the bar at a bistro for a drink, that he fancied himself blending in as much as any Parisian native.

And when he'd met Isabelle Rouen, surely, the blessings of Allah were shining down upon him. Tall, thin, blonde. A French-Canadian, working in the fashion industry in Paris. Marketing was her field, but in Izo's eyes she was beautiful as any model he had ever seen. And of all the men she could have had, of all those who had wanted to be with her, *he* had been the one she'd said "yes" to.

He never could figure out what she managed to see in him, short and rotund as he was; whenever he had asked her about it, she would always laugh and tell him it was what she couldn't see that mattered most.

After a brief courtship they had married, and she had moved into his apartment off the avenue Foch. He had known he had married outside the laws of Islam, but he didn't care. It didn't matter to Isabelle, so why should it matter to him?

Shortly after the wedding, the offer came from Birktec. He had been shocked when they contacted him, and flattered, too. The substantial increase in salary. The furnished apartment in the city center. Computer equipment. Certainly, the firm had many Saudi connections, perhaps that was where they had heard of him. His new job gave him the opportunity to return to his hometown of Riyadh from time to time, and he enjoyed that. It was there, on one particular business trip, that he'd stumbled across his old friend, Rashid.

Somehow, Rashid had known about his job with Birktec. Talked to him of future rewards, promotions, if he promised to help Rashid and his friends from time to time. Help with what— Rashid would not say. But with a beautiful wife at home who was bound to be tempted by other men, those who could offer her what he could not—an open checkbook, matinee-idol looks, expensive homes and automobiles—who was he to deny such a harmless opportunity? The cause was secondary. A thing as distant to him as the Arab robes he had left behind.

He trusted Rashid. And so an agreement had been reached.

He had thought Isabelle would be pleased, but she was not. His new job required much travel, and so the time they were able to spend together was limited. She continued to travel for work as well: London, New York, Montreal, and there were lonely times when he wondered just whose company she kept when he was not by her side.

His suspicions born of insecurity led to arguments.

Arguments to out-and-out fights.

The fighting, finally, to a separation. With Isabelle swearing to Izo that she would never have him as long as he persisted with his ridiculous claims of her supposed infidelity.

He had moved out.

Too exhausted to get a divorce, and with not enough trust to fully reconcile, their relationship had foundered. She would take him back on occasion, briefly rekindling the passion they once shared, but always it would end the same, with her blonde locks flying and her face twisted in anger as she showed him the door.

Until that last time.

"Mr. Mufti, what was your wife doing on Flight 180?" It was the tall woman speaking, the one with hair dark as midnight and eyes that seemed to reach into him, grabbing for his soul.

"I believe she had business in Montreal. A retailers meeting."

"I'm so sorry that I can't make this plane with you, darling. Damn client. I promise, I'll join you in Montreal in just a few days. You'll be at the Regency?"

The dark woman, Catherine Phillips, seemed to believe him. Good.

"Tell me, why weren't you listed as next of kin? We might have contacted you sooner."

Izo fought to maintain a calm, cool exterior. Just answer their questions, and get rid of them. "We'd been having problems on and off."

"We need you to help us, Izo. One last time. What do you care about that bitch? She's done nothing since the day you were married but cheat on you and laugh about it, behind your back."

A tight smile. "You know how it goes. We'd only just gotten back together again."

"This time it will last, won't it, Izo? I don't think I could bear it if we parted again."

"You know how I feel about you, Isabelle. With us, it is forever."

"Do you work for Birktec Electronics?"

"No," Izo answered, more sharply than he'd intended. Uh-oh. So much for the dark one buying his story.

"Oh, but you do," Phillips said, drilling him with the sapphire chips of her eyes. "You're a consultant, working with them on an exclusive basis."

Izo gulped, hard. How had they found that out? "I have many clients," he hedged, feeling the perspiration break out on his brow.

"Don't worry, Izo. As a consultant you'll be safer this way. And of better use to the cause."

"I'm sure you'll be able to prove that to the authorities if necessary, correct?" Phillips lifted an eyebrow to him.

"Of course," he insisted, insulted. Just how he would, he

was uncertain. But Rashid had never let him down before. He would deliver.

"Well," Phillips continued, flipping through some papers that the smaller woman had handed her, "what do you know about Birktec manufacturing electronic timers?" Her face remained impassive, but he could see a flash of anger spark behind her cold stare.

"Wha—" Izo felt his bowels turn to water. "Who knows?" He waved a dismissive hand towards his visitors. "Possibly. I don't keep track of every inventory item they have."

"It will be quick and painless, Izo. They won't know what hit them. And the authorities will never be able to figure out what happened."

The tall woman took a step closer to him. She bested Izo in height by at least a head, and knew it. She was using that advantage to intimidate him, to try and get him to crack. No. It wouldn't work.

"Mr. Mufti," she said, her voice so low and close that he could've sworn he felt her breath on his face, "Did your wife own a black, hard-sided Sky King suitcase?"

"The taxi is here, darling. Are you ready? All packed?"

"Yes. Just let me use the toilet once more. God, you might think I've never flown before. It's...it's just that I'm so excited, Izo. We'll be together again for a romantic getaway—just the two of us. I can't wait."

"Neither can I, Isabelle. Now don't worry. You go ahead. I'll bring your luggage down."

"The suitcase, Mr. Mufti. Did she own one?"

"NO," He roared, turning his back on the accursed woman so she could not see him shaking. What should he do? It was bad enough that Isabelle was gone. He had told himself that he wouldn't feel for her. That it was justice, after all.

But these past weeks without her...it was a heartache, a sense of loss so exquisite and profound that he never could have anticipated it for himself. So different from the times they had been separated.

So...final.

Since Isabelle had died, he had begun to doubt himself.

Doubt the cause. Doubt what Rashid had told him. While at the same time, the one thing that grew in his conviction was a phantom love for a woman he could no longer possess.

She had told him she would wait for him there, in Montreal. Maybe, Isabelle had said, with a glint of mischief in her eye, the time would be right to start a family.

Instead, he had sent her to her death. And once he had seen her on the plane, that late foggy night at Charles de Gaulle, he had rushed back home and quickly gotten on his computer, sending the message to Rashid that they had agreed upon.

The gift is on its way.

"Mr. Mufti." A soft voice behind him.

He felt a hand on his shoulder. It was that other woman, the smaller one who spoke French.

"When that plane went down, 210 people lost their lives. Women. Children." A pause. "Your wife. Doesn't that mean anything to you?"

"Please," he said, his voice breaking, "you must go. Now. Or I shall have to contact the authorities." For the love of Allah, was he crying? Angry with himself for this show of weakness, he used the heel of his palm to wipe away his tears.

"We're staying here for the next couple of days," Phillips said, and he heard a pen scribbling on paper. "If you decide you want to talk, call. It will go better for you if you do, Izo. Believe me."

Footsteps moved away, and he heard his door open. "El Yousef won't get away with this," Phillips vowed. "I promise you that."

Izo spun around just as the door clicked shut. *No. The Chosen One. She had spoken his name.*

Panic jolted through Izo's system like an electrical shock. What should he do? Who could help him now? He raced into his bathroom and splashed trembling handfuls of cold water onto his face, panting, fighting to rein in his galloping heart. What if those women came back? Rashid would protect him, certainly, but he was so far away. And Isabelle was gone...gone.

He stared at his image in the mirror: balding, fat, his normally dark complexion a jaundiced yellow under the fluorescent light. It would be typical for an average man like himself to get stuck taking the fall. He had seen it happen before, countless times. Simply grab the most convenient suspect, and leave it at that. Perhaps he should talk to those women after all. Maybe he could confuse them, throw them off the trail? It was worth a try. Better to deal with them now, than to wait for the police to get involved. The tall one had threatened that, after all.

A soft knocking at his door.

No. No. Fear clutched at Izo's gut. Could it be the women, back already? Very well. He would tell them just enough to cover his tracks. And then run like bloody hell to Rashid, and take his chances there.

"Who...who's there?" he asked, his voice unusually high and querulous.

"A friend," came the muffled response. "My name is Omar. Rashid sent me."

Izo was stunned. Of all the luck—why, Allah hadn't deserted him after all. "Come...come in," Izo cried, sagging in relief.

He flung open the door to admit his visitor, a man taller than himself, dark skinned, with a mustache. A strong odor of cigarette smoke clung to him, and instantly Izo found himself craving a *Gitanes;* Isabelle had made him quit. Omar wore the clothes of a westerner: brown slacks, a sport shirt, and blazer, but Izo instantly recognized him as being a brother Arab.

"May peace be upon you," the man said, stepping inside and giving Izo the traditional greeting and embrace, along with a brush of lips upon his cheeks.

"And upon you be peace," Izo replied, grinning from ear-to-ear like a silly schoolboy. He was saved. He knew that Rashid would come to his aid.

"Rashid sends you his warmest good wishes," Omar said, smiling broadly.

"Thank you, Omar, thank you." Izo ushered him into the living room. "And your timing could not be better."

"Really?" Omar eyed the little man curiously. "How so?"

"Well..." Izo began, finally getting a grip on himself. "You first. What brings you here to Paris?" He hesitated. "To me?"

"The cause, my friend, the cause." Omar let his gaze roam around the room, taking it all in. "How goes it with you, Izo?" He returned his attention to the smaller man. "It was some sacrifice you made for us...the Chosen One is pleased. But surely...you miss your wife?"

Izo was taken aback. "Yes, er—no. What I mean is—that's what I want to tell Rashid."

"Yes." Omar's voice was soft, soothing, urging Izo on.

"Omar." Izo's eyes darted nervously from side to side, and he drew closer to his visitor, whispering. "The authorities are on to Birktec. To...to the device I put in Isabelle's suitcase. They suspect *me*, Omar."

"Sssh. Don't worry, my friend." Omar gave Izo's arm a comforting squeeze. "We'll take care of everything. Now tell me. What authorities, Izo. Who?"

"They were just here." Izo scurried over to the table by the door and picked up a piece of paper. "From the airline. They wrote down where they are staying. They wanted me to talk to them, but I refused." He waved the paper triumphantly.

"Good." Omar smiled. "We knew you would be loyal to us, Izo. To the cause."

"Of course, my good friend." Izo laughed heartily. All would be well. Those women who had so unnerved him only a short time ago—hah. They were merely specks of sand in the desert wind. Allah would provide.

"Has anyone else contacted you?" Omar plucked the paper from Izo's outstretched hand.

Izo wagged his head in the negative. "No. But what shall we do, Omar? What if they come back—"

"There, there, my brother." Omar's manner oozed calmness, comfort. "Leave it to me. You have your laptop here?"

"Yes." Izo brightened, motioning towards the bedroom. "Shall we send a message to Rashid? It's not the normal contact time but..."

"Yes," Omar softly replied, stepping behind Izo as they walked into the bedroom. His eyes narrowed into two darkened slits. "Why don't we do that?"

Izo never saw the flash of metal in Omar's hand. Was never

able to fully process what had happened to him.

There was only a sharp *thump* in his back that took the wind out of him, and then he was sprawled face down on the floor. Had he fallen? He tried to draw in a breath, but strangely, it would not come. A pair of shoes glided past his line of vision—that would be Omar, moving to help him up, of course.

He felt a warm, sticky moistness creeping across the middle of the shirt on his back. Had his fall caused him to spill something? And the pressure—the thunderous weight he felt in his chest, pressing in on him, swamping him.

Sluggishly, he struggled to make sense of it all, but could not.

Omar.

He needed his help.

He reached out a hand, only to see it flop uselessly by his side. "Help me," he wanted to say, and was baffled when his throat produced only a gurgled moan. He focused upon the brightly colored carpet on which he lay; the rich weaves of gold, blue, and rose reminded him of the floor covering in his childhood home in Riyadh. The carpet needed cleaning, and he smiled at that. It had not been done since Isabelle had left. She would be home soon. She would help him...she would take care of everything.

But the colors faded, even as the smile froze on his face. He heard a voice, so far away, and yet close enough that it seemed to breathe into his ear. He listened...and heard the words he now knew in his heart to be true.

"Walk with Allah, my friend. Your loyalty has been rewarded."

Chapter
13

Catherine and Rebecca walked slowly along the rue Bonaparte back to their hotel, moving without hurrying, simply breathing in the sights and sounds of Paris in the evening. A few streets away from their destination, they passed through the spacious square ringing the church of Saint Sulpice, the "cathedral" of the Left Bank. A number of cafés were still open, as well as several smaller restaurants. Tables in the square were filled with patrons, dining, drinking; their faces animated by candles flickering in the light evening breeze. Mouth-watering cooking smells and strains of music wafted on the air towards them, offering an invitation.

"Want to get a drink or something to eat?" The pilot looked down at her quiet companion. Rebecca's mind was elsewhere, completely oblivious to the temptations surrounding them.

"No thanks," Becky replied, smiling faintly. "I feel kinda tired. But if you want something—"

"I'm good." Kate casually draped her arm around the smaller woman's shoulders and gave her a squeeze. *Well, that's a first,* she thought. Rebecca Hanson never turned down the opportunity for a food encounter, let alone a fresh shot at Parisian delights. She teased her companion about her appetite on occasion, but secretly, she loved to watch Rebecca eat. The flight attendant attacked her plate—and those dishes around her—with passion and joy, eating with a bottomless abandon as though each meal might be her last. No, if Rebecca wasn't hungry, then something was definitely on her mind.

The sounds of the square faded behind them as they turned a corner and headed down the last block towards their hotel. The two friends walked in silence, Rebecca's brow furrowed deep in thought, Kate giving her the space that she needed.

"Well," Becky spoke at last, gazing up at the strong profile of her lover in the twilight, "what do you think?"

Kate thought about the question for a moment, knowing instantly what Rebecca was talking about. Hanson was her friend. Her colleague. Her confidante—and more. Kate had an opinion, all right. The blunt and honest truth. She owed her that.

"What do I think?" Kate sighed. "I think he helped kill his wife and 209 other people, that's what. He's a murderer, Rebecca, plain and simple. And now he's afraid."

"And alone," Becky added, pursing her lips. "I think he misses her." She stuck her hands into the pockets of her pants. "Isabelle, I mean."

The pilot stiffened. "Well he should have thought of that before he planted a *plastique* explosive in her luggage."

They had arrived in front of the Hôtel de l'Abbaye, its stone façade softly illuminated by recessed floodlights, a glowing fortress offering them sanctuary against the gathering gloom.

"Let's get some sleep, okay?" Kate guided Rebecca through the great wooden doors and into the fieldstone lobby. "It'll all be better in the morning." She offered Rebecca a tired grin.

"'Kay," Becky said, smiling, snuggling into the warmth of the tall body next to her. "If you say so."

They tumbled into bed, exhausted. Kate slept soundly, for once, comforted by the feel of the small blonde lying in her arms after too long an absence. It was Becky who slept fitfully, her dreams troubled by herky-jerky flashes of being lost in a raging storm. The crashing thunder, the jagged streaks of lightning exploding against a darkened sky, sounded a note of terror that struck at the very core of her being.

And Catherine Phillips was nowhere to be found.

* * * * * * * * * *

The next day dawned bright and fair. A warm breeze parted the thin, gauzy curtains of their window, stealing into the hotel room where Rebecca Hanson lay curled on her side in bed, and tickled her on the nose.

"Mmnpf." Becky twitched her nostrils, feeling the tug of consciousness, and flung her arm out behind her, groping into thin air.

Something, or someone, to be precise, was definitely missing.

"Kate?" she mumbled, edging herself up on an elbow.

"Hey, sleepyhead." Catherine Phillips, wearing nothing more than the suit she was born in, sauntered out of the bathroom toweling her hair. "Rise and shine."

"Ugh." Becky made a show of shielding her eyes from the sunlight streaming in, the better so she could covertly eye her partner's breathtaking form. "What time is it?"

"Nearly 0800 hours."

"WHAT?" She sat up in bed as though she'd been shot. "You mean we've been in asleep over ten hours?"

"*You* have been," Kate said, planting a kiss on top of the younger woman's head.

"You should have gotten me up."

"What makes you think I didn't try?" The pilot grinned mischievously, and turned back towards the bath. In truth, Rebecca had seemed so exhausted the night before that she hadn't had the heart to waken her. Instead, she'd allowed her to sleep in, catching a few more moments of rest.

"Oh...you." Becky tossed a pillow at the retreating back of her lover. "If you did, you didn't try very hard."

"We can debate that later," Kate laughed, easily dodging the missile. "Right now we've got things to do. They serve breakfast in the garden downstairs. I figure we can grab something there, and then head over to the Sorbonne."

"Ahmed lives near there, right?"

"Yeah, according to the address Miskha gave you," a disembodied voice echoed from the bath. "Maybe he's taking classes

there, who knows. We'll see what we can find out from him, and
then pay another visit to Mr. Izo Mufti. Based on what we find
out today, we'll take it all to Inspector Girard and see about the
data tap."

"Sounds like a plan," Becky yawned, ruffling a hand
through her short blonde hair. She swung her legs over the side
of the bed, just as her stomach let loose with an ungodly rumble.

"Kaaate?"

"Mnnn?"

"What do you think they'll have for breakfast?"

* * * * * * * * * *

The garden of the Hôtel de l'Abbaye was in an interior
courtyard, surrounded on all sides by the one-time convent. Covered walkways supported by delicately scrolled columns lined
the perimeter, and a small fountain with a sculpture of a beatific
Madonna and Child gurgled at the center of a flower bed.

Tables topped with crisp white linen cloths were spaced discreetly throughout the garden; they were about half filled with
guests from the hotel as well as customers from the public; an
iron gate at the far end of the enclosure led from the portico to
the rue Cassette.

"This must have been the cloister at one time," Becky said,
diving into her third croissant of the morning. "It's so peaceful
here, so quiet." She reached for a shallow bowl of apricot pre-
serves, proceeding to spread them liberally on her croissant.

"It is," Kate said, her eyes traveling around the courtyard at
their fellow diners. A group of elderly women. A young couple.
Several tables of businessmen. And a single man, smoking, his
face obscured by a copy of *Le Monde.* "I'm glad you like it."

Becky paused, her croissant hovering in mid-air. Her eyes
flickered from the pastry to Kate, and then back again, thinking.
Carefully, she parked the croissant on her plate.

"Kate," she said, her eyes finding the pilot's and locking in
on them, "I—I'm glad you picked this hotel. This...area. I mean.
I know you just as well could have set us up at the Paris Hilton
or something."

"I know." Kate's tan face colored slightly. "This place was convenient, though," she said, reaching for her *café noir,* struggling to remain professional. Detached.

Rebecca silently dipped her head closer to the pilot's, a look of skepticism skipping across her face. "And...?"

Busted. "And," the corner of her mouth curved up in the beginnings of a smile, "I thought...you might like it."

"Well, I do." Becky smiled happily, returning her attention to her croissant. "It was very...romantic of you."

"Hey," Kate said crossly, even as the smile took over her face, "what's that supposed to mean?"

"Relax, sweetie." Becky's voice was patient. "It was a compliment, okay?"

Kate motioned for the waiter, her blue eyes sparkling. "Says you."

"Mnnn—hang on." Becky crammed another bite of croissant into her mouth. "Let me finish this."

"Either make it to go, or leave it, Champ." Kate stood, smirking. "We've got to get moving." She signed for their breakfast, and then waved a beckoning hand at the smaller woman. "Let's go."

"Okay, okay." Becky took a last swallow, trailing after Kate through the garden and out the gate leading to the rue Cassette. "Can we walk?"

From behind an unfolded newspaper, where a thin wisp of smoke twirled a lazy pathway towards the sky, a pair of dark eyes flashed and watched intently as the two women left.

* * * * * * * * * *

The irony did not escape Omar.

As he took the elevator to the floor indicated on the slip of paper he'd taken from Izo, he smiled at the thought that he had so easily been able to track down these women from Orbis Airlines—their names, where they were staying. And written by one of their own hands, no less. Looking down at the bold script slashing across the paper, confirming the room number, he guessed that the writing belonged to the tall one. Regardless, he would find out what he needed to know from them. Starting with a simple survey of their hotel room. For Rashid had warned him it would be best to avoid further bloodshed, unless the situation called for it.

He slipped a hand into his pocket, feeling the smooth coolness of his switchblade. Just let one of them get in his way. Then, he would be *sure* to have an excuse to kill them. They were trouble. He knew that from the first moment he'd seen them, standing there at Izo's front door. Omar had no rational reason for his concern, just a gut instinct that had served him— and the cause—very well over the years. He would not stop relying on it now.

Getting into the room was easy; the ancient convent doors had locks on them only slightly newer than the abbey itself. He slipped inside, clicking the door shut behind him, sweeping his eyes about the room like a cat seeking its prey.

In his eyes it was a rather modest accommodation, charming, he supposed to some, but inferior to his acquired luxurious tastes. The bed was unmade, a damp bath towel lay draped over the side of an upholstered chair, and from the open window he could hear the muffled sounds of traffic coming from the street below.

Next to the window was a simple wooden table with a single drawer attached, and he moved there, first.

Nothing.

A clothes chest by the door, likewise, was empty. A nightstand near the bed held a phone and memo pad; he flipped through the pad and found no indication of any notes being made. Hmnn. He'd seen the women leave, carrying portfolios; what if whatever information there was to be had, they kept with them?

No matter. He would deal with that if and when he needed to.

Patient, unhurried, he stepped over to the closet.

He quickly checked the pockets of the clothes hanging up, producing only a tissue and a stick of gum. His eyes lit upon the two travel bags stacked neatly on the floor of the closet. They were unlocked and, to his dismay, empty.

Sighing, he was about to check under the bed, when he saw it. A less thorough man might have missed it, but not he, Omar. He, who left no detail unattended to. There, in the rear of the closet, behind a crude excuse for an ironing board, he spied a black leather computer bag.

Aaah, he thought. What luck. He could not have asked for a better information source as to the activities of those Orbis women. He thought about leaving with the laptop immediately, but Rashid's cautionary words still rang in his head. Better to make sure it was worth taking, rather than risk an unnecessary early exposure.

Gently, as though crooning to an infant, he lifted the bag and removed the computer. Fighting the urge to light up a cigarette, he turned the power on.

****

"Oh, shoot," Becky cried, holding a hand to her forehead. She and Kate had gotten no more than a few steps down the sidewalk of the rue Cassette. "I forgot Mishka's letter."

"Forgot it—how?" Kate froze in her tracks. "As in back at the hotel? Or as in back in the States?"

"Tsk—oh ye of little faith." Becky playfully elbowed her taller companion. "It's in our room, ya big skeptic." She was already starting back for the gate. "Look, I'll run back upstairs and get it. Why don't you just wait down here, and have another cup of that...oil you've been drinking?"

"It's called *café noir,* for your information," Kate said stiffly. "You ought to try it, Miss 'Broaden Your Palate.'"

"No way," Becky laughed over her shoulder, pulling away from Kate and moving towards the elevators. "I figure I'll actually *need* the use of my stomach for the next fifty or sixty years."

"Chicken," Kate called after her, grinning. She eased her lanky frame down into a garden chair. Another café? Well, why not. And she lifted her hand in the air.

****

Rebecca jogged down the hall to their room, breathless. How could she have forgotten the letter? Granted, she had put it in a safe place, but leaving it behind like this sure didn't make her look good in front of the boss. She hurried, fumbling for the key in her pocket, knowing how Kate's moods were as changeable as a quick moving cloud skipping over the sun on a summer's day. It didn't take much for the pilot's short fuse to blow, and she had so wanted to get this day to get off to a good start. So far, it had.

Standing in front of their door, Becky turned the antique-looking key in the lock, and tried the knob.

Only to find that the door didn't budge.

Well, that was strange. Somehow, she'd locked it. Yet she distinctly remembered the overly cautious Kate checking the door when they'd left for breakfast. Perhaps the maid had come and gone and left it unlocked?

Whatever, Becky didn't give it much thought as she inserted the key again and heard the tumblers turn. She pushed open the door and stepped into the room.

And gasped, her heart skipping a beat.

All right...now this was *very* strange. A dark-haired mustachioed man, wearing black pants, white shirt, and a gray blazer, was crouched in front of the closet. Next to him on the bed, the laptop lay open, its screen flashing. The man turned his black eyes to her, but they did not register surprise. *Anticipation,* Becky thought later, if she'd had to put a name to it.

"What the—" Her jaw hit the floor. All logical explanations for the man's presence crashed and collided together in her mind, nearly shorting it out.

One by one, they were rejected.

He was definitely not the maid. And if he were, where was his cart, anyway? He was no one she'd seen at the hotel, although he could be security or some such. Or what about a guest? Might he possibly have entered their room in error? Just a simple tourist, who'd made a mistake?

If so, what was the laptop doing out—and on?

"I'm sorry, *Mademoiselle,*" he said, speaking in English. He moved quickly towards her, his teeth flashing. "Perhaps you can help me." His voice was calm. Soothing. And his glittering smile was one Becky vaguely remembered from...somewhere.

There. She found herself stupidly returning the smile. *Now he'll tell me his logical explanation, and everything will be okay.*

And then he was on her, the smile bleeding away from his face, turning it into a cold mask of hatred. In a movement so quick, so practiced, that Becky was powerless to defend herself, he shoved the door shut behind her, grabbed at her left arm and spun her around. Twisting her arm so brutally that she thought he might tear it from its socket, he threw her up against the wall, hard.

What might have been a scream flew out of her mouth sounding instead as a strangled cry, thanks to the force of the impact. *Uh-oh,* Becky thought dully as spots swam before her eyes. *I think I have this all figured out.*

****

Catherine Phillips closed her eyes and let the sun hit her full in the face. This was a hotel she could get used to, that was for certain. Rebecca seemed to like the place. And it *was* in a good location, despite the ribbing she'd taken from the flight attendant earlier. This might be just the spot to stay when she brought Hanson back here for an extended vacation.

Kate took in a deep breath and released it, already planning in her mind's eye the delights she would treat Rebecca to when they returned for pleasure. Once this damned case was over with.

The tables around her were being cleared by the wait-staff with a quiet efficiency; the service for *le petit-déjeuner* was nearly through. She took another sip of her *café noir,* relishing the strong, robust flavor of it as it seared a path down her throat. Leave the *café au lait* for wimps. Nothing but the hi-test stuff for her.

All around her there was still the scent of coffee brewing, of fresh bread baking, mixing with the delicate, fragrant scent of the roses and tulips blooming in the garden. Eyes closed, she focused in on her breathing, and listened to the murmurs of French conversation.

The language of love.

Hmnn. She'd have to get Rebecca to teach her a bit more of it. Hey—she was willing to learn. And, thinking of Rebecca— where was she, anyway? Maybe she *did* have to go back to the States after all. Kate sat up and opened her eyes, checking her watch. It was getting late. Well, she'd give it a few more...

What the fuck was that?

A—a what? A *feeling* of...of something, stabbed at Kate's heart and clutched at her gut. God, too much coffee on an empty stomach? Maybe Rebecca was right. Her eyes fell upon a table near where they'd been eating before. A single man had been sitting there, as she recollected. Reading. Smoking. Now, the table was empty, save for a discarded *Le Monde* riffling in the breeze.

C'mon. Snap out of it. She chided herself. A chill skittered down her spine, despite the warmth of the sunlight heating the cobbled garden stones. She found herself with no explanation for why she was rising, heading back through the courtyard to their room. Passing by the empty table, looking at the discarded butts in the ashtray, a memory tickled at the based of her skull, and she quickened her pace.

I just want to get her moving, she told herself, deciding to take the stairs instead of waiting for the elevator. *Rebecca, where are you?*

* * * * * * * * *

Swallowing her initial shock at being assaulted, Rebecca was finally able to collect her wits and her wind, and she screamed. God, what else was there to do? Instantly, a hand roughly clamped down over her mouth, cutting her off in mid-yell. She felt her arm being twisted further behind her, and she was shoved painfully into the wall.

"Where is your friend, eh? Where is that bitch?" Gone was the intruder's gentlemanly voice, replaced by a coarse, low growl.

Kate. He means Kate. Oh God. Oh God. A new fear blossomed in Becky's chest, propelling her into action rather than paralyzing her. Mustering what leverage she could, given her awkward position, her reply to her attacker's question was the sharp stomp of her heel onto his foot.

He yelped in pain, slightly releasing his hold on her. "You fucking whore."

She twisted desperately in his grasp, panting wildly, tears springing to her eyes as her shoulder moved in a direction it was never meant to go. But it was enough. With a chop of her elbow towards his Adams apple that nearly struck home, suddenly, she was free.

"Help," she screamed, racing for the door. "Help me, please." She was so close. Sobbing, her hand reached out for the doorknob.

But then her body was rocked by what felt like a linebacker slamming into her, arms snaking around her middle, driving her down to the floor in a tackle that very nearly crushed the life out of her.

She lay there dazed, gasping, knowing she should be fighting for her survival; wanting to, but unable to direct her body to respond.

Pressure from behind.

Grinding her face into the woodwork.

Oh God, he was on top of her now, straddling her, grabbing at her arms and pinning her to the cold, wooden floor.

"Now, you will tell me," the intruder panted, leaning down, close to her ear, "what information did Izo Mufti give you?" He gave a tug on her hair, pulling her head towards him, and Becky groaned at this latest violation.

Okay. So this was not your normal hotel thief. His breath was overpowering, reeking of strong coffee and stale cigarettes, and for a moment Becky thought she might be ill. In hopeless desperation she cried out again, weaker this time, and once more a hand covered her mouth, and nose too, smothering her.

Frantically, her mind raced over her limited options, quickly settling on one.

With a strangled cry, she bit down for all she was worth on the hand imprisoning her.

"Aaah." There was an enraged bellow behind her, and her head was sharply, painfully smacked against the floor for all her efforts, but at least she could breathe again, and she did so in grateful, hitching pulls.

"You infidel bitch," he roared, and she felt him move slightly.

From her position she could not see what he was up to, but she heard a dry click. *No.* Dread washed over the flight attendant like an icy-cold wave, and she froze. There was a flash, she managed to see that, of finely honed metal catching the light from the window.

*What? Oh...*Her mind fuzzily put the pieces together as soon as she felt the sharp pressure of a blade at her throat.

"Another move," his voice was a harsh rasp, "and I slice you open like a squealing pig."

"Oh God," Becky whimpered, squeezing her eyes shut. This was it. *I love you, Kate. Don't be angry with me, please.*

And then she heard the crash of a door nearly wrenched off its hinges.

"Rebecca." A hoarse, panicked cry.

She couldn't see her, but God, how good it was to hear her. *Kate.*

Becky felt the man's weight shift on her back, and the pressure on one of her arms was somehow lighter. "Stay back or I kill her now."

"You're the dead man," the pilot replied, in a voice so cold and lethal that Becky could scarcely recognize it as Kate's.

The intruder was definitely distracted by this sudden change in the odds, by that damned tall bitch he'd been worried about, standing there calmly in the doorway as though he posed no threat to her or her little friend whatsoever. Well, he would show her.

He took a deep, steadying breath, reassessing his strategy, unaware that his knife bobbed slightly away from his victim's throat.

It wasn't as much clearance as she would have liked, but she didn't care. Becky jerked an arm free, putting it between her neck and the blade.

"What the—"

It was all the opening Kate needed.

In the dizzying blur of motion that followed, Rebecca was hard-pressed to figure out just what had happened. As if by magic, the crushing weight was removed from her body and the knife clattered to the floor. She rolled over onto her side, her breath coming in aching spurts, and was in time to see an enraged Kate, her long dark hair flying, toss her attacker into the chest of drawers.

The man scrambled to his feet, his eyes wild, watching the chest teeter precariously. Disarmed, with this crazy woman at his throat, he saw his escape. He pulled the chest down behind him. Wood splintered and drawers came whizzing out of the cabinet, sliding across the floor and blocking Kate's path. The intruder tore out the door, retreating without a backward glance.

The pilot, nearly blinded by her fury, started after him.

Until she heard a soft, mewling cry. "Kate."

And she stopped. With her heart pounding, her chest heaving wildly, she turned her eyes from the life or death hunt she found so intoxicating, and let her gaze fall upon the small figure crumpled on the floor behind her.

In a flash of grounding recognition, her anger and rage melted away.

"Oh, God...Rebecca."

Immediately she was by her side, holding her, stroking her hair, whispering the meaningless nothings that soothed heart-stopping fears from trembling limbs. "There. Sssh, it's okay. I'm here."

"Kate, I...oh God, I didn't know...he, he—" Suddenly, it all hit Becky like a sledgehammer: what had happened, what nearly had happened, and she dissolved into tears. "Oh Kate," she sobbed, "I was so scared."

"Ssssh, it's all right, I got ya now." Kate squeezed her tight, rocking her like a small child. She fought to control the pounding of her own heart, to quell the abject terror she'd felt at bursting into their room and seeing Rebecca on the floor with that bastard on top of her, holding a knife to her throat. *God...for a moment there...*She swallowed, hard. She had to get a hold of herself. She couldn't fall apart, not now. There was no time for that.

Rebecca needed her.

They sat there on the hardwood floor for a few moments, clinging to one another, recovering.

Finally, "Are...are you okay?" Misty blue eyes searched moist green.

"I—I think so," Becky hiccuped, rubbing her aching shoulder.

Kate gently reached out and stroked the younger woman's neck, testing. Probing. "Are you sure?"

"Yeah," Becky said, laughing without mirth. "Just a little shaken up, that's all. Sorry I lost it like that."

"Hey," Kate kissed away a tear from a soft, pale cheek, "you were entitled, okay?" She paused, sweeping her eyes around the disordered room. "C'mon," she said, helping Becky carefully, solicitously, to her feet. "We've got to call the police."

As if on cue, the phone on the nightstand shrilly sounded.

"Here, sit." Kate maneuvered Rebecca to the edge of the bed. "Probably the neighbors wondering what all the commotion is about."

"Tell 'em I'm not home." Becky flashed a pained grin.

"Oui." Kate smiled back, relieved beyond all measure to see that Rebecca's shock seemed to be wearing off, that glimpses of her normal self were returning. And God, after what she'd just been through. The internal strength, the resolve of the smaller woman never ceased to amaze her.

Kate grabbed the phone. *"Bonjour,* hello," she said. "Yes, this is she." Two dark eyebrows furrowed. "Mn—hmn. Mmn hmn. Yes."

"Who is it?" Becky whispered, leaning closer to Kate.

"Really." Silence, as the party on the other end continued speaking. "When?" The pilot turned slightly, her eyes falling on Rebecca, her face set like a stone. "Thank you Inspector, we'd appreciate that. Actually," she hesitated, "we've just had a break-in in our hotel room, and my colleague was attacked." The muscles in Kate's jaw flexed at that, and she nodded, listening to the inspector's words.

"Very well. We'll wait for you here. *Merci."* She slowly replaced the phone in the receiver.

"That...was the police?"

Kate regarded Rebecca intently. Saw the confusion in her eyes; the reddened nose and the pale face where the tears had nearly dried. This woman who was her everything. "Yes," Kate replied quietly, sitting down on the bed. "Inspector Girard." She released a heavy, quaking sigh. "We can forget about needing the data tap, Rebecca."

Becky's eyes widened and then clouded over as the realization of Kate's words struck home. "No..."

"Izo Mufti was found murdered this morning."

It was not until the police at last arrived at their doorway that Catherine Phillips finally let Rebecca Hanson out of her arms.

Chapter
14

It took some time to be rid of Inspector Girard and his associates; the French police inspector was nothing if not thorough. He wanted to know word for word Mufti's conversation the day before, and agreed with Kate and Rebecca that the man they'd seen on the elevator at Mufti's building, the very same one who had attacked Becky, was currently the prime suspect in Mufti's murder.

The man was obviously after something.

"Information?" Girard puzzled in passable English. "About the plane crash?"

"Well, he did want to know what Izo Mufti had told us—but there was nothing *to* tell, really," Becky said.

"You had no other information about the investigation here in this room? Papers? Lists?"

"Besides what was on the laptop—no. Everything else was in our portfolios, and we had them with us."

"The letter..." Kate said, lifting an eyebrow at Rebecca. She hadn't left the flight attendant's side, sitting next to her on the bed, keeping a protective, reassuring, hand on the small of her back as the inspector quizzed them both.

"Oh, gosh." Becky gingerly got to her feet and moved to the closet where the discarded laptop bag lay. She unzipped an inside pocket, and withdrew a sealed envelope. "Phew," she breathed, sagging back down onto the bed.

"That is—?" Inspector Girard flipped open his note pad; the pages were already filled with his earlier jottings.

"Just...just some travel documents of ours," Kate quickly volunteered, silencing Becky with a look. "Tickets and such."

"Oh, I see." Girard snapped the pad closed, satisfied.

"Well," Kate added, anxious to move on, "whatever he was after, he didn't get it."

"Yeah. I mean, when I walked in on him, the laptop had literally just been turned on. I could tell by the screen."

Girard leaned closer to Becky, eyeing her carefully. "Are you sure you're all right, *mademoiselle?*" A fatherly concern flickered in his gray eyes.

"Yes." Becky mustered up a tense smile. "Really."

"Don't you think you should go to the hospital at least, just to get checked out?" Kate could not resist another opportunity to suggest that her companion seek medical treatment. Her shoulder was obviously bothering her, and the purpled beginnings of a bruise had started to color the young blonde's jaw. It had taken several frowning hotel staffers quite a bit of time to bring some semblance of order back to the room, installing a state-of-the-art lock on the door in the process. Judging by the level of disarray, it had been quite a struggle between Rebecca and her attacker. Just to be on the safe side, she really wished the younger woman would agree to a check-up.

"*No,* I don't think so," Becky said, reaching out and tugging impishly on the sleeve of Kate's blouse. "And that's my final word on the subject, Captain Phillips."

"Very well." Inspector Girard motioned his team towards the door, oblivious to the glower on Kate's face. "We'll be leaving, then. I would advise you to stay in touch, *Mademoiselle* Phillips, and have a care while you're here. We wouldn't want any further...complications."

"No, we wouldn't" Kate sourly replied, folding her arms in front of her chest.

"You'll be here for how long?" The inspector swept his eyes from Kate to Becky.

"Another day or two, at the most." Kate walked the inspector to the door.

"Well, ah, we'll let you know if we come up with anything."

"Merci," Kate said, closing the door behind them. She leaned her back against it and sighed, her gaze tracking to Rebecca. "This has been some morning, eh?" She checked her wristwatch. "Or, should I say, afternoon?"

"Yeah," Becky agreed, working her sore shoulder. "This was definitely not included on the tour itinerary."

"I think you should take it easy for the rest of the day," Kate said, pushing herself off the door and moving towards the desk. She found some papers there and, eyes lowered, fiddled with them. "Tomorrow is soon enough to find Ahmed—"

Before she knew what was happening, Rebecca Hanson was by her side, her green eyes on fire. "This is *my* lead on *our* case," she said, waving the envelope in Kate's face. "There's information out there that people are willing to die for. To kill for." She thrust out her chin defiantly. "Judging by this morning, we must be getting pretty damn close, Kate." Becky ran a hand through her hair, fuming. "And I *don't* like the idea of getting messed with in my own hotel room."

"But—"

"El Yousef is still out there, Kate." Rebecca cut her off, her eyes sparking. "Let's go get him."

****

Against Kate's better judgment, Becky rejected a taxi, insisting that going on foot would help to work the kinks out of her pummeled body. As a compromise, they walked back past the church of St. Sulpice to the Mabillion metro, and took it three stops down to the Latin Quarter.

Home of one of Europe's most prestigious universities, the Sorbonne, the Latin Quarter derived its name from the ancient university tradition of studying and speaking in Latin, a practice that died out after the French Revolution. A uniquely bohemian enclave in what otherwise was a cosmopolitan city, the *Quartier Latin* was populated with students and would-be academics who filled the air of the local cafés with their grandiose ideas—and tobacco smoke.

The district was perched on a roller coaster maze of steep, sloping streets, with buildings cut precariously into the hillside, stubbornly clinging to their bit of ground in defiance of the laws of gravity. The sidewalks were crowded with artists selling their wares, craftspeople, book salesmen, even the odd fortune teller. Resisting the urge to stop and browse, the women pressed on until they arrived at a tumble-down building off the rue des Carmes—obviously student housing. The first floor housed a café, and even at this mid-afternoon hour, the tables were nearly filled. Students, mostly, engaged in various debates, grabbing a quick bite, or studying.

"Upstairs, I think," Kate said, leading Becky through a rabbit's warren of rooms to a narrow, winding staircase.

"Third floor," Becky said, breathlessly. "*Numero trois.*"

"Got it," Kate said, glancing back over her shoulder to where her companion followed, leaning heavily on the staircase. "You doing okay?"

"Yeah," Becky huffed, her face flushed. She caught the pilot's eyes and grinned. "I could use the workout."

"Okay." Kate forced herself to do the impossible—to stop worrying. She breathed a silent prayer of thanks when they got to the third floor landing, with Rebecca none the worse for wear. The walls had decades old beige paint peeling off of them, and the bare wooden floors in the hallway, sagging slightly in the middle, were worn shiny-smooth by a century's worth of feet tramping over them. It was warm in the hallway, not a surprise considering there was no visible means of air circulation and, judging by the smell in the air, someone was apparently cooking garlic and peppers.

"Here we are," Becky said, stopping in front of a scarred door with the number "3" spray-painted on the top of the frame. She spared a quick glance at Kate. The pilot nodded, giving Becky the green light.

Returning the nod, she lifted her hand to the door, ready to give it a good rap with her knuckles, when it suddenly burst open.

A young man with a scruffy black beard, carrying a backpack, nearly ran into them. *"Pardon, "* he cried, as surprised to
see them as they were to see him.

"Bonjour, hello." Becky lurched backwards and nearly lost
her balance but for Kate's steadying hands. "Êtes vous...er, are
you Ahmed Dushan?" she asked, her French failing her.

"Ah...yes, I am," he replied in nearly accent-free English.
He eyed them carefully now. "Who wants to know?"

"Can we talk to you for a little bit?" Kate stepped forward
from behind Becky, taking in the young man's jeans, tattered tee
shirt, and black engineering boots. There was nothing about him
that would differentiate him from the thousands of other students
here in the Latin Quarter; nothing that would otherwise label him
as an electrical engineering genius turned refugee from the Balkan war.

"I—I'm late for class," he said, growing nervous. "I'm
sorry. I must go." He started to push past them.

"Please, Ahmed." Becky grabbed at his forearm, stopping
him. "We won't take long, please." She lifted a pair of pleading
green eyes to him. "Mishka sent us."

And at that, the Kosovar sagged against the wall and closed
his eyes, muttering something in his native language that Becky
could not identify. But she could see the lone tear that escaped
the corner of his eye and trickled down his face and, finally, she
heard him cry, "It's over...it's over."

* * * * * * * * * *

Quietly, with a look of drawn resignation hollowing his face
and slumping his shoulders, Ahmed had led the way back downstairs to the little café on the first floor of the building. There,
the three had procured a corner table and ordered drinks and
sandwiches. Exchanging silent glances, Kate and Becky had sat
and waited while Ahmed read through Mishka's letter.

"Mishka said you could help us," Becky said, watching the
wind lightly lift the flap of the envelope Ahmed had torn open.
"We hope you can."

"You know, I thought by leaving Kosovo, I could leave it all

behind me." He folded the letter and replaced it in the envelope.
"But that's not true, I've found." He turned his sad, brown eyes
to them. "I was happy to take their money. Happy to work with
them, travel with them before the war broke out, experimenting,
playing the scientist. As for their cause," he sighed, "I can't pre-
tend that it didn't interest me. After all, I am a Muslim."

"But you weren't KLA," Becky stated, referring to the Kosovo Liberation Army that had done battle against the Serbs.

"No." he smiled faintly. "I was too intellectual, too much
the independent thinker, to affiliate myself with one particular
organization. But I was there. I saw what the Serbs did to our
homeland, to our families, to our friends..." His voice shook. "I
hated them for it."

"Ahmed." Becky reached out a hand to him. "Mishka told
us...about his little sister, Natasha. And you." Her heart went out
to the thin-faced young man before them. The things he had
seen. The suffering he'd been through.

"Yes." Ahmed blinked back the tears that threatened to
claim him. "Even so, I had no idea what they would use those
polymers for. They never said."

"And you didn't ask," Kate said, her voice hard. "People
died."

"No," the engineer shook his head, "I didn't ask. You're
right. I should have." He hesitated, biting his lip. "Maybe a part
of me didn't want to know."

Kate let her eyes travel around the café, absorbing the faces
of the clientele, watching the people move through the street
beyond. "When was the last time you had any contact with El
Yousef's people?"

"Not since I got out of Kosovo. Their money...blood money,
helped me with that," he said. "I thought I'd keep a low profile
here, take a few classes here at the Sorbonne and at the Arab
Institute...and try to forget. I knew what had happened with
Mishka, saw what El Yousef's people were doing with the technology I developed, but I didn't know what to do, or who to
trust." The dark curls of Ahmed's hair framed a face that was
ashen with grief, with suffering. "If there were a way I could
make it all right, I would do it.

"You can't keep running forever," Kate said firmly. "They'll just keep using the technology you developed, with or without you. They don't even need you anymore. To them, you're just a liability."

"I don't care," Ahmed cried miserably. "Let them come and get me. At least it would end this torture."

"They're tying up loose ends, Ahmed. Turning up the heat." Kate's blue eyes searched Ahmed's, struggling to touch that part of him that was still able to feel. "One man has already been killed. You could be next."

"I tell you I don't care." Ahmed dropped his eyes.

"Innocent people are at risk, Ahmed," Kate said through gritted teeth. "How many more have to die?"

"It doesn't have to be that way," Becky said earnestly, following Kate's lead. "You can help us. We're trying to break El Yousef's encryption code, track down his network of terrorist cells...expose his sham corporations."

"We're giving you a chance to make good." Kate's heart pounded in her chest. This was as close as they had ever gotten to penetrating El Yousef's defenses, and they could not have chanced upon a more valuable, viable contact. Well, not "chanced," the pilot corrected herself. It was Rebecca's smart detective work that had gotten them this far.

"I can never make up for what has happened," Ahmed said, gulping for air, his lower lip trembling. "But you're right. I can try to prevent it from ever happening again. To try and make up for what I've already done." He tapped the letter and raised his eyes to Rebecca. "And how is Mishka?" A wan smile skipped across his face.

"He is well."

"He says," he picked the letter up, "that I should trust you. And do whatever you ask."

Rebecca's eyes widened in surprise. "He...he's a good man, Ahmed. He saved our lives." she glanced sideways at Kate. The tall pilot sat rigidly still, her eyes fixed upon the young engineer.

"Mishka says," he sighed heavily, "that he's found a peace in prison, in taking responsibility for what happened." Tears filled his eyes once more. "I swear, we didn't know..."

"Ahmed," Kate leaned forward, "Where did you get the cash? That's the place for us to start. If you told us, we might be able to track it back to El Yousef."

Ahmed took a gulp of his coffee and swallowed hard. "I can do better than that," he said, squaring his shoulders and rubbing the tears from his eyes. "For the people on that plane—for Natasha—I can take you to the bastard myself."

Chapter 15

What the hell am I getting us into?

Catherine Phillips stretched out her long legs, taking care not to jostle the seatback in front of her. The interior of the Boeing 737's cabin was dim; most of the passengers were taking advantage of time between the end of the in-flight movie and their arrival in Karachi to steal an hour or two of sleep. Kate found the droning hum of the aircraft's big Pratt & Whitney engines vaguely comforting, but she refused to allow that ease to penetrate her defenses, to weaken her resolve. No, sleep was not for her.

How quickly things had fallen into place. Ahmed had offered to take them to El Yousef, and Kate had jumped at the chance. She had fought the battle within herself and won...beaten down the niggling voices in her head that told her it could be a trap. That it was too dangerous. That only a fool would follow a virtual stranger into one of the most unstable regions in the world, hunting a dangerous international terrorist.

It was an absurd idea.

Insane, really.

And yet, from the moment Ahmed had proposed his plan, Kate knew there would be no turning back. To have an opportunity to get this close to El Yousef, she'd waited too long, worked too hard, seen too many people die, to pass it up. To delay, to instead go through the "proper" international channels—it would take too damn much time, and possibly allow El Yousef to once again slip through their grasp. That, and the fact that, thanks to Mishka's letter, Ahmed seemed to trust no one save for herself and Rebecca, compelled her to act immediately. On their own. If the authorities were brought in now, Ahmed would turn and run. She'd seen the fear in his eyes that told her as much.

As a young, fast track intellectual within El Yousef's organization, Ahmed Dushan had easily, effortlessly, found himself in an orbit drawing closer and closer to El Yousef's inner circle. And so he'd traveled on behalf of the cause: worked a semester abroad at Birktec Electronics, helped to fine-tune a communications post in Athens and, finally, just before returning to his native Kosovo, aided in establishing the Chosen One's newest stronghold in Birat.

Ahmed swore to Kate that he would be able to get her in and out of El Yousef's camp, undetected. It wouldn't be easy, and there would be hardships along the way, but the young Muslim was confident they could safely penetrate the camp's defenses, get to the communications array hidden in the hills above the sleepy mountain village, and secure the information that would permanently bring down El Yousef.

"Would you like some water?"

A soft, lilting voice at her elbow roused the pilot from her thoughts. An airhostess dressed in conservative maroon slacks and a long tunic top smiled down at her, proffering a tray of water.

"Thanks," Kate said gratefully, feeling the scratchy dryness of the recycled air against the back of her throat. She took one cup of the cool liquid for herself, and another for the blonde-headed form slumbering at her side. The attendant floated away down the aisle, her image blending into the murk of the darkened cabin. "Prayers in the Air," Kate and her fellow pilots had jokingly referred to this particular Pakistani airline, as much for their aged fleet of planes as for the on-time performance of their arrivals and departures—inconsistent at best.

Still, Kate had had to agree with Ahmed; flying on an Orbis

Airlines jet right the hell into Karachi was not exactly the best idea just now. Keeping a low profile was paramount. And God, if Cyrus found out what she was up to...shit. Well, she'd cross that bridge when she came to it. And that bridge would be in Peshawar, the gateway to the fabled Khyber Pass—their entrance into Afghanistan. Kate had promised Rebecca she would contact Cyrus then, just to let him know where they were and what they were doing. *Of course, it will be too late by then to stop us,* she thought grimly.

But a promise was a promise, and she would keep it. Kate sighed deeply and drank a mouthful of the chilled water. She angled her head to better regard her traveling companion. In the gloom of the aircraft's interior, she could not prevent herself from lifting a hand and lightly running her fingers through the tousled wisps of Rebecca's hair. The sleeping woman shifted slightly at the contact, unconsciously moving closer to Kate.

Oh God, what am I getting you into, Hanson? Catherine felt a wave of emotion well up within her—powerful, intense—and she was struck breathless by the force of it. The desire to hold, to cherish, to protect...and more, that she dared not put a name to. She swallowed hard, trying to gulp down the raw, visceral feelings that threatened to swamp her. *Damn it.* If there was a fly in the ointment of her plan to crush El Yousef, it was her fear for the safety of the small body curled up peacefully next to her.

Rebecca Hanson.

She who had insisted she would not be left behind and who had vowed to follow the pilot to hell and back, if necessary. *And I hope it doesn't come to that.*

"What?" Two sleepy green eyes flickered at her in the darkness.

"Sorry. I didn't mean to wake you," Kate said. She forced a half-hearted smile to her face and struggled to get her emotions under control. It would never do for Rebecca to know of her uncertainty, of her concerns.

She had to be strong.

For the both of them.

"You didn't," Becky replied, blinking away the cobwebs. "At least," she yawned, smiling, "I don't *think* so."

Kate pushed a plastic cup of water towards the flight attendant. "Here. Have something to drink."

"Thanks. I'm parched." Becky quickly emptied the cup of its contents and turned to press her nose against a darkened window. "Where are we? It's awfully black down there."

"Over the Caspian Sea, would be my guess." Kate's pilot instincts kicked in. "Just a little while longer, and we'll be there."

Becky returned her attention to the dark-haired woman by her side. "Have you ever been to Pakistan before?"

"Nope," came the simple reply. "And I sure as hell have never been to Afghanistan." A pause. "But Ahmed seems to know what he's talking about." Kate let her eyes drift forward in the cabin to the area where she knew the young scientist had a seat. Given his concern for secrecy, Kate had thought it best that they not sit together, at least on the flight into Pakistan. Of course, thanks to international sanctions against Afghanistan, flying directly into that troubled land had been out of the question entirely.

"Do you trust him, Kate?"

The pilot thought about that before answering. "I...I don't really have a choice, now do I? I have to." She looked down at Becky's upturned face. "But you do, don't you." Kate posed the question as a statement of fact.

"Yes." Becky's voice was barely a whisper. "There's something about him. I mean, I know he's done some awful things in his past—"

"That's an understatement," Kate interjected.

"But he's trying to make up for it. To put things right." A small hand found Kate's own and gently covered it. "He deserves a second chance. Everybody does, now and then, don't you think?"

The irony of that statement was not lost on the tall pilot and, chastened, she slowly nodded her head in the affirmative. "Yes, Rebecca," she agreed. "But with El Yousef, make no mistake about it, there won't be any second chances."

And as the plane droned onward, cutting through the bleak indigo sky, Becky tightened her grip on Kate's hand. The pilot returned the squeeze, with as much assurance as she could muster. Her eyes stared sightlessly ahead at the seatback in front of her, and silently she chanted to herself over and over again that she was doing the right thing.

One chance at El Yousef. That was all she needed. Just one shot at the monster. She would have that opportunity soon enough.

Be careful what you wish for, Phillips.

****

The airport at Karachi was a blur of activity, even at the early morning hour in which the plane landed. Pakistan's busiest airport was crowded with travelers, many wearing the traditional Islamic dress. Processing at customs and immigration was agonizingly slow, and additionally Kate found her patience sorely tried by the close quarters and the still, muggy air. She consoled herself with the knowledge that the temperature would cool soon enough once they headed to the northern, more remote region of the country. Finally, with Ahmed leading the way, they boarded a Fokker F-27 for their connecting flight to Peshawar.

The aircraft seated approximately forty people and for this route, which was only flown once a day, the plane was nearly full. Some of the passengers were Pakistani natives, to be sure, but also there were a number of young people wearing western-style hiking clothes, laughing and talking merrily amongst themselves.

"They're trekkers," Ahmed said, picking up on Becky's curious stare. "The North-West Frontier Province has some of the most rugged and beautiful scenery in the world. Some climbers even use the area as a jumping off point for the Himalayas."

"I thought you said the region where we're going is wild and dangerous," Becky questioned, noting that some of the would-be trekkers looked to be barely out of high school.

"Oh, it is." Kate joined the conversation after finally giving up on her attempt to stow Becky's laptop into a tiny overhead bin that was already filled to bursting. With some annoyance, she thrust the black bag under the seat in front of her. "But that doesn't keep some crazies...like us, for instance, from going there."

"For these people," Ahmed thrust a thumb at the hikers taking their seats, "it's the beauty and the danger that draws them. The thrill of the challenge."

"You're right. Not so much different from us after all," Becky said softly, turning her eyes toward Kate's.

It was a quick hop from Karachi to Peshawar's tiny airport, perched in between two spire-like mountain peaks. The small valley that was Peshawar was barely visible until they were right on top of it, and the buildings sprang from the earth like a rickety tinker-toy town. With snow-capped summits visible in the distance and the lands below them the color of ochre and vermilion, the stark beauty of it all took Rebecca's breath away, like frosty air on a crisp winter's morning. With ghostly hands of mists rising skyward, reaching for pillowy clouds above, the flight attendant found herself reminded of the fabled land of Shangri-La. "Wow," was all she could say, speechless for once, and Catherine silently agreed, nodding her head and gazing out the small window of the Fokker.

The magical atmosphere continued on their ride from the airport to the hotel. They rode in a makeshift taxi that had last seen its prime during the days of the imperial *Raj,* Kate guessed, but for Rebecca's sake she was glad the driver took them on an impromptu mini-tour through the Old City of Peshawar. For there would be no time for sightseeing on this trip, the pilot thought, her eyes narrowing as she considered their purpose here.

Peshawar was a blend of the old and new, tracing its origins back through the millennia, stubbornly eking out an existence in the thin air and rocky landscape. It was obvious, however, that at least some modern conveniences had not passed Peshawar by. A Range Rover here, a satellite dish there, and there was a riot of bazaars and turbaned vendors along the route who sold everything from tribal jewelry and oriental rugs, to TVs, VCRs and leather pistol holders. The streets were choked with foot and bicycle traffic, as well as plodding horse-drawn tongas driven by fierce-looking Pashtuns—the predominant local tribe.

The driver chattered away, describing the sights in what he must've thought was passable English, although the women could understand little of it thanks to the sharp, unfamiliar dialect.

"Are you getting any of this?" A grimace edged across Kate's face as she watched the cab narrowly avoid a stand of squash set close to the road. The gap-toothed, turbaned driver was oblivious to the near miss, turning back frequently to stare at his passengers, Rebecca in particular.

"Not a bit of it." Becky grinned happily. "Just go with it, Kate."

"He's telling us where the good shopping deals are to be found," Ahmed said, shaking his head. "At least I think so. Special discount, he can get us. Especially for you, Miss Rebecca."

"Wha—hey. Watch where you're going, buddy." Kate poked the driver in the shoulder as the cab weaved once again, barely avoiding an old man leading a balky goat by a tether. Reluctantly, the driver faced forward, still prattling excitedly.

"Jesus. What is his problem?"

"You'd better get used to it," Ahmed told the pilot, a faint smile dancing across his narrow, bearded face. "Western women are not usually found in these parts," he explained, "and a blonde woman," he looked pointedly at Becky, "is a rare sight indeed. You should prepare to be stared at."

"That's ridiculous," Kate snapped, her nostrils flaring. "For God's sake, we're dressed conservatively enough." She gestured towards the khaki pants and beige, long-sleeved blouses and field jackets that both she and Rebecca wore. They'd made a point of quickly obtaining clothing better suited to the cooler, more rustic environment prior to leaving Paris. "Why, if that's not a bunch of bulls—"

"Hang on, Kate," Becky's eyes lit up as the taxi lurched towards a dry goods vendor. "I've got an idea."

****

Catherine Phillips had been involved in her share of "special operations" in her days with the Air Force. Little "unofficial" or "ad hoc" missions, as Cyrus liked to call them. He had used her because she was good, one of the best; because she was discreet—she had no one to tell; and because she was always willing to give it a go, to play full out. "No" simply wasn't in her vocabulary. Despite the some times extreme levels of risk involved, she'd never backed down. Maybe, she'd wondered later, it was because in those days she'd felt she had nothing to lose, really.

Libya. The Philippines. Somalia.

And that damned no-fly zone above Iraq. Or "go-fly," as Kate and her colleagues had called it. There was that one hellish time when one of her sorties had gone bad. She and her wing man had been flying a couple of F-16 Falcons on what was supposed to be a quick in and out. She'd taken a few rough hits but hadn't had to bail, unlike her wing man, who had gotten nailed one time too many and went down. It had been a pitch black night with no moon; the only light in the sky had come from the Soviet-made Iraqi fighter who'd come out of nowhere and let loose on them, unprovoked. She'd soon fixed that, burying an AIM-9 missile in the bastard.

Damn, that night had been one hell of a fuck-up. She'd seen her fellow pilot eject, but hadn't been able to make contact with him. The terrain below was exposed desert. So the pilot, if he had survived, was exposed too. She'd stayed above him, maintaining a sweeping, circling pattern, coordinating the retrieval effort from her position despite the static she was getting from base to bring her damaged aircraft home. But it was as if she hadn't heard. No way was she leaving her man behind, defenseless. And so, somehow, she'd fought off two more enemy jets until the rescue choppers signaled that they'd picked up the pilot; unconscious, with two broken arms, but alive.

It all seemed like so long ago to Kate, but on days like these, in the middle of a strange new land with a mission weighing heavily on her mind, it seemed like only yesterday. Even now, as she reflected back on her covert operations, she marveled at them with a mixture of awe, accomplishment, and a "what in the *hell* did you think you were doing?" She'd thought when she'd taken Cyrus up on his offer and joined Orbis Airlines that she'd left those dark, dangerous days behind.

She'd been wrong.

It was funny now, in a way, how quickly she'd found herself shifting into her old special ops mode. The tight, clenching feeling in her gut. How her heart raced every time she thought of what their success might mean. The way in her mind's eye that she was able to see things more sharply, more clearly, focusing on the mission at hand and on nothing and no one else.

Well, almost no one else.

For this time, she had a partner along. And that made things...different somehow. No better, no worse, just different. And Rebecca Hanson did not plan on simply being extra baggage along for the ride; she'd already made that perfectly clear. She planned to contribute, to bear equal responsibility for their mission. Already, the pilot had found she'd had to check her ego at the door and acknowledge that the younger woman *did* have a say in all this, one that she'd do well to listen to.

Like their clothes, for instance. While Kate had been busy blustering on with the reasons why the locals should simply treat them as peers in their conservative, western dress, Becky had already been directing the driver towards a vendor where they were subsequently able to purchase more traditional garb.

Now, sitting in the relative quiet of the restaurant in the Pearl Hotel, both she and Rebecca wore the *shalwar kameez*—a long, loose, non-revealing garment worn by men and women alike. It fit nicely over their clothes, providing an added layer of warmth against the mountain chill. Becky's was of a buff-colored cotton, with a green head-scarf and trim on the sleeves and bottom, while Kate's was less decorative; a plain, functional garment the color of slate. Becky had picked up a copper bracelet in the market too, and the bangles glittered warmly in the light of a small candle that lit their table.

Gazing at her companion as they both ate an early dinner of *dhal*—a lentil mush—curried lamb, cabbage and rice, Kate could not help but notice how Rebecca's native attire suited her. Wayward strands of her blonde locks still peeked out from under the head scarf and, despite their long travels and the uncertainty of what lay in store, the young woman's face fairly glowed with a peaceful serenity that Kate herself found strangely calming, soothing.

Noticing her stare, Becky paused in mid-bite, a spoonful of the sweet-smelling mush hovering in mid-air. The blonde's gaze took in the pilot, quickly dropped down to her food, and then at last skipped around the half-full restaurant. "What? Do you see something?"

The words effortlessly flew out of Kate's mouth before she could find either the strength or desire to stop them. "You're so beautiful," she said simply, plainly.

Immediately, a red flame ignited Becky's cheeks, and she replaced the spoon in her bowl. "Gee, in this old thing?" Hands went to smooth out the folds of light-colored cloth and to push stray hairs off her forehead, but her green eyes sparkled in appreciation.

"Yup." Kate felt a smile spread its way across her face. She reached out to playfully twirl Rebecca's bracelets. "You are."

"Thanks." Becky released an explosive burst of air, gratefully returning Kate's smile. "I needed that. It's been a long couple of days."

"And they're gonna get longer." Even as the words escaped her lips, Kate hated herself for ending the moment. She saw Rebecca stiffen and nod in agreement. Well, it was true, wasn't it? It was only fair that Hanson know what they were in for.

"You're right, Kate," Becky said, her face gone still. Serious. "And I'm ready." She turned towards the doorway that connected the restaurant to the hotel bar. "I wonder what's keeping Ahmed?"

"I don't know." Kate glanced at her watch, feeling impatience tickle at the base of her skull. "He was supposed to meet his so-called friend for that drink an hour ago."

"But he said it might take a while, didn't he?"

"Yeah," the tall woman grudgingly replied. Pakistan was officially a dry country. But there were exceptions. The bar in their hotel was one of the few places in the area where alcohol was served, and even at that there were forms to be signed in triplicate before the first beverage would even appear. Ahmed had arranged the meeting with an acquaintance of his from his past life in this border region, an Afghan trader who ran supply convoys through the pass from Peshawar to Jalalabad and Kabul. Hopefully, he would be willing to take a couple of discreet foreigners along with him on his next trip. For a fee, of course. It had been Ahmed's idea to let him broach the delicate subject with his contact alone, at first, over a rare, friendly drink. And then, if the man were agreeable, to introduce him to the two western women.

Kate pushed away from her food, no longer hungry. "Hell, how many drinks does it take to get a yes or a no?"

"Give Ahmed some time, Kate. He'll be here." The flight attendant could see that the pilot was rapidly becoming agitated. And here, in a foreign land where the locals were unused to the likes of Catherine Phillips, that was not necessarily a good thing. "It's going to be rough going, isn't it," she changed the subject, "making our way over the pass and getting, somehow, to Birat."

"That's putting it mildly."

"Well, Ahmed thinks it's possible, and I believe him." Becky held her head high, challenging her friend with that statement.

"Me too. Or else I wouldn't be here," Kate replied, quietly considering whether, if pressed, she could accurately describe just where the hell "here" was. "More importantly," she looked squarely at her young companion, "I wouldn't have dragged you here with me."

"Dragged is hardly the word I would use." Becky haughtily lifted an eyebrow. "I seem to recall quite clearly insisting that you take me with you to this..." she waved her hand about the high-ceilinged room, "...place."

"Oh yeah. You did, didn't you?" Kate offered her companion a faint grin, knowing that there had been no question but that Rebecca would accompany her, not really.

"Kate," a moment's hesitation, "you're going to call Cyrus tonight, aren't you?" Becky's voice was quiet, without reproach.

"Yes," Kate sighed. "Like I promised."

"You know," Becky traced small patterns with her spoon in the bottom of her bowl, "it occurred to me that nobody, besides you, I mean, knows where I am."

A shadow briefly passed over the blonde's face, one that did not escape Catherine's notice. In the months that they'd been together, the one thing that the older woman knew above all was that Rebecca Hanson was a sensitive soul, despite her rather feisty attempts at times to demonstrate otherwise.

Ah hell, Kate thought. *Let me give this a shot.* "You mean, like your family?"

"Well, yeah." Rebecca sat up straight in her chair, doing her best to appear strong. Ready for anything. "It's not that I'm homesick, of course," she added quickly. God, the last thing she'd wanted to do was to give Kate the impression she wasn't up to the job. "After all, I know we've got work to do here, important work."

"You wanted to come," Kate said, her voice betraying no emotion. It was the truth, plain and simple.

"And I wouldn't have had it any other way," Becky fiercely replied, her feistiness rearing its blonde head. "Heck," she softened her voice, "someone's gotta watch your back, Captain."

"And that someone would be you?"

Rebecca found herself on the receiving end of a blue-eyed gaze. "Yes," she said quietly, boring her eyes into Kate's with an honesty of emotion that rocked the pilot back on her proverbial heels. "It's, it's just..."

"What?" Kate urged her on.

"Here, in this place, we're so very far away from...from what and who we know. The people we care about. Mac, Rory, and—"

"And Dottie?"

"Yeah, even her." A grin suddenly appeared on Becky's face and fled just as quickly, before she continued. Just being able to talk about it—the isolation, the risk—made her feel better. "But now, after all the hard work we've done, that *you've* done, it's come down to just you and me, Kate. If anything were to happen to you—"

"No—stop thinking like that," Kate hushed. "You and me...we're enough to see this thing through, Rebecca," Kate said, her eyes shining in the candlelight. "Believe in that, like I do. Okay?" She anxiously searched Becky's face for her answer, knowing she would go no further on this mission if her friend were not one hundred percent committed, confident.

"Yeah," Becky said, smiling at last. "I do." She shook her head. "You know me, Kate. I'm such a worrywart at times. It's what I do best, you know?" she laughed helplessly.

"It's okay. It's kinda nice for a change, having someone who gives a damn," Kate said, barely holding back a chuckle when she saw Becky's eyes widen as a waiter walked by with a tray bearing a head of mutton.

"Oh my." Becky swallowed hard, holding a hand up to the side of her face, blocking her view. "What was that?"

"Dinner?"

"Oh, you." Becky reached out and impishly slapped at Kate's shoulder.

"Hey." The pilot pushed up the sleeve of her *shalwar kameez* to check her watch. "Just wait a few days, when we're on the trail. You'll see."

"*Never,*" Becky muttered, turning a shade of green that matched the color of her scarf.

"That's it." Kate stood abruptly, her chair almost tumbling over backwards. "I wonder how many drinks Ahmed is buying his friend on my tab?" She took several long steps towards the bar. "Be right back."

"Kaaate," Rebecca warned, her stomach lurching at the sight of the diners at a nearby table tucking into the lamb's head. "You know ladies aren't allowed in there."

The tall pilot did not break her stride. "Fine," she called back over her shoulder, and Becky could hear the smirk in her voice, "because I'm no lady."

****

The appearance of the tall, dark, and mightily annoyed woman in the bar of the Pearl Hotel provided just the impetus that Ahmed and his friend needed to leave the men-only, smoke-filled bar area. It was either that, or provoke an international incident.

"We were just about to come over," Ahmed protested, desperately hoping that the pilot would not notice another tray of drinks heading in their direction.

"Sure you were." Kate's tone was skeptical as she ignored the angry stares of the bar's patrons. "Let's go." She bowed slightly towards the doorway leading to the restaurant. "After you, Mr.—"

"Ceru. Nayim Ceru." A short, bearded man wearing wire-framed spectacles examined Kate curiously, as though she were a creature unlike any he'd ever encountered before. His skin was dark, like his eyes, and he wore an oversized woolen jacket over dusty-brown slacks and a shirt. "And you must be Catherine Phillips." He spoke in a sing-song English accent.

"Nice guess," Kate said dryly, following Nayim towards the restaurant.

"Oh, no guessing necessary, I assure you, ma'am." Nayim smiled merrily at her. "Ahmed has told me much about you."

"Has he?" Kate gave the Kosovar a dark look. "You'd better cancel that last drink order, Ahmed. You won't be able to take them into the restaurant, right?" Her voice was icy cold.

"Ah...yes. Quite right," he said sheepishly, realizing his next round had not escaped Kate's notice. He turned to hurriedly toss a handful of rupees at a rather confused waiter.

The small group finally settled in at their table in the restaurant, Kate taking a moment to reassure an anxious Rebecca with a sidelong wink of an eye.

"Well," Kate leaned forward on the table after introductions were completed, "tell me, Nayim. Are you willing to get us through the pass and take us to Birat?"

To Kate's chagrin, the middle-aged man released a roar of belly laugh that echoed throughout the restaurant, temporarily distracting the nearby diners from their head of mutton.

"By God, Ahmed," Nayim swabbed tears of laughter from his eyes, "she's just as you said, and more."

"*What?*" Kate could feel the anger building in her gut like the pressure within a volcano. If she were subjected to much more of this bullshit, she would blow.

"Please, Catherine," Ahmed said in a panicked voice, his eyes darting back and forth between her and Nayim, "There's a certain...protocol we have to follow here."

"Really?" Kate said tonelessly, crossing her arms in front of her chest. "Such as?"

"Such as," Ahmed frantically searched for the right words, "one does not enter lightly into such an agreement. There should be a bit of conversation, bargaining, good humor..."

"And a spot of tea would be delightful." Nayim gazed pointedly at a passing waiter. "I'm dry as the lowlands in early spring."

"I wouldn't know why, after all the time you spent in that bar," Kate grumbled, flagging down a waiter.

"Kate," Rebecca admonished her companion, "Please." She turned to the older man. "Mr. Ceru, Ahmed's told us you've been back and forth through the pass many times. You must be quite an expert."

"Yes I am, dear lady." He removed his glasses from the bridge of his nose and cleaned them with his napkin. "And I don't mind saying so. If you want to get through the Khyber, I'm the man to see. There are permits to be obtained, and with the fighting among the local clans, you must be careful about which convoy you ride with. Not to mention the dangers to be found along the way. The thieves, the land mines. Make one mistake," he raised a stubby finger at her as a cup of piping hot tea was placed in front of him, "and it could be your last."

"You're a very brave man." Becky smiled engagingly.

Nayim shrugged his shoulders. "So some might say. But I feel it is my duty to do what I can to supply the rebels with grain and other supplies."

"I thought the war was over?"

"With Russia, yes. But within the country, there is still much infighting between the tribes. Oh, the Taliban has control of Kabul," he explained, describing the ruling political party, "but they're little more than an armed militia, or so some of us think." He took a sip of his tea. "They moved into the vacuum the Russians left. With a common enemy gone, various groups of *mujahideen* turned on one another. The Taliban were the strongest. In time, they overran our bombed-out capital and hanged the former Soviet-backed president. They simply took over." He sadly shook his head. "They're zealots really, banning women from work and girls from school. They have public executions, amputations, and whippings—in stadiums no less, as if one were simply watching a cricket match. Oppose them, and you're publicly executed. I've seen it," he said, falling silent.

"Sounds just like the sort that would welcome an Abbado El Yousef," Kate said quietly, softening some towards Nayim. Obviously, he'd been through his own brand of private hell at the hands of the Taliban.

"Don't think your United States is without blame here." Nayim turned dark, flashing eyes towards the pilot. "The CIA helped to create and support the likes of the Taliban. Your American Presidents sending 'aid' to the rebels—billions of dollars before and after the Soviets finally left, most of it to obtain arms. Some say the CIA is still meddling in our affairs."

"But without that American aid, the Russians might be in Afghanistan still," Rebecca objected.

"Possibly," Nayim allowed, "possibly. But the aid was not democratically parceled out to all Afghan tribes and states. For some reason," he laughed bitterly, "it flowed only to the tribal and political leaders friendly to Pakistan. It was under these conditions that the Taliban came to power."

"I—I'm sorry," Becky said, the anguish she felt over the situation in Nayim's homeland clearly etched on her face.

"Don't be, dear Miss Hanson," he assured her. "Of course this is not your fault. And what you and your friend are trying to accomplish with your little trip to Birat, can only help us. Those of us who believe in freedom, that is." He paused. "*Taliban.* It is Farsi for 'seekers of the truth.' How I wish to Allah that were true."

"Birat," Kate gently pressed. "Can you take us there?"

"I don't have a convoy heading through the pass for another three weeks. I am sorry," Nayim said woefully.

Kate's shoulders slumped. To have traveled all this way, and for nothing.

"*But,*" the Afghan trader flashed his teeth in a grin, "a business associate of mine has a convoy leaving tomorrow morning for Jalalabad. I planned on being on it. There's a small village northeast of there called Duristan. It's on the road that can take us towards Birat. As coincidence would have it, Duristan is my hometown. With a little *baksheesh,* " he rubbed the coarse skin of his palms together, "I could get you on the convoy as well."

"You mean a bribe." Kate bristled at the thought. Still, at this point she would do whatever it took to get over the damned Khyber.

"I mean a key." Nayim benignly smiled, correcting her. "With the right *baksheesh,* " he waved a hand through the air like a magician, "there is no door that will remain closed to you."

Catherine Phillips thought about that for a moment, before coming to a conclusion.

She held out a hand to the trader, her lips quirking into a grin. "So...do you take traveler's checks?"

Chapter
16

"Okay, that's it," Kate, closed the door to their small hotel room after handing a 100 rupee note to the hotel's version of a bellman. "They'll store the rest of our things until we return." Kate turned and stood with her hands on her hips, her appraising eyes taking in the backpacks and other trail gear strewn across their bed. "I don't want to hear it about that laptop," the tall woman said, eyeing the computer that Rebecca insisted on bringing along on their journey.

"You won't," Becky smugly replied. "At least *one* of us believes in being prepared."

"For what?" Kate's voice was incredulous. "Do you think a rogue board meeting might break out in the middle of the Khyber Pass?"

"Funny." Becky primly zipped the computer into its black leather bag. "Just remember, *when* you need it, Missy, I won't say 'I told you so.'"

"That's what I...like about you so much, Rebecca." The pilot moved behind the smaller woman and encircled a pair of long arms about her waist. "You're ever so gracious." She planted a kiss on the top of the flight attendant's blonde head and she lingered there, contentedly nuzzling her hair.

Becky felt her body relax into Kate's, drawing nourishment from her partner's strength and warmth as though it were the most natural thing in the world to do. Come to think of it, it was. "Thanks," she said softly, letting her head fall backward against the pilot's shoulder. They stood that way for a time, in the plain, sparsely furnished room, moving only at the shrill sound of the telephone on their bedside table.

"I'll get it," Kate said, reluctantly pulling away from Rebecca. "Probably the connection to Cyrus went through." She was at the phone before it completed its next set of double-rings. "Hello?"

"By God, Katie, where the hell are you?"

Kate held a palm over the receiver. "It's Cyrus," she mouthed to Becky. "Nice to hear from you, too, Cyrus." She returned her attention to her caller.

"That's not funny, Katie."

"It wasn't meant to be. Now, do you want to have a conversation with me or not? It's late here and I'd like to get to bed sometime soon."

"Wha..." the retired Air Force colonel sputtered. *"I haven't heard from you in days, and neither has your office. I've been left holding the goddamned bag here, trying to explain where the hell you are. To tell the truth, I'm slightly curious myself."*

"I don't want to say too much over the phone." Catherine knew that a terrorist without borders such as El Yousef had an electronic network of listening devices that reached far and wide. Best to play it safe. "I can tell you we're somewhere in Pakistan."

"Paki-- what the hell, Katie. And who is 'we?'"

"Myself, Rebecca, and...a former associate of El Yousef's that I..." she considered the young scientist asleep in the room across the hall, "...would rather not name. We're hot on his trail, Cyrus. We're closer than we've ever been."

"Katie," Cyrus' voice was ominous, *"what the hell are you up to?"*

"We know where he is," Kate explained. "We're going in."

"In."

"To Afghanistan. We know how to get to him, Cyrus. We're going to shut him down." The pilot was surprised to hear her own voice break with emotion at that last statement. The goal that had been so long out of reach was now within her grasp. And it meant everything to her. A redemption of sorts, for a personal past that she wasn't necessarily proud of. Now...now at last, she could finally make it right.

"No, Katie, no." She could hear Cyrus' groan across the miles. *"You— you can't. The Taliban are some harsh sons of bitches. They'll never let two western women into the country."*

"That's *if* they know we're trying. We're dressed as locals, and we'll be traveling with an Afghan trader who says he can get anything from diamonds to luxury cars into the country undetected. Getting Rebecca and I in? For this guy, it's like a day off for him. We're leaving first thing in the morning."

"No. Give up this...this damn fool mission. That's an order."

"Getting El Yousef *is* my mission," Kate said stonily. "You hired me for that, remember?"

"Katie, you don't understand."

"What? Tell me Cyrus. After all we've been through together." Kate could feel a stab of pain behind her eyes. Not another fucking headache. She had no time for this. "What don't I understand?"

Nothing.

Only the crackling hum of the line. And then, *"Ah, the hell with protocol. Katie."* His voice grew hushed, as if by that singular act he could ward off any would-be electronic eavesdroppers. *"My contacts at the Pentagon tell me they feel fairly certain they've located El Yousef's main stronghold. His communications post. Terrorist training ground and all that good stuff."*

"No shit," Kate said blithely. "Me too."

"Katie, listen to me. They're planning a missile strike against it."

"What?" Fire surged through her veins. "No. No way, Cyrus. They can't do that. They'll only be striking at the tail of the snake. Blowing up a few oil drums and buildings isn't the answer. You've got to strike at his head. And that means information," Kate raged on. "Breaking his codes. Uncovering his web of spies and contacts. The so-called legitimate companies that are fronts for his operation. Hell, Cyrus, you know this guy isn't just another zealot with a gun. He's a fucking international entrepreneur with a multi-million dollar bankroll and sophisticated covers bought and paid for. He'll simply set up shop somewhere else, and we'll have missed our last, best chance."

"Don't you think I know that, Katie?"

"You've got to stop them, Cyrus," Kate pleaded. "At least until we can get in and out."

Her boss laughed mirthlessly. *"Katie, you sorely overestimate this old man's sphere of influence. We've got an election year coming up. Why, the impact of the PR generated by an attack on the terrorist who supposedly brought down Flight 180? Priceless. Polls will go through the roof. Those talking heads in Washington will never back off of this."*

Kate was silent for a moment, letting her gaze fall upon the concerned face of one Rebecca Hanson. The younger woman had moved to her side when Kate had raised her voice, and now rested a hand against the small of the pilot's back, listening.

"When will they bomb?"

"I don't know, Katie. But soon."

"Then I'll just have to make sure I'm out of there when they do."

"Katie, please," Cyrus' voice was hoarse, *"I'm begging you. Stay away. Leave this to the authorities."*

"The authorities?" Kate sightlessly swept her eyes around the little hotel room. "Where are they now, Cyrus? I don't see 'em. And where the hell were they when Flight 180 was blown out of the sky?"

"Katie...you could get your ass killed. Please. Don't."

The ache in Kate's skull was a pulsating throb now, and she squeezed her eyes shut against it. "Hmnn...me risking my life and disobeying orders, seems like old times, Cyrus."

The pilot could hear the heavy sigh of her former mentor from far across the miles. Helpless. Resigned. *"Just...just be careful, will you, Captain?"*

"I'll be in touch as soon as I can...Sir," Kate said quietly, ending the connection. "Goodbye." She replaced the phone in its cradle. "Well," she turned to Becky, "you heard most of that, right?"

The young flight attendant grimly nodded.

"They're planning on bombing El Yousef's camp. Cyrus isn't sure exactly when. I'll have to tell Ahmed and Nayim but, regardless, I'm still going in." The pilot lowered her dark head, the pain shifting from behind her eyes to the center of her gut. "I—I'd understand if you didn't—"

Rebecca placed a silencing finger against Kate's lips. "Sssh. Don't say it. Don't even *think* it." Her green eyes blazed with emotion. "You and me. We're in this together, period. We're enough to see this thing through, Kate." Becky echoed the pilot's own earlier words. "Believe in that, like I do, okay?"

Kate removed Becky's finger from her lips, and proceeded to open up the small palm as though it were the bud of a delicate flower. She kissed it, relishing the vibrant warmth she found there. Overcome with relief, and with a bewildering sense of amazement at the faith that Rebecca Hanson had in her, she gathered her up in a tight, possessive embrace.

"I do, Rebecca, I do. Always."

* * * * * * * * *

Kate didn't know what precisely she'd imagined their Khyber Pass convoy would be comprised of, but never, not in her wildest dreams could she have pictured the stream of vehicles, both wheeled and footed, that made their way over the narrow mountain road.

Military trucks and jeeps that had seen better days. Automobiles: both boxy Eastern European makes as well as the odd Chinese manufactured vehicle. Broken-down hippie-style vans, including a small yellow school bus with nearly all of its interior seats removed to make room for cargo. And at the side of the road, trailing next to the modern-day caravan, there were bellowing, over-burdened camels, and wagons drawn by donkeys, even the occasional hand-drawn cart.

The entire convoy was "guarded" by a number of fierce looking, turbaned men, who seemed to sport more cigarettes and guns than they did teeth and good sense. Three times already, Kate had politely declined their offers of opium. And though

scorched craters pockmarked the road, telltale signs of land
mines, the guards led the convoy onward with an appalling lack
of regard for the potentially catastrophic consequences. In that
sense, Kate was glad they were positioned about halfway along
in the train of vehicles.

Nayim had told them that the journey through the pass
would not be a quick one, and he'd been proven correct. They
slowed down every time they hit a tunnel. And as they climbed
higher into the mountains and the air grew thinner, they'd had to
stop their whole bedraggled juggernaut every hour or two, not
only to offer Muslim prayers, but also to pay "tolls" to scruffy
looking characters who emerged from tiny ancient forts that dotted the route. During such stops, greetings and *baksheesh* would
be exchanged, and the men would let off salvos of small arms
fire into the sky, shouting religious slogans and slapping each
other on the back.

"Christ," Kate swore, watching this performance yet again,
making sure she and Rebecca were protected in the covered jeep
that Nayim Ceru's reputation within the convoy community had
obtained for them. "Don't those assholes realize that what goes
up, must come down?" Kate threw an arm around Becky's shoulders and hunkered down in the rear of the vehicle.

"They are happy to be returning home, Miss Catherine,"
Nayim said as he shifted the jeep into idle, "despite the hardships they know await them there."

"Well, they'll never make it if they don't angle those bullets
away from the convoy," Kate said testily. She'd come too far to
be taken out by some damn fool trigger-happy, hopped-up, holy
warrior.

"There are an awful lot of toll stops," Becky's muffled
voice sounded. "Whose jurisdiction are we in, anyway? Afghanistan's or Pakistan's?"

"Jurisdiction?" Nayim chuckled, and Ahmed's laughter
joined him. "Tell, them, Ahmed."

"This is the only jurisdiction in these lands," the young
Kosovar replied, letting his hand drop down to caress the rifle
Nayim had casually placed between them. "The people here
don't recognize borders...countries...not like we do. There are

no Afghans or Pakistanis." He let his eyes track to the front windshield and the breathtakingly beautiful snow-capped peaks that lined their route. "Here there are only clans. Tribes. Pathans and Pashtuns. Chitrali, Taliban, and Tajik. Fighting nature...and each other, for what they believe in. We'd do well to stay out of their way."

"It is the curse of my people," Nayim said with some regret as the convoy slowly, laboriously, pulled out, another toll satisfied. "That which should bring us together, instead drives us apart."

Food was eaten on the fly: *chapattis* and *nan* rolled with cold spicy spinach and rice inside, and water from plastic bottles that looked suspiciously re-filled; they'd had little choice but to drink it anyway. *Hell,* Kate thought, taking a healthy swig, *this should be the least of my worries.*

"How ya doing?" Kate forced a smile as she gazed down at her smaller companion. Somehow, Becky had managed to doze off a bit from time to time, and was the better for it, no doubt. A bone-chilling coldness had crept into their vehicle, and it seemed to Kate that there was not a rock or a rut in the road that was missed by the small jeep. Gears ground incessantly as Nayim adjusted to the varying tempos of the caravan, and the pilot could feel her head starting to pound once more. The sun had set; there were just a few faint shards of sunlight reflecting off the mountains, and fat snowflakes had appeared, peppering the windshield and the road ahead of them.

"Okay," came Becky's answering yawn, and she stretched as best she could in their cramped quarters. "Oh look, it's snowing."

"It will be an early winter, to be sure." Nayim bobbed his head knowingly.

"This won't slow us down, will it?" Kate took Rebecca's hands in her own, warming them. With darkness nipping at their heels, the sooner they were out of these mountains, the better.

Nayim stuck his head out the window of the jeep and sniffed at the air. "Not likely," he concluded, bringing a few snowflakes back inside with him. "We'll be out of the pass before it can do much."

"Just think," Becky sniffled slightly, looking out the window, "we're traveling the same path that Alexander the Great did over 2300 years ago."

"I wonder if he had to pay as many tolls," Kate said dryly as the convoy shuddered to a halt once more. The by-now routine shouts and shots came again from the head of the line.

"How much more of this do we have left?" Kate tightened her grip on Rebecca, feeling suddenly uneasy, hemmed in by the rocky walls rearing up to either side of the convoy, trapping them.

"Another couple of hours, at most," Nayim replied. "Then we'll be heading out and down. It will be warmer there, at least. We'll leave the convoy and be able to stop for the night."

More shouts came from the front of the line, and to Kate's ear they sounded different than before.

Angry.

Insistent.

The gunfire moved closer.

"Something's wrong," Kate said firmly, her senses on full alert.

"My dear," Nayim swiveled around to face her, "there's nothing to—"

At that moment, the ground shuddered and the *whomp* of an explosion rattled the jeep. Kate flung her body over Rebecca's, pressing her to the floor of the vehicle, as disembodied shrieks and screams sounded from the gloom up ahead. Dirt and rock and God knew what else pinged down upon them.

"A land mine," Nayim shouted hoarsely. "It has to be."

More yells, drawing closer now, and the *pop-pop* of rifle fire.

"What's happening? Can you make out what they're saying?" Kate peered over the tattered seatback, her heart pounding in her chest.

"So sorry to have to tell you this," behind his spectacles, Nayim's dark eyes were open wide, "but this is an ambush, I fear. Some enterprising mountain tribes take 'toll' collection to a whole new level, and this is the result of it."

"Can I get up now?" Becky's far-away voice came from the

floor of the rear seat.

"Stay put," Kate responded sharply, pushing Rebecca down. "Look," she hissed in Nayim's ear, "what are they saying?"

The trader cocked his head towards the window before answering. "It sounds as though they're looking for tolls from each...vehicle. And if they don't get what they like..."

"Great. Is it money they're after?"

"Money...and more, if you know what I mean. And they are, what you would call, 'royally pissed off,' you'll pardon my saying, since one of them accidentally stepped on a land mine. They're blaming us for that."

"Fuck. You'll pardon *my* saying," Kate muttered.

From her rather uncomfortable position on the floor of the jeep, Becky was shocked to see the pilot reach under her *shalwar kameez* into the pocket of her jacket, and withdraw a pistol.

"Kate." Her voice was breathless. "Where did you get that?"

"Guest services at the hotel?" Kate tried, giving Becky a sly smile in the half-light. "Look. Stay here, will ya? And keep your head down." She pressed the pistol into Ahmed's hand. "Watch out." Blue eyes pinned him against the door of the jeep. *"Nothing* happens to her, got it?"

The young scientist silently shook his head "yes" as his gaze darted ahead. Amid the approaching shouts a donkey brayed, and there was a voice that even in a foreign language Kate could tell was imploring mercy. Another gunshot, and then nothing.

"Nayim, you're with me." She nodded at him to grab his rifle as the two of them exited the jeep.

"What...what exactly is it we're doing?" The smaller man was not afraid, rather, he seemed curious at Kate's plan of action.

"I figure in an area where muscle counts, the best defense is a good offense."

"Ah...we play poker now, do we?" He'd seen thieves like this before, and knew how unpredictable they could be. Some would let you pass with a smile and a wave, while others would just as soon shoot you where you stood. The American woman's strategy was as good as any.

"Exactly." Kate smirked, grabbing a carton of water bottles from the rear of the vehicle and placing it on the ground next to them. As an afterthought, she reached back into the front of jeep to Ahmed. "Give me your arm," she demanded.

Obligingly, he extended it to her. "Wha—" Quickly, she slid his watch off his wrist. "Hey. Why don't you use your own?" He settled indignantly back into his seat under the heat of Kate's threatening look.

"Because Rebecca gave it to me." *Hell,* she thought, turning to face the approaching highwaymen, *it's a good-enough reason to me.*

In the encroaching darkness, Kate could see that a number of the criminals had taken up positions on high ground overlooking the convoy, rifles stolen from dead Russians at the ready, while the main group—about a dozen, heavily armed—worked their way down the line.

Nayim casually leaned against the side of the jeep, his rifle negligently pointed to the ground, but Kate could see that his eyes were sharp, following the thieves and their conversation. Kate was at a double disadvantage she knew, being a woman and a foreigner at that. Ah, well. She'd been in worse situations than this. But none where she'd had the added responsibility of looking out for one Rebecca Hanson.

What the hell. "Ready?" She muttered under her breath as a man stepped forward, their leader, she supposed, wearing a heavy overcoat and a turban that did little to control the dark, wild hair that blew about his face. Interestingly enough, he had piercing blue eyes that looked her over from head to toe, before he turned to address Nayim in a harsh, guttural voice. He finished with a grab at his crotch and a derisive laugh.

"Please pardon, Miss Catherine," Nayim began, "but he wants to know if you're good in bed. And, if you are, would I be willing to share you with him."

Kate fought to keep her temper in check, instead lifting a hand to pull her head-scarf down, fully exposing her face to the elements and to the ringleader. "Tell him..." her thoughts flashed to Rebecca crouched on the floor of the jeep, "...tell him that he'd do better to fuck a sheep than to try his hand with me. But

that we would be willing to share this bottled water with him."
She kicked the side of the carton she'd placed on the snowy
ground.

Blushing, Nayim repeated Kate's words to the bandit.

A shocked expression appeared on the leader's face as he
absorbed Nayim's statement, but he quickly recovered, grinning
like a man with a crude secret. He gripped his rifle tightly in
grubby, blackened fingers, and turned it towards Kate, speaking
rapidly.

"He says he'll take you *and* the water, and there's nothing
you can do about it. Oh, and he wants to know if you're English.
He says he's always wanted an Englishwoman."

Kate laughed aloud at that, a deep, rumbling laugh, causing
the bandit and his men to shrink back a bit in surprise. "Tell him
I'm *your* Englishwoman, and you'll never let me go. So leave us
pass through, and we'll throw this into the bargain."

She tossed Ahmed's watch onto the carton. Immediately the
leader snatched it up and twisted it onto his wrist, holding it up
proudly to the appreciative "oohs" and "aahs" from his men.
Once more he turned to Nayim, smiling, but the tone of his voice
was menacing, betraying him.

"He says that...that now he can tell it's time for us to die."
Nayim subtly raised the barrel of his rifle.

"No...not yet, my friend," Kate said calmly, hoping the bandits had not noticed the threatening move. "Tell him it is instead
time for he and his men to die. If he doesn't let us pass, we'll set
off more of the bombs we've hidden. Many of his people will be
killed, and the rest will hate him for it."

"Wha—oh, yes, of course," Nayim said, catching on.

"And be loud about it when you tell him." Kate eased back
against the jeep, assuming an "I don't give a rat's ass" posture.
She could see the flicker of fear dance across the bandit's eyes as
Nayim spoke, could hear the first grumbles of discontent from
the rest of the gang surrounding him.

The leader moved closer to Nayim, shouting in the little
man's face now, before whirling to confront his increasingly agitated band.

"He thinks we're bluffing, but a part of him is frightened

too, Miss Catherine. However his pride won't let him back down, I fear."

"Tell him," Kate bit her tongue, thinking quickly, "that in appreciation for his letting our convoy pass by, as an acknowledgment of his wise leadership, choosing to protect his men from the wrath of our...bombs, we would have one more gift for him. One that will place him high above all other tribal leaders in the land."

The bandit's icy blue eyes narrowed and sparked as Nayim relayed the message. Perhaps there was a way out of this after all, preserving both his reputation and his dignity. He gestured wildly at Nayim, stomping his feet hard against the rocky ground.

"He wants to know what this wonderful gift is." The trader curled the corner of his mouth at Kate. "Me too, for that matter."

"No," Kate said firmly. "We must have his word of honor first, as the great leader that he is, that he'll let us pass."

The bandit was silent. His breath came in steaming plumes from his nostrils and his brow furrowed as he weighed the offer. Finally, with a broad smile that revealed a mouthful of rotting teeth, he nodded in agreement and extended his hand to Nayim.

"Very well," Nayim said, the relief plain in his voice. "First, the gift, then he'll let us through."

The pilot moved to the rear of the jeep, lifted up the flap, and pulled a small, black leather bag out of the jumble of supplies there. She could see Rebecca in the rear seat, watching her, and silenced her outraged glare when she saw what she was doing, with one of her own.

"Here." Kate moved back to Nayim. "Give it to him. A computer."

Playing along, Nayim made a great show of presenting the laptop to the bandit. If the wristwatch had been impressive to the thieves, the computer was the equivalent of Allah come down from heaven.

"Aah." The bandit leader sighed, awkwardly removing the laptop from its bag. "Macintosh?" He looked hopefully at Kate.

"Um..." Kate half-flirted with the idea of trying to fool him, but thought the better of it. "No. IBM."

The bandit considered that for a moment, before smiling and shrugging his shoulders. "IBM. IBM." he crowed, hoisting the computer up into the air as through it were a war trophy. His band took up the cheer, thrilled beyond all reason with this prize. How great their leader was, to have been gifted with such a fine thing."

Melting into the embraces and congratulations of his men, the bandit turned and shouted something back at Nayim.

"He says we can go."

"Good," Kate sighed. "We don't need to be told twice."

"Well done, Miss Catherine." Nayim looked at her with a newfound sense of appreciation and respect. "I could use you along on my next convoy."

"I'll think about it," Kate replied, her face serious but her eyes sparkling.

They scrambled back into the jeep, Nayim shouting ahead and waving. The convoy once again roared to life and moved out, slowly passing by still, bloodied bodies at the side of the snowy road. Only when they were out of sight of the bandits did Kate allow Becky to sit up. "I'll take that pistol back now," she said, holding out her hand to Ahmed.

Next to her, Kate could feel a shiver run through Rebecca, as the gravity of the situation they'd been through at last dawned on the smaller woman.

"Oh God, Kate." she shook uncontrollably.

"It's okay," she pulled Rebecca close, willing her warmth into her companion, "we made it. We're out of there," she cooed, until the trembling subsided. "Rebecca?"

"What?" Came the faint, thin response.

Kate gave her partner a reassuring squeeze. "About that laptop. You can tell me 'I told you so,' if you want to."

****

Several hours later, at the base of pass, the main body of the convoy continued on to Jalalabad, while Nayim, after sharing an effusive "goodbye" with a grateful convoy leader, peeled the jeep northward, towards Duristan. Kate and Rebecca were more than happy to leave the treacherous pass and the jangled nerves that went with it, behind.

Although it was significantly warmer now that they were out of the mountains, Becky still felt chilled, and was content to doze on and off in the arms of her companion. The times when she'd woken up, temporarily disoriented, she'd found Kate still wide awake and alert like some nocturnal creature of the forest, her strong profile barely visible in the darkness.

Rebecca awakened yet again, but it was different this time. Very different. And then she realized why: the silence. No grinding of gears or groaning of motor; no crunch of rock and gravel against hard tires. All was still.

She heard doors opening, soft voices speaking, the bark of a dog. "Where are we?"

"Home," Nayim said, hopping out of the jeep. "We'll rest here overnight before continuing on in the morning."

Heck, it's got to be nearly morning as it is, Becky considered, stumbling on sleepy legs out of the back seat. But there was Kate's hand on her elbow, steadying her.

"Some day, huh?" The pilot's low, rumbling voice sounded in the inky blackness of the star-less night.

"I'll say," Becky replied, hugging her arms in front of her waist. She breathed in the cool, crisp air that carried on it the scent of wood smoke and spices, and fought to control her drooping eyelids.

Too tired to pick up much of the conversation going on around her, the young blonde meekly followed Kate and the others into a single story building, moving through the shrouded darkness to a rear room where blankets were quickly arranged on the floor.

More distant conversations and the flickering of a candle, and Rebecca found herself tucked beneath one of the warmest blankets she'd ever had the pleasure of wrapping herself in. Fuzzily, she debated with herself whether she should remove her boots, and soon, as vague consciousness gave way to deep sleep, it simply ceased to matter.

****

Rebecca Hanson was dreaming. It made no sense, although it was a good dream. Images. Bursting into view and fading away just as quickly. Flashes of this. Snatches of that. Nothing that her mind's eye could arrange into any sort of order. And just as well, considering how tired she still was. That, and the fact that she felt too darn comfortable to even think of moving. Of waking up. *Just a little while longer...*

Except...except for...something, intruding upon her pleasant dream. A voice? No. A sound? Not likely. Rather, a touch, soft and gentle. Kate? Wait...the touch was more of a jab now, sharp and prodding. What the—

Reluctantly, Rebecca allowed herself to be tugged into wakefulness, and she lifted open one bloodshot green eye, then another.

To see two dark brown eyes, round as saucers, staring back at her. The eyes were attached to a little girl, no more than five or six years of age. She wore a colorful pants set and tunic, and her rich brunette hair was plaited neatly behind her head. In her hand she held a spoon, which had served double duty this morning as Becky's alarm clock.

The flight attendant edged herself up on her elbows, releasing a long breath of air. "Good morning, honey. What's your name?"

Upon hearing the nonsensical syllables pouring from the mouth of this strange, sleepy lady whose hair was a most unusual color, the little girl shrieked with laughter and scampered away.

Well. "Oh, that's a nice name," Becky continued to herself, feeling slightly put out at the child's reaction to her. She held her hand out to thin air. "My name's Becky. Pleased to meet you." She pushed off the warm blanket and sat up, for the first time taking in her surroundings.

Sunlight poured in from a small window behind her; the walls were whitewashed and free of any decoration, and a small wooden table with a doused candle on it stood to the left of the doorway. Other blankets had been neatly folded and moved to the side of the room, with small pillows arranged on top of them. Where the heck was everybody?

A giggle, and Becky looked up to see the little girl poking

her head around the doorway, absent-mindedly chewing on the lip of her spoon.

"Guess I overslept, huh?" She used her fingers to brush her hair into what she hoped was a presentable arrangement and, groaning, got to her feet.

This action elicited another gale of laughter from the child, and Becky could hear the pattering of her feet as she trotted off, jabbering something excitedly to the rest of the house.

*Now then...*Becky looked down at her feet and realized she was bootless. *Funny. I don't remember...*Another, more detailed scan of the room still had her coming up empty. No boots. *Oh well. Time to venture off and figure out what's what.* She started to move towards the doorway, just as a woman appeared.

"Uh, hello. Good morning." Becky thought she'd try it again. To her relief, the woman, dressed in an adult version of the little girl's ensemble, smiled and motioned that she should follow her. "Thanks." Becky returned the smile, and padded in sock-covered feet after the woman.

As they moved through the sparsely furnished dwelling, Becky could see more children underfoot, both boys and girls, in addition to the little one who was obviously regaling her fellows with tales of her encounter, still pointing and laughing in her direction. Following the older woman towards the front of the house, Becky's stomach growled as the first scent of food cooking reached her nose. God, when was the last time she'd eaten, anyway? And where were Kate and the others? Had they just freaking left her here in the middle of Afghanistan with a semi-hysterical child and no boots?

They passed through the main doorway and into an open courtyard encircled by a mud and straw wall. The cooking smells were strongest now.

"Oh. There you are."

Squinting against the bright sunlight, Becky saw a low table laden with food, with Kate, Ahmed, Nayim and several more children sitting on cushions around it. On the far side of the courtyard a cook fire burned, and the woman who'd retrieved Becky returned to it, stirring a large pot that hung over the fire.

"I was wondering if you'd ever wake up." Kate rose and

ambled over to her, grinning.

"You should have woken me," Becky said crossly, conscious of the stares upon her and the titters of laughter coming from the table.

"Nah, we had the time, and besides," Kate licked her palm and did her best to tame an errant cowlick on the top of Becky's head, "I thought you could use the beauty sleep."

"Oh yeah," Becky's tone softened when she saw the mischievous twinkle in her friend's eyes, "I'm a regular sleeping beauty. And a starving one at that."

"C'mon. Let's get you something to eat." Kate led her towards the table.

"What I'd really like—Ow," Becky yelped after stepping on a rather large pebble, "are my boots. You haven't by chance seen them walking around here, have you?"

"Right there by the doorway." Kate pointed the way and indeed, there were the wayward boots. "They were pretty wet after our snowy trip last night. Thought I'd let them dry off a bit. Nothing worse than waking up and sticking your foot into a damp boot."

"Oh, thanks," Becky replied, feeling somewhat chastened. She never would have thought of such a thing herself, and today instead would have bemoaned the state of her soggy feet. She quickly retrieved her footwear and sat down at the space Kate made for her at the table. She tied her bootlaces. "Now, what have I missed?"

"What you have missed," Nayim waved his arms expansively around the courtyard, "is my home and my family. Please, be welcome here. My wife, Rabia," he nodded towards the woman by the fire, who had since been joined by another, younger woman, "our children, and my brother, his wife and their children, all live here," he finished proudly.

"How many people is that?" Becky reached for the piping hot cup of tea that Kate poured for her.

"Oh, about ten or twelve."

"Ten...or twelve." Becky nearly choked on a swallow of the strong, spicy tea. "Uh...you're not sure?"

"It varies," Nayim chuckled, "and with all these children,

they are my poppy flowers. My seeds of joy. It is our way."

"You're fortunate that your brother is here when you're away," Kate observed, chewing on a sweet made of dry milk solids that in a short amount of time this morning she'd developed quite a taste for.

"This is so true, Miss Catherine." Nayim grew solemn. "Particularly during the Russian occupation. Duristan was once twice the size of this. If Masud had not been here when I could not..."

Gazing out past the courtyard, Kate could see other small buildings, little more than huts, really, all buzzing with activity.

"Where is Masud now?" Kate wanted to know.

"With some of our boys, out grazing the sheep in the high pasture. They won't be back for another several days."

"Well, we're sorry to have missed him," Becky said. She tore a piece of brown bread sprinkled with sesame from a nearby loaf. "Maybe we'll see him when we come back."

Nayim nodded agreeably. "This is true, Miss Becky."

"Speaking of which," Ahmed had been fairly silent to this point, "we really need to talk about this last stage of the operation—getting in, and getting out."

"You're right," Kate agreed, detecting the strain on the thin young man's face. Perhaps it was the memories of what he'd done in the service of El Yousef, but the closer they got to his stronghold, Kate noted the more quiet he'd become. And while Nayim still sported his oversized woolen coat, Ahmed had changed into a sleeveless tunic that he wore over a long-sleeved, flowing white shirt, looking more like a local inhabitant than ever.

Nayim issued a few stern commands in his native tongue, and the various children who had gathered 'round the table backed away, reluctantly leaving the adults alone. The trader reached into the pocket of his coat, and produced a well-worn map, which he carefully unfolded. He delicately opened it on the tabletop, smoothing it flat, minding the tattered edges. "Not that I even need this map, you understand," the wisps of his dark beard moved as he chuckled, "but I thought you might like to see where you're going." He eyed Kate and Rebecca carefully over the top of his glasses. "Of course, this is nothing new to Ahmed."

"Of course," the young man agreed, looking past the little courtyard towards the distant, hilly horizon.

"It's fairly open ground between here, Duristan," he stabbed at the map with a crooked finger, "and the northeast region where we're going." A thumb marked the spot. "We'll have to have a care."

"How long will it take us to get there?" Kate asked, trying to gauge the distance on the rudimentary map.

Nayim turned an eye towards the sun. "We'll leave here within the hour, after loading up the jeep with fuel and supplies. It will be rough going, some of it off-road, becoming more mountainous as we go. And then there are the land mines to watch out for, not to mention El Yousef's people hanging about, the closer we get to Birat. I'd say," he thoughtfully massaged his beard, "approximately two, two and a half day's journey at most."

"That's a point, regarding El Yousef's people." Kate pushed away from the table and rocked back on her heels. "We can't just drive right the hell into Birat."

"No," Ahmed agreed. "The town itself is like a miniature country, completely loyal to...the Chosen One. We'd be spotted instantly. I'm confident that if we can get to within nine or ten kilometers of Birat, we can travel the rest of the way in on foot, under cover of darkness." His dark eyes captured Kate's in a weighty stare. "I know exactly where the communications post is hidden in the hillside. Allah knows I helped to set it up myself. They won't be expecting...visitors in the middle of the night, crawling out of the mountains. We can surprise them, get the data we need on here," he produced several computer discs, "and get out. If we do this thing right, we can be out and away before the alarm is raised. And with the right information, data I know how to retrieve," Ahmed tapped the discs, "El Yousef will be out of business."

"Let's talk about the 'getting out' part of the operation some more," Becky said, pulling her knees up under her chin. "I'm still a little fuzzy on that."

"I know a secluded spot about nine kilometers away from Birat where it would be possible to keep the jeep out of sight," Nayim volunteered.

"Good. That'll do." Kate rose. "Then that's where Ahmed and I will meet you and Rebecca once we get out of Birat. If we're not back within twelve hours, or if it looks like things have gone bad," she looked evenly at Nayim, "then I want you to take off. Get yourselves to safety."

"Whoa. Wait a minute." Becky held up the palms of her hands, her face looking like the sky before a thunderstorm. "I don't think we discussed this part of the plan, Kate."

"No, we didn't," Kate replied, her mouth set in a thin line. "And it's not open for discussion. Period."

"But, Kate," the younger woman protested, leaping angrily to her feet, "Rory told me what to look for—the hidden directories, encryption codes...the file extensions. I can *do* this thing."

"I know you can," Kate said quietly, avoiding the wrath of her lover's gaze, "but Ahmed can do it better."

"Kate..." Becky's voice cracked as the sting of Kate's words struck her like a slap in the face. "Please..." The blonde was acutely aware of the scene she was making in front of Ahmed and Nayim, but she didn't give a damn. She tugged on the pilot's arm, spinning her around to face her. "I thought we were in this together."

"We are."

"Then don't shut me out now."

"I'm not Rebecca, believe me." The pilot lifted pained, blue eyes to her. "Stealth is the key to this mission. If we're lucky, El Yousef won't even know we've been there. The more people involved, the greater the risk we'll be detected."

Becky faltered, hard-pressed to argue with that logic. "But, Kate," her eyes grew moist as she took in the tall, impassive figure standing in front of her, "what if...if you need me?" *Oh God*, she thought with no small degree of mortification, *I will not cry. I will not cry.*

"What I *need*," Kate reached out a hand to clasp Becky's shoulder, "is to know that you and Nayim are safely waiting for us, so we can make a quick getaway and make sure El Yousef gets the punishment he deserves."

"But what if the missile strike happens before then?" *Darn it.* Kate's image was starting to swim before her eyes.

"Then what you and Nayim do for us becomes even more important. We'll double-time it back to you," Kate said calmly, as if it were the most logical, certain thing in the world, "and you'll have to have that Jeep fired up and ready to go. Right, Nayim?"

"Oh, absolutely, Miss Kate." The trader smiled. "We take off like Luke Skywalker."

"There, you see?" Kate grazed Becky's chin with the crook of an index finger, forcing the smaller woman to look her in the eye. "Please," the pilot's voice dropped low so that only Becky could hear. "I need you to do this one thing for me. Promise me, okay, Champ?"

Conflicting emotions swirled within the flight attendant. She'd imagined herself sticking by Kate's side through the whole thing, but now...heck, what her friend was saying made sense. And, she wouldn't be left alone. Nayim would be with her, too. Such a sweet man. Still, it hurt to be left out of the final exercise, no matter how much she tried to rationalize those feelings. More than that, she knew what lay at the core of her distress. It was her concern for the well being of Captain Catherine Phillips. Why, just the thought of something happening to Kate made her stomach seize up as though she'd been on one hell of a roller-coaster ride. Well, whenever and wherever Kate needed her, she would be there. She would not let her down.

"I promise," Becky said at last, biting her lip and blinking back the tears. "But you promise me something, too."

"Anything."

"Come back to me, Kate."

"Are you kidding?" The pilot pulled her into an embrace at that. "The devil himself couldn't keep me away."

Chapter
17

Two days of hard driving and two nights of rough sleeping later found the little group about a half day's ride away from the spot Nayim suggested as a rendezvous. They had encountered no one in passing save for a stray goat or two, and though the surrounding countryside was beautiful in a stark, barren way, there were constant reminders of the terrible battles that had exacted such a toll upon the land. The roadside was littered with war debris: supply drums, empty shell casings, burned out field guns. Electrical pylons lay on their sides like fallen giants, the power cables long since harvested for other usage, for electrical power was nonexistent in this part of the land unless it was generator supplied. Infrastructure of any sort was but a fleeting memory.

The lowlands gave way to higher pastures and steppes, bisected by icy-cold streams supplied by the great mountains to the north. Birat lay somewhere in those hills, waiting. As they had the night before, they'd set up two small pup-sized tents and constructed a tiny fire. It was too much to ask that the willowy tongues of flame do much in the way of generating heat, but it was enough to boil water for tea, cook rice, and warm a bit of spiced beef and mutton.

Becky had watched Kate's face in the firelight: the warm glow that emanated from her eyes, the shadows of her cheeks, the hollow of her neck. Though the pilot was physically near, she remained remote, unresponsive.

There hadn't been much conversation between them at all over the past couple of days, and Becky had told herself that this was simply Kate's way of focusing, of preparing. She'd watched her companion gradually withdraw and had let it happen; it was all part of the plan, wasn't it? There were the quiet conversations between Kate and Ahmed; that pistol that Kate carried, and the rifles, too. Becky had seen them, and said nothing. She was in Kate's world now, and there was nothing for it but to simply trust her to do what was right and good.

The alternative was too horrific to contemplate.

And so she'd clung to the thinnest of emotional tethers between herself and Kate; telling herself that it would be enough, yet fearing at the same time that in the darkness where Kate now dwelt, their connection might be severed and the pilot would simply slip away.

Finally, they'd tumbled into their sleeping bags, exhausted. Ahmed and Nayim were in one tent, and Becky and Kate in the other. If the two Muslim men noticed anything...different, about the two women's relationship, they'd kept it to themselves. Perhaps they were too tired to even care. Weariness plagued them all. And it wasn't over yet. They were to be up at dawn for the last leg of the journey, and from there, Kate and Ahmed would strike out on foot for Birat.

By this time tomorrow, Becky thought, gazing up at the battered green canvas above her, *maybe we'll be on our way back to Duristan, and all this...stuff...will be behind us.* That's what she told herself anyway, while at the same time wondering why, if she were so confident, she was lying here wide awake in this tent with her stomach churning, when she might otherwise still have been sleeping?

Rebecca checked her wristwatch. If Nayim were running true to form, it would be at least another hour before she heard the pots and pans being knocked about in preparation for breakfast.

Damn.

She drew in a deep breath of air, feeling the chill that had

descended during night, knowing too that part of it came from
the distance she felt between herself and her partner. Oh, she'd
fallen asleep in Kate's arms as she always did, marveling at the
warmth the taller woman generated even in this far-off place, but
there was a barrier between them, just the same.

She wondered if Kate felt it, too.

Her vision had adjusted to the dark, and she rolled over onto
her side, her eyes fastening on Kate's face. Her heart leapt in her
chest as it did every time she awoke and saw Kate like this,
which wasn't often enough; the pilot invariably rose before her.

It was always a secret delight of Rebecca's to see her in
repose, her face relaxed and expressionless. Unguarded.

It was insane, she thought dimly, here in the middle of a
virtual war zone, but she could not help herself. She reached out
and let her hand gently caress Kate's face, then travel down her
throat, along the line of her shoulder, to the corded strength of
her arm. That touch, that feeling, was something she'd been
missing, and desperately craved.

Becky did not turn away when she suddenly found two blue
eyes peering at her in the darkness. She silently challenged her
lover, knowing she'd won when she saw the flash of amusement
in those eyes. For one dizzying moment her world turned topsy-
turvy, and then she found herself seated firmly astride Kate's
body. She saw the film of desire that glazed the pilot's eyes, felt
the air rush from her body at the shock of the heat radiating up
from the tall woman's naked skin, for even here in the wilder-
ness she'd insisted on sleeping unencumbered.

Kate's lips parted and Becky could hear the tempo of her
breathing quicken; it matched the pounding of her own heart.
She lowered herself down to Kate, stretching free of the clothing
the pilot's expert hands quickly removed from her, relishing the
electrifying contact of skin upon skin. Their mouths met in a
slow, lingering kiss that nearly made Becky's heart catch in her
throat, so thrilled was she at this tangible affirmation that her
bond with Kate was still everything she'd told herself it was, and
more. She wanted to laugh and weep at the same time, for the joy
of it.

The sleeping giant had awakened, and Becky felt the intensity of the kiss change, deepen, even as powerful hands roamed over her body, teasing her, driving her to distraction, and then finally possessing her as none had ever before. Kate was everything she'd ever wanted in a lover, body and soul, always giving, and never taking but what was freely offered.

Their passion set the air within the tent on fire; there was a furnace of energy and heat rising from their bodies. The heady scent of their perspiration mingled with the earthy aroma of the ground beneath them and the bittersweet fragrance of dying apple blossoms, carried in on the wind from a distant meadow.

Becky rolled back on top of Kate, letting her full weight rest upon her body. The pilot's damp skin clung to hers, and she felt long arms tightly wrap themselves around her smaller form. She returned the embrace, holding on for dear life as she thrust toward climax, kissing the silent woman beneath her with her mouth open as she came, crying out Kate's name.

Becky stayed on top of her, feeling the tension drain from her own body with that release, helpless to stave off the sleepiness that quickly followed such an outpouring of emotion and the passion that accompanied it. And still Kate's hands continued to roam of their own accord all over her body, holding, stroking, finding her most sensitive places. As their breathing slowed and their hearts steadied, Becky took confidence and strength from the arms that held her fast. And as her eyes slipped shut, as she drifted off to the sleep that worry had previously denied her, she released her vow into the faint, glow of the light before dawn.

"I love you, Kate. And I always will."

She didn't need to see the pilot's face as she spoke the words, didn't require any sort of response. The fact that they were here, together, and connected in the most intimate of ways, was enough.

****

For about the tenth time in as many minutes, Rebecca Hanson checked her watch and looked nervously to the north. Give them twelve hours, Kate had said. Okay. So that meant they had eleven left.

Plenty of time, right?

It was the not knowing that was killing her. She'd known that they couldn't risk any communication device where El Yousef's people could pick up the transmissions, but God. What she wouldn't give for a cell phone right now.

"Please, Miss Becky," Nayim glanced up from where he sat on a low rock, making much needed repairs to his *pakol,* a woolen hat favored by many of the former mujahideen. "Don't be a bundle of nerves, yes?" He grinned at her as he threaded a needle through his hat. "You will wear yourself out in no time flat. And then where will you be when your friend returns? No use, I say. You will be of no use to anyone."

"I know," Becky slumped against the rocky overhang which partially obscured the Jeep from prying eyes. "I'm sorry. I...I can't help it, I guess." She sighed heavily and crossed her arms, gazing out in the direction she'd last seen Kate and Ahmed. They'd set out in late afternoon, each bearing light backpacks and armed with Kalashnikovs, hoping to make most of the distance to the hills outside Birat before darkness firmly took hold.

The going would be rough: in staying off the main road they'd have to traverse rocky plains and narrow gorges, all the way to Birat itself. Then, it would simply be a matter of watching, waiting, and striking.

Nayim took pity on the young blonde. He had seen back in Duristan how much the thought of being left behind had pained her; knew as well as she did that the odds of this mission succeeding were "iffy" at best. But fighting the odds was something Nayim Ceru understood well: whether it was the guerrilla warfare against the hated Russian invaders, or the struggle from within to overthrow the hated demagoguery of the Taliban. One had to try...to have hope. Without that, what point was there in living? Now, the pieces in the final act of this play were set in motion. All he and the girl could do was bide their time and stay out of sight. But that didn't mean they had to go stir crazy in the process.

"Something to eat, Miss Becky?" He put the *pakol* aside and reached for his backpack.

"No. I'm not hungry, thanks."

"Would you like to read?"

"Have you got something with you?" Becky turned hopeful eyes upon the little Muslim.

"No," he replied, shaking his head. I thought you might have..."

"Well, I don't." Becky tried to keep the nervous irritation out of her voice. She knew the trader was only trying to help.

"I don't suppose..." Once more Nayim reached for his backpack. "It is forbidden of course, but I have always been tempted by that which is denied to me." He rummaged around in his sack, at last proudly producing a battered deck of cards. "Do you know how to play?"

Becky's eyes widened at the sight. "Do I?" she exclaimed, sidling up to the trader and plucking the cards from his hand. She plopped down next to him, pushing up the sleeves of her robe. "We're going to play the most exciting, thrilling card game I know. It requires great skill, cunning, and nerves of steel."

"Are we going to play poker?" Nayim was fairly quivering with delight at the prospect of playing the forbidden game.

"No." Becky's green eyes narrowed in the late afternoon sunlight. "Let me tell you about a little game I like to call...Go Fish."

****

"That's Birat, over there." Ahmed pointed to the northwest. There, shimmering like a mirage against a horizon that was a blazing palette of purple, rose, and gold, was their objective. "We'd better stay here and wait for full dark before we try to draw any closer, don't you think?"

"Agreed," Kate said, watching the young Kosovar sit down heavily on a graded hillside. He tiredly popped open a canteen of water. They'd pushed themselves hard, crossing the open, hard-scrabble ground between the rendezvous point and Birat, taking care to swing wide and approach El Yousef's stronghold from the southeast. Along the way, they'd had to stay on alert for El Yousef's patrols, of which they'd seen several, as well as watch for hidden land mines. The mines were particularly worrisome; they'd had to keep a sharp eye out for telltale signs: small stone piles, craters marking areas of prior explosions—while at the same time struggling to keep their footing while crossing the difficult terrain.

The patrols were of less concern; they seemed to be operating routinely and sticking to the main road leading to and from Birat. The pilot and Ahmed had steered clear of the road, taking care to keep it always at least a kilometer or two to the west.

"Drink?"

"Thanks." Kate reached for the canteen, and took several deep drafts before handing it back to him. She sat down next to Ahmed, catching her breath and stretching out her legs. She ran the arm of her robe across her forehead, in a vain effort to remove some of the perspiration that had formed there.

This damn thing.

She looked down at her now-soiled tunic, fighting the overwhelming urge she had to rid herself of the native attire she wore on top of her khakis. Gritting her teeth, she resisted, knowing how important it was to maintain at least some attempt at disguise, lest they be spotted from a distance.

"So, how long has it been since you were here last?" Kate asked, opening her backpack and pulling out a battered pair of Russian field glasses that Nayim had supplied her with.

"Oh, about a year and a half, I think." Ahmed leaned back on his elbows, his eyes fixed on the last flickers of sunlight disappearing beneath the horizon. "Though it seems a lifetime ago."

"I wonder how much the layout has changed since then." Kate peered through the binoculars, bringing Birat into focus. The village itself looked like a more modern version of Duristan: concrete block houses replaced mud and straw; and there were more vehicles on the street than camels and horse-drawn carts. The glow of lighting shone through some of the windows; generator powered, Kate surmised, all this a result of El Yousef's well-laundered funds pouring into the village. People roamed the dust-clogged streets—women with their faces covered, men fully bearded, and there were children too, occasionally pulling along goats with bells about their necks. Kate could almost hear the thin jingling sound of them on the early evening breeze.

To all outward appearances, Birat was a typical Afghan village, if a bit more prosperous looking than most. But it was the blight at the edge of the village that drew Kate's attention: El Yousef's compound. There had to be at least forty tents, outbuildings, a drilling field, trucks, and a munitions depot, not to mention the armed, uniformed men crawling throughout the encampment. And, of particular interest to Kate, was a well-worn trail that led out from the facility and up into the hills. Somewhere, in the rocky gray-brown hillside, lay the communications center: her ultimate objective.

"Let me have a look." Ahmed crawled next to her.

Kate handed him the binoculars.

"No," he said, bringing the village into focus, "it looks pretty much the same as I remember it. And why would the Chosen One worry about such things? This is his adopted home. The villagers are his followers now, selling their identities for full bellies, a warm hearth and a cold rifle. He feels safe here," Ahmed lowered the glasses and turned to Kate, "and that will be his downfall."

"I'm counting on it," Kate said, and she shoved the glasses back into her bag.

"Catherine..."

Something in Ahmed's voice gave her pause, tugged at something deep inside of her, and she raised her head in time to catch the haunted, haggard look that had no right to be on the face of one so young.

"I...I want to thank you for...for letting me come along. For giving me the opportunity to make good on...what I've done."

"I think you've got that the wrong way around," Kate replied quickly, earnestly. "We couldn't do this without you, Ahmed."

"I wonder," he said, gazing off into the horizon, "if even this will be enough. The debt I owe is so great. I've hurt so many—" He rubbed at his eye with his fist. "I hear them at night, you know. The spirits of those I've wronged. They demand justice."

"What's done is done. There's nothing you can do about it

now, no matter how much you may want to," Kate said, understanding this truth so well herself. "The important thing is, that you regret what you've done, and you're trying to make it right. Just think of the people whose lives will be saved because of the work we do here."

"I know." Ahmed picked up a loose stone and tossed it down the hillside, watching it loosen other small pebbles along the way and raise gentle puffs of dust in its wake. "But I wonder. Will it be enough?" He lifted his head to Kate and captured her in a stare that reached into her very soul. "Justice...will have its day."

Kate silently nodded, feeling his pain and knowing there was nothing she could do about it. The young scientist had made more than his share of mistakes and had gotten himself caught up in something bigger than he could have ever possibly imagined. Had stumbled into a world where his science was used on behalf of terrorism, with frightful consequences. It was not her place to judge him, although somehow she suspected there was no sentence any court could render that was worse than the misery he'd imposed upon himself.

"Ssssh." Kate suddenly cocked her head, listening. "Do you hear that?"

"What?" Ahmed's demeanor instantly changed, and he stiffened, recovering himself. "What is it?"

The pilot turned towards the south, as the distant *thump-thump-thump* drew closer. "A helicopter," she said grimly, gulping back the fear inexplicably gripped her. It was flying from the direction of the rendezvous. "Take cover."

* * * * * * * * * *

"Jack of diamonds." Nayim looked warily over his hand of cards towards the young blonde sitting opposite him.

Rebecca carefully examined the few cards she held, before answering. "Go fish," she said at last, her voice as hard as her stare.

Nayim sighed, and plucked a fresh card up from the pool. He shook his head. The new card did him no good.

"All right." Becky took a sip of the tea that Nayim had prepared for them both, and licked her lips. "Three of clubs."

"Three of clubs," Nayim repeated, scanning his hand. He gave Rebecca a baleful glare. "Three of clubs." Reluctantly, he pulled the card from his hand and flung it towards his opponent. "There. I hope you two will be very happy together."

"Oh, we will." Triumphantly, she laid down the complete set of four "three" cards, emptying her hand. "I win again."

"Damn," Nayim swore, then remembered himself. "You'll pardon me for that, Miss Becky. But this is a most challenging game, this Go Fish." He gathered the cards up. "We play again."

"Are you sure?" Becky asked dubiously. "That makes it ten games to nothing."

"No, no, no." Nayim waved her off. "One more game, please. I think I'm just getting the hang of it. Then," he grinned devilishly at her, "you wait and see how I will simply demolish my brother, Masud. He will stand no chance."

"Oh, I see," Becky chuckled, reaching for a refill from a battered teapot that had clearly seen better days.

"Wait." Nayim's hand shot out, stilling Rebecca's. "Listen." The tension was plain in his voice.

"Wha—" Becky fell silent, her hears straining, and then she heard it. A distant thumping sound. "Why, that sounds like—"

"Helicopter." Nayim bolted to his feet, the cards spilling from his hand. He frantically kicked dirt onto the small fire, trying to extinguish it.

"Here." Becky tossed the remaining liquid from the teapot onto the flames, and with a sputtering sizzle, the fire gave up its last.

"Quick...take cover under that ledge." Grabbing their backpacks and bedrolls, Nayim directed them both towards the rocky overhang that partially concealed the jeep. "Get down," he cried, pressing Becky low against the ground.

The helicopter had to be right over them now, buzzing like an angry bumblebee that would not abandon its prize flower.

"Stay perfectly still," Nayim's voice hissed in her ear.

Becky was worried now. They hadn't seen anyone in two days. They'd figured it should have been safe to build the small fire, even if they were only 10 kilometers outside of Birat.

Or maybe not.

"Do you think he spotted us?"

Nayim tightened his hold on her. "I'm not sure..."

Suddenly, the ground in front of them seemed to pucker and writhe, kicking up a furious line of dirt and dust that reminded Becky of a fast-approaching hail storm. But this was no hail.

Rat-a-tat-a-tat-tat-tat!

Becky screamed.

****

Darkness had descended upon Birat like an old blanket, snug and providing adequate cover in some areas, thin and threadbare in others. The village itself was tucking in for the evening, the household sounds diminishing and the lights winking out. But Kate noted with some consternation that the area surrounding the compound was still fairly well illuminated.

They had crept closer to the stronghold after the helicopter had passed them by, and now they were positioned in a small depression on a rocky incline that ran all the way down to the edge of the camp. Staying low, they would be invisible to any eyes scanning the hills from below. But their position afforded them a good view of El Yousef's complex, and was adjacent to the hillside where Ahmed said the communications post lay hidden in a cave.

Kate checked her watch. "Still too damn much activity," she said.

Soldiers were still in plain sight within the camp: tinkering with vehicles, casually conversing, moving up and down the hillside from the communications post. One large tent, centrally located, had much activity centered around it; Kate suspected it had to be El Yousef's. A large generator was visible at the rear of it, and the tent fairly glowed from within, humming with an incandescent energy all its own. *The bastard's in there,* Kate sighed. *I know it.* She tightened her grip on the rifle by her side. Taking out El Yousef wasn't part of the mission, she knew. But if he happened to get in the way, well, that would be his misfortune.

"We've got time, Catherine," Ahmed said. "We can afford to be patient."

"I know. But we've got to be on the move and out of here by 0300 hours if we want to make the rendezvous."

"No problem." Ahmed's white teeth flashed in the darkness. "I won't be a minute, once I get my hands on his computers."

"I'll hold you to that." Kate returned the smile. "Hey—here comes another patrol."

Sure enough, snaking its way towards the camp on the main road was another miniature convoy. An armored personnel carrier, a couple of Russian-made trucks with machine guns mounted in the rear and...

Fuck.

Kate grabbed the binoculars from her bag, knowing they wouldn't do much good in the dark. *What I wouldn't give for a pair of night-vision glasses.* Instead, she willed the patrol towards the yellow-white glow of the artificial lighting bathing the central area of the compound. If they would just head there.

They did. The little convoy motored down the main thoroughfare of the camp. And with that, Kate had her worst fear realized. A broken-down, covered jeep chugged along behind one of the trucks.

"Is that—?" Ahmed's voice, strained in the darkness.

"I think so."

She's gotta be okay. She will be fine.

Soldiers tumbled out of the vehicles, laughing and slapping one another on the back. From the jeep, three soldiers emerged, dragging a woman behind them. Her hands were tied behind her back. She wore a green-trimmed *shalwar kameez*, spattered with darkened stains. *Blood.* One of the soldiers shoved her from behind; she stumbled and nearly fell. But it was enough to dislodge the scarf from her head, revealing short, blonde locks.

"Oh God, it's Rebecca," Kate groaned, feeling her stomach do a flip-flop.

"What in Allah's name could have happened?"

"I don't know." Kate struggled to get a grip on her emotions as she watched her partner being roughly escorted to a tent at the edge of the camp. "Maybe the chopper spotted them. Or maybe the patrol...if we'd only known they ranged that far out of Birat." Her heart sank. *No. Stop it. This is not the time for second-guessing. Focus.*

Surrounded by soldiers, Rebecca walked with her head held high. She turned her dirtied, tear streaked face towards the hills. Kate's heart lurched when she saw the emerald eyes she knew so well seem to scan the terrain in the darkness, searching, but not finding.

I'm here, Kate wanted to cry out, to reassure her. But the words died in her throat.

A hand on her arm. "Is there any sign of Nayim?"

The pilot tracked the binoculars back to the convoy, watching the soldiers for long minutes as they stowed their gear and powered down the vehicles. "No," she said at last. "I didn't see him."

Ahmed sat back against the side of the ravine, his palms resting on his thighs. He looked as though the air had been blown out of him. "Well, perhaps he's still out there. He got away, somehow."

Kate turned moist blue eyes to the distraught scientist. "Do you really think he would've left Rebecca alone?"

Ahmed stared at Kate and said nothing; his silence was the only answer he could give. Finally his shoulders sagged, as he resigned himself to the implication of the pilot's words. He pulled up his knees to his chin, and rested his forehead against a fist he'd propped against his kneecap. "What do we do, now?" he asked, his voice muffled, trembling.

"Good question."

Well, the mission was fucked.

Nothing new about that, Kate thought, she'd been in such tight spots before. But now...God, what Rebecca must be going through at this moment. She had to get her out of there. And yet, rescuing the girl would surely raise an alarm. They would have no shot at getting to the cave undetected. The objective of the mission would be lost.

Damn.

Kate sat back on her heels. It had all come to this. To travel all this way, to have made so many sacrifices, to be this close to the goal.

Getting El Yousef. Bringing him down. Destroying him.

He was her obsession. The fire that fueled her. He was a cold-blooded killer who had no right to a life on this earth. She had wanted to personally dispatch him to hell, she could admit that to herself now.

She looked up at the sky above, where only a few stars were visible among the clouds, and breathed in deeply. On the air she could taste the pungent tang of the ancient earth that surrounded her—timeless, enduring. She was vaguely aware of Ahmed next to her, his dark eyes fixed upon her, expectantly. He would do whatever she ordered, there was no doubt of that now.

This was her mission, as it had always been. Ahmed had simply been another tool she'd used to bring her closer to her goal, but she would have gotten here eventually, one way or another, she was sure of that. Zeroing in on her target like a smart-bomb, maneuvering her way through the twists and turns of the chase until—*blam*—mission accomplished.

Kate released a deep, shuddering breath, letting it go, letting it all go. The choices were clear. She could penetrate the communications post and destroy El Yousef, possibly saving countless lives in the bargain. Or she could rescue the frightened young blonde in the tent down below, who'd gotten herself involved in an operation where she had no place being.

It wasn't even close.

Kate shouldered her rifle and tilted her head towards the compound. "We've got to get down there."

Chapter
18

Rebecca Hanson squeezed her eyes shut against the images that kept playing before her mind like a bad movie.

The helicopter swooping down on them.

The bullets flying.

A scream—her own—so loud and so long that it had only ceased when she'd run out of air.

And then she was frozen, unable to breathe at all, and had simply huddled there, waiting to die. Nayim had thrown himself next to her, trying to press her as far under the rocky ledge as he could. He was shouting at her...something, but she could not hear him for the whining sound of the helicopter, and the blinding whirlwind kicked up by the rotor blades.

Eventually, the firing stopped and the helicopter set down. And then there was a new sound...motor engines.

Wheels grinding against gravel.

Feet hitting the ground and running.

Shouts.

The sound of firearms being slapped into hands.

"Nayim, we've got to get out of here." She'd found her voice at last, choking against the bitter dirt that filled her nose and mouth, blinking back the tears that streamed from her eyes as she struggled to regain her vision.

"Nayim."

But the trader had not answered her.

More shouts, and suddenly she'd felt the weight of him roughly removed from her. She'd been pulled to her feet, coughing, wheezing, and when her vision finally cleared, she'd wished to God that it hadn't.

Half a dozen rifles, pointed at her.

A man in fatigues standing scant inches from her, his deeply lined face twisted in fury, screaming demands in her face in a language she had no hope of understanding.

And then there was Nayim. Lying on the ground amidst the scattered deck of cards, staring sightlessly at the sky through broken spectacles.

She'd felt herself go numb as they tied her hands and threw her in the back of the jeep; she'd allowed it to happen, welcoming the numbness. Anything was better than embracing the reality in which she now found herself. This wasn't supposed to be happening. None of it was real. But the scene played on and on, as indelible upon her consciousness as the blood, Nayim's blood, which stained her tunic.

"I ask you again, what were you doing out there? Where were you coming from?"

They'd figured out fairly quickly, what with her blonde hair and green eyes, that she wasn't a native, and once they'd gotten her back to Birat they'd produced a soldier who spoke passable English to question her. But he kept on asking her the same questions, over and over, getting angrier by the minute.

Well, that was his problem. She would never tell him the truth.

"I—I was just looking around."

"Liar."

She never saw it coming. He slapped her, hard, and as her head snapped sideways she nearly fell.

"You are a SPY," the soldier roared, taking a threatening step towards her.

Becky flinched, hating herself for it, and wondered for perhaps the thousandth time since she'd been captured where Kate was, and was she safe. She'd seen no sign of the pilot and Ahmed since she'd been brought in, nor had her captors mentioned having any other prisoners. So that meant that perhaps there was still a chance that the mission could succeed. And the mission was all that mattered now. Perhaps she could keep these terrorists distracted down here, while Kate and Ahmed got in and out of the communications center. *I can still help,* the flight attendant thought, and she made the decision to focus on that objective.

She had to try.

For Kate.

"No. You've got it wrong. I—I'm a writer. Working on a story." Becky thought fast. "I want to...to let the world know of the troubles of the Afghan people."

"You lie." The solider raised his arm again, as if to strike.

"Enough," A deep voice sounded behind her.

"But Rashid. She is lying, can't you see?"

"I said enough, Mazar," the man said, stepping forward from the shadows, his hand moving to the pistol he wore at his side.

Becky turned slightly to see a tall, bearded man standing there, wearing fatigues and a turban. His eyes were dark, like his skin, and in another life Becky might have found him attractive.

"I'll take over from here," he said smoothly, pushing the soldier back on his heels, away from Becky.

"Sorry about that." He offered her a cold smile. "Now. You will tell me please. Who was the man traveling with you?"

"He...he was my guide."

"Guide? From where?"

"From...Jalalabad, I think," Becky said, worrying that Nayim's family might be at risk if she divulged the correct information. "My...my editors set up the deal."

"Well...*writer*," he smiled again, "what is it that you will tell your readers about our troubles?"

The man spoke perfect school-boy English, Becky had to give him that, and as he stepped slowly around her, looking her up and down, she noticed with a sinking feeling that he had her backpack in his hand. Well, there was nothing for it but to play out the string.

"I—I would tell them that war has torn this land apart," she

stammered, shifting the position of her arms slightly to relieve
the pressure of the rope digging into her wrists. "But there are
good people here, people who are suffering terrible hardships
now, but who are willing to work together to bring about a
peace."

"Interesting," he said, pausing for a moment as if to consider her words. "Well," he shrugged, 'I am from Saudi Arabia,
actually, so I can't say I really give a damn about all of that rot.
But I find it curious," he reached into her backpack and pulled
out her wallet, "that *you* say you are a writer, but your identification indicates you are in the employ of Orbis Airlines."

Rashid tossed the wallet onto a table in the middle of the
tent. It landed with a dull *thunk,* flopping open and displaying
Becky's smiling Orbis photo ID.

"Oh, that," Becky said faintly, feeling her head starting to
spin.

Rashid dropped all pretense at civility, and his features
turned to stone. Omar had told him of his little misadventures in
Paris with the woman before him. He knew well the risk she
posed to the cause. She and her colleague, that irksome pilot.

"You can talk to me, Miss Rebecca Hanson," Rashid stepped
closer to her, his dark eyes glittering, "or you can speak with the
Chosen One. And I can assure you, the latter would be most
unpleasant."

* * * * * * * * *

"Okay." Ahmed pressed his back against a storage crate, his
voice a breathless whisper. "I don't think we can get any closer
Catherine, and not be detected."

"She's still got to be in that tent," Kate said in a low rumble. "We haven't seen anyone leave for quite a while." The pilot
checked her watch: nearly 2400 hours. Fighting every instinct in
her body that had told her to charge down into the camp and free
Rebecca, she'd forced herself to stay with Ahmed up in the hills
and wait until activity below decreased. As the compound had
quieted down, she and Ahmed had crept closer, until now they
were in some sort of storage area facing the tent where the flight

attendant was being held.

"The communications center is right up there," Ahmed pointed to a spot about halfway up the hillside behind them, "and there's a series of camouflaged satellite dishes on the top." A dusty path trailed upwards towards the post, and from their vantage point the entrance to the cave was visible as a slight change in coloration from the rocky ground surrounding it. "They've got blackout curtains shielding it. If you didn't know it was there—"

"You wouldn't," Kate finished for him, gazing wistfully at her one-time objective. "Okay," she said, sucking a deep breath and returning her attention to the rescue at hand. "Same plan of attack, different target. I want to get in and out of here, undetected. And if we can get a hold of one of their vehicles," she bobbed her head towards where a number of jeeps and trucks were parked, just off the main camp road, "so much the better."

"But that guard doesn't look like he's going anywhere." Ahmed cast a glance towards the armed soldier standing outside the tent. "And there are at least two more men inside the tent." The young scientist's dark eyes tracked back to Kate. "What do we do?"

Kate rubbed the back of her neck, thinking, detecting the perspiration there despite the coolness of the night. "I don't want to wait any longer," she said flatly, not letting her mind consider what might be happening to Rebecca inside that tent. "We're going in."

Foot traffic in the camp was nearly nonexistent, and had been for the last hour or so. Clearly, as Ahmed had suggested earlier, El Yousef and his people felt that the barren land around Birat held no threat to them. Oh, there were guards posted at the main entrance to the camp at the village's edge, and several soldiers walked patrol routes through the compound at intervals that Kate had already timed. But she'd seen military installations on heightened states of alert plenty of times before, and this base was not one of them.

"Well, we can't just walk in there," Ahmed hissed in the darkness, his eyes flashing.

"Oh, yeah?" The pilot gave him a sly tilt of her head. "Why not?"

* * * * * * * * * *

Malik Haqqani restlessly shifted his weight from one foot to the other, and tried to get his mind off his growling stomach. It had been hours since dinner, and his relief was late. For the love of Allah, where was he? Malik's mouth watered uncontrollably as he thought of making a quick detour by the cook-tent on his way back to the barracks for the night. His past midnight forays there had always proven successful, and he saw no reason why this night should be any different. Some apricots, cheese, a bit of the lamb left over from the evening meal—all washed down with goat's milk. He'd get away with it again; that lazy cook, Pahlawan, was never any the wiser.

Malik peered down the dirt road of the camp; still no relief man. And no one about that he could ask to go fetch him. Malik toyed with the idea of leaving his post—what harm would it do, really—but thought the better of it, knowing that Rashid was still inside. Past experience had told him that crossing the Chosen One's right-hand man, might cost him the loss of his own hand, or worse.

No, better to wait until Rashid or that wretched lieutenant of his, Mazar, came out. They'd been in there for some hours, questioning the girl, and from time to time Malik had heard voices raised. Several times, he'd heard the woman cry out. He couldn't speak English so he couldn't be certain of what was being said, but he knew that one way or the other, Rashid would get what he wanted out of the prisoner. He always did.

Malik sighed, turning his gaze up to the starless night. He sniffed at the air, detecting the faint hint of rain. The chill told him that the fall season was on its way, and with that, the rains and snow would not be far behind. Hmnn...perhaps, if there was still a cook fire burning, he would heat the goat's milk, instead.

"Hey. You there."

At first, Malik thought it was his relief. But the soldier approaching him looked more like one of the armed volunteers from Birat, dressed as he was in an Afghan man's tunic, vest, and turban. And he spoke in the native *Dari,* rather than the language of the Chosen One and his closest advisors.

The soldier was not alone.

"We've got another one here for you." He had his rifle pointed at a new prisoner, another woman. She was tall, taller than any female Malik had ever seen. Her hands were tied off at the wrist, and her features were properly covered by her *burqa.* All Malik could see were two eyes flashing at him in the darkness. For a brief moment he felt fear at the wrath of the woman's stare, but he chased that away by tightening his grip on his AK47. He and his fellow soldier were more than enough to handle this woman. And once Rashid and Mazar got their hands on her, well, that would be that.

"Always room for one more," Malik replied, laughing at his own joke. Perhaps he could get this fellow to hunt down his relief for him or, better yet, take over.

"You can have her." The soldier gave his prisoner a rough shove, and she fell to the ground in a heap.

Malik chuckled at the woman's distress, and the soldier's laughter joined in. He walked over to her, and gave her a nudge with his boot. "Clumsy, are we? Come on. Get up, before I lose my patience with you." Malik turned to the soldier, smiling. He seemed like a good sort. "Listen," he began, "I wonder if you wouldn't do me a favor." Out of the corner of his eye, he saw the prisoner struggling to her feet. "I've been waiting for my relief to—"

A *crack* sounded in his ears, and Malik dully realized that something hard had made contact with his own skull. As the darkness descended, his hunger pangs were forgotten.

* * * * * * * * * *

"Be right back," Kate whispered, looking furtively up and down the deserted compound. Ahmed took up watch at the tent as though he were the guard, and the pilot quickly dragged the unconscious soldier back behind the storage crates where they'd been hiding. There, she gagged him and bound him securely with the rope that had been loosely tied around her own wrists. *So far so good*, she thought, grabbing the rifle she'd left there. Now, they would have to move quickly. Once they'd gotten Rebecca free, she wasn't sure how long a guardless prison tent would remain unnoticed.

Glancing both ways up and down the compound, she crossed over to the tent where Ahmed stood guard. "Okay," she said tightly. "Same deal. You lead me in. That should give us a few seconds to figure out who's who, before the surprise wears off. Got it?"

"Got it," Ahmed said hoarsely, his eyes wild in the night.

"Listen." Kate put a steadying hand on his shoulder. "Don't fire your weapon unless you absolutely have to, okay?"

The young scientist gulped, and nodded in the affirmative.

"Good."

Kate slid her rifle inside her *shalwar kameez,* and pressed her wrists together as though they were bound. It would do. All she needed was a second or two, at most.

"Let's go."

She burst through the tent flap, giving the illusion of having been shoved. Ahmed was hard on her heels, babbling something, she knew, about her being his prisoner.

Kate's eyes scanned the interior like twin laser beams, instantly locating Rebecca. The young woman was sitting in a chair in the middle of the tent, her back facing her, her head bowed. *Guards...*There were only two that she could locate. A tall man, bearded, standing right next to the flight attendant, his hand raised as if to strike her.

And another man, shorter, with ferret-like eyes, leaned casually against a nearby table, apparently enjoying the show.

The pilot instantly concluded that the bigger man presented the most imminent danger, at least as far as Rebecca was concerned, and so she continued her tumble directly into him, taking him off his feet. Ferret-man leaped forward, alarmed, and from the corner of her eye Kate saw Ahmed slip next to him, lifting the butt-end of his rifle towards the back of his head.

Kate pushed off from the big man, and in one smooth motion swept her rifle free from her robes and regained her balance. The man was furious, his dark eyes fastened upon her, shouting something unintelligible that the pilot guessed was not a pleasant greeting. His turban askew, the big man clawed for the pistol at his side, freeing it from his holster.

"Move, and she dies," he screeched in English at last, and he pivoted on his back towards Rebecca. But before he'd even completed the sentence, Kate had anticipated his move and was on him, her scarf fallen away from her head, towering above him like a dark avenger.

"I don't *think* so," she growled, bringing the stock of her rifle down hard across his jaw. The big man slumped to the ground, blood flowing freely from his mouth. Kate kicked the pistol clear, and turned to confirm that Ahmed had indeed taken out his target. Ferret-man lay sprawled facedown in the dirt. *Well. That all came back to you easily enough.*

Drawing in a deep, hitching breath, only then did Kate fully focus her attention on Rebecca Hanson. She'd dared not do so before, for fear that what she might find would distract her from securing the tent. Her heart pounding, she dropped to her knees in front of her. The young woman hadn't moved during the fracas, and now Kate could see why. She removed a knife from the sheath she had in her boot, and cut the girl's arms free from where they'd been tied behind the chair.

"Are you okay?" Kate's shaking hands worked their way over Rebecca's body, pressing, feeling, assuring herself that her partner was here in front of her now, alive and breathing.

"I...I'm fine, Kate." Small hands found the pilot's face and lifted it so that green eyes might gaze into blue. "Really."

But the young blonde didn't look fine. Blood spattered the left side of her tunic, and the dirt that marred her features did not fully conceal the telltale signs of abuse: a slightly swollen lower lip, bruising on her cheek and along the line of her jaw.

"What happened?" The grief that swept through Kate at the punishment Becky had endured was quickly followed by a simmering rage. "Who did this?"

"The...the blood's not mine, Kate." Becky grabbed Kate's hands and held them.

"It's Nayim's." Ahmed's voice sounded tonelessly.

"Yes." She lowered her head, biting back the tears. "It happened so fast. One minute we were laughing and talking, and the next minute there was this helicopter...he tried to save me and—

" She started to cry.

"Ssssh." Kate opened her arms and Becky fell into them. "There's nothing you could have done, Rebecca," she said, calmly stroking the blonde head.

"I...I guess I know that," Becky said, drawing in a deep quaking breath and pulling away. "But that doesn't make it any easier. I keep thinking of his wife...his children..."

"He knew the risks," Kate said, thumbing away a tear from Rebecca's bruised cheek. "We all did. And do. But right now..." she swung her eyes quickly around the tent, "we've got to get moving." She gave Becky's arm a squeeze. "Think you can make it?"

"Sure," the smaller woman gamely replied, allowing the pilot to help her to her feet. "Kate," she grimaced as she limped towards the door on Kate's arm, feeling the circulation return to her aching limbs, "did you and Ahmed get everything you needed?"

"No."

"What do you mean, *no*?" Becky halted, forcing Kate to do the same.

"No, meaning we didn't get into the communications post." Kate refused to look Becky in the eye, instead busying herself with her rifle, re-shouldering it. "C'mon, now." She started forward again.

"Wait just one minute, Captain Phillips."

Kate drew up short at the anger in her companion's voice, the edge of steely authority. The pilot turned on her heel to find herself assaulted by two blazing green eyes.

"Why didn't you get into the cave?" Becky demanded, fearing she already knew the answer. "Was there a problem?"

"Rebecca," Kate sighed, "We couldn't get into the communications post without raising some sort of alarm eventually, and the same could be said for busting in here." She waved a hand at the prone figures of Rashid and Mazar. "There was a choice to be made, and I made it. Now come on, let's go."

"No." Becky stood her ground, her chest heaving. "You can't Kate. What about the mission? All those people out there whose lives depend on us."

"If we don't get out of here now," Kate said grimly, "we're not getting out at all. Tell her, Ahmed."

"It's true, Miss Rebecca," the Kosovar admitted. "It would take too much time...someone would come looking." He shook his face sadly. "Maybe I can think of another way—"

"No," Becky repeated. "There is no other way. You said so yourself." She turned back to Kate and gripped her tightly by the arms. "Please, Kate. You've got to try. Please."

"I—I can't," the pilot got out in a choked voice. God, if Rebecca only knew how much she wanted to. But she couldn't risk it. Her own life meant nothing to her. But Rebecca's...that was her everything.

"Kate, you've got to do this thing. You've just *got* to." Becky bored her eyes into Kate's searching for some spark there of the woman who'd told her so many times that she was committed to bringing down El Yousef—no matter what. "Otherwise," she continued, "all this will have been for nothing. All the sacrifices we've made. The lives that have been lost."

"Rebecca, I—"

"For God's sake, Kate," Becky's voice was ragged, "what do you think I've been spending all night doing? Besides getting slapped around and lying through my teeth about what I was doing here?"

"I—I don't—"

"I'll tell you." The flight attendant swallowed hard, struggling to maintain her composure. "All I could think about, was that no matter what was happening to me, you and Ahmed still had a chance to complete the mission and get away. That you'd make it."

"What?" Kate felt as though she'd been punched in the gut, so astounded was she by Becky's revelation. "Rebecca," she said softly, despairingly, "you couldn't think that I'd just...just leave you here."

"You made a choice for the both of us, Kate," Becky said, feeling the dark-haired woman's pain rip through her like a jagged knife.

But she would not back down. There was too much at stake.

"It's one that I don't happen to agree with."

Catherine Phillips fell silent, considering Rebecca's words. Once again, she'd somehow blundered her way into underestimating the inner strength of her partner. And broken all her own rules in the bargain.

There were always choices in life, always options. You just had to want to find them badly enough. Hell, she'd spent the better part of her life finding ways to do the impossible, coming up with solutions others had been blind to. And yet...when she'd been confronted with the thought of Rebecca being in danger, instantly she'd made it an either-or decision. Had never considered that there might be other options, ones that could have saved both Rebecca *and* the mission. Instead, she had zeroed in on getting Rebecca out of there—to the exclusion of all else.

Damn.

She should have trusted in herself more.

And trusted in Rebecca, most of all.

"You and me...we're enough to see this thing through, Rebecca. Believe in that, like I do. Okay?"

How her own words mocked her now.

The pilot straightened her back. "You're right," she said, releasing a shaky breath. "We're not leaving here without making a try for the communications post." She turned to Ahmed. "You okay with that?"

The young Muslim smiled thinly, but his eyes shone with renewed hope. "I'm with you."

Kate swung back to Rebecca, rubbing a hand up and down the younger woman's arm. "How about you? Are you with me?" Kate gravely inquired, realizing this had to be her decision as well.

Moist green eyes sparkled up at her, and through the dirt, blood, and bruises, a smile lit Becky's face. "I never left you."

Kate felt a tightness in her throat, preventing her from responding. Instead, she simply gave her friend's arm a final squeeze, and stepped towards the tent door.

She never made it.

At the same instant a terrible roar sounded through the camp, the earth violently undulated beneath their feet. She grabbed for Rebecca, finding instead only thin air. A concussive shock wave rocked through them, knocking them to the ground like bowling pins.

The bombardment's begun, Kate thought dizzily, trying to unscramble her brain cells. *We're too fucking late.*

****

Within moments, the sleepy terrorist camp at Birat had turned into a scene of smoking, burning chaos.

"What's happening?" Becky gasped, crawling next to Kate at the tent's entrance.

"It's the missile strike," the pilot replied, coughing. "Tomahawk cruise missiles, I'd guess." The pilot cast an eye towards flaming streaks illuminating the night sky like lighting. "Probably launched from ships in the Persian Gulf."

Panic fueled the response of El Yousef's people.

In the confusion and disorder they were firing anything and everything they could into the air, futilely hoping to intercept the enemy barrage: rocket propelled grenades, hand-held mortar launchers, and even lighter small arms. Kate saw soldiers throwing the tarps off two truck-mounted anti-aircraft guns.

And of greater concern to her were the "Stingers" she saw several teams of men scrambling to activate—the lightly armored, highly effective, shoulder fired surface to air missiles. They wouldn't do much good against the Tomahawks. But when they fell back to earth after failing to hit a target—ouch. The pilot didn't want to be around for that result.

"Ahmed, grab those extra AK47s," Kate said, willing to trade her single action rifle for the more sophisticated automatic firepower of the guards they'd overcome. "We've got to get ready to make a break for it."

She had half considered bailing out again when the barrage had begun, but the fact of the matter was that the attack now provided them with the best cover they could have possibly hoped for.

"And let's get rid of these." Kate shrugged off her *shalwar kameez,* happy to be free of the damned thing, and she helped Rebecca to do the same. She could tell by the younger woman's haste that she was not sorry to discard the bloodied garment. Now they each wore only their khaki pants, shirts, and jackets. In the confusion, they'd draw less attention to themselves dressed as ersatz men as opposed to native women.

But that blonde hair of Rebecca's... "Here," Kate said, grabbing Rashid's turban from the floor and tugging it down over Becky's head, grinning. It would have to do.

"Ugh." Becky turned up her nose distastefully. "Do I have to?"

"Yes," the pilot firmly replied. "Besides," her eyes twinkled, "it suits you."

"Here you go." Ahmed joined them, bearing a total of three AK47s. He gave one to Kate and kept one for himself, offering the third to Rebecca.

"No thanks." She blanched, holding up her palms even as another explosion rocked the camp. "I— I'll just stick close to you guys." She grabbed her backpack from the floor where Rashid had tossed it, and slid it over her shoulder. "If you don't mind, that is."

"We don't," Kate said, understanding that Rebecca's peaceful nature and an assault weapon did not go hand-in-hand. "Okay," she eyed her two companions carefully. "Here's what we're going to do. We're just gonna charge up that hillside, telling everyone we see that...the Chosen One wants everyone to...to meet him at his headquarters immediately for new orders. Same thing when we hit the communications post, plus telling 'em that the missiles will be targeting them. The Chosen One wants everyone out, and down here." Kate looked at Ahmed carefully. "Can you handle that?"

"Yes." Ahmed swallowed hard, but his voice was steady.

"Good." Kate flashed them a rakish, confident smile. "Then let's go."

The air was full of sounds as they stepped out of the tent, all thunder and crackling like a violent electrical storm. Kate felt a tingling at the back of her neck, an excitement in her belly that flamed her drive as nothing else did. The mission was on, and she was ready.

As she'd expected, the frantic soldiers racing about the

compound had little time for them. Other tents were down or in flames, and Birat itself was in trouble from what Kate could see; smoke rose ominously from several locations in the middle of the village. Well, there was no time to worry about that now.

"Lead the way," Kate shouted at Ahmed, and he took off towards the path. Becky followed, with Kate bringing up the rear. The path was well-traveled and the going would not normally have been difficult. But the impact of the missile strikes shook the ground like angry earthquakes, causing them to occasionally loose their footing. Debris rained through the air; shrapnel, rock, and spent bullets, and a smoky haze made vision and breathing difficult.

"Keep it moving," Kate cried out, anxious to get under cover.

"We're almost there." Ahmed spared a quick glance over his shoulder, making sure his companions were still with him.

Kate looked up, her eyes scanning the hillside in the darkness, trying to penetrate the murk. Suddenly, out of the gloom, a large form appeared. "Ahmed—watch it," she shouted, but she needn't have sounded the warning. One of El Yousef's soldiers barreled down the pathway from the cave, obviously running for his life. He didn't challenge them as he scrambled past, not daring to look them in the eye. The man was obviously on a self-serving mission of his own.

"That's one less we have to worry about." Kate laughed without humor, gasping as her eyes watered in the acrid smoke.

They clambered up the path, their harsh breathing drowned out by the whistling screams of the incoming Tomahawks and the explosive sounds of anti-aircraft guns firing off in angry protest, like so many Fourth of July fireworks.

"Aaah." Becky stumbled on the loose gravel but Kate was there to catch her, prodding her along.

And then they were there, bursting through the black-out curtain into the communications center. There were six soldiers that Kate could see, turning to face the new arrivals with mouths agape. Clearly, they were frightened, and Ahmed's agitated shouting did little to alleviate their fears.

"Quickly. Quickly," he cried at them in *Dari*. "The bombs

are coming this way. Out. Out. You must leave immediately. The Chosen One has commanded." For emphasis, he swung his AK47 towards the entrance. "*Now*, you fools. Run for your lives."

Four of the soldiers didn't need to be told twice. They fell over themselves as they pushed for the entrance. The fifth soldier hesitated. Then, another bomb hit nearby, shaking a fine cloud of dust down upon them from the cave's ceiling, and he scrambled after his comrades.

The last soldier, probably the officer in charge, was not as easily persuaded. Kate could hear him questioning Ahmed, and she saw that the young scientist was becoming increasingly flustered. Finally, the terrorist gestured towards her and Rebecca, and reached for a 2-way radio on his desk.

"Un-uh," the pilot mumbled, quickly closing the distance between herself and the soldier. She knocked the radio out of his hand with a forearm chop, and gave him a solid taste of the butt of her AK47.

"Nighty-night."

The man grunted and slid, unconscious, onto the paneled floor of the cave.

"Okay—you two get going." Kate jogged to the doorway to stand watch. "We don't have much time."

"We're on it," Becky replied, her face a mask of concentration. She followed Ahmed to a central computer console and the two of them began working.

Kate crouched down in the entranceway, leaned back against the cool rock wall, and slightly parted the curtain with the barrel of her AK47. Now she had a clear view of the pandemonium on the ground. The bombing was getting more intense, she could tell that much. *Those damn suits in Washington must have a helluva lot to prove,* she thought bitterly.

The flames lit the camp nearly as bright as day, and with some dismay Kate saw that the vehicle depot had taken a direct hit. Many of the other jeeps and trucks throughout the encampment were already disabled. The closest usable vehicle, as far as she could see, was a supply truck parked about halfway across the compound. Even in all that mayhem, it would be a difficult run, getting there undetected. They could always just slip back into the desert, but the pilot didn't really like those odds. Particularly considering what a rough time she and Ahmed had had just walking those last nine or ten kilometers to Birat. *But...* Kate's blue eyes narrowed as she detected another transportation option.

"How's it coming?" She called over her shoulder. Becky and Ahmed were working furiously at the computers, the *tap-tap* of their fingers on the keyboards mingling with their softly murmuring voices.

"It's coming," Becky tightly replied, not lifting her head. "But we need more time."

"We might not have it," Kate muttered, letting her eyes travel around the interior of the cave. Ahmed had been right; this was some installation. The dust that clouded the air earlier had already been cleared, thanks to the climate and ventilating system. There was enough computer hardware about to make the place the closest thing to a geek heaven that the pilot had ever seen. And at the rear of the cave she saw piles of ominously marked crates that she was sure contained Stinger missiles and mortars rather than hard drives and printers. *With that kind of firepower stored up here, it's only a matter of time before...*

Kate stiffened her back against the cave wall. "We've got company," she yelled over the pounding bombardment. Scrabbling up the hillside were half a dozen heavily armed soldiers, their AK47s brandished directly at the post's entrance.

Fuck. There were too damn many of them. She couldn't take them out one-by-one as she and Ahmed had handled the guards earlier. And there was no goddamned way she was letting them get inside this cave. Not with Rebecca here.

Kate's mind worked furiously, examining and discarding a multitude of options, until her instincts and training drove her to the only one that made any sense.

She hated it just the same.

She let them come closer...closer...Suddenly the lead soldier shouted something and pointed at the entrance. *Double fuck.* She'd been spotted. And in that same instant, her finger squeezed the trigger of her assault rifle. The first three terrorists went down like dominoes. Kate tucked and rolled away from the cave's entrance, drawing the fire of the remaining soldiers as she went. She smacked hard into the face of a rock about eight meters from the mouth of the cave, one that helped obscure the entrance from below. Wincing as its sharp edges dug into her side, from her prone position she returned the enemy fire, and she saw two more men tumble backwards and slide bonelessly down the hill.

Now...where was that last bastard? Kate edged forward on her elbows, moving back towards the cave, but she kept her eyes peeled downhill. In the dark and smoke it was difficult to see. The sounds of the bombardment fizzled away.

There was shouting coming from within the cave, but Kate couldn't make it out. She knew at least that no one had gotten past her. There was nothing but the pounding of her heart, her finger poised upon the trigger, the heat and metallic stink rising up from her recently discharged weapon.

To the pilot the whole scene had a unearthly feel to it. At that moment, she inhabited a world that straddled the line between what was in this plane of existence and the next—where people moved about like ghostly ships in an impenetrable mist, searching, but not finding. Was she a mere witness to their passing? Or had she, too, become one of them? She continued her belly crawl, angling her course to take her towards another rocky outcropping on the far side of the path.

Something told her...

She saw the barrel of his rifle before she actually saw him.

It slipped above the rocks like the head of a cobra, sniffing at the air. She flung herself violently to her right, firing, just as she saw the flash and heard the *rat-a-tat-tat* of his AK47. She heard his cry and the dry clattering sound of his rifle hitting the rocky ground, and then—nothing.

"Kate. Oh, God, *Kate.*"

More shouts, coming behind her now.

Who was that?

And who were they calling for?

Dully, she realized that *she* in fact was Kate. And that the person yelling was—

"God, Kate, are you okay?" Hands on the back of her shoulders, rolling her over.

"Uh...yeah, Rebecca?" Kate edged herself up on her elbows, shaking her head as if to clear it. "I—I'm fine," she told herself, gazing up into two concerned green eyes. "Just got one hell of a headache."

"No wonder," the flight attendant said shakily, reaching a hand out to touch an angry red gash that streaked along the pilot's left temple. "You've been shot."

"Ow." Kate flinched, slapping away Becky's blood-covered fingertips. "It's just a scratch." She fought to get her breathing under control, to focus. Now was not the time fade out.

"Scratch my ass, Kate," Becky objected, watching the pilot push herself to her feet.

Kate smiled engagingly.

"Okay. Maybe later."

Ignoring Rebecca's pained groan, she grabbed her rifle and nodded at the bodies littering the hillside. "There will be more of them on the way, I'm sure of it."

The ground around them rocked again with another close impact. "C'mon." Kate grabbed Becky by the elbow. "We've got to get going."

"Ahmed was just about done," Becky said, coughing, and they darted back into the cave.

"Ahmed *is* done." Standing behind the main console, sporting a grin that ran from ear-to-ear, the young man held up a handful of discs. "Encryption codes, contacts, bank accounts, business interests, operations sites, satellite feeds—it's all here."

The news did more for Kate than a deep lung full of the clean air inside the cave ever could have. "Thank God." The pilot squeezed her eyes shut for a moment, fighting off the annoying buzzing in her head. "That was some work, Ahmed." Kate took the discs and placed them carefully into a small pouch at her waist.

"I had help." His voice was relieved, exultant. "Wonderful help, isn't that right, Becky?"

"We're a team." The tired blonde grinned. "Now," she turned to the tall, dark woman next to her as another explosion rattled the cave, lightly touching her arm, "how do we get out of here?"

    Kate's eyes glittered. "Follow me."

Chapter 19

The air around them was alive, a living, breathing thing, screaming its misery into the night. Debris flew in every direction, pummeling the heaving earth like hot, furious fists.

"Go. Go. Go," Kate shouted hoarsely as they stumbled down the hillside, feet moving, always moving, until they reached the edge of the compound.

"What now?" Becky's eyes were wide as silver dollars as they slid to a stop behind a jumble of crates.

"El Yousef's helicopter." Kate sucked in a choking breath of air. "It's on the far side of that storage building." The pilot nodded towards a structure opposite them. Flames shot out from its roof and the windows had been blown away.

"Are you sure that's a good idea?" Rebecca turned a sweat and soot-streaked face from the blazing compound to the pilot.

"I don't much like the alternatives," Kate grimly replied, throwing an arm around her companion and ducking as another explosion ripped through the camp. "We'll have to make a break for it. Just keep your heads down and keep moving. Don't stop until you get to the chopper, okay? And leave the rest to me."

Ahmed ran a hand over his thin face, tugging at his beard. "Then what?" His voice was strained. "Can you fly helicopters?"

"Depends on who you ask." Kate gave the young scientist a

lopsided grin. "But I think I can handle it."

"I know you can," Becky let her eyes rest evenly on her partner, reaching a hand out to squeeze her shoulder. "After you."

A renewed surge of energy pulsed through the pilot, blowing away the throbbing ache in her skull and the exhaustion that dogged her limbs. If Rebecca Hanson believe in her, then anything was possible. "Okay. What we'll do is—*fuck.*"

"What is it, Kate?" A stab of fear shot through Rebecca at the alarm she heard in her partner's voice.

"The damn chopper," Kate swore, and now Becky could hear the *whump-whump-whump* of rotor blades firing up. "It's getting ready to take off."

Cursing, Kate looked both ways up and down the compound. El Yousef's people looked otherwise engaged in desperately trying to extinguish fires. Others were shooting their rifles and mortars angrily at the sky towards an enemy that assailed them from above. "Across the compound," Kate instructed, her face set in fierce determination. "Behind the building—to the chopper. On three.

"One." Kate held up a finger.

"Two." She pulled her Kalashnikov to her chest.

Before "three" had left her mouth, the dark-haired woman had burst from behind the crates and sprinted across the compound, laying down a screen of covering fire as she went. Becky followed, leaping from their hiding place, with Ahmed trailing behind.

They cleared the compound and skittered past the burning storage building. Hot embers rained down upon them, and thick, black smoke obscured their vision. But they kept moving, like planes flying in formation, each person focused only on the individual in front of them, leading each other through the clouds until—there it was. The helicopter sat like a fattened duck in a clearing just in front of them.

A pilot was in the cockpit, throttling up the chopper. So far, he was oblivious to the presence of three bloodied, dirty, slightly scorched trespassers.

Take out the pilot.

It was Kate's only thought as she motioned her group forward, their sole chance for survival now. She moved across the rocky earth, her eyes locked on the helicopter, heedless of the bombardment that stormed around her.

Until a great roar sounded to their rear. *The storage building. It's been hit again,* Kate guessed. "Get down," she cried, knowing Becky and Ahmed could not hear her. She started to dive as the air exploded around her, and then a rolling wall of sizzling heat slammed into her from behind, and she felt her feet leave the ground.

The earth bucked beneath her, like an indignant bronco trying to throw its rider, and she did her best to shield herself from the wood and rock and concrete chunks that whirled through the air as though whipped by an unseen cyclone.

Finally, the wave passed, and Kate blinked open her eyes, coughing. By God, the chopper was still in one piece. It was a Sud Alouette, she could now tell by the looks of it.

God bless the French.

The pilot's eyes were on her, his mouth in an open "oh" as he caught sight of her. Startled he lunged for the throttle.

No. God damn it, NO.

She pushed herself to her feet, every bone in her body shrieking at the abuse. A quick glance behind her showed that Ahmed was next to Rebecca, helping her up. They looked okay, and Kate breathed a silent prayer of thanks at that, but she knew that none of it would matter soon if she didn't get her hands on that chopper. Spitting out the dirt and soot that was gagging her, she staggered towards the cockpit.

Faster and faster the helicopter blades rotated, kicking up a painful whirlwind of dust and debris. Kate could tell by the whine of the turbine engines that it was only a matter of seconds until the pilot would have generated enough lift for take off. She pushed her body forward, calling upon her last reserves of energy, reaching for that dark, competitive part of herself that was unwilling...unable to accept defeat.

She saw the pilot's eyes widen, saw the anger and fear in his eyes, and she flung herself through the open door, batting his hands away from the control column. She felt his knee come up and strike her middle, blowing the air out of her, but that only fueled her more. She grabbed him by the collar of his jacket with one hand, and with the other launched a roundhouse punch to his jaw, knocking him out cold.

"Not today, pal," she gasped, feeling the burning in her gut as she took in a wheezing breath of air.

She roughly grabbed the pilot's body and carelessly tossed him out onto the rocky ground. "Let's get going," she called to Rebecca and Ahmed, seeing them drawing closer to the helicopter, heads down. The flames of the burning storage building danced behind them, driven by the wind of the aircraft's rotors.

Oh God, Noooo.

Silhouetted against the inferno a tall, dark form moved. Kate grabbed for her AK47 and realized with a sinking feeling, that it wasn't there. She'd dropped it in the explosion, and she saw it now, lying on the ground outside the helicopter, useless.

A flash of light as an exterior wall sighed and collapsed in on itself, and Kate could see his face then, twisted in fury, bent on revenge. Rashid.

"Rebecca," she desperately cried out, her heart leaping into her throat, choking her. She reached for the pistol she'd stuffed into her jacket, cursing, knowing she would not be in time. Rashid's weapon glittered in the firelight, pointing directly at the young blonde who slowly turned, following Catherine's wild-eyed gaze to her killer.

I love you, Kate, was all Becky could think. There was nothing else, not the Tomahawk missiles sailing overhead, not the hell burning around her, not the smoke stinging her eyes and cutting off her breath. She squeezed her eyes shut, conjuring up an image of her lover, wanting that to be her last conscious thought. She heard Rashid's pistol fire, at the same instant an unknown force slammed into her, driving her to the ground. *I wonder if this is what death feels like?* And then she heard more shots, coming from the helicopter, this time.

Feet pounding on the ground, drawing closer.

Hands on her body.

Holding.

Caressing.

"Rebecca...oh, God. Talk to me, baby. Please."

Interesting, Becky curiously thought. *I suppose I'm not dead after all.* She blinked open her eyes to see the tear-streaked face of Catherine Phillips hovering above her.

"Thank God," Kate said, sagging back on her heels. She took a steadying breath. "You okay?"

"F- fine, I think." Becky rubbed her right shoulder that had taken much of the impact. "What happened?"

"Ahmed happened," Kate said sadly, moving to the young Kosovar's side. He lay sprawled on his back, his breath coming in a series of rapid, shallow gasps.

Kate had nearly gone insane when she'd seen Rashid take aim at Rebecca. But before she'd been able to draw her own weapon, Ahmed had detected the danger and thrown himself in front of Becky, shoving her out of the way. And, in the process, taken the bullet meant for her. Kate had seen the look of triumph denied on Rashid's face, and as he'd turned his gun to her, the pilot had been only too happy to cut him down.

The fucking bastard.

She'd torn out of the idling helicopter, holding her breath until she'd seen two green eyes flicker open at her.

"Ahmed, no," Becky sobbed, crawling next to the young man and grabbing his hand. With the other she pressed down on the gaping wound on his chest. His soft gray vest and white shirt were soaked through with blood, dark and glistening wet in the light of the flames.

"*Do* something, Kate, please. Help him."

"I—I can't," Kate choked out, hating herself for saying that, and wishing more than anything that it were not true.

"We...we'll get him on the helicopter. Get him back to Duristan. They'll help him there." Becky's fervent hopes tugged at Kate's heart, devastating her, knowing as she did that the young man would probably not even be able to make it to the chopper alive, let alone a friendly village.

She opened her mouth to respond, when she felt a weak touch on her wrist.

"Leave me..." Ahmed rasped, his thin face gone pale.

"No," Becky insisted. "We'll get you out of here."

"There's no...no time. GO," he said more firmly, his dark eyes flashing defiantly.

Kate sighed heavily, knowing Ahmed was right. Any moment, more of El Yousef's men might show. "We'll never forget you." She paused, feeling her throat constrict at the thought of what she'd nearly lost but for the young scientist's heroic act. "And from the bottom of my heart," she said, her voice catching, "I thank you."

A smile spread across Ahmed's face, and Kate was amazed to see the anguish and the pain bleed away, freeing him. "My...my debt is paid," he said, his eyes locking onto Kate's. She forced a smile to her own face, and nodded.

"In full," she assured him, and she kept her eyes upon him as the light in his went dark.

****

God, she hated what this was doing to Rebecca. Hated every goddamned minute of it. She knew it had been the girl's choice to be with her here, in this place.

But not *here.*

Someone like Rebecca...she should never have to witness such violence, such destruction as she had this day, let alone bear the burden of seeing two friends killed.

If Kate could have taken all of the young blonde's pain, all her suffering, and borne it on her own shoulders, she willingly would have done so. After all, she was damaged goods already. What difference would a few more dents and bruises make?

But there wasn't a damn thing she could do about it...about any of it. Not about Nayim and Ahmed, not about Rebecca's grief, and not about her own personal obsession that drove them all to this godforsaken place to begin with. It was too late for regret, for recrimination. The time for that had passed. The only thing she could do, or even felt she was capable of at this point, was to make sure she got Rebecca, herself, and those damned discs onto that Alouette and the hell out of Afghanistan.

Kate grabbed her fallen AK47, and then turned to pull Rebecca to her feet. "We've got to move."

Becky bit her lip and nodded. Numbly, she collected her backpack and shouldered it, choosing to leave behind her fallen turban. Kate didn't argue.

They sprinted towards the chopper, ignoring the missiles that continued to fall, striking more towards Birat and further west, now. That would at least give them better odds during lift-off, the pilot thought. Kate pushed Becky quickly into the cockpit and then hopped in after her, securing their safety harnesses.

*Okay...*Kate quickly scanned the controls of the French-made helicopter. *No time for a standard pre-flight,* she thought grimly, as the sound of rifle fire seemed to close in upon them. She'd never flown an Alouette before, but she knew that they weren't necessarily the speediest or the most maneuverable craft in their class. Still, this bird had been retrofitted with a sideways firing 20 mm cannon, so how bad could it all be?

"Kate."

The pilot lifted her head to see several of El Yousef's men turn the corner of the decimated storage building, weapons drawn.

"We're outta here." Kate seized the throttle. The chopper jerked fitfully like an elevator starting to move, and then they were off, gaining altitude before swooping away towards the blackened southwest.

"Shit."

Bullets pinged an insistent beat against the hull, tapping like tiny hailstones, and not for the first time in her life did Kate reflect on the many reasons why she infinitely preferred the power and speed of her fixed-wing F15s and F16s, as opposed to these lumbering birds. She stayed relatively low to the ground, hoping to avoid not only the incoming Tomahawks, but also any of El Yousef's wild mortar or Stinger fire.

As the blazing terrorist stronghold receded into the distance, Kate allowed herself a steadying breath. "Damn," she shouted over the whine of the rotating blades, "that was close." She turned to her companion, but Becky said nothing, simply staring straight ahead into the inky darkness, her bruised, tear-streaked face lit by the greenish glow of the instrument panel.

They'd made it, the pilot thought, but at what cost? She

wiggled and wagged some of the controls, getting a feel for the chopper. It wasn't a bad machine, not really, and it appeared as though it had been fairly well maintained. And if the gauges were accurate, they might just have enough fuel to get them to a safe harbor.

Kate coughed, ridding herself of some of that horrid grit and ash that had threatened to choke her. She settled down in her seat for the ride back, and idly wondered if Rebecca had anything for the headache she had—no thanks to the damn bullet that had creased her thick noggin.

There was no way she could have seen the Arab man with dark, dead eyes, staring with a blazing fury at the winking lights of the Alouette as it whirled away from the camp. He was surrounded by overly zealous guards, taking care to shield him from any falling debris. Standing in the smoking, empty space that had once housed his personal helicopter, the Chosen One angrily shoved his lackeys aside.

"Out of my way," he cried, and his men stumbled over themselves in order to comply. He fell to his knees next to a still form lying on the rocky ground. Long, manicured fingers reached out to touch a body already grown cold, despite the flames from the storage building burning nearby.

"Rashid," he sobbed quietly, mourning the loss of his confidant, his lieutenant, his friend. How dare they. The Infidels. To come into his house, to destroy his property, to hurt his people. They would pay. All of them, he would make them pay.

With a roar of outrage sounding from deep within the bowels of his blackened soul, Abbado El Yousef rose to his feet. He thrust his arm outwards, pointing towards the horizon, his robes billowing in the swirling winds, standing like a living, breathing messenger of death itself. "Destroy them."

****

Tiny, illuminated dots bleeped at Kate from the radar display, demanding her attention. They were way too low to be any of the Tomahawks she'd been keeping an eye on, and too damn high to be any of El Yousef's rocket-fired mortars. Her pulse quickened, and with a sinking feeling in the pit of her belly, she realized what they were.

"Stingers," Kate declared with a low intensity. "El Yousef's trying to shoot us down."

"Can we get out of the way?" Becky looked over her shoulder, as if attempting to spot the missiles in the darkness.

"I can try, but it doesn't look good."

"What?" Green eyes flew open wide with alarm.

"Brace yourself." Kate stiffened. She could see the Stingers zooming in on them. At least three or four, streaking towards the Alouette. Maybe if they'd been farther away from the compound, or had had a chance to gain more altitude. But flying as close to the ground as she had been, limited the pilot's options. There wasn't enough time, not enough space, to maneuver her way out of it.

"Damn," Kate swore, watching the bleeping Stingers converging in on their target.

Too close to the rocky earth below, she tried for more speed, abruptly pulling up. She knew it was a dangerous move and she risked a stall, but the alternative was even less attractive. The rotors screamed and the engines whined and huffed against the abuse thrust upon them.

Kate's mouth went as dry as the barren earth beneath her, and she feared her pounding heart might burst through her chest. Maintaining a death grip on the control column, she worked the rudder pedals furiously and, for half a second, believed she had gotten clear, the fox desperately trying to evade the hounds.

Until a grinding, metallic explosion hit the rear of the chopper.

A hard, hot slap that wrenched Kate's hands from the controls and sent the Alouette skidding across the sky. The pilot thought she heard Rebecca scream, but she couldn't be sure; her own eardrums were close to bursting from the sound of the blast.

The chopper vibrated and roll to the left.

Not a fucking stall.

Kate tried to recover, cutting back the power and reducing airspeed, but nothing would respond. They were spinning out of control, heading for the ground. *What is it with me and helicop-*

ters? she thought testily. She blew out her RPMs to the maximum allowable limit and pounded the hell out of her pedal trim, to no avail. Still, she would not give up.

If I could just coax a little more lift out of this thing...

But when the turbine engine sputtered and died, she realized that too was no longer an option. Now there was just the *whoosh* of the air blasting through the damaged chopper, and they were going down, down in a free-fall, like some godly hand had simply reached out and dropped them from the sky.

The last thing she remembered was throwing her right arm across Rebecca's middle, as though that small, pathetic gesture would somehow be enough to keep them both alive.

****

Rebecca Hanson's anguished ascent back towards consciousness was not a gentle one. She felt prodded, poked. Rather than fighting it, she ran towards it, embracing it, fully understanding that by doing so there would only be more pain, more fear. It was precisely the fear that drove her most of all, the uncertainty, the not knowing of it. No matter what it cost, no matter how much it hurt, she had to know.

"*Kate...*" The name tore from her lips as she struggled to orient herself. Dirt, there was that, and something vaguely minty smelling, or was that catnip?

"*Ugh.*"

She pushed herself up to a half sitting position, from wherever "down" was, which happened to be a stand of low scrub brush. *What the—*

She reached a hand to her forehead, and felt the beginnings of a good-sized swelling there. *Wonderful,* she thought dizzily, *it'll go great with my cuts and bruises.* She took in a deep breath of air, desperately trying to clear the fogginess from her mind.

It was then she smelled the smoke.

An alarm sounded inside the young blonde.

"Kate," she yelled, at last putting the pieces together. The missiles, the hit they'd taken. They were going to crash, she'd known that, and braced herself, felt Kate's strong arm holding her fast. And then...

"Oh God." She swiveled around, ignoring the aching pull in her lower back, and saw the helicopter. It was crumpled on the ground like a broken child's toy. Orange and red flames licked at the rear of it; the front cockpit area had accordioned in on itself upon impact.

"Kate," she cried again, panic seizing her.

She got shakily to her feet, and had to mentally walk herself through the process as she forced one foot forward after the other, moving towards the aircraft. "Kate, please. Answer me." She cast frantic eyes around the harsh, lunar-like landscape, pleading with whatever gods might be listening that Kate, too, had been thrown clear. But there was no answer, no sign of her, and the pull of an undeniable life force continued to propel the flight attendant towards the burning fuselage. Realization struck her like a sharp blow to the gut; she knew what she would find there.

"No," Becky groaned, breaking out into a shambling run.

The heat from the flames was intense as she drew close, stinging her, but she paid it no heed. For there in the cockpit, slumped over the controls, was Catherine Phillips.

"C'mon, Kate." Becky boosted herself over the side of the awkwardly pitched chopper. "Wake up. We gotta go." But Kate did not move.

The safety harness that had failed Becky had only partially disengaged on the pilot's seat. The shoulder harness was detached, but Kate was still belted in at the waist.

"C'mon." Becky gripped her by the shoulders and pulled her back, away from the control column, and it was all she could do to keep from crying out. Kate's dark hair and face were streaked with blood, and now the smaller woman could see that her right leg, from the knee down, had gone through the floorboards of the helicopter. Jagged and torn metal, sparking wires, and shattered glass were all that remained of the front console area.

"Kate."

Becky took her face in her hands, slapping her lightly, peering closely at her closed eyes. Kate's head simply lolled to one side, unresponsive.

"Okay. I...I've got to get you out of here."

Becky swallowed hard, ignoring the tearing of her eyes. Whether it was from the smoke and heat, or from her worry over Kate, she cared not. She crawled further into the cockpit, wincing as a sharp piece of the control column stabbed at her arm. "Sorry," she gasped, reaching over Kate and trying to release the belting mechanism. She pulled and pushed, but it refused to snap free.

"Damn it," she cursed in frustration. "Now's a hell of a time to be doing your job." Her eyes scanned the cockpit in a panic. *My backpack.* There it was, still intact. Crying out in relief, she grabbed at it, pulling out the Swiss Army knife that she always carried with her when traveling.

"See. I told you," she coughed, "that this would come in handy." She threw the pack clear, and began cutting Kate free. "Like I've always told you, Kate, you can't be too prepared." With a final slashing cut, the belt fell away.

"Okay." Becky snapped the knife shut. "I'll have you out of here in a jiffy." She returned her attention to Kate's trapped leg, pulling away at the metal surrounding it as best she could. She worried that she was doing her partner further damage, but she had no other choice, not now. The smoke was so thick and black that she felt as though she and Kate were lost in a storm cloud. And the heat...Becky didn't bother to look behind her to see how close the flames were. Frankly, it didn't much matter. She would stay here as long as it took to get Kate out. Or...or whatever.

"Now, you're gonna have to work with me here, big stuff." She edged as far behind Kate as she could, giving herself the best leverage possible in the shattered cockpit. Working her arms under Kate's shoulders, she took in a choking breath. "Since you like count-offs so much, that's what we're going to do. We're gonna go on three." She paused, her eyes tracking to Kate's slack, bloodied face. "Together, okay? Because I'm not going anywhere without you, you got that?"

She swabbed the tears out of her eyes with her shoulders, and then began counting.

"One." She pulled Kate sideways from her seat, and she cringed inwardly as her mangled leg came into full view.

"Two." Panting, she slid the pilot towards the door. But the angle the chopper rested at was steep, and Becky was working against gravity now, her muscles straining.

"Three," she cried, lunging for the wrecked exit with all her might, hoping it would be enough.

It wasn't.

"Oh God." She slipped backwards into the cockpit. Kate's body was lodged half in and half out of the door, and Becky's strength had reached its limits. The flames had to be almost upon them now; she could feel the hairs on the back of her neck curling and burning, surely she must be on fire. She was breathing, but not getting any air. Her booted feet still pedaled, looking for traction that wasn't there.

No, she thought stubbornly. *It will not end like this.*

"Did you hear me, Captain Phillips?" Becky gathered herself for one final attempt. "I said *three*, God damn it." And with that she surged for the door, dragging Kate along with her, felt nothing but thin air for a millisecond, and then hit the ground with a bone-jarring *crunch.* The pilot collapsed next to her.

"Okay...okay..." Becky kept up a constant patter of conversation to herself as she weakly got to her knees, her feet, and then hauled Kate's battered body away from the burning helicopter.

"If this thing blows now, Kate," Becky laughed hoarsely, "then we'll know for sure this really wasn't our day."

It was a graceless operation but effective. She maintained a grip on Kate's upper body while dragging her torso and legs behind. The pilot's boots left twin tracks on the dusty ground like two snails snaking their way along, marking their path as they passed by. Becky stumbled, falling back onto her rear more than once, each time apologizing to her conspicuously quiet companion for any discomfort she might have caused.

Finally, they had pulled clear enough of the flaming wreckage to satisfy Rebecca. Her arms shaking with the effort, she gently lowered Kate down, and dropped onto the ground next to her.

She let her eyes run up and down her lover's still form, realizing she had to find the strength now to do what before she had resisted, simply because she hadn't felt herself capable of dealing with the potential consequence.

"Please Kate, please."

A soft whimper.

Becky reached a trembling, burned hand to the pilot's neck, feeling for a pulse. Her heart fluttered; at first she could detect nothing. And then...there it was. Faint, thready, but there just the same.

"Oh." Becky closed her eyes and allowed herself to release the breath that she'd been holding. She basked in a relief that washed over her parched spirit like a rainstorm in the desert, then stared out into the dying flames of the crashed helicopter, the fuselage fully consumed now. How they had both survived that...Becky shuddered uncontrollably in the night chill. She turned back towards Kate, and brushed back the matted hair from her face, gone all shadowed and dark in the flickering light.

And so still.

What do I do now, Kate, huh?

Rebecca Hanson had never felt so helpless.

But with the barely discernible rise and fall of Kate's chest she knew the pilot was alive, at least.

Well, it was a place to start.

"Thank you, God." She lowered her head into her hands and cried, acutely aware that no one, not on this earth, anyway, would hear her. "Thank you."

Chapter
20

The black horizon to the east gradually turned a deep, oceanic blue, and when subtle touches of rose and gold glowed at that place where the land met the sky, Becky's heart gladdened. She knew that dawn would not be far off. And with that new daylight, perhaps there would be hope. Or, at a minimum, an end to this interminable night.

It had taken some long moments after the crash for Becky to get a grip on herself, to calm herself down. Her breath had wanted to hitch, her heart to pound, but she wouldn't let them.

She had a job to do: Kate needed her. And she could not...would not, let her down.

Once she'd been able to focus on that, her Orbis Airlines first aid training had quickly kicked into gear. That, and a little bit of the Girl Scouts, too. Do what you could, with what you had.

She'd cleaned Kate up as best she could, given the circumstances, and cut a spare shirt from her backpack into bandage strips. Kate's leg was her main concern. If it was broken, she couldn't tell. But it was bleeding profusely, the skin on it shredded and torn, and so she'd done what she could to tie the strips tightly around the injured area. But still the blood was seeping through. The cuts on the pilot's face and scalp had bled a lot but were shallow, and Becky guessed that these had been most likely caused by the shattering glass of the cockpit. There were a few burns, too, but there was little Becky could do for them, other than to try and keep them clean. If there were any more injuries to be dealt with, they would have to wait until Kate could speak for herself.

And I hope that's soon. Becky sighed and turned a bleary eye to the northeast. Birat, or what was left of it, still cast an eerie orange glow into the sky, the only sign of the town that Becky knew to be there. Kate had managed to get them some kilometers away from the compound before, well, they were stopped, and the flight attendant hoped that El Yousef and his people had bigger problems on their hands this early morning than chasing after a helicopter they'd blasted out of the sky.

What now, Becky-girl?

She ran her hands up and down her shirt-sleeved arms, warming herself. She'd given Kate her field jacket as a sort of blanket, and some bit of heat did still radiate from the skeletal, metallic frame of the burned out Alouette. But Catherine Phillips, she who had always sported an internal engine that revved degrees higher than anyone else's—was cold. Her face was so pale under the cuts and bruising...her skin so cool and clammy, and getting worse.

A number of dark thoughts bobbed to the surface of Becky's mind, but she forcefully pushed them aside. Sure, they were in a jam right now. But they would get out of it. They always did. And Kate would be right there with her, every step of the way.

Well, maybe there wouldn't be a whole lot of stepping on Kate's part. Becky let her eyes fall on her eyes on her partner's wrecked leg. She'd been able to slow the bleeding but not entirely stop it, and that wasn't good. She raked a hand through her blonde hair, sighing. She had to get help, but how?

With the coming dawn, her own aches and pains had become more starkly evident. It had been a constant battle through the night to keep her thoughts focused; her head felt as big as a melon, and her body ached as though she'd been in a twelve round prize fight. She had no memory of how she'd gotten the burns on her hands, but she did remember slicing open her fore-arm arm as she'd tried to free Kate, and though she'd tied and wrapped the darn thing, it still throbbed painfully.

A quick inventory of her backpack showed her that they did have some food: a couple of bruised apples and a hard cake of dried mullberries and walnuts that Rabia, Nayim's wife, had given her. Becky smiled at the memory of how the trader's wife had quickly recognized her sweet tooth, and covertly slipped her a little something extra for the journey. But Becky's smile soon faded, thinking how the events of the past several days had made Rabia a widow, her children—fatherless.

Water—that would be a problem. Becky had only her canteen, and it had been about two/thirds full when she'd started working on Kate. Now there was only half a container left, and she'd already resolved to preserve this portion for her friend, should she regain consciousness. Then there was her Swiss Army knife, some tissues, a near-empty bottle of aspirin, and some Band-Aids. Becky chuckled humorlessly as she remembered how she'd thought bringing that bottle would make for a lighter load, and at the tiny adhesive strips she'd thought she might need for a little cut or two. The darn things were next to useless now.

The sun peeked above the horizon, and Becky turned, lifting her face to it. "Oh, God, I hope today's a better day."

"It will be." A low, raspy rumble sounded next to her.

"Wha—" Becky swung herself around, needing to see with her own eyes what her disbelieving ears had told her. "Kate. You're awake."

Two bloodshot blue orbs blinked up at her.

"Thank God." Becky gulped back the tears of joy that threatened to drown her. "Oh God, I was so worried. Don't move, all right? You've been banged up a little, but you'll be okay. And don't try to talk, either. Just take it easy. Now...where...where does it hurt? No, wait—" she shook her head, flustered. "I just asked you not to talk, didn't I? Here, you should drink some water." She reached for the canteen, but her eyes had gone so blurry that she could not find it.

"Hey...slow down, Champ."

Just the sound of Kate's voice brought her to a screeching halt, and she fell silent.

"How are you?"

This is so typical. She's the one lying there half-dead, and she wonders how I'm doing? Becky rubbed the tears out of her eyes and turned to look at Kate. "I'm fine," she replied, a tense smile tugging at her lips, "now."

"You don't look so fine, short stuff," Kate observed. "Look at you." She reached out a weak hand to touch the swelling on Becky's forehead, and then let it drop down to brush the back of the younger woman's burnt hand.

"Don't call me short." Becky's voice was indignant, but her green eyes were warm. She paused. "Here," she said softly, "let's get some water into you."

She lifted Kate's head up, and the pilot was able to take a few choking swallows before waving Becky off and lying painfully back down. "I suppose that wasn't a good idea," she said, chuckling through the agony.

Becky pursed her lips. "Kate," she began, "you need help. But...but I don't want to leave you here, not like this."

"Then I'll go with you." Before Becky could stop her, Kate had started to push herself up.

"Aaah." A deep, guttural moan tore from the tall woman, twisting like a knife in Becky's gut.

"Kate, don't."

The pilot sagged back down onto the ground, her injured leg flopping awkwardly to one side.

"Fuck." Kate grabbed at her middle, her breath coming in shallow gasps. Beads of perspiration sprang to her forehead.

"Kate, please. You'll hurt yourself," Becky cried, wondering how it was possible for the normally dark skinned woman to grow even more pale.

"Too...too late for that now," the pilot wheezed, squeezing her eyes shut.

"Kate?"

The pilot did not answer at first.

Becky placed the palm of her hand against Kate's battered face. "Kate, are you with me?" A hint of panic colored her voice.

"Still...still here," Kate mumbled, forcing her eyelids open. "Did I mention that my headache's gone?" She turned the corner of her mouth up in a small grin.

"Thank God for small favors," Becky replied, sighing. She leaned back a bit, relieved. For a moment there, she'd thought that Kate had passed out.

"Listen, Hanson." Kate settled cloudy blue eyes on Rebecca. "I— I need you to do something for me, here. I don't feel so good, you see," she said calmly, evenly, "and I'm going to need for you to go and get help."

"But Kate—"

"Most of all," the pilot coughed, and painfully reached for the small pouch she wore at her waist. "Take this." She snapped it free. "Get these discs back to Cyrus. He'll know what to do with them."

Becky shook her head. "No," she cried hoarsely, stunned with the realization of what Kate was asking her to do.

"Just a kilometer or two east should be the road we came up on. Stay on it...follow it south. If there's traffic coming from the north, from Birat, you *run,* you got me?" The pilot's eyes blazed fiercely. "But if it's from anywhere else, flag 'em down." Kate paused, her breath coming in painful spurts. "It'll be risky," she continued, "but it might be the only chance you've got."

"Don't ask me to leave you, Kate," Becky said stiffly. "I won't do that."

"I'm not." Kate dropped her eyes. "You're in better condition to watch out for those discs, that's all. You'll go get help, come back here for me, and then we'll all get out of here, right? That's the plan. Promise me you'll do that for me, Rebecca. Please...." And at that, she caught Becky's eyes in a searing, blue-eyed gaze. "Promise me."

Rebecca Hanson felt the breath leave her body. God, this wasn't fair. How much of this could she take? How much more could she bear? To just...just leave Kate behind. Who knew what sort of wild animals lurked in these badlands anyway? Or what if El Yousef's men found her? Or thieves? Or...what if Kate took a turn for the worse? She would be helpless out here, in the middle of nowhere.

Still.

Becky let her eyes run up and down the form of the wounded pilot before her, the woman she loved. This mission, getting El Yousef, had meant everything to Kate, she knew that. There had been times, more than once, when she'd felt she had taken a back seat in Kate's life to her damned obsession, but she knew that that was only a part of who the pilot was, and what she stood for.

The lives of so many were at stake. And the lives of so many had already been sacrificed. If the mission were lost and Kate's life saved, Becky knew that the pilot would never be able to live with herself. To survive, and to be forced to watch more people die at the hands of El Yousef's brand of terrorism, would slowly kill her.

Rebecca made her decision. "I promise," she said gravely. "But you promise me something, too."

"Anything." The pilot's mouth quirked, remembering their long-ago conversation in Duristan.

"Promise me you'll be here waiting for me, when I get back."

"I promise," Kate vowed, offering her a smile that died before it reached her eyes.

Rebecca quickly busied herself with preparations for her departure, making sure Kate was as settled as possible before she took her leave. She'd been insistent upon leaving her knife with Kate, as protection, until the pilot had pointed out that she still had her own pistol. Kate had refused to keep the canteen, and finally they'd compromised. Becky agreed to take the canteen, and leave the apples with the Kate. The pilot convinced her that after her last ill-fated attempt at swallowing, it would be better to stick to sucking on pieces of moist apple, instead.

"Besides, you probably won't be gone that long anyway," Kate said, trying to reassure her. "After all, people will probably be heading this way, wondering what's happened in Birat."

"Probably." Becky's eyes flickered, and she lowered her head.

"Hey." Kate forced a cheerfulness into her voice that she did not feel. "While you're out there walking, I want you to start thinking about all the things you want to see when I take you back to Paris."

"Paris?" Becky chuckled, shouldering her backpack.

"Sure. You know, Eiffel Tower, Louvre, Left Bank—all that stuff." Kate held back a grimace as a stab of pain spiked through her.

"Don't think about that now." Becky dropped to her knees, placing a hand on Kate's now-feverish brow.

"I—I just want to remind you, Champ," the pilot gasped, "that I keep my promises."

"I know." Becky sat there for a time, absorbing the comforting feeling of her nearness to Kate. She knew it was time to leave, yet she had no clue of how she could ever find the strength she needed to tear herself away.

"I'm counting on you, Rebecca." The voice was low, the eyes, closed.

And that was enough. That was all the conviction she needed.

"C—can I get anything for you before I leave?" Becky swallowed hard and squared her shoulders.

"How 'bout a shot of that good Irish Whiskey you've been holding back on me?"

Becky was confused at first, not quite understanding what she'd heard. But then a bright smile skipped across her face, reaching her eyes, shining twin sparkles of light back upon the injured pilot. "Sorry. The bar's fresh out. But I'll give you a rain check."

"Nah." Kate's voice sounded like sandpaper. "In that case, I'll settle for a kiss."

Rebecca leaned down, pressing her lips gently against the pilot's own, feeling the heat, the energy that pulsed from them. Every time she felt it, that bond, that connection, just as she had that very first time they'd kissed, so long ago in Rome.

Becky wanted to pull Kate to her, to tell her everything she meant to her.

No. She struggled to hold it all together. *I can't do that, not now. I'll fall apart, and I can't. I have to be strong.*

For Kate.

Instead, she simply breathed in deeply of Kate's scent, wanting to remember it forever. Finally, she pulled away, arranging a few loose strands of the pilot's dark hair neatly back on her head.

"Be careful, Hanson." Blue eyes locked upon her.

"Back at ya." Bones crackling, Becky pushed herself to her feet and started to move away.

"Rebecca."

She stopped, turning at the catch in Kate's voice.

"I...I just wanted to tell you," she gasped, "I love you. I...have...always...loved you. And I always will." Kate's head fell back after that effort, and she closed her eyes.

Covering her mouth with her hand, there was nothing Becky could do but what she had to, what Kate needed for her to do. She continued on her course, moving east, towards the new day's dawn.

Towards hope.

****

The air warmed as the sun drew higher in the sky, and after a few hours walking, Becky no longer missed her field jacket. Luckily, Kate had been too out of it to notice that she had left without it. The thought of the wounded pilot alone, shivering at night...Becky forced that vision from her mind. No way. She would have thrown her own jacket away first, before wearing it herself. Not while Kate needed it.

As usual, the pilot had been right, and Becky had found the gravelly road just a kilometer or so east of where they'd crashed. The smoke of Birat had faded away behind her, and in front of here there was nothing but a vast vista of barren ground; low mountains rising up in the east, rocky desert towards the west, low hills and scraggly bushes straight ahead. All of it, shades of gray and brown, streaked with ochre.

It had taken them over two days driving to reach the outskirts of Birat from Duristan. Walking? Becky didn't want to think about it. All she could do was hope that she'd find someone willing to help...to go back with her to Kate...to save her.

Bruised, battered, and burned, the flight attendant continued on her way, her mind drifting, unsure of just how long she'd been moving along the rocky tract. She felt the dusty dryness in the back of her throat, but had resolved to drink the water as sparingly as possible. The longer she could hold out, the better her odds of making it, she figured. The separate aches in her body had merged and blended into one great, numbing sensation, and she felt herself lapsing into a bit of a trance as she walked, beating a comforting, mesmerizing pattern out with each step she took.

And then she saw it.

A dust cloud in the distance. Closer...and then she saw it for what it was. Coming up the road from the south.

A truck.

No, more than one. It was a convoy, of sorts. Trucks, and a couple of jeeps.

South.

That would be a safe direction, so Kate had said. God, could it be? Help?

Becky stood her ground in the road, waving. She maintained her composure, unwilling to let her guard down yet. The convoy slowed as it drew closer, and only then did the flight attendant grow alarmed. Several of the jeeps had machine guns mounted in the rear. The men traveling in the convoy were dressed in a hodgepodge of clothing, both traditional and western-style, but they all were heavily armed. Bandoliers were strapped across their chests, rifles were at the ready in their hands. Their faces were dirtied from their days on the road. Not exactly the sort of rescue party she'd had in mind, she considered, feeling a tightness grip her chest.

The convoy ground to a stop in front of her. There were shouts...yells, as the men leaped out of their vehicles.

"We—we need help," Becky said haltingly, shrinking back a bit as the men confronted her, their voices raised. Angry? Excited? Threatening? She had no idea.

"My name—" she started as one of the men circled around her, jabbing her in the shoulder. Another tugged at her blonde hair, and she slapped his hand away. "My name is Rebecca Hanson. Does...does anyone here speak English?"

The word "English" they understood, and the tempo of their shouting escalated. The men grew even more agitated, pointing their weapons at her, and then towards the north. *Oh God. What if these are El Yousef's men? Or more bandits...or—*

The door to the lead jeep slammed shut, and an Afghan man stepped out, shouting in a voice that over-rode those of his compatriots. They quieted down as the man moved slowly toward Rebecca. He was dressed completely in Islamic *hijab,* up to and including the scarf he wore, covering his face. Only his piercing brown eyes were visible to Becky. He stood in front of her now, eyeing her carefully, before he pulled a pistol from his gun belt. He waved it in the air with a flourish, shouting, and his men let out a cheer.

He turned back to Rebecca, still waving his pistol at her, and took her by the arm.

I've failed, I've failed, and Kate's going to die.

The floodgates of despair opened in Becky's heart. "Oh, Kate," she cried aloud, exhaustion and defeat at last claiming her pummeled body. "I'm so sorry."

And with that, she fainted.

****

If the helicopter crash hadn't killed Catherine Phillips, saying good-bye to Rebecca Hanson damn near had. All the things she'd wanted to say, had wanted to show her, but there hadn't been any time. Not for the both of them, and not for Kate, most of all. In the end, telling her at last that she loved her, would have to do.

Kate had no idea how long she'd been lying there on the rocky ground, fading in and out. The apples and sweet cake sat by her side, untouched. Excruciating pain wracked her body, from the mangled leg that she knew was broken, through a stabbing pain in her gut and the bruising pressure on her chest, to the fuzziness in her mind that she knew was due to a concussion—or worse. Shock was setting in, and after that?

She was going to die.

She knew that, and was unafraid.

Instead, she took heart from the fact that she'd finally been able to talk Rebecca into leaving and saving herself, as well as the mission. She hoped, prayed even, that Rebecca would make it. Because the thought of the young blonde in trouble out there in the wilds of Afghanistan, lost, injured...God, it was almost too much to bear.

Kate closed her eyes against the dimming sunlight, and felt two tears leak out the corner of her eyes, tracing a path across her temples and tickle her ears. She pulled in another tortured breath, thinking how easy it would be to just let go, to just let herself slip away.

"You've got to get back up on it." A man's voice.
Firm.
Insistent.
"No."
"Get back up on it, I say."
"No."
A little girl, a child, wailed pitifully. She had long dark hair pulled back in pigtails, and moist blue eyes that seemed entirely too large for her small face. A child's bike lay on the ground next to her, and the girl shrank back from it as though it might bite her.

"You'll never learn to ride a bike if you don't get back up on it, Katie." The man was tall, over six feet, with midnight black hair and dark skin, courtesy of his Greek forebears.

"But Daddy, I don't want to," the little girl cried. She looked down dubiously at her scraped knee, with tiny pebbles from the street still ground into it, and rubbed at the bruise forming on her elbow.

"You will."

"Noooooo," The girl bawled helplessly next to the offensive bicycle.

"Nicholas—leave her be." There was the girl's mother, standing on the stoop of their row house. Her hands were planted firmly on her hips in a pose that the girl had learned from past experience to fear, and there was a scowl on her mother's face to match.

"Stay out of this, Meghan," her father said. "The girl's got to learn."

"Nyah-na-nah, na-nah, nah. Katie can't do it. Katie can't do it. Her older brother Peter whirled in circles around her on his bike, ringing his bell.

"Here, Katie." Her father picked up the bike, and dusted off the seat of her shorts with a gentle pat.

The girl's sobs subsided as her blue eyes flickered from her father to the bike. She wanted so much to please him. But she had tried so many times before with this darn bike, and had the cuts and bruises to prove it. Why should this time be any different?

She hiccuped, gazing longingly towards their house, wishing more than anything that she could just...just quit. Who needed to know how to ride a bike, anyway? Just 'cause all the big kids did it. So what. She didn't care. Not a whit.

"C'mon, Katie, you can do it." There was her little brother Brendan, his fair, freckled face shining in the sunlight, sticking a cherry lollipop into his mouth. He clapped at her with his chubby hands. *"And me, next."*

"Heavenly days." Her mother clicked her lips. *"Not another one."* She shook her head and went back inside, slamming the door shut after her.

The little girl's lower lip trembled and her face grew stormy, disappointed that her mother no longer wanted to watch.

But then there was her father's soft, warm voice buzzing in her ear, telling her she could do anything, if she tried hard enough.

She felt herself climb back onto the bike, keeping one tippy-toe down on the ground for good measure. *"That's it,"* her father said, and they moved. *"Concentrate."*

She started pedaling, working up her speed, her little cheeks flushed and puffing with the effort.

Her father stayed right with her, jogging beside her, one beefy hand on her handlebars, keeping her pointed straight ahead, another on the seat of her bike, holding her steady.

"You've got it, Katie, you've got it."

She hadn't even been aware of the exact moment when it happened. All she knew was that suddenly...suddenly she was free. Riding her bike, all on her own. She shrieked with the pure *delight of it all, hearing the cheers and claps of her father, Peter, and Brendan behind her. She pedaled more furiously, feeling the wind rush through her hair, faster. Faster. So fast that she was flying now.*

Up into the air.

She could reach out and touch it, the crystal blue sky above.

It was so close.

So damn close.

"*Katie!*"

Leave me alone.

"*Kate!*"

Go away.

"Catherine Edwina Phillips. You answer me right this minute."

"*Mother?*"

"Kate, it's me, Becky. Can you hear me?"

The pilot groaned. "Rebecca." She forced open eyes cemented shut with dirt and grit. "What have you been doing, reading my driver's license again?"

"Nah," said the pale face hovering above her. "Just trying to get your attention, baby." The shakiness of her voice belied the smile on her face. "Hey—look who I found."

Kate forced her bleary eyes to focus on the Afghan man who crouched down next to Rebecca. He was of average height and average build. He pushed back the scarf concealing his features to reveal an average-looking face, tanned by the elements, and average brown hair, but his deep brown eyes sparkled with above-average intelligence.

What the?

Kate struggled to pull the bits and pieces of her foggy mind together in an attempt to reconcile a face she *should* remember with the face before her now. At last, she was able to make sense of it.

"Jesus Christ," Kate moaned. "Who the fuck do you think you are—Dan Rather?"

"At your service." Josh Greenfield grinned. "Do you realize I've been trailing you halfway around the world, trying to get a story?"

"Well, you've got one now." Kate shuddered, and she could hear Rebecca's far off voice calling for a blanket.

"And then some, Catherine," the CIA operative solemnly replied, placing his hand on her arm. "Good work."

"You're welcome." Kate let her eyes slip shut, knowing that Rebecca was near. She could hear her, smell her, feel her tucking the blanket in around her, telling her everything was going to be fine. Just fine.

Well.

If Rebecca Hanson believed that, then it must be so.

****

(Associated Press--New York) U.S. Mounts Missile Strike Against Terrorist Stronghold

United States Defense Secretary James Roberts announced today that a missile strike was mounted against the Afghan-based terrorist camp of exiled Saudi, Abbado El Yousef. The raid took place at 1730 EDT, about 0200 hours local time in Afghanistan. Secretary Roberts said the attack was timed to reduce potential casualties to innocent civilians, who might otherwise have been killed or wounded in the attack. It was disclosed that El Yousef's stronghold was located in the remote mountain village of Birat, in northeastern Afghanistan.

Roberts said he would not release any details of the attack, other than the fact the strike was carried out by U.S. Naval ships situated in the Persian Gulf, firing an unknown number of Tomahawk cruise missiles. The strike was launched on the unanimous recommendation of the National Security Council, with the President's full knowledge.

Abbado El Yousef's international terrorist organization has claimed responsibility for a number of terrorist acts against western governments and has been implicated in other incidents, including the hijacking of Orbis Airlines Flight 2240 in March, and the Flight 180 bombing in July.

While Roberts was unable to confirm whether El Yousef

himself had been killed in the missile strike, he said the United States was now in possession of vital electronic data that, when fully analyzed, could potentially destroy El Yousef's world-wide terrorist organization.

An official statement from the ruling Taliban government in Kabul declared the attack an outrage, and a blatant violation of Afghanistan's sovereign rights.

Roberts closed his briefing with strong words assuring the global community that Washington would continue its economic and diplomatic assault on the Taliban, and on any other nation or political party who lends its support to international terrorism.

Chapter
21

The tall, dark-haired woman sat on a balcony, high above the most wonderful city in the world, to her eyes, anyway. With its belching buses, crazy taxi drivers, and people—too damn many people to even think straight—she loved it all. Funny, how until you nearly lose something...or someone...you don't realize how vitally important it is to you. It becomes something you jealously guard and protect, and once you have it, you don't ever want to let it go.

From the safe, secure aerie of her Manhattan high-rise, Catherine Phillips could look down upon it all: the traffic, the crush of people, the spit and the litter, the sweat and the grime, and claim it all for her very own. She liked it here, on this earth, and she had no desire to leave it any time soon.

She leaned back in her chair and closed her eyes in the late afternoon sun.

Warm.

Healing.

She shifted her aching right leg to a more comfortable position on the cushioned footrest, an item that her partner had dragged out here after realizing that even the frosty fall air would not keep the pilot off of the balcony. No, there was something about just being outside, and breathing in the crisp, free air, that Kate had to have. Every day, in fact.

It had been a blur of hospitals after Josh Greenfield had found them.

It turned out that the CIA operative had been keeping tabs on the Orbis Special Operations team for months, hoping they'd find some unconventional means of getting to El Yousef in a way that the Agency had been unable to.

Fortunately, for everyone concerned, save for Abbado El Yousef, he'd been right. After Afghanistan, Kate and Rebecca had hop-scotched from hospitals in Rawalpindi to Incirlik, from Wiesbaden to Washington.

And then, finally, to New York.

And home.

The pilot had been banged up even more than she had thought, and it was not until she'd heard the doctors going over a litany of her maladies one morning—or was it afternoon?—in Turkey, and seen the blood drain from the face of the blonde woman sitting at her side, that she'd realized just how close it had been.

"Did you fall asleep out here again?"

A voice sounded behind her, the voice of an angel.

Sleepy blue eyes glanced casually over one shoulder. "Nah," she said, smiling. She sat up straighter in her chair as Rebecca stepped through the sliding door and out onto the balcony. The flight attendant brushed her lips against Kate's cheek before draping a small throw blanket around her shoulders.

"Watcha doing?" Becky pulled her thick sweater tightly around her middle and sat down on the arm of Kate's chair.

"Oh, a little of this, and a little of that." Kate offered her partner a mischievous grin as she busied herself with the computer balanced on her lap.

"Who would have thought it," Becky laughed aloud. She'd been shocked at first when the pilot had requested a laptop while still in the hospital. Later, when Kate had continued her convalescence at home, she'd amazed Rebecca with the focus she'd shown, going after a thorough knowledge of all things computing with a vengeance. Well, if this was a way to keep Kate's agile mind occupied during what, of necessity, would be a lengthy recovery period—so be it.

As it was, the way Kate had bounced back was a miracle in itself, amazing the doctors and astounding her friends. Cyrus, Mac, Rory—even Dottie West—all had been subjected to lengthy e-mails from the recuperating special operations director. Just in the last week, Becky had been finally able to detect a healthy glow to the pilot's face that had been missing for far too long.

"Okay." Kate's tongue poked out thoughtfully from between her lips. "Now...watch this." Her hands flew over the keyboard, tapping at length, until finally she pressed "enter." "There." She grinned triumphantly, infinitely pleased with herself. "I did it."

"Did what?" Becky played with a lock of Kate's hair.

"Just made reservations for us in Paris next month."

"Paris?" Becky's voice was a high-pitched squeak. "Kate, are you crazy? Will you be okay by then?" Her eyes darted to the crutches leaning against the balcony railing.

Kate snapped the laptop closed and took Rebecca's hand in her own. "I'll have good reason to be, won't I?" She gave the hand a squeeze. "I promised you I'd take you back there, and do it right."

Becky swallowed hard and said nothing. She simply threw her arms around Kate's shoulders and rested her head against the dark woman, allowing herself to get lost in the closeness. They sat that way for a time, silently watching the palette of the autumn sky change from blue to amber to violet.

Then Kate detected the tremor run through the small body next to her, felt the warm splash of moisture on the back of her hand.

"Hey. Hanson. What the—Jeez, don't cry."

Kate gamely searched for a tissue and, finding none, used the cuff of her cotton sleeve, daubing it at the younger woman's cheeks.

"Aah, I'm sorry, Kate." Becky hung her head, embarrassed. "You know me." She threw up her hand helplessly. "I'm like an old leaky bucket."

"Yeah." Kate lifted her chin with her index finger, and smiled into her green eyes. "But you're *my* leaky bucket. Now tell me," she lifted an eyebrow at her partner, "what's the matter?"

Becky sighed. "It's just that...I can't help but think about...*it* sometimes, you know? What happened. And what if—"

"Ssh." Kate pressed a silencing finger against her lips. "*What if* didn't happen, Rebecca, thanks to you. You saved my life. And you know what that means." She released a low, rumbling laugh, trying to lighten the mood.

"What?" Becky sniffled, looking at Kate as though she held the answers to all the questions in the world.

"It means you're stuck with me, forever."

A smile lit the young blonde's face at that, chasing away the clouds like a warm summer breeze. "Sounds like a plan, Captain Phillips. Sounds like a plan."

Be sure to read the first two books in this series by

Belle Reilly:

Darkness Before the Dawn

A troubled Captain Catherine Phillips plans for this flight to Rome to be her last in the employ of Orbis Airlines. Unfulfilled by her job and adrift in her personal life, the only solution she sees is to quit—to run away—as she's done in the past. But a band of terrorist hijackers, as well as a gutsy young flight attendant Rebecca Hanson, throw a wrench into Catherine's plans. The pilot is forced to come to terms with the demons of her past even as she struggles to save her crippled aircraft and the lives of all aboard.

Roman Holiday

Orbis Airline pilot Catherine Phillips grudgingly decides to spend a lay over in Rome with Rebecca Hanson, keeping a protective eye on the recovering flight attendant. The two women are soon caught up in the magical splendor of the eternal City, seeing the sights and drawing ever closer to one another in the process.

These books may be ordered through your favorite local or online booksellers.

Available soon from

RENAISSANCE ALLIANCE

And Those Who Trespass Against Us
By H. M. Macpherson

Sister Katherine Flynn is an Irish nun sent by her order to work in the Australian Outback. Katherine is a prideful woman who originally joined her order to escape the shame of being left at the altar. She had found herself getting married only because society dictated it for a young woman her age, and she was not exactly heartbroken when it didn't take place. Yet, her mother could not be consoled and talked of nothing except the disgrace that she had brought to the Flynn name. So, she finds great relief in escaping the cold Victorian Ireland of 1872.

Catriona Pelham is a member of the reasonably affluent farming gentry within the district. Her relationship with the hardworking townspeople and its farmers is one of genuine and mutual respect. The town's wealthy, however, have ostracized her due to her unorthodox ways and refusal to conform to society's expectations of a woman of the 1870's.

As a bond between Katherine and Catriona develops, Catriona finds herself wanting more than friendship from the Irishwoman. However, she fears pursuing her feelings lest they not be reciprocated. And so the journey begins for these two strong-willed women. For Katherine it is a journey of self-discovery and of what life holds outside the cloistered walls of the convent. For Catriona it is bittersweet, as feelings she has kept hidden for years resurface in her growing interest in Katherine.

Coming Home
By Lois Hart

A triangle with a twist, Coming Home is the story of three good people caught up in an impossible situation. Rob, a charismatic ex-fighter pilot severely disabled with MS, has been steadfastly cared for by his wife, Jan, for many years. Quite by accident one day, Terry, a young writer/postal carrier enters their life and turns it upside down. Injecting joy and turbulence into their quiet existence, Terry draws Rob and Jan into her lively circle of family and friends until the growing attachment between the two women begins to strain the bonds of love and loyalty, to Rob and each other.

Vendetta
By Talaran

Nicole Stone is a narcotics detective with a painful past that still haunts her. Extremely attractive, yet reclusive, she has closed her heart to love and concentrates solely on her career. After someone tries to kill her partner in cold blood, she meets her partner's sister, Carly Jamison. An unmistakable attraction catches both of these women off guard. Can Nic protect her partner and Carly from the clutches of a ruthless drug lord bent on revenge and still open her heart to the one woman who could change her life forever?

Other titles to look for in the coming months from RENAISSANCE ALLIANCE

You Must Remember This By Mary A. Draganis

Staying In the Game By Nann Dunne

Blue Holes To Terror By Trish Kocialski

Restitution By Susanne Beck

Full Circle By Mary A. Draganis

Bleeding Hearts By Josh Aterovis

Anne Azel's Murder Mysteries #1 By Anne Azel

Gun Shy By Lori Lake

High Intensity By Belle Reilly

New Beginnings By Mary A. Draganis

A lover of travel and adventure all her life, Belle (Bel-wah) Reilly currently lives in southeastern Pennsylvania, where she enjoys a somewhat less perilous existence than the exciting characters she creates. "It's been a really fun process for me, " Belle says, "with each new story, seeing what interesting direction Catherine and Rebecca will go in, and what the next 'curve in the road' will be for them. One thing's for sure: those ladies always get in the last word!"

Printed in the United States
982000003B